A PLACE FOR GOOD AND EVIL

Also by STACEY HORAN

STANDALONES (Young Adult)

Inland

Sycamore Lane

THE ELIXIR VITAE ADVENTURES SERIES (Young Adult)

Book One: *Ortus*

Book Two: *Juvenis*

Book Three: *Adultus*

Book Four: *Senectus*

Book Five: *Mortem*

A PLACE FOR GOOD AND EVIL

An Old City Mystery

STACEY HORAN

Ghost Bridge Press LLC

Cover design by James T. Egan of Bookfly Design

ISBN: 978-1-964473-01-7

For Matt

A PLACE FOR GOOD
AND EVIL

Life is neither good or evil,
but only a place for good and evil.

—Attributed to Marcus Aurelius (*n.d.*)

Prologue

The knock at the door signaled the end of Sidney Stone's old life and the beginning of her new one, although she didn't know it yet.

Sid had been home only a few minutes, tiptoeing into the condo and making her way to the kitchen as quietly as she could so as not to wake her husband and daughter. She guzzled a glass of water, trying to clear away the remnants of the beer buzz that she'd diligently maintained all evening at Manny's farewell party. After putting her glass in the sink, she started down the hallway that led to the bedrooms. The knock at the front door was so loud that Sid jumped and pressed her hand to her heart, trying to steady its now frantic beating.

She threw open the front door and hissed, "Shut the hell up! People are sleep—" Sid stopped, her eyes going wide and her mouth falling open.

"Sidney," said her husband's boss, Sheriff Travis Colquitt. He took a hesitant step forward, looking down at her with bloodshot eyes, and ran a hand through his thick blond hair. "Can I come in?"

She held up her hands. "Sorry, Sheriff. Come on in." Stepping back, she motioned for him to enter. "Must be important for you to come out here at this time of night. I'll go get Wes."

"Sid, wait." The sheriff reached for her.

But Sid didn't wait; she slipped through his grip, turning and jogging down the hall to the master bedroom. It wasn't unusual for Wes to get dragged out of bed and called into work, but usually the sheriff's office just called his cell phone. They didn't send the sheriff himself to come and collect her husband.

"Wes!" she whispered as she entered the bedroom. The bed was empty, the room dark and untouched. Sid sighed and continued down the hall to Iris's room, knowing she'd find Wes in there asleep on Iris's bed with their little girl tucked up against him. They'd probably fallen asleep reading a story or watching a Disney movie.

"Wes!" she hissed again as she opened Iris's door. The little girl's room was also dark and untouched. Returning to the hallway, she saw Sheriff Colquitt approach. "I'm sorry, Sheriff, but they must not be home yet." Sid shook her head slightly, trying to clear it. Either she was drunker than she realized, or she was mistaken about Wes and Iris leaving the party an hour or two ago, well before her. It had to be one or the other, right?

"Let's sit down, Sid." Sheriff Colquitt took her by the elbow and led her back into the living room. "I know where they are."

"Really? Where?" she asked, picking up one of Iris's picture books from the sofa cushion and placing it on the coffee table next to the orderly stack of papers she'd been marking earlier in the day and her lesson plans for the following week. Sid's tidying was so compulsory that even two beers more than she usually enjoyed couldn't keep her from the habit.

Sheriff Colquitt waited until Sid was sitting down before taking a seat next to her on the sofa. She noticed his eyes were bloodshot. Two sheriff's deputies now stood at the open front door. "Sidney, I am so sorry to have to tell you this . . ."

Sidney Stone didn't remember much of the conversation that followed. She'd let the sheriff say what he'd come to say and then asked him to leave. No, she didn't want him to call anyone. No, she didn't want a deputy to stay with her. Fine, someone could come by in the morning to pick her up.

"Are you sure you don't—" began Sheriff Colquitt, but Sid held up her hands to stop him, unable to bear his attempts to soothe her.

"Get out! Get out! Get out!" She screamed those words, slammed the front door, and watched from the window as the two vehicles—one patrol and one unmarked—drove away.

The silence in the condo was louder than a jet engine, and Sid covered her ears. Her breaths were getting shorter and shallower, her heart thumping harder and faster. Any lingering buzz from the party was now gone, replaced by panic and nausea.

She sprinted for the bedroom and yanked open her dresser's bottom drawer, tossing items onto the bed. Swiftly shedding her sundress, she pulled on running clothes, not caring if anything matched. Then, she laced up her running shoes, grabbed her spare key, and locked the front door behind her. Only once she stepped onto the driveway did she notice that Wes's car was missing. Tears streamed down her face, and she tried to suck in breaths of the hot, sticky night air.

The realization of the sheriff's words hit Sid square in the chest, like a punch from a prizefighter, and she almost went down. Almost.

Instead of falling to her knees, she threw her head back and let out a long, agonizing scream, stopping only when her throat was raw and lights came on in the neighboring condos.

And then Sidney Stone ran.

She didn't know where she was going, and frankly it didn't matter. In the past, running had always cleared her mind. But even if it were possible to run forever, Sid knew the sheriff's words would never be wiped from her memory. Nevertheless, she pushed forward, as hard and as fast as she could. Running was her only solution; she had no other answers.

Chapter One

Leo stood by the trunk of the car and stared at the elderly couple sitting side by side on the porch swing of the bright yellow house across the street. The woman lifted her glass of iced tea in salute to him, the clinking of the ice cubes ringing out like wind chimes, while she stroked the fur of a gray tabby cat stretched across her lap. The man smiled and waved, and Leo noticed his dapper dress: light gray seersucker suit, pressed white shirt, and pale pink bow tie. Leo flashed a quick smile and looked away, focusing instead on the large, clapboard house right in front of him.

Leo hesitated for a moment but finally silenced the music blaring in his ears. He removed his headphones and hung them around his neck, slipping his phone into his back pocket. He hoped the man across the street would not come over and try to speak to him. Now was not a good time. If he did try, Leo would put the headphones back on and crank up the music again. It was his only defense, flimsy as it was, to keep the man at bay. Leo knew the man would approach him eventually. People like him always did.

Leo's gaze roamed over the front of the clapboard house, just in time to see the front door fly open and another man appear.

"There you are!" bellowed Burt Roberts as he clomped down the porch steps. He wiped his hands on an old apron with "Sauce Boss" written across the front in large letters. "You're early!" He threw his arms open wide, and Leo couldn't help but smile as his grandfather wrapped him in a bear hug and lifted him an inch or two off the ground.

"Hi, Grandpa," said Leo, his arms pinned to his sides.

Burt smiled at the boy, who stood almost as tall as he did, at an even six feet. "Lordy, you've grown since the last time I saw you. Fifteen now, am I right?" He stood with his hands on Leo's shoulders, beaming at him.

Leo nodded. "Yeah. But you saw me last year, Grandpa, and I haven't grown that much since then."

Burt held up a finger. "I beg to differ. A good two inches, I'd say."

"More like three." A woman exited the car and pushed her sunglasses up on top of her head. She smiled weakly as she leaned to crack her back. "He's grown out of everything. Pants, shirts, shoes. In fact, I'm pretty sure he grew another inch on the trip down here, and we only left yesterday."

Leo frowned and looked away from his mother, glancing back at the porch swing across the street. The old woman was still sipping her iced tea and stroking her cat, but the old man was no longer sitting next to her. Leo swallowed hard as his eyes scanned the street, searching for the man. The old man was gone . . . at least for now.

"Nice to see you, Trisha," said Burt. His face fell as he studied his daughter-in-law. She looked tired, pale and thin.

She sighed. "I'm not going by Trisha anymore. I'm using my middle name. I told you that."

Burt nodded. "Right, right. Sorry. Paisley, is it?"

"With a Z," added Leo, still scanning the street and the neighboring yards. "Paizley with a Z."

Burt's brow furrowed. "Your parents named you Paizley with a Z?"

Paizley pinched the bridge of her nose and sighed again. "No, they spelled it with an S, but I changed it to a Z. It's all part of my new brand."

"I understand," said Burt with a nod, although it was plain by the look on his face that he didn't understand at all. "How was the drive?"

"Long," grumbled Leo under his breath.

"Fine," answered Paizley. "We made good time. We hit some Friday rush-hour traffic yesterday, but traffic today wasn't bad at all." She wiped sweat from her upper lip. "I forgot how hot it is here."

Burt held up his arms, spreading them wide. "Welcome to Florida in July—where there's never a break from the heat, and the humidity is so high it's like trying to breathe underwater."

Paizley's hand fell limply to her side. "You should be in advertising, Burt."

He chuckled and clamped his hand on Leo's shoulder, the smile returning to his face. "Well, let's get you settled."

Burt reached to pop open the trunk, and Leo's gaze swiveled away from the street and back to the car, the driveway, and the two-story detached garage behind his grandfather's house. Something moved in one of the windows on the second floor of the garage. Leo saw the pale face of a woman with long, dark hair. She stared down at him, and Leo thought she might be scowling. When the woman realized that Leo was staring back at her, she moved away from the curtains.

"That's just Sid," said Burt as he looked up at the window.

Leo raised an eyebrow. "Is she—wait, you can see her?"

Burt smiled. "Who? Sid? Of course I can see her." He winked at his grandson. "She's my tenant. She's renting the garage. Well, she's not exactly paying me at the moment, but that's another story. Anyway, she lives in the apartment upstairs, and I helped her set up an office downstairs. You'll get to meet her later. She's good people, but she's had a rough time of it the last few years. Very sad." He shook his head. "She'll be all right . . . eventually."

Burt bent to grab hold of the strap on the large, battered seabag that was wedged in the trunk next to Paizley's pink suitcases, but Leo got there first. "I got it," said Leo, hoisting the heavy bag over his shoulder.

Paizley opened the back door of the car and pointed to two large storage bins placed side by side across the back seat. "Leo's bin is the blue one, Burt. Can you grab it?" He nodded and did as she asked. She collected Leo's backpack and assorted trash from the passenger seat.

Burt led the way into the house through the front door and up the stairs to the second floor. "I fixed up your dad's old room, Leo. Hope you're okay with that. I got a new mattress for the bed and new sheets, but I left his posters up on the walls. Thought there might be some you'd want to keep." He nudged the door open with his hip and stepped inside.

Leo hesitated in the doorway, his eyes darting around the room, looking for spirits. There were none, and he felt his body relax. He had been expecting to see his father sitting on the bed waiting for him, and that thought had sat like a rock in the pit of his stomach during the entire two-day car ride. In a way, he'd been hoping his dad would be here, even though seeing spirits—any spirits—scared him. But Gunner Roberts had not appeared, not here or anywhere else. Not once in the entire year since he died.

Leo dumped the seabag, which had been his father's, in the

corner of the room, and Burt placed the storage tub at the foot of the twin bed. The bedroom was a time capsule, and Leo imagined that most of it looked exactly as his father had left it at eighteen when he enlisted in the navy.

Paizley remained in the doorway, glancing around the room that had belonged to her husband when he was a boy, and held out the backpack. "Here, Leo. Take this." She wrapped her arms tightly around herself and leaned against the doorframe for support. "Burt, do you still have Gunner's old concert T-shirts?"

Burt rubbed the stubble on his cheek. "His old T-shirts? Why do you ask?"

Paizley stopped hugging herself and stood up straight. "I'd like to take them. I'm planning to wear them on my trip, as part of my new brand. I think it would be a cool image, sort of nineties grunge meets boho chic." She tucked a loose strand of hair behind her ear and smiled.

"Sorry, darlin'," said Burt with a slow shake of his head. "I tossed those shirts long ago. They were covered with holes and stains, and if I'm bein' honest, no amount of washing would have gotten those suckers smellin' good. I donated them to the local thrift shop, although I can't imagine anyone would buy 'em to wear 'em. They're probably being used as dustrags by now."

"Are you kidding me?!" squawked Paizley. "Well, that's just great. Now, I have to rethink my entire wardrobe." She turned on her heels and stomped off down the hallway, making as much noise as possible as she tramped downstairs.

Leo shook his head. "She's been talking about those T-shirts for the past month. They were supposed to be part of her new image. She's gonna be so mad now."

Burt put his hand on Leo's shoulder and steered him

toward the door. "She'll get over it, son. Besides, it gives her an excuse to go shopping. What woman doesn't want that?"

They found Paizley in the kitchen making a sandwich. "Hope you don't mind me helping myself, Burt." The edge in her voice, as she struggled with the lid of the mayonnaise jar, indicated that her anger was in no hurry to subside.

Burt took the jar from her and opened the lid with a satisfying pop. He set it down gently on the counter, but Paizley grabbed it up and scooped a large mound of mayo out with a knife. Burt took three plates out of the cupboard and placed them on the table that was built into a little nook in the corner of the kitchen. "Get the chips out of the pantry, please, son," said Burt, "and help yourself to a soda in the fridge. I've got all kinds."

Leo found a giant box of assorted chip bags on the bottom shelf of the pantry and pulled out one of each kind. He dumped them all on the table and grabbed a cream soda from the refrigerator. Sliding into the bench seat, he opened a bag of corn chips and sipped his drink as he took in his surroundings.

He had only visited the house once in his life. He'd been seven years old at the time, and his father had gotten leave while on shore duty. The three of them had driven down to St. Augustine from Norfolk, Virginia, making the drive in one painfully long day, and stayed with Burt and Camille, his grandmother. They went to the beach, the alligator farm, and the old fort, and Leo's dad had bought him a slice of pizza and a waffle cone as they strolled along St. George Street. It was a great vacation, the best one he'd ever had. The only one he'd ever had, actually. Leo smiled at the memories: his dad swimming with him in the ocean, his dad racing him across the lawn next to the old fort, he and his dad trying on all the different pirate hats in the little museum shop.

Leo jumped back to the present as his mom dropped the knife in the sink with a loud clang.

"I have to get back on the road," announced Paizley as she swaddled her sandwich in plastic wrap. She plucked two cans of soda from the refrigerator. "Do you have a shopping bag or something I can use to carry this stuff?"

Burt nodded and pulled a small, insulated lunch bag from the top shelf of the pantry. "Are you sure you won't stay the night, Trisha? I . . . uh . . . I mean, Paizley? I've got ribs marinating in the fridge. Not to brag, but my sauce is legendary. And I've invited some friends 'round to welcome you both. Kitty, from across the street, is making a red velvet cake." Burt winked at Leo, whose mouth watered at the thought of ribs and cake.

"Can't," said Paizley. She shoved the drinks and the sandwich into the lunch bag and grabbed two bags of chips from the table. "I need to make it down to Boca Raton by this evening. There's still a lot to be done."

"But don't you want to make sure everything is settled here first?" asked Burt, the question sizzling with frustration.

"It's fine. He's fine." She waved in Leo's direction. "It's all fine." Her voice cracked a little, and she cleared her throat to try to cover it up. "He's already set up with his homeschooling plan, and he knows exactly what he has to do. He's taking all virtual classes, so everything will be done online. School starts in August. I can't remember the exact date, but Leo knows. We went over everything. I've given him some spending money and . . . oh, right. Almost forgot . . ." She marched out of the kitchen and found her purse hanging on the newel post at the bottom of the staircase. She held the lunch bag and chip bags in one hand as she fished out a plain white envelope with the other.

"Here," she said, holding out the envelope to Burt. "Nine hundred. That's three months' worth, as agreed." It was a lot of money, but it probably wasn't nearly enough. She knew she should be paying Burt more, but he'd fought her on it. He'd originally refused to accept any money at all, and it had taken her breaking down in tears before he finally relented. They'd agreed on $300 per month, a sum she could afford now that Gunner's military death benefits had come in, but she doubted it would even cover the cost of food for Leo. Paizley cleared her throat. "It would be really helpful if you could set up your digital wallet so that I can pay you electronically going forward. It's not going to be easy to mail a check from the road, so please just set it up. Leo can help you."

Burt took the envelope. "Okay." He folded it and put it in his back pocket. "Are you sure I can't convince you to stay just one night? I think it would be good for the boy."

"Can't," answered Paizley before he could finish. "I have to go. He'll be fine. It will all be fine." Her voice cracked again, and she bit her lip, fighting back tears.

Burt wrapped his arms around her and whispered, "Of course it will, darlin'. Everything will be all right. I'll take good care of him, but you have to take care of yourself, too." He felt her stifle a sob as she pressed her forehead to his chest. "You go do what you need to do, and we'll see you back here when you're done." She nodded, her head still pressed against Burt's chest. "You keep in touch now, okay? And anytime you want to come home, you're welcome here. There's a bed waiting for you and a home-cooked meal. Like I said, my sauce is legendary."

Paizley snorted with laughter and picked up her head. Burt took her face in his hands and wiped her cheeks with his thumbs. He kissed her forehead and then took the lunch bag, chip bags, and purse from her. "I'll put these in the car for you." He winked at her and stepped out onto the front porch.

Leo was standing in the living room, his hands shoved into the pockets of jeans that were now more than an inch too short for him. He smoothed the fringe of the threadbare rug with the toe of his old sneaker, which was also too small for him.

"Come give me a hug," his mother ordered, holding out her arms and trying to lighten her voice. He shuffled over and wrapped his arms around her, bending down to touch his forehead to her shoulder. Her little boy was grown up, almost as tall and just as skinny as his father had been when she first met him at age eighteen. She hugged Leo tightly, breathing in the familiar scent of teenage boy and trying to memorize the feel of her son's hug. "Make sure you do your schoolwork, okay? And mind your grandpa. He'll take good care of you, but you have to do what he tells you. Got it? And stay out of trouble, please."

"'Kay," mumbled Leo. He released his grip on his mother and rubbed his eyes with the back of his hand. "You stay out of trouble, too."

She laughed and pressed her hand to his cheek. "I will. You'll be able to see it all on social media anyway." She hooked her arm through his, and they headed outside. "You understand why I have to do this, right?" He nodded, although he really didn't understand. Paizley squeezed her son's arm. "I'll see you when we stop in St. Augustine in about a month or so, give or take. I'll keep you posted."

"And then I can come with you?" he asked, his face lighting up with hope. When his mother hesitated a moment, his face fell again.

"We'll see, Leo," she answered. "Let me get my bearings first, okay?" He nodded and held the car door open for her. She kissed him on the cheek and slid into the driver's seat. "Be good."

Leo tried to smile, but he couldn't manage it. "You too."

Paizley backed the old Honda Civic out of the driveway, honked the horn twice, and waved out the window as she drove off. Leo didn't wave back. He and Burt stood on the driveway and watched as her car turned the corner and disappeared from view. Burt rubbed his hands together. "How about some lunch? I'm starving."

"Sure," answered Leo, wiping his eyes. He followed his grandfather across the backyard. As he climbed the four wooden steps to the kitchen door, he noticed a swish of curtains in a window above the garage. He stood for a moment and waited, but he saw no movement other than a cardinal landing on the wrought iron fence that framed his grandfather's corner lot. The cardinal took flight again, momentarily alighting on the roof of the garage, and then vanished into the branches of the giant live oak next door.

Burt held open the back door. "Ham and cheese okay with you?"

"Yeah, fine," answered Leo. As he turned to enter the house, he saw the curtain move again, and the pale face of the woman with the dark hair appeared. A second later, the curtain fell back into place.

There was another blur of movement, and Leo saw the dapper man in the seersucker suit emerge from around the corner of the house. The man stood on the driveway, smiling and waving at Leo.

Dead people, thought Leo. *Why did they always seem to find him?* He groaned and, without waving back, hurried inside his grandfather's house.

Chapter Two

A few hours later, while Burt Roberts was in the backyard manning the grill, Leo sat on the sofa in the living room sandwiched between Kitty Lonigan, the elderly woman from across the street, and Eli Williams. Eli was a large man, six foot four and well over two hundred and fifty pounds, most of which resided in his broad shoulders and back and his impressive beer belly. His smooth, dark brown skin only creased with lines when he smiled, belying his age. Only his white hair and the groans he made when sitting or standing up indicated he was not a young man. When he laughed, which was often and loudly, his voice boomed through the room.

The two chairs opposite the sofa were occupied as well. Cesar Hernandez sat in one of them. Cesar was a short, slightly built man with long, gray hair tied back in a ponytail and thick, bushy eyebrows that framed amber-colored eyes. His skin was leathered from the sun, and he wore cargo shorts and a short-sleeved, collared shirt with a busy print that included palm trees and bikini-clad women. Cesar sat back with his legs crossed and sipped his beer.

In the other chair sat Guppy Goodwin. Guppy was Leo's height, with light brown skin, hazel eyes, a bald head and thick forearms with ropey muscles. His leg bounced as he sat on the edge of his seat and explained to Leo that the other members of the group had nicknamed him Guppy when he joined six years ago because he was so much younger than they were.

Guppy had recently turned sixty years old. Cesar was sixty-eight, Leo's grandfather Burt was sixty-five, and Eli was the patriarch of their little troupe at the venerable age of seventy. Together, these four men made up the rock band Recent Geezer. They played locally in St. Augustine at least twice a month. Their set lists consisted mostly of covers from the seventies and eighties, with a few of their own songs strategically slipped in when they thought they could get away with it.

And at the tender age of eighty-six, Kitty Lonigan was the band's most loyal groupie, as she was quick to admit. Leo had a vague recollection of having met her before when he visited on vacation all those years ago. Her husband had been alive then, but Leo couldn't remember his name. Leo's father had introduced him to the couple, but the meeting was brief. Nothing more than a wave and a few kind words exchanged across the street from their front yards. Sitting next to Kitty now, he marveled at how tiny she was. Not much more than five feet tall, rail-thin, with white cottony hair that was perfectly curled and coiffed. A bright pink sweater was draped over her shoulders even though it was nearly a hundred degrees outside.

The only other person in the room was Kitty's husband. Leo tried his best to ignore the spirit, but that was hard to do given that the old man was hovering at the entrance to the living room near the end of the sofa where his wife was seated. Periodically, Kitty would adjust her sweater, pulling it more tightly around her neck and shoulders. Leo understood why.

Out of the corner of his eye, Leo watched as the spirit drifted closer to his wife, occasionally stroking her hair or her cheek, causing Kitty to shiver and tug on her sweater.

The spirit wasn't causing trouble and seemed perfectly content to hang out with Kitty and the band, so Leo did his best to ignore him. So far, Kitty's husband had not tried to engage with Leo, and Leo was happy to keep it that way. He was still wearing his headphones around his neck and had his phone in his pocket, ready to blast music if necessary to keep the spirit out of his head, but he was hoping it wouldn't come to that.

Kitty patted Leo's knee and smiled at him. "Now, young man, how do you like Florida? What are your plans? When is your mother returning?" She nodded at him, encouraging him to start talking. "We want to hear everything."

Cesar tipped his beer bottle toward him. "Burt's told us a little, but I think he left out a lot of details."

Leo's gaze swung around the room. The four adults were waiting with smiles on their faces. Guppy's leg bounced to a quick rhythm only he could hear. Leo shrugged. "Not much to tell, really."

Eli sat back and stretched his long arm over the back of the couch. "Give it a try. We've got all evening." He chuckled, and the deep sound rolled across the room. Guppy sat back as well, his leg still bouncing away, and Kitty shifted her position on the sofa so she faced him while still being nestled among the cushions.

Leo sighed in defeat. He opened his mouth to begin, but he stopped before the words could leave his lips. The woman with the dark hair had entered the living room.

"Just in time," said Eli, nodding to her. "Leo here is getting ready to tell us his story."

Guppy leaped up. "Here you go, beautiful. Take my seat." He winked at her and waved to his empty chair.

The woman rolled her eyes at him as she took the offered seat. Now that Leo could see her up close, it was obvious that she was, in fact, not a spirit, but she was pale. Odd for someone who lived in Florida year-round, thought Leo. Her long, straight hair was pulled back in a ponytail and was in desperate need of a wash. The color reminded him of the strong coffee his father used to drink. So dark it was almost black. A few silver streaks caught the light and sparkled like tinsel. Her face was smooth, save for some fine lines and creases at the corners of her dark brown eyes and around her mouth as well as one deep groove between her eyebrows.

Despite the smile lines, Leo got the impression this woman didn't smile much. The deep groove between her brows and the dark circles under her eyes told a very different story, as did her clothes. She wore yoga pants with a few pinpricked holes in one knee and a faded, oversize T-shirt that was either blue or gray. Leo wasn't sure which. The shirt was wrinkled and misshapen, as if it had been washed a thousand times but never properly folded or ironed, and there was a faint stain on the front that looked like it might have been mustard.

Guppy pulled a chair from the dining room table and positioned it next to her, grinning widely as he did so. She shook her head at him and tried to suppress the smile tugging at her lips.

Kitty placed a hand on Leo's arm. "Have you two met yet?"

Leo shook his head. "No, ma'am." Kitty raised her eyebrows at him, and Leo took the hint. He stood and held out his hand to the woman now seated across from him. "I'm Leo."

The woman leaned forward and shook his hand. "Sid." She released his grip and sat back. "I didn't mean to interrupt your story."

Leo sank back into the sofa, wishing he could disappear.

Kitty leaned toward him and whispered loudly, "Go ahead, dear."

Leo took another look around the room, all eyes on him. "There's not much to tell. I used to live in Norfolk with my mom, but now I'm going to be living here with my grandpa while my mom is on the road." He shrugged and stopped talking, lowering his eyes and wishing someone would change the subject.

"What does your mom do?" asked Sid. Leo looked up, and she fixed him with her gaze. Her eyes were so dark that they were almost black, like her hair.

Leo rubbed his hands down his thighs. His palms were sweating, as was the rest of him, from either the heat or the inquisition. He wasn't sure which, but it was probably both. "She's a travel blogger." He dragged his lower lip between his teeth. "Well, she's trying to be. She and her friend are starting a travel blog."

Sid frowned, the groove between her brows deepening. "Is she going overseas?"

Leo shook his head, frowning at the question. "No. She's on her way to Boca Raton." The adults glanced sideways at each other.

"Not much to write about in Boca," muttered Sid.

"That's where her friend is," explained Leo. "She's meeting up with her friend, and then they're going to drive down to Key West and start from there. Her plan is to go to various places in Florida, take pictures, and post them online."

"Without you?" Sid crossed her legs, wrapping her hands around her knee.

Leo's face heated, and he looked away from her scowl. "For now. Mom wants to get things set up and figure it all out first, and then I'll join them later."

Sid continued to stare at him. "Who's *them*?"

Through a clamped jaw, Leo answered, "My mom and her friend."

"Boyfriend?" Sid raised an eyebrow.

"No!" barked Leo. "Just a friend of hers from high school. Someone named Brooklyn." He rolled his eyes. "Well, it's Brooke. Brooke Lynn Something-or-Other. But she's changing it to Brooklyn—one word. It's part of their brand."

Sid's eyebrow rose just a bit higher. "Brand?"

"Yes, *brand*," snarled Leo. "Their online brand. Mom is now Paizley—with a Z—instead of Trisha. And Brooke is Brooklyn. And there's Brooklyn's dog, Jezebel. It's some tiny, white, fluffy thing that can fit in your hand or purse or teacup or whatever. She's very photogenic, apparently. The dog, I mean." He inhaled sharply, nostrils flaring. "Brooklyn bought a little camper, and she and Mom are having it painted and fixed up. And Brooklyn bought a jeep to match it and tow it around and stuff. They're going to travel all around the United States and take pictures and post about places to eat and shop and whatever." He wiped his hands on his jeans again. "I drew the logo for them and helped them set up their website and social media handles."

"What is it?" asked Sid, folding her arms across her chest.

Leo felt a bead of sweat roll down the back of his neck. "What is what?"

She continued to fix him with her stare. "Their logo. What is it?"

Leo's nostrils flared again. "It's a yellow picnic basket with a pink bow on the handle and a little white dog poking its head out of the basket. And the writing is in turquoise: 'PB&J Buffet.' That's their name. And under that is their catchphrase: 'A Medley of Travel, Food, and Fashion.'"

Sid frowned. "P, B, and J. Like the sandwich?"

"Yes, like the sandwich," barked Leo. "It stands for Paizley,

Brooklyn, and Jezebel." He wasn't sure why this woman was getting so deep under his skin, but there she was, like a splinter he couldn't tweeze out.

"But no L for Leo?" Again, her eyebrow lifted.

Leo felt his face flush even more, which he didn't think was possible, and he ground his teeth so hard he worried they might break. "No."

"Hmmm." Sid's mouth pressed into a line, her lips going white as she fought the urge to let loose all the choice words that seemed to be racing through her mind. She leaped to her feet and clenched her fists so hard her knuckles turned white. "I'm going to go help Burt." She turned and left the room. The kitchen door slammed shut a few moments later.

Leo gaped and glanced at the others. Cesar stared out the window and sipped his beer. Guppy stared at the floor and rubbed the back of his neck. Kitty picked some invisible lint from the sleeve of her sweater.

"Sid takes some getting used to," said Eli, clapping his big hand on Leo's shoulder. "She's . . . she's had a hard time of it herself, and it's made her a little . . . a little testy." He pursed his lips. "She's got a short fuse these days. But she means well."

"Does she?" Leo frowned, staring at Sid's empty chair. "Doesn't seem like it." He inhaled deeply, trying to calm himself, and added under his breath, "Doesn't feel like it."

"She's just a bit sad," offered Guppy.

Cesar lifted his beer bottle to his lips. "And lost."

Kitty patted Leo's hand. "She'll come around. You'll see."

Leo pursed his lips. He didn't care if Sid was sad or lost or having a hard time. He didn't want to see if she'd come around. In fact, he didn't want to see her at all.

Chapter Three

Sid barged through the kitchen and stormed into the yard, letting the door slam shut behind her. She smoothed her hands down her face and growled a few choice words as she paced back and forth. Burt sat at a small, wrought iron table under the shade of the neighbor's giant live oak, which stretched over the fence into his own yard. He didn't look up at her, content to keep playing Solitaire on his phone while the ribs cooked on the grill next to him. Sid stalked toward him, throwing up her hands. "What the hell, Burt?!"

"Keep your voice down, Sid," replied Burt, continuing to stare at his phone. "And 'what the hell' what?"

At a loss for words, Sid shook her head and pointed toward the house. She kept pointing, jabbing her finger in the direction of the kitchen door, until Burt looked up. "She just left him here?!"

Burt sighed, lowered his phone, and placed it face down on the table. "Yes, Sid, but she said it was only temporary."

"And you believe her?!" Sid resumed her pacing but kept her glare fixed rigidly on Burt's face. He looked tired. She knew he had been working hard to fix the place up for his grandson and daughter-in-law's visit. There had been weeks of planning and shopping, trimming and weeding, painting and repairing. The house had never looked so good, and Burt had never looked so weary.

"I don't know." He shook his head slowly. "I do think it will be for longer than she promised him, though."

Sid's mouth opened and shut, words failing her.

Burt stood and opened the lid of the grill. Savory smoke poured out around him. "He's welcome to stay here for as long as he wants. As long as he needs."

Sid stepped over to him and tried to keep her voice low. "That woman just left her son. Drove up, chucked his bags out of the car, and took off. He's in the house right now telling the Geezers all about her stupid name and her stupid friend and some stupid dog. She's got a brand, Burt. A *brand!*" Sid waved the smoke away from her face. "Who needs a brand when you have a teenage son who needs *you?*" She watched as Burt silently turned the ribs on the grill. "Did you know he designed the logo for her asinine plan? A picnic basket with a little dog. And the name. Ha!" She threw up her hands. "Do you know what she's calling this . . . this . . . little adventure? PB&J. Like the sandwich. Have you ever heard of anything so absurd? It's their initials, Burt. Hers and her friend's and even the stupid dog's. But not his. There's no L for Leo. No room for her son in this ridiculous life crisis. He even set up her website. Did you know that? He created her logo and set up her website. He actually helped her with her damn *brand*. What the hell is wrong with that woman?!"

"She lost her husband, Sid." Burt flipped the last of the ribs and closed the grill. "Everyone grieves in their own way. You know that." Sid glared at him as she paced back and forth. "Trisha—I mean, Paisley . . ."

"With a Z!" snapped Sid. "It's Paizley with a Z. That's not even a name, by the way. It's a made-up word. The whole thing is ridiculous."

Burt pressed his lips together and watched the rage roll off her in waves. "Paizley was a kid when she met Gunner. Just turned eighteen. They got pregnant right away and were married only a few months after they started dating. She thought marrying a sailor meant that she would see the world. But all she saw was the naval base at Norfolk. Gunner was gone for most of their marriage. Went to sea every chance he got. Left Paizley and Leo by themselves. Her parents threw her out of the house when they found out she was pregnant. They never gave her any help or support. She worked two jobs. Camille and I sent money to help them out. Made a few trips a year up there to see Leo and give her a break. After Camille passed, I made the trips myself. Not as often, mind you, but I still went." He shook his head as his shoulders sagged. "Gunner's death hit them both real hard. Hit me hard, too. So, if Trisha—I mean, Paizley—if she needs to travel around, snapping pictures of food and sea turtles and whatnot, in order to move on, well, so be it."

Sid stopped pacing and stared at him, her fists at her sides. "She could have taken him with her. What is he supposed to do while *Paizley* is off becoming a travel blogger with a *brand*?"

Burt smiled weakly. "He's going to stay here with me. He's going to have a home. He's going to be loved and cared for. He's going to get some sun and make some friends and have a little fun. And I'm going to help him." He hooked a thumb toward his chest. "Me and the Geezers and Kitty. Even you, Sid." He shook a finger at her. "We are all going to help that boy. All of us. He is going to not only survive but thrive while he's here."

Sid's nostrils flared. "And how do you propose to make a

kid thrive, one who has lost his father and been abandoned by his mother?" she asked. "Do you have a plan?"

Burt smiled. "As a matter of fact, I do."

The kitchen door swung open, and Cesar poked his head out. "How are those ribs coming, Burt?"

"Just about done." Burt lifted the lid again to inspect the ribs. "Ask Leo to set the table, would you, Cesar? And help Kitty put out the potato salad and the other stuff. Sid and I will be right in with the these."

"Got it," replied Cesar, lifting his empty beer bottle in salute.

Burt handed a large platter to Sid, who took it and stepped up to the grill. "Just hold your tongue, Sid. Please. I'm asking this as a favor to me." He raised an eyebrow at her. "That boy has enough on his plate at the moment. He doesn't need you making him feel worse."

Sid pressed her lips together until they were a thin, white line. With a quick nod and a low grunt, she held the platter out while Burt filled it with ribs.

———

The conversation at dinner was colorful, to say the least. The members of Recent Geezer entertained the others with tales of their musical escapades. Eli had been playing music the longest, since he was a boy growing up in New Orleans, but Cesar had the craziest stories, having toured with a couple of rock bands in the eighties. A few of his more debauched tales made Kitty blush darker than her pink sweater. Burt had to ban him from saying anything further for fear that the elderly woman might faint.

Leo couldn't remember the last time he had laughed so hard. His sides hurt, and the tears that spilled from his eyes were the first joyful ones he'd shed in a year. For a moment, he forgot about the pain and sorrow, the loss of the life he used to have and the limbo he found himself in now.

After dinner, he helped clear the table as the Geezers unpacked their instruments for their biweekly jam session. They usually played at Burt's house on Sundays—it was their day to brainstorm and learn new songs—but in honor of Leo's arrival, they had agreed to do it on Saturday instead. Wednesday practices were always held at Guppy's place. He owned a small house on several acres just west of downtown, across the San Sebastian River. Wednesdays were full-on rehearsals. They performed in town at least every other week, more frequently if they were asked to fill in for a band who'd cancelled their gig. Tonight, the members sat around the living room and tuned up while Burt, Sid, and Leo cleaned the kitchen and Kitty made coffee.

"Thanks for dinner, Burt. I'm going to head out," announced Sid once the last of the dishes had been washed and dried.

"Oh, no, you're not, sweetheart." Kitty smiled as she poured coffee into a carafe. "Not until you've had dessert. I simply slaved over this cake. You have to have a slice." She waved a hand over the four-layer red velvet cake, proudly displayed on a cut-glass cake stand. "Now, if you two will be dears and take this into the living room for me, I'd appreciate it." She pointed to Sid and Leo and then to the cake stand and a serving tray piled high with coffee mugs, plates, napkins, and forks.

Sid sighed and reached for the tray.

Burt stepped forward, drying his hands on a dish towel. "They'll bring everything in a minute, Kitty. I just need a quick word with 'em first." The elderly woman nodded and exited the kitchen carrying the carafe of coffee.

"I have a proposal for the two of you." Burt leaned back

against the counter and folded the towel, studying his grandson and his tenant. "Sid, now that you've got your license and are all official, you'll be needing some help. And Leo, you'll be needing something to do in your spare time. Therefore, the two of you are going to work together." He folded his arms across his chest, resting them on his round belly. "Leo, you'll help Sid with whatever she needs. And Sid, you'll show him around and teach him a thing or two. Sound good?"

They both stared at him, mouths agape. A moment passed before they both blurted, "What?!"

Burt smiled and nodded. "See? You're in sync already."

Sid shook her head and held up her hands. "I can't have him working for me. I don't even have any work right now."

"You do so." Burt smiled.

"Only small jobs. Nothing of any significance." Sid scowled, hands on her hips. "Besides, he's not old enough. There are rules and laws and requirements. And I can't pay him. I can't even pay you!"

Burt nodded, undeterred. "You don't have to pay him. I will. Leo, you'll get a weekly allowance from me if you keep up your schoolwork once your classes start and you help Sid out at least fifteen hours per week. That will give you some spending money, and it will help you meet people and learn your way around town. And Sid, you'll give him tasks to do. Nothing that violates any laws, of course. He's a smart kid, and he'll learn quickly. Show him the ropes. It will give you some room to get out there and drum up business."

"This is insane." Sid ran her hands over her face. "I can't do this, Burt." She glanced at the boy, standing there in his jeans that were too short and his T-shirt that was too small. His wavy, brown hair flopped over his forehead and almost covered his dark gray eyes. He needed a haircut. He needed new clothes.

He needed his mother. Sid's heart squeezed. "No offense, Leo, but I can't take you on. I just can't."

Leo stood there, brow creased in confusion and mouth open but at a loss for words. Burt moved to pick up the tray of cups and plates. "You will take him on, Sid. If you don't, I'll start charging you rent. And not just going forward. You'll owe me for all the months you've been here and didn't pay."

Sid growled, "That wasn't our deal, Burt."

"I'm changing our deal, effective immediately." Burt picked up the serving tray and turned to face them both. "I think this arrangement will be good for both of you. I think each of you may be just what the other needs." He nodded to them and left the kitchen.

The other three members of Recent Geezer began playing in the living room, and the sounds of "I Won't Back Down" by Tom Petty drifted into the kitchen.

Leo and Sid stood staring at the spot vacated by Burt and then slowly turned to look at each other. Sid shook her head. "He's nuts. I can't do this. I'm not even sure if it would be legal. And I barely know what I'm doing. How can I possibly take you on and train you?" She closed her eyes and shook her head again.

"I'm sorry, but what are we even talking about?" Leo asked, frowning. "What do you do exactly?"

Sid began pacing back and forth, but the kitchen was small and allowed for only two steps in any direction. She mumbled under her breath and rubbed her temples. After a few moments, she halted and pointed a finger at Leo. "Fine. I'll do this, but I want you to know up front that this is not a joke. What I say goes, even if it doesn't make any sense to you. You'll do what I say, or this ridiculous arrangement is off. I won't be responsible if you get yourself hurt." She strode to the back door. "And I am not a babysitter."

"I don't need a babysitter," barked Leo. "I'm not a child."

The music from the living room seemed to grow louder, and Sid spun to face the teenager. "But you are a child, Leo. You are a child. That's the whole point."

"I am not!" Leo's face grew red. He hated this woman, whoever she was, whatever she did. He hated her. "I don't want to work for you, doing whatever it is you do. And I do not need a babysitter!"

"Really?" Sid threw up a hand. "Maybe you do, given the circumstances."

Leo took a step back. "What does that mean?!"

Sid shrugged one shoulder.

Leo pointed a finger at her. "Oh yeah?" he sputtered. "Well, you need a shower!"

Sid clamped her mouth shut and looked down at her clothes, noticing the mustard stain for the first time today. "No, I don't." She paused and wondered if she had taken a shower today, if she had taken one in the last few days. Surely she had, hadn't she? Sid pressed her lips together and glared at Leo, who stood with his arms crossed, looking very satisfied with himself. She grabbed the doorknob and shoved open the kitchen door. "Tomorrow, come to my office in the morning."

Leo smirked. "You mean the garage?"

"I mean *my office*," said Sid through gritted teeth. "Nine o'clock. Don't be late."

Leo huffed. "Tomorrow is Sunday."

"I work seven days a week, smart-ass. And now, you do, too."

Chapter Four

At ten minutes after nine on Sunday morning, Leo begrudgingly stood before the door to Sid's office in Burt's two-story garage. He raised his hand to knock, but he couldn't do it. Rather, he didn't want to do it. Lowering his hand, he looked around, stalling for time. The morning was quiet. Someone down the street was mowing his lawn, but the noise wasn't loud enough to drown out the birdsong coming from the trees in the yard.

His grandfather's house sat on the northeast corner of Saragossa and Sevilla streets. The house faced Saragossa, but the detached garage faced Sevilla. A plain, beige, two-door sedan sat in front of its automatic door. The sedan looked almost as old as his mom's car, Leo noted, but without the rust or scratches—or stained seat cushions, he noted, as he peered inside. Burt's silver pickup truck sat on the semicircular drive-way, both ends of which opened onto Sevilla.

The house itself was old, built in 1901, but it had been updated over the years. The clapboard house and garage had been painted since Leo's last visit. They were now pale blue with navy-blue shutters and white trim. The wrought iron fence running around the yard butted up against the sidewalks on Saragossa and Sevilla and was entwined with star jasmine. An oak tree stood tall and wide in the front yard, and several crepe myrtle trees lined the driveway. There were small patches of grass in the yard, but most of it was covered with plant beds overflowing with azalea bushes and large philodendrons. The effect was more primordial than manicured, and the air was scented with the ripe, earthy smell of soil and decomposing flowers, made even more potent by the oppressive summer heat. The neighboring yards had large live oaks and six-foot wooden fences running along the property lines, which provided Burt's yard with privacy and shade. Despite the shadows cast by the trees and plants, the Florida sun still seeped through gaps in the shade and turned everything a Technicolor green.

It was a pretty house, and it had seemed almost magical on Leo's first and only visit all those years ago. Now, it was the place his mother had dumped him so that he'd be out of the way, so that he couldn't hold her back as she set out on her adventures. The magic of the old house that Leo had felt all those years ago was gone, vanished the moment his mother pulled out of the drive and headed south without him. A muscle flexed in his jaw, and he breathed in and out slowly to calm himself.

A flash of movement caught his attention. Leo swung his gaze to the corner sidewalk. On the other side of the jasmine-covered fence stood the spirit of Kitty's husband, looking dapper as always in his seersucker suit and pink bow tie. He smiled and waved to Leo, who promptly turned around and banged on Sid's door.

Leo reached for the headphones around his neck, ready to place them over his ears and blast his music, but Sid's voice bellowed from inside, "It's open!" Leo flung open the door and stepped inside, quickly shutting it behind him. If the old man was so inclined, he could follow Leo into the office. No door would keep a spirit away, especially not one who was hellbent on trying to communicate with him. Leo waited, heart banging against his ribs, but the spirit didn't appear.

Once Leo felt he was safe, he glanced around Sid's office, taking note of his grandfather's handiwork in the renovated space. It no longer resembled the cluttered garage he remembered from his visit years ago. He leaned against the door, grateful that the room was pleasantly cool, and suspected his grandfather had outfitted the place with air-conditioning. The inside had been drywalled and painted the color of French vanilla ice cream, and a white ceiling fan whirled lazily overhead. Transom windows ran along both side walls and allowed enough sunlight into the room that the overhead lights were not needed at this time of the morning. He smelled freshly brewed coffee and the faint, artificial scent of some sugary-sweet air freshener that resembled baked apple pie. He inhaled deeply and smiled at the surprisingly pleasant combination.

From where he stood at the door, Leo studied the office, running his gaze clockwise around the space. Immediately to his left on the same wall as the door, Sid had tacked up several maps of the local area and decorated them with colorful sticky notes. A transom window sat just above the maps. The adjoining wall had once been the garage's opening, but the automatic door was sealed shut now and merely decorated the outside. Inside, along that wall, stood three mismatched file cabinets and an artificial paradise palm. In front of the file cabinets sat an old metal desk, its wood veneer top scratched and one metal side dented. Two guest chairs faced the desk. One was a faded, green wingback chair covered in a crushed-velvet fabric that was now more crushed than velvet. The other was a

Queen Anne dining room chair, its dark wood legs cross-hatched by years' worth of dings and scratches. The padded seat cushion had been recovered at some point in its life and now boasted a pink-and-blue floral print. A squat end table covered in water rings sat between the two chairs.

The next wall, directly across from Leo, hosted a makeshift kitchen complete with a mini fridge, a coffeepot, and a short, plastic shelving unit bearing a few chipped mugs, several mismatched drinking glasses, an assortment of boxed cookies and crackers, and an enormous bottle of ibuprofen. Light spilled in from the second transom window directly above the kitchen setup. A narrow, metal staircase stood next to the fridge in the corner of the room, spiraling upward into the studio apartment above the office. There was no door at the top of the stairs—the staircase just disappeared into an opening in the ceiling—and Leo couldn't see into the apartment. Sid's muffled swearing, however, could be heard as she banged around upstairs.

The last of the four walls, on Leo's right, was covered by heavy curtains that were a shade darker than the wall paint and hung from a wooden rod near the ceiling. Leo reached out and carefully pushed aside the nearest edge of the curtain to peer behind it. All he could see was a door, its casing flush against the corner. Leo scanned the room again and realized it was smaller than the footprint of the garage. This door must lead to a storage area, he reasoned. Leo let the curtain drop back into place and shoved his hands into the pockets of his too-short jeans.

He shook his head at his surroundings. His mom, if she were here, would have joked that the décor was from the "Early Yard Sale Era." Leo's chest tightened as he thought of his mom. She hadn't called him last night. He had broken down and sent her a text at midnight to ask if she had made it safely to her friend's house, and his mom had texted back immediately with the thumbs-up emoji and nothing else. She hadn't shared any details, hadn't asked how he was doing, nothing. Leo lowered his head, letting his hair fall across his forehead as he squeezed his eyes shut. He didn't want to be here. Not standing in this sad excuse for an office, not living at his grandfather's house, not stranded in St. Augustine. He wanted to go back home to Norfolk. Life there hadn't been great, but at least he was used to it. Leo turned to leave, but he was interrupted.

Sid clomped down the metal staircase, coffee mug in hand. Her wet hair was tied up in a bun on top of her head, and she was wearing yoga pants and an oversize yellow T-shirt. She'd spilled coffee down the front of her shirt and had tried to wipe it off to no avail. Leo frowned and wondered whether this was her uniform for whatever work she did or if she was merely a slob. "You're ten minutes late," she said as she sat in the squeaky desk chair and placed her mug on a file folder that already sported several coffee stains.

"You can take it out of my paycheck." Leo moved farther into the room but didn't sit down.

Sid leaned back, studying him for a long moment. Leo glared at her in return. She reached for her mug and waved to the empty guest chairs. "Have a seat."

Leo chose the wingback chair and sank down into its sagging seat. He was sitting so low that he had to look up at Sid, who smiled as she sipped her coffee. He pulled himself up and out of the wingback chair and moved to the dining room chair with the floral-patterned seat cushion. It was lumpy and rocked awkwardly due to one leg being shorter than the rest, but at least he was sitting high enough to be able to see over the desk.

"Nice office," he smirked.

"Thanks." Sid returned her mug to the stained file folder. "So, did Burt tell you what I do?"

Leo shook his head and scanned the top of her desk. On the corner nearest him, a stack of business cards sat in a clear plastic card holder. He picked one up and read aloud, "Old City Investigations. Sidney Stone, Private Investigator. Licensed and Insured." His eyebrows shot up, and he looked across the desk at the woman in the stained T-shirt. "Are you undercover?"

Sid frowned. "No, not at the moment. Why?"

Leo's gaze snagged on the coffee stain. "No reason. Just curious." He smiled at her and placed the card back in the holder. "Private investigator, huh?"

Sid sighed. "Yep. Long story for another time." She leaned forward, her chair emitting a high-pitched squeal, and rifled through the half-dozen folders on her desk. She selected one and held it out to Leo. "You can help me with this one."

Leo took the folder and opened it, scanning the one-page client intake form inside. "You want me to find a missing cat?" Leo kept reading. "A sixteen-year-old, one-eyed cat named Sherlock." Leo looked up. "Are you serious?"

"As a heart attack," replied Sid. "This case came in yesterday morning. Mrs. Kessler down the block suspects her husband let Sherlock out of the house on purpose because he never liked the cat. Was always jealous of him. And, truth be told, according to Mrs. Kessler, Mr. Kessler has good reason to be jealous because Mrs. Kessler does love Sherlock more than her own husband." One side of Sid's mouth ticked up in a half smile, revealing a small dimple in her right cheek. "Mrs. Kessler is beside herself with worry and asked me to find Sherlock." Sid picked up her coffee mug and saluted him. "And now it's your job. Find Sherlock and return him safe and sound to Mrs. Kessler."

"But the cat's name is Sherlock." Leo closed the file and

placed it on the edge of the desk. "Surely he can find his own way home."

"One would think," agreed Sid as she sipped her coffee.

Leo sighed. "What if he's dead?"

Sid raised an eyebrow. "The cat or Mr. Kessler?"

Leo fought to suppress a smile. "The cat."

"We are to find Sherlock and return him home, dead or alive." Sid shrugged. "But, if he's dead, it's probably best to wrap up the remains before returning him home. That would be the nice thing to do." Leo groaned with disgust, and Sid took another sip of her coffee. "The details are in the file. You can start today. Keep track of how much time you spend on the case. I've already agreed to a flat fee with Mrs. Kessler, so I won't be billing your time, but I'd like to know how long you spend on this one all the same. Mrs. Kessler emailed me about fifty photos of Sherlock, so I'll forward those to you." Sid patted a pocket on the side of her yoga pants and swore. "Left my phone upstairs. I'll be right back." She stomped up the metal staircase and disappeared.

Leo picked up the folder again and tried to read through the notes. Sid's handwriting was mostly illegible. He recognized the street name, Saragossa, but not the house number. Most of the other words were just a series of squiggles and smudge marks. Leo closed the folder and felt a chill settle around him. He didn't turn around, didn't move, didn't breathe.

"What's your email?" asked Sid, clomping down the stairs again with her phone in hand. When Leo didn't respond, she waved her phone in front of him and set it on the edge of the desk. "Here, just put in your contact info." She plunked down in the chair and shivered, pulling a long cardigan from the bottom drawer of her desk and wrapping it around her. "I've got to convince Burt to get someone out here to look at the AC. The damn thing blows ice-cold air at random. I swear, sometimes I'll turn it off completely, and I'm still freezing."

Leo shook his head slowly as he stared into the corner behind the desk. "It's . . . it's not the air-conditioning."

Sid followed his line of sight toward the corner. "It's not?"

Leo shook his head again, eyes wide. Sid leaned forward, studying him. Color had drained from the boy's face, and tiny beads of sweat dotted his forehead and upper lip. "What's wrong, Leo? Are you all right? Are you sick?" The boy pressed his lips together and didn't answer. "Leo? Do I need to call Burt?" Sid stood and came around the desk, taking his hand and prying the case file from his grip. She pressed her fingers into his wrist and felt his pulse racing. "Leo?!"

Leo blinked as the figure in the corner moved toward them. He hated it when spirits approached him. So far, Kitty Lonigan's dead husband had kept a respectful distance. Even last night in Burt's living room, the old man had stayed a safe distance away. However, this spirit in Sid's office had no qualms about getting up close and personal. The spirit said nothing as it came to stand next to Sid. Leo leaned away from it, but Sid held fast to his wrist with one hand as she pulled the sweater tighter around her with the other.

"You can see me."

It wasn't a question. It was a statement. The voice was soft and gentle, and yet it was not really a voice at all. It was more like a message downloaded directly into his brain, and that message came with sound. What he heard was something that sounded friendly, not frightening. And female. Most definitely female.

Sometimes the spirits communicated in words, as in this case, but more often it was through symbols or images. Most of the time, the messages were cryptic and made no sense to him, but the spirits always seemed to get this particular point across: he could see them, he could hear them, and they knew it. Leo closed his eyes, shook his head ever so slightly, and gripped the arm of the chair with his free hand until his knuckles turned white.

A knock on the door startled them both. Leo's eyes flew open, and he pulled his arm away from Sid.

"Come in," Sid called out as she handed the file back to Leo.

The office door swung open. A man wearing sunglasses and a dark blue sport coat stepped inside, and the spirit of the little girl vanished.

Chapter Five

"Good morning, Sheriff." Sid leaned against the desk and crossed her arms in front of her. "To what do I owe the pleasure?" Her voice was flat, and Leo noticed she was frowning. Her brows drew together, deepening the crease between them.

"Sidney, good to see you." The sheriff removed his sunglasses, closed the door behind him, and stepped farther into the room. His gaze roamed over her, taking in the yoga pants, coffee stain, and messy hair. "Hope I'm not interrupting anything."

Sid sighed, repulsed by his ogling and yet not surprised by it. It was the same thing every time she met him—a thinly disguised full body scan—no matter where they were or who was around. He'd even surveyed her figure in front of his own wife and daughters. When the man's eyes finally reached hers, she held his gaze. "Of course not, Sheriff. Nothing important happening around here." While she schooled her face to remain as expressionless as possible, she couldn't hide the flinty tone in her voice. Sid flicked her hand in Leo's direction. "This is Burt's grandson, Leo. He's going to be staying with Burt for a while, and he'll be helping me out a bit."

The sheriff extended a hand to Leo. "Good to meet you, son. I'm Sheriff Travis Colquitt. Welcome to St. Johns County."

Fumbling with the file folder, Leo rose from his chair and shook the sheriff's hand. "Nice to meet you, sir." When the sheriff released Leo's hand from his bone-crushing grip, Leo hugged the file folder to his chest.

The sheriff wasn't an overly large man, but he seemed to fill the room with his presence. He was the same height as Leo, just shy of six feet. And at around two hundred, he had a good fifty pounds on the boy. He had a full head of dark blond hair, bright turquoise eyes, and sun-kissed skin with faint tan lines at his temples from the frames of his sunglasses. Sheriff Colquitt wasn't wearing a uniform this morning. Instead, he looked like every other former frat boy turned reluctant adult, sporting pressed khaki trousers, a starched white shirt, dark blue blazer, and a bright blue tie with orange stripes. A gold pin in the shape of an open-mouthed alligator's head was stuck into his lapel. Leo recognized it as the logo of the University of Florida.

Leo stared at the man, guessing him to be a bit older than his mom, who was thirty-three. Maybe he was Sid's age, but he had no idea how old Sid was. If Leo had to guess, he'd bet the sheriff was younger than Sid but probably not by much. Strangely, something about him made him seem older than he looked. Maybe it was his summer tan and tailored clothes. Maybe it was his cocksure manner. Maybe it was the threat of the power he wielded as sheriff. Whatever it was, it seemed to have no effect on Sid, who was practically scowling at him.

Leo wondered how someone as young as Sheriff Colquitt could achieve such a position. Surely sheriffs were supposed to be old, grizzled lawmen who had been on the job for decades.

The man staring back at him was neither old nor grizzled. He was smooth, polished, and youngish.

The sheriff also felt wrong. It was not something Leo had ever felt before, and he couldn't put his finger on the problem. He felt himself becoming increasingly nervous and unsettled, like his lungs were straining and his heart was racing. He also felt a sharp pain in his right forearm. Leo wrapped his left hand around the site of the pain and squeezed, trying to make it stop. Something was wrong, but Leo couldn't make sense of what he was feeling. Was the sheriff a bad man? Dangerous, a threat to their safety? Or maybe he was carrying around some personal trauma? Leo didn't know. He'd never experienced anything like this with a living person. Usually, these types of sensations happened when spirits were around, and often they signaled how a person died or some other suffering they endured. But the sheriff was definitely not dead, and Leo was at a loss to understand what was happening. All he could do was stand there and dig his fingers into his forearm.

As soon as the sheriff broke eye contact, the pain vanished, and Leo's breathing eased. Sheriff Colquitt took in the low-budget office. "I take it business is good then, if you're hiring an associate." The sheriff swung his gaze back to Sid and grinned, but his smile didn't reach his eyes.

"You know me, Sheriff. Busy, busy, busy." Sid remained where she was, leaning against the desk with her arms crossed, and tilted her head to one side. "What can I do for you?"

"Well," began Sheriff Colquitt. He slowly unbuttoned his blazer, spread the front of his sport coat, and placed his hands on his hips. The movement caused his sleeves to tighten over his muscled shoulders and arms, and the butt of a revolver in a shoulder holster became visible. Leo held his breath and took a few small steps backward until he bumped into the wall. The sheriff's gazed flitted over to the boy, and the man's grin grew a bit broader.

Sid, for her part, didn't so much as blink. "Sheriff?" she prodded, drawing the man's attention back to her. "You were saying?"

Sheriff Colquitt took a step toward Sid. "I have a job for you, assuming you're not too busy."

Sid smiled. "Surely the sheriff of St. John's County has an entire department of deputies at his beck and call. What could you possibly need me for?"

Sheriff Colquitt chuckled and licked his lower lip. "Well, Sid, it's not me who wants to hire you. I'm merely the messenger." He pulled a folded piece of paper from his breast pocket and handed it to her.

Sid unfolded the paper and read the name and address scratched across it in an overly slanted hand. "Why does J. T. need a private investigator?"

"I think it's best if he explains it to you himself." Sheriff Colquitt glanced at his watch and buttoned his blazer. "He wants to meet you tomorrow morning at ten o'clock in his office. There is an appointment in his calendar under your name. You know, concerned citizen stuff." The sheriff winked at Sid and then turned toward the door. "J. T. will tell you everything you need to know at your meeting."

"What if I don't want the job?" asked Sid, sounding a bit like a child who's tired of being bossed around.

Sheriff Colquitt paused with his hand on the doorknob. "It's an easy job, Sid. High profile, well-connected client. Good money. His situation is delicate, and he will pay handsomely for your discretion." He smiled. "I'm the one who recommended you for the job."

Sid's eyebrows shot up. "Why?"

He chuckled. "J. T. and I go way back. We knew each other

at UF. He's a . . ." The sheriff shrugged. "He's a friend. Don't overthink it, Sid. You're a PI now." He glanced around the office and smirked. "And I thought you could use a break. After all, it's kind of hard to make a living finding lost pets." He winked at her again, opened the door, and stepped out into the bright Florida sunshine.

"Who's J. T.?" whispered Leo after the door closed. He didn't want to speak at full volume in case the sheriff was lingering outside.

Sid had no similar qualms. She crumpled the piece of paper and tossed it over her shoulder onto the desk, her eyes still boring holes into the door. "Jasper Theodore Clement," she said with a heavy sigh. "Asshole county commissioner for District Five, covering downtown St. Augustine, St. Augustine Beach, and Vilano Beach."

Leo reached for the crumpled piece of paper and smoothed it out, noting the address was for an administration building. "Is that his official title? Asshole County Commissioner?"

Sid nodded. "Yep. 'ACC' for short."

"Are you going to take the case?" Leo sat back down in the dining room chair and waved the piece of paper in the air. "The sheriff said it was good money. You could use it." Sid turned her head slowly toward him and raised an eyebrow. Leo smiled. "You could buy yourself some decent office furniture. Maybe some new T-shirts." He pointed at the coffee stain.

Sid glanced down and groaned. "I forgot about that." She looked over at Leo, taking in his appearance as well. His hair flopped in his face, and he was wearing those jeans that were too short for him, but she smiled at his black Pearl Jam concert T-shirt. She pointed to the logo in the center. "Nice shirt."

Leo looked down, as if he didn't remember what he was wearing. "Thanks. It was my dad's. He had a whole collection of them. Grandpa told Mom that he got rid of them, but he lied to her." A smile tugged at his lips, and he ran his hand over the logo. "Grandpa said he wanted me to have them since my dad loved them so much."

Sid's heart squeezed in her chest, a sensation that was all too familiar to her, and she swore silently to herself. After clearing her throat, she asked, "Do you own any shorts?"

Leo shook his head. "I have a bathing suit, but it's old. Not sure it even fits me anymore. But that's it."

"We're going to have to remedy that." Sid grabbed her coffee mug and headed to the staircase. "Go tell Burt that you need some spending money. Tell him I'm taking you to buy some shorts and, well, whatever else you need." She waved a hand to shoo him away. "This is Florida, Leo. It's hot as Hades here and twice as humid. If you're going to do PI work, you need to dress the part of a Florida teenager. Otherwise, you'll stick out like a tourist. Meet me at the car in five minutes."

———

Later that afternoon, Leo strolled along the sidewalk, heading west on Saragossa Street. He scrolled through the photos of Sherlock on his phone, all forty-eight of them. He deleted most of them, including all the blurry ones, the ones taken at a distance, and those of Sherlock as a kitten. The cat was sixteen years old and was likely dead by now, having escaped the house and crawled off somewhere to die in peace rather than be dressed up in a bow tie for yet another photo shoot with Mrs. Kessler. Sherlock should be easy to identify if found. He was a skinny orange tabby with his left eye sewn shut and a stubby tail that was the result of a partial amputation as a kitten. Poor Sherlock had had a rough start to life, but he'd been spoiled rotten by Mrs. Kessler ever since she brought him home from the animal shelter fifteen and a half years ago.

Leo took out the hand-drawn map that Sid had given him. She'd marked several spots where Mrs. Kessler had found Sherlock during his half-dozen escape attempts over the years. Leo would start with those locations first, then stroll up and down the surrounding blocks looking for an old cat that likely didn't want to be found. He checked for traffic, crossed to the other side of Saragossa Street, and headed west.

As he walked, he turned up the music in his headphones just a little bit. Kitty Lonigan's husband had been sitting on the front porch swing a few minutes ago, and Leo didn't want to take any chances. He was listening to Pearl Jam, even though he had traded the concert tee for a plain white one that he had bought with Sid. They had been to Target and the local Goodwill shop to purchase items that Leo would need: several pairs of cargo shorts in an assortment of drab colors from dark gray to light tan, half a dozen plain T-shirts in similarly drab colors, a pair of previously owned but never-worn running shoes, a new pair of flip-flops, two pairs of sunglasses, and a slate-gray backpack. He had declined the suggested baseball caps, telling Sid he hated wearing them because they made his thick hair curl outward around his ears. When she insisted that he needed one for work, he agreed to wear one of his dad's old hats that were stored in the closet of his bedroom. His plan, however, was never to wear one.

So here he was, working undercover, wearing his new plain white T-shirt, tan shorts, aviator sunglasses, and gray backpack while looking at Sid's map, listening to music, and hunting for a missing cat. Leo smiled to himself. This was not what he had expected to be doing on his first full day in St. Augustine. His thumb hovered over his phone, and he thought about calling his mom to tell her about it. He still hadn't talked to her since she hugged him goodbye yesterday, but he closed his phone and slipped it into his pocket. He'd tell her about his day when she called him. He was sure she'd call tonight. She would want to check on him, make sure he was all right. He'd wait for her to call him.

Leo slowed his pace as he passed the Kesslers' house, a two-story Spanish-style house with a red tile roof. He scanned the yard but saw no sign of the cat. He continued walking and consulted his map. The first stop on the tour of Sherlock Kessler's favorite feline haunts was a house on Riberia Street, the next block up. Leo turned left on Riberia and strolled down the sidewalk, glancing about for any sign of the cat. He slowed his pace again as he approached the house in question. It was a two-story clapboard house that had been divided in half down the middle, creating two apartments. The left-hand apartment looked unkempt, with broken blinds in the window, a dead plant in a chipped pot by the front door, and three days' worth of newspapers lying in a pile on an old welcome mat.

By contrast, the right-side apartment was well kept to the point of being fussy. A dozen or so potted plants were clustered outside the front door, and flower boxes lined the railings of the front porch. All of them were overflowing with colorful blooms. Frilly curtains framed the front window, and a spotless welcome mat sat in front of the door. The welcome mat was in the shape of a kitten, complete with a pink bow around its neck and a ball of yarn under its front paw.

A sudden chill ran up Leo's spine, and a flash of movement to his right caught his eye. He turned and saw the spirit of the young girl from Sid's office standing right next to him.

"You can see me."

It was the same statement as before. The same friendly voice.

Leo's skin grew clammy, his heart pounded against his rib

cage, and his breathing became ragged. He reached for his phone, ready to crank Pearl Jam even louder, but he stopped when he heard the voice again:

"*Cat.*"

The little girl drifted into the yard and up the porch steps. She stopped at the door of the right-side apartment.

"*Cat.*"

In his mind, he saw an image of Sherlock curled up in the lap of an old woman. The cat was most definitely Sherlock, with his left eye sewn shut. The old woman, however, was not Mrs. Kessler. The woman in his mind was small and frail, more like the diminutive Kitty Lonigan than the rotund woman holding Sherlock in most of the forty-eight photographs. Unlike Kitty, this mystery woman had short, black hair.

With shaking hands, Leo slid his headphones off and let them hang around his neck. His heart was still beating a frantic rhythm, but he took a shaky breath and pulled his phone from his pocket. He turned off the music and scrolled through the photos, looking for the best one of Sherlock. When he looked up, the spirit of the young girl was gone. He climbed the porch steps, searching for the little girl but not finding her, and finally knocked on the door of the right-side apartment. No one answered. He knocked again and then a third time.

A faint voice from inside the apartment finally responded. "Yes?"

Leo cleared his throat and leaned toward the door. "Hello, ma'am. My name is Leo. I live around the corner. I'm looking for a missing cat."

"Who?" asked the voice.

He frowned. "Leo. My name is Leo Roberts. I live around the corner with my grandfather. You may know him. Burt Roberts?" He leaned over the plants and tried to peer into the window.

A face suddenly appeared in front of him, and Leo stumbled backward, almost knocking over a pot of geraniums. Leo waved at the old woman staring at him through the window. It was the same woman he had seen in his head. The short, black hair was most definitely a wig. "I'm Leo Roberts. My grandfather is Burt Roberts. He lives around the corner in the blue house." Leo pointed toward Saragossa Street.

The old woman's face disappeared, and she opened the door just wide enough for the security chain to pull taut. She couldn't have been more than five feet tall. "I know Burt. You're his grandson?" She looked Leo up and down. Leo saw a flash of orange on the floor behind the woman and heard faint meowing.

The spirit of the young girl appeared right behind the woman, and Leo's breath caught in his throat.

"Cat."

Leo swallowed hard, took a step forward, and nodded, as much to the spirit as to the old woman. "Yes, ma'am. That's right. I'm hoping you can help me." Leo gave her his brightest smile and stretched himself up to his full height in order to pull the woman's gaze upward. As he did so, Leo slid his foot forward into the open space between the door and the frame. "I'm looking for a cat. It's gone missing, and I've been asked to help find it. Maybe you've seen it?"

"Missing cat?" The old woman blinked rapidly. "Nope. No, haven't seen it. Sorry." She moved to close the door, but Leo's foot was in the way.

As the door hit his foot, Leo was glad Sid had convinced him to wear the running shoes rather than the flip-flops. She'd jokingly asked him what he'd do if the search for Sherlock had turned into a foot chase. Leo had replied that he hated running, and his choice of footwear wouldn't change that. But eventually he'd given in to her nagging and worn the running shoes. Now, as the old woman banged the door against his foot, Leo almost wanted to tell Sid that she'd been right to insist that he wear them. He wouldn't tell her, of course. But he almost wanted to.

"Ma'am, please," said Leo, trying to look over her into the apartment.

"Stop that! Stop that right now!" yelled the woman. "Remove your foot."

She tried to slam the door on Leo's foot, but he braced the door with his arm. "Ma'am, I haven't even told you what the cat looks like yet. How do you know whether you've seen it or not? You don't even know which cat I'm talking about."

"I haven't seen her cat," cried the woman, pushing on the door with all her strength as Leo pushed against it. "The only cat in here is my cat, Willy."

Leo was eager to remove his foot from the doorjamb, but he held firm. "How do you know it was a woman who lost the cat? I didn't tell you that." The old woman growled in frustration, leaning against the door with her full weight, which wasn't very much.

A loud yowl came from the other side of the door, and a flash of orange flew past Leo's foot. Sherlock had squeezed himself through the opening in the door.

"Willy! No!" the old woman wailed when she saw Sherlock on the other side of the door. The old cat had stopped at the top of the steps, rocking back and forth, trying to decide whether to jump or not.

Leo slid his foot from the doorjamb and turned, scooping

up Sherlock and cradling the cat to his chest. He bolted for the sidewalk and sprinted down the street and around the corner until he reached the Kesslers' front door. Leo paused to catch his breath and looked down at Sherlock. The old cat stared up at Leo with his one eye and meowed.

"Good boy, Sherlock." Leo rubbed the cat's cheek with his thumb, and Sherlock leaned into Leo's touch, purring with appreciation. Leo held Sherlock to his chest as he knocked on the Kesslers' front door.

Chapter Six

L eo strolled into Sid's office and dropped Mrs. Kessler's check on the desk in front of her. "She said this is what she owes you. She already paid you half up front."

Sid picked up the check for fifty dollars and slid it into the top drawer of her desk. "Alive or dead?"

"Alive," answered Leo as he plopped down into the dining room chair. "Found him at a house on Riberia Street. Some old woman with a black wig."

Sid nodded. "Mrs. Murphy. She used to have about half a dozen cats. Her last one passed away a few months ago, I think. She found Sherlock once or twice when he ran away before, but she always returned him to Mrs. Kessler. I guess I'm not surprised she wanted to keep him for herself this time."

"She was calling him Willy," said Leo.

"As in One-Eyed Willy from *The Goonies*?" Sid smiled in amusement.

Leo shrugged. "I don't know. What are the Goonies?"

"Lord, give me strength." Sid pinched the bridge of her nose and shook her head. "How long did it take you?"

He shrugged. "I don't know. Half an hour. Forty-five minutes at most. That includes getting the check from Mrs. Kessler and waiting for her to box up some cookies for me." He pulled a plastic container of chocolate chip cookies from his backpack and opened the lid. "She said she just made them this morning." He took one and placed the container on the desk.

Sid reached for a cookie and studied Leo as he leaned back and took a large bite of his own. "Drinks are in the fridge. Help yourself."

He nodded and walked over to the mini fridge. "Want one?" He held up a generic cola. Sid nodded with her mouth full, and Leo brought her a soda, handing it to her across the desk. "So that was pretty easy."

"From now on, you can handle all of the missing pet cases." She smiled at him, and Leo saw that she had slight dimples in both cheeks. She popped the top on the soda can and asked, "How did you find Sherlock? Tell me about it."

Leo reached for another cookie and told her what had transpired, minus the part about the spirit helping him. Sid remained quiet throughout the story and continued to stare at him after he stopped talking. She simply nodded and sipped her cola, and Leo reached for a third cookie.

A chill ran up Leo's spine, and he watched Sid reach for her sweater and wrap it around her shoulders. Leo looked to his left, and the little girl was standing next to him.

"Cat." Her voice was light and musical. It almost sounded like giggling.

The spirit of the little girl reached out and placed her hand on his. The sensation was like holding an ice cube.

"That damn air conditioner," muttered Sid as she threaded her arms through the sleeves of her sweater. She watched as the color drained from Leo's face again. "Leo?!"

Leo swung his gaze to her. He placed his soda can on the

desk with a shaky hand and stood up. "I gotta go." He picked up his backpack from the floor and strode across the room to the door.

"Hey!" Sid picked up the plastic container. "What about your cookies?"

"Keep 'em!" Leo flung open the door and darted outside.

Sid raced after him. "Leo! Wait, Leo!" She jogged across the backyard and caught up with him as he waited with his hand on the doorknob. He stared at the ground and was breathing like he'd just run a marathon. She handed him the container of cookies. "You okay?"

He nodded. "I have to go."

"All right," she said. "I just wanted to say that you did a good job today. A really good job."

Leo looked up at her through his mop of hair, his gray eyes wide. "Thanks."

"I've decided to take the new case. The ACC." Sid watched as a smile tugged at the corners of his mouth, but his gaze darted around the yard. "I have a meeting with him in the morning. Should be interesting." She gave him an overly dramatic eye roll. "Come see me tomorrow afternoon. Let's say two o'clock. I'll brief you on the meeting with the ACC, and we'll go from there. Sound good?" Leo nodded, and Sid took a step back.

He opened the door, stormed through the kitchen, and disappeared into the living room. Sid stood in the doorway and heard Burt's voice call out, "Leo, my boy. How was your first day on the job?"

There was a muffled, "Fine," and then heavy footsteps bounding up the stairs.

"In or out, Sid. No sense in cooling all of Florida." Burt sauntered into the kitchen with an empty glass. Knowing Burt, it had probably been his third iced tea of the day.

Sid stepped into the kitchen and closed the door. "What's wrong with Leo?"

"Nothin's wrong with him," answered Burt.

She sighed. "Then what are you not telling me, Burt Roberts?"

Burt crossed the kitchen to the refrigerator and took out a pitcher. "Sweet tea?"

"Fine." Sid took a seat at the table in the corner of the kitchen as Burt placed a glass of tea in front of her. "So?"

"Cake?" offered Burt, removing the lid from the cake stand that held Kitty's leftover red velvet. Sid waved him off and waited for him to start speaking. Burt busied himself with cutting a slice, cleaning the knife, and wiping the counter, so it was a full five minutes before he sat down and faced her.

"How much do you know?" asked Burt.

Sid raised her eyebrows. "Let's assume I know nothing. Start from there."

Burt ran his hands through his thinning gray hair and sighed. He met Sid's stare and whispered, "Leo sees ghosts."

"*What?!*" mouthed Sid, opting not to vocalize for fear that she'd have no control over her volume.

Burt nodded. "He sees ghosts. Hears 'em. It freaks him out sometimes. He can't control it. It's why he's always got those headphones on. Apparently, loud music helps dampen the voices. His dad taught him that." Burt placed his hands on the table, spreading his fingers wide. "Gunner saw ghosts, too. Always struggled with it. I could never help him, and neither could Camille. Gunner inherited it from his dad, Camille's first husband. But he died when Gunner was only two, so he wasn't around to teach Gunner anything. And Gunner wasn't able to teach Leo much about it either." Burt shook his head and stared down as he curled his fingers into fists. "I've always wondered if the whole seeing-dead-people thing had something to do with Gunner's death." He shrugged. "Probably not, though. The navy ruled it an accident. Anyway, Leo struggles with seeing dead people."

Sid raked her hands down her face, leaned forward, and placed her elbows on the table. "Is he . . . is he mentally . . . is he stable?"

Burt frowned. "Of course, Sid. He's not crazy."

"He just sees dead people." Sid threw up her hands. "How often does this happen?"

"I have no idea," answered Burt. "With Gunner it was a constant thing. Whenever there were ghosts around, he saw them. It wasn't a choice. Some places had more ghosts than others."

Sid leaned across the table. "And Leo's mother brought him to St. Augustine?! Is she nuts?! This place must be lousy with them."

Burt nodded. "Gunner had a hard time growing up here. Said they were everywhere. It's the reason he enlisted in the navy as soon as he turned eighteen, so he could get out of this town and try to find some peace."

"For Chrissakes, Burt!" Sid threw up her hands again. "What is Leo going to do? How is that poor boy going to survive here?"

Burt smiled at her. "We'll help him. Keep him busy. Maybe find someone who has the same gift that he has, someone who can give him some pointers." He shrugged and took a sip of his tea. "We'll figure it out, Sid."

"We?! Not we. Don't put this on me, too."

"We, Sid. *We.*" Burt lifted a forkful of cake and frosting. "I could use your help. Leo could use your help. And, frankly, you could use some help yourself. So we'll figure this out together, all of us."

Sid pressed her lips into a hard line and shook her head. "You should have told me, Burt."

The man shrugged. "I figured I'd tell you when it came up."

"Well, it came up," replied Sid. "In my office. Twice. And here I am thinking that Leo has a mental health issue or an electrolyte imbalance or some other physical ailment that causes him to go as white as a sheet with his eyes bugging out of his head. But *nooooo*." She leaned forward. "Nothing like that. Apparently, there's just a ghost in my office."

Burt's eyebrows shot up. "Really?"

"Yes, really, Burt!" Sid said. "He got freaked out. Twice." Burt nodded and stared at his cake, and Sid moaned. "Excellent. That's great news. Just great." She gripped the edge of the table, her fingertips turning white. "Did he bring it with him, or was it here already?"

"The ghost?" asked Burt. Sid stared at him, nostrils flaring. He shrugged and answered, "I don't know. I would guess the latter, but I don't know."

Sid stood and paced around the small kitchen. "So my office is haunted?!" she whispered. "Fan-fucking-tastic!" She spun to face Burt and shook her finger at him. "You . . . he . . . you . . ." She clenched her hands into fists and pressed them to her eye sockets. "You should have told me, Burt."

With that, Sid stormed out of the kitchen and crossed the yard to her office. She paused when she reached the door, hesitant now to open it. She whispered to herself, "It's not haunted. It's not haunted. It's not haunted." Glancing up at the house, Sid saw Leo's face in one of the windows on the second floor. He ducked out of sight when he realized she saw him. Sid's heart squeezed yet again, something that was becoming a regular occurrence around the kid.

Sid took a deep breath, opened the door, and peered inside.

Chapter Seven

The following day, Sid sat in the small reception area outside County Commissioner J. T. Clement's office in the county administration building a few miles north of downtown St. Augustine. The young receptionist ignored her as she alternated between typing on her computer and scrolling on her phone.

Sid fidgeted with the tag of her short-sleeved, navy-blue sundress. She hadn't worn the dress in over three years and had forgotten how itchy the tag was on the back of her neck. The dress probably wasn't even in style anymore. Was it a little too short? A little too tight? Were the ruffles in the wrong place? Were there too many of them, or not enough? She had no idea. If she was really going to do this PI thing, she'd have to invest in some new clothes, but that was hard to do without money. And Sid had almost none. She smoothed the soft material over her thighs and stared at the clock on the wall, its second hand silently ticking away. Sid had been waiting for half an hour and vowed to include this time in the ACC's bill.

She pulled her small, leatherbound portfolio out of her handbag. The portfolio had been a gift from her mentor, Edwin Lewis Murdock III, upon his retirement last month. He was known as Trip to everyone who loved him and even those who didn't, and Sid had worked for Trip for two years, putting in the time she needed to apply for her Class C investigator's license. Trip had been eyeing retirement when Burt Roberts introduced them almost two and a half years ago. Being kindhearted and having no solid plan for his retirement, Trip agreed to keep his PI office open so he could train Sid. Having no other plans and no interest in doing much of anything at that time, Sid had reluctantly agreed to come work for him. She worked all of his cases, which steadily dwindled over her two-year tenure due to Trip's lack of interest in drumming up new business. He'd become famous early on in his PI career for solving a missing child case, but most of his cases involved a cheating spouse. That had been Trip's bread and butter.

Sid put in her time, and as soon as she was fully qualified and had passed her state license exam, Trip closed his shop and moved to Key West to spend his retirement years helping with his son's fishing charter. At the time of his retirement, there had been only two minor files still open, both of which were flat fees that had been paid in full, and Sid closed them quickly on her own. Now, thanks to Leo's closing of the Sherlock Kessler case, she had no clients, no open cases, and no good ideas for how to bring in new business.

On the day Trip Murdock left for Key West, he helped Sid move his three file cabinets, artificial palm, and old metal desk into the garage office that Burt Roberts had renovated for her. The portfolio was hidden in one of the file cabinets, wrapped in graduation paper with a giant white bow on top. Sid ran her fingers over the soft leather cover and chuckled to herself. Trip had chosen a rosy-pink cover, and Sid could just imagine him picking it out. He'd probably spotted it, decided that all girls must love pink, and marched to the register to pay for it. Sid hated the color, but she loved Trip, so here she sat with her pink notebook, ready to meet her first big client. She bit her bottom lip and wondered what the job would entail. If J. T. Clement wanted her to find his lost Pekinese or prize-winning calico kitten, she might just scream.

The receptionist's desk phone rang, and she picked it up, tossing her bleached-blonde hair over her shoulder and glancing up at Sid as if she'd forgotten there was anyone in the room with her. She replaced the receiver and smiled at Sid. "You can go in now." She turned back to her computer and continued typing.

"So soon?" asked Sid, not bothering to hide her irritation. "But he's only wasted half an hour of my time. Are you sure he doesn't want to keep me waiting longer?" The receptionist didn't look up, but Sid could see her roll her eyes.

As Sid entered J. T. Clement's office, she found him typing away on his phone. "Come in, come in. Have a seat." The councilman pointed to the padded leather guest chairs facing his desk without glancing up, much less offering her a handshake.

J. T. Clement was thirty-nine years old with thinning blond hair; a ruddy complexion that burned rather than tanned in the sun; and a round, soft body that had never been muscular. He looked older and fatter than his official photo on the St. Johns County government website. The Clement family had money, acquired years ago when J. T.'s grandfather had sold large swaths of family-owned land along Florida's Treasure Coast to real estate developers. It had made the Clement patriarch obscenely wealthy, and J. T. was enjoying the trickle-down effect of that family fortune.

He put the phone face down on his desk and leaned back in his chair. A smile crossed his lips as he watched Sid take a seat, his gaze roaming over her slender figure and bare legs. He nodded at her, as if in approval.

Sid willed herself not to pick up the nearest heavy object and hurl it at him. Trip had taught her to size up her clients quickly, and it took her mere seconds to realize that J. T. Clement was a first-class pig. She could use that to her advantage, though.

"Good morning, Councilman Clement." She removed a business card from her portfolio and leaned forward. She slowly slid the card across the desk toward him, smiling at him as she did so. "I understand that you are in need of some assistance and some . . . discretion." She sat back and crossed one leg over the other.

J. T. grinned at her legs as he picked up the card and began to play with it absentmindedly. "Indeed, I do." He paused and glanced at the card. "Sidney Stone." His smile never faltered, but Sid noted the beads of sweat around his hairline and on his upper lip. He looked at her and stammered. "Was it . . . your . . . your husband?"

"Yes. Yes, it was," answered Sid, cutting him off. She smoothed the material of her dress over her thigh and tried to take a deep breath, but the rapid thumping of her heart made that difficult. "Why don't you tell me about your situation, and then we can talk about how I might be able to help you?"

J. T. glanced at the business card again. "You're really a PI?"

"I am. Honestly and truly." Sid tilted her head to one side. "Licensed and everything."

J. T. looked her over once more and nodded as he slipped her business card into the breast pocket of his blue dress shirt. "Okay then, Ms. Stone. Or should I call you 'missus'?"

Sid paced back and forth in her office, wishing she had more floor space. She'd pushed the guest chairs and end table up against the wall to make more room, but it still wasn't enough. Still in her running clothes and sweating from the ten miles she'd mostly run through the historic downtown district, over the Bridge of Lions, into Anastasia State Park, and then back again, Sid wiped her face with a towel and guzzled more water. If the weather had been cooler or less humid, she could have run the whole way today, but it was the middle of the day in late July in Florida, and the jaunt had felt like running through water. Sid almost never ran during daylight hours in the summer because heat stroke was no joke, but today she'd needed to clear her head so she could think about what to do next.

Sid had run cross-country in high school, but after graduating, she lost interest in the sport and only participated in the occasional 5K fun run—that was, until one day almost exactly three years ago. In the early morning hours of that particular Sunday, after the police had left her alone for the very first time in her condo, she'd laced up her running shoes and taken off. She'd run for hours, until her thoughts had gone fuzzy and she had completely exhausted her energy and her tears.

Since then, she ran to cope, to ease her anxiety, to remember that she was alive and well during those times when she didn't feel that she was either. She ran whenever she couldn't think of anything else to do or any other way to solve her problems. She did her best thinking on her runs, and today she'd reached a decision around mile seven. Now, dripping sweat and pacing back and forth in her office, she was trying to convince herself that the decision was the correct one.

The knock on the door didn't slow her pacing. "Come in,"

she barked, wiping the back of her neck with the towel and glancing at her watch. Leo stepped into the office. "You're early."

He frowned. "Yeah, well, yesterday I was ten minutes late. Today I'm ten minutes early. I guess there's just no pleasing you."

"Being on time." She stopped her pacing to look at him. "That's what pleases me."

Leo shrugged. "Know what pleases me?" She raised an eyebrow, and he grinned. "Showering."

"I just came back from a run and didn't have time to shower." She grabbed her water bottle and took a swig. "You might want to think about running. It's good for you. Clears your head."

"I don't think about running unless I'm being chased." Leo sat in the dining room chair pushed up against the wall. "So, what do you want me to do today? Got another missing pet? Maybe you can make it more of a challenge this time, like a hamster or a parakeet."

Sid tossed her towel on the staircase banister and grabbed two sodas from the mini fridge, then handed one to Leo. "I had an interesting meeting with J. T. Clement this morning."

Leo snorted. "The ACC?"

"Yeah, him." Not wanting any barriers between them for what came next, Sid pulled her squeaky chair around the desk and positioned it in front of the makeshift kitchen so she and Leo were facing each other across the room. "But before I tell you about the case, you and I are going to have an honest conversation. We're going to lay our cards on the table before we go any further."

She pulled two snack bags of cheese crackers from the plastic shelves and tossed one to Leo. The chair squeaked in protest as she leaned back. She ran her hand through her long, damp ponytail and let out a long breath. "I am going to tell you what you need to know about me, and you are going to tell me what I need to know about you. It seems to me that we both are keeping a lot of secrets, the kind of stuff most people would never know about us if they met us on the street. Stuff most people wouldn't understand." She pressed her lips into a thin line as Leo's eyes went wide. "I don't want to tell you what I'm about to tell you, and I am willing to bet that you don't want to tell me anything either. But you and I are going to do this. Right here, right now."

Leo shook his head. "No, that's not a good idea. You're gonna think I'm crazy."

Sid shrugged. "I don't think you're crazy, and nothing you say is going to change that. You might think I'm crazy, though."

A smile ghosted the boy's lips. "I already do."

Sid opened her bag of crackers and popped two in her mouth. She motioned for him to do the same. It took several long moments before Leo's trembling fingers got the bag open. Sid waited patiently as he chewed.

"Your grandfather told me that you can see ghosts." Leo stopped chewing, stopped breathing. Sid leaned forward, placing her elbows on her knees. "I can't imagine how terrifying that must be for you. And I must confess that I don't know anything about ghosts, or what you can do or what you go through on a daily basis, but I have seen what happens to you in this office. Twice now, you've looked like, well, like you've seen a ghost." She held his gaze, fairly certain he still wasn't breathing. "So, did you?"

Leo nodded slowly and forced himself to swallow the crackers he'd been chewing, chasing them with a sip of his soda. "Spirits," he mumbled. Sid frowned, and Leo cleared his throat. "I call them spirits, not ghosts."

"Is there a difference?" Sid forced another cracker in her

mouth, trying to act like this was no different than a simple conversation about the weather.

"Sometimes people use both words to mean the same thing, but I think of them differently. Spirits are people who have died and crossed over. But ghosts . . ." He chewed his bottom lip as he thought for a moment. "Ghosts are stuck. They haven't crossed over. Something is holding them here, or they may not even realize they're dead. There may be other differences between them, but that's how I distinguish the two. I haven't come across many ghosts. Mostly what I see are spirits."

Sid kept her voice even and her gaze fixed on the boy. "Which kind have you seen in my office? Is there more than one?"

Leo shook his head. "It's a spirit, and I've only seen one."

"Okay," said Sid. She wanted to run from the room, but she kept her voice as calm as she could. "You can see it?"

Leo nodded again.

"Can you hear it, too?"

"Yes." He sipped his soda. "But it's more like a *knowing*, knowing what it's trying to say rather than hearing it with my ears. Sometimes it's words; sometimes it's images. Most of the time it doesn't make a lot of sense to me."

"And the music helps tune it out?" Sid pointed to the headphones around Leo's neck.

His fingers reached for them reflexively. "Sometimes. Not all the time, though. Not as often as I'd like."

Sid glanced around the room. "Is the spirit here now?"

Leo shook his head, and Sid breathed a silent sigh of relief. Leo could see her visibly relax, and he smiled a little. He had to give this woman some credit. She was doing a good job of hiding how nervous she was, better than almost anyone else he'd ever talked to about this stuff—which was why he never talked about it.

"Sometimes they are transparent, like I can see through them," he offered. "But sometimes the spirits look solid. Real. Just like regular people. When I was a kid, I sometimes had a hard time recognizing who was alive and who was dead. I'm pretty good about it now. Some spirits look fine, normal. There's nothing wrong with them. But others look like they did when they died, all bloody and mangled and stuff." He looked down at his sneakers, the nearly new ones they'd bought the day before. "I really hate it when they look like that."

Sid let him take another sip of his soda and swallow a few more crackers before she continued. "What does the spirit look like, the one in my office?"

Leo shook his head slightly and kept staring at his shoes.

"Leo, I'd like to know if there is a spirit living with me in here."

"It's why you're cold," he muttered, finally looking up at her. "It's not the air-conditioning. You feel a chill when the spirit is around."

Sid thought back to all the times in the past two and a half years that she'd felt chilled in this office and in her apartment upstairs. It happened all the time—most days of the week, sometimes multiple times a day. She squeezed her eyes shut for a beat and then forced the corners of her lips up into a slight smile. "Well, Burt will be happy to know he doesn't need to call a repairman." Leo dropped his gaze. "Why don't you want to tell me about it? Do you know the person? The spirit?"

He shook his head. "I don't know her."

"Her?" The crease between Sid's brows deepened, and she bit her bottom lip.

"She's not bad," blurted Leo. "I don't get the impression that she's mean or angry or wants to harm you, if that helps."

Sid smiled. "Good to know, Leo, but I'd still like you to tell me what you saw."

He sighed heavily, his shoulders sagging. "You sure? Most people think they want to know, but they really don't."

Sid pursed her lips and raised an eyebrow, waiting for him to answer her question.

Leo tipped his head back against the wall. "It's a girl. A little girl." He swallowed hard. "She looks exactly like you."

Chapter Eight

All color drained from Sid's face as she sat motionless, staring at Leo across the small office. Leo studied her, waiting for a scream or a string of colorful swear words. That's what usually happened when he told someone this kind of news. But Sid didn't move, didn't say anything for a good long minute.

When she finally did make a move, it was to stride to the wall with the floor-to-ceiling curtains. She stood in the middle of the wall, pressing her face into the curtains and bunching the material in her fists. She took a few deep breaths, trying to calm the rising sense of panic. Leo quietly set down his drink and bag of crackers and watched her. Sid shook her head, mumbling something under her breath, before finally straightening herself and squaring her shoulders.

"Does she look like this?" Sid pushed the curtain panels back so that most of the wall was revealed.

Leo stood, eyes going wide, and then he walked slowly toward her. He stared at the collage of photos and newspaper articles that were arranged on the wall. Sid tapped the photo of a little girl with sable hair and dark brown eyes sitting on Sid's lap. The child was wearing a yellow dress with white polka dots. Rows of embroidered red strawberries decorated the neckline and the little cap sleeves. She was smiling at the camera. A happier version of Sid was kissing the little girl's cheek.

Leo nodded and tried to clear the lump from his throat. "That's her," he croaked. "That's the little girl I've seen here. She was wearing this dress."

"This is my daughter, Iris." Sid pressed her fingers to the photo. She didn't cry, not anymore. Not after that first night when she'd gone running after the cops had left. "My husband, Wes, took this photo of us at a party. They died later that night. Car accident. Drunk driver." She pressed fingers to another photo on the wall. This one was an official portrait of a man in a law enforcement uniform. "Have you seen him? His spirit?"

"No, I haven't. Just Iris. But your husband looks like he was a nice guy," offered Leo.

"He was the best." Sid smiled fondly at the photo. "Wes was kind and smart and nice. So, so nice. And, God, was he good-looking."

Leo studied the photo and the ones around it. Wes Stone had been handsome in a rugged, outdoorsy sort of way. Blond and square-jawed, with light brown eyes, broad shoulders and bulging biceps. Leo glanced sideways at Sid. She was sort of pretty, he thought, for someone as old as she was. While Wes had been blond and tan, Sid was raven-haired and fair-skinned. She was also tall, slender, and athletic. And there were the dimples in her cheeks when she smiled, which Leo had only seen once. Smiling made her look like a different person; a much nicer, gentler person. Maybe that's why she didn't do it so often. After all that she'd suffered, maybe she didn't want to be nice and gentle. Leo frowned as he studied her. If she would only shower and wear something other than workout clothes with food stains on them, she would probably be attractive. To old guys, at least.

Sid pressed her fingers to a wedding photo, her in a white dress and Wes in a tan suit on a sandy beach. She had flowers in her hair, and they were both barefoot. The image made Leo smile.

"Wes and I had been married for fifteen years when he died. Iris was only five. She had just started kindergarten. We tried for almost ten years to have a baby before Iris came along. Wes and I had given up hope and were getting ready to try to adopt when we learned I was pregnant. Iris was the light of our life, so funny and happy and always laughing." She tilted her head to the side and pressed her fingers to a photo of the three of them at the beach, building a sandcastle.

Leo scanned the wall. Its vanilla-cream paint was covered with family photos, newspaper clippings, crime scene photos, and handwritten sticky notes. In the center of it all was the photo of Iris sitting in her mom's lap. "I'm so sorry, Sid," he whispered.

"Is Iris . . . does she seem . . .?" But Sid wasn't able to finish the question. She bit her lip and shook her head.

Leo studied Sid's profile. She wasn't crying. Usually people were crying by now, but not Sid. "Iris seems happy. Peaceful. She was even laughing."

"She was always laughing." Sid smiled. "Does she look—"

"No," blurted Leo. "She's fine. She's normal. She's not hurt or anything. She looks just like this." He tapped the photo in the middle of the wall.

"Good. That's good," said Sid. She took a deep breath and shook her head once to try to clear her thoughts. The fact that she was having this conversation with a teenage boy was crazy. They were talking about Iris haunting her office, and she was showing Leo her wall. If she was honest with herself, she wasn't sure what she'd expected from a conversation about ghosts or spirits or whatever it was that Leo could see. Sid took a step back, paused, and then took another. "I call this my Wall of Shame."

Leo stepped back to stand next to her, his eyes scanning the photos and newspaper clippings. "Why?"

Sid wrapped her arms around herself, squeezing hard as if to hold on to the pain. After all, it was all she had left of her previous life.

Noticing her movement, Leo glanced around. There were no spirits. Sid wasn't cold. She was just sad.

"Like I said"—she nodded to the photo of her and Iris—"we went to a party that day. It was the weekend after Labor Day. Wes was a deputy with the marine unit of the sheriff's office. Labor Day weekend was always a busy weekend for him. The last summer hurrah, everyone boating and drinking and doing stupid, dangerous stuff. Wes's partner was Manny Sandoval, and they had worked together for years. Manny always threw a big party the Saturday after Labor Day, when things were quieter. This year, the party was big. He was a marine sergeant deputy and had just turned fifty-five, and because he was eligible for retirement, he decided to take it. He and his wife, Emily, were planning to move to Orlando to be close to their twin daughters, both of whom were married and had little kids. Manny's plan was to take a part-time gig driving a ferry around the Disney resorts and spend the rest of the time with his grandchildren."

Sid rocked back on her heels. "That party was a huge bash. Lots of deputies from the sheriff's office stopped by to celebrate Manny's retirement as well as Wes's promotion. He was being promoted to marine sergeant deputy to take over for Manny, and he had been assigned a new partner. The party lasted all day and late into the night. Manny's wife, Emily, was my best friend, and I was so sad that she was moving. I drank too much that night, and I kicked up a fuss when Wes wanted to leave. It was almost eleven o'clock, and Iris had fallen asleep on his shoulder, but I wanted to stay, to be with Emily until the last possible moment. I offered to stay and help clean up, and Manny would drive me home when we were done."

Sid squeezed her eyes shut. "Soon after Wes got home from the party, he called me to tell me that he was going to pick up his new partner at the all-night gun range on Big Oak Road, a few miles north of where we lived. My phone was in my purse, and I didn't hear the call. It went to voicemail. All Wes said was that he had gotten a call telling him that the new guy was drunk and he needed to go pick him up. Since I was still at the party, and Wes couldn't leave Iris home alone, he took her with him.

"Wes's car was found off Big Oak Road. They were both dead. A drunk driver in an old Camaro hit them from behind and pushed them into a concrete barricade along the side of the road, where some work was being done on a drainage swale."

Sid opened her eyes and sighed heavily. "Iris was in her booster seat behind Wes. When they were hit, the mechanism in Wes's seat failed, and it collapsed backward. Iris was crushed."

When Sid didn't continue, Leo asked, "What about Wes?"

Sid stared at her husband's photo. "Wes died of a gunshot wound to the head."

Leo's gulp was audible. He scanned the headlines taped to the wall, searching for confirmation. "Someone *shot* him?"

"Suicide." Sid shook her head. "That's what the coroner ruled it. Shot himself in the head. Said it looked like it happened after the accident, so he was injured but still alive after they were hit."

Leo glanced sideways at Sid. "I'm really sorry."

"Don't be." She waved her hand in the air, like she was

shooing away a fly. "He didn't kill himself. Wes would never do that. He was a law enforcement officer. If he was alive after that accident, he would have tried to help Iris. He would have tried to help the person in the other car. And if he was seriously injured and not able to get himself out of the car, he would have at least tried to call it in. He would never have shot himself. Never." She shook her head once. "Someone killed him that night. And if I hadn't been drunk and whining about my best friend moving to Orlando, I would have gone home with them. We would have put Iris to bed. Iris would still be alive. Wes might still be alive, too."

Leo stared at the wall, at all the photos and clippings and sticky notes, and he understood how much guilt she felt. He could feel it coming off her in waves. She felt guilty for staying at the party and not going home with Wes and Iris, for not keeping them from being in that accident. But she hadn't called it her wall of guilt.

"I don't understand why you call this your Wall of Shame." He shook his head. "Why are you ashamed of their death?"

Sid sighed. "I'm not ashamed that they died, Leo. I'm ashamed that *I'm* that the one who lived."

Chapter Nine

"So that's my story." Sid pulled the curtains closed over the Wall of Shame. When the photos and newspaper clippings were hidden from view once again, she turned to face Leo. "What do you think?"

"I think it's awful," he answered. "I'm so sorry."

Sid smiled ruefully and shook her head. "No, not about that, but thank you. I meant about working together. I know your secret, and now you know mine." She pointed to him and then to herself. "Do you think we can work together?"

Leo nodded.

Sid placed her hands on her hips and took a step toward him. "Then this means no more secrets. If you see a ghost or a spirit or whatever, regardless of who it is or what it looks like, you have to tell me. No more of this breaking out in a cold sweat and running away. Agreed? Can you do that?"

Leo chewed on his bottom lip. "You want to know about all the spirits I see?"

"And hear and feel and whatever," she replied. "However it

works, whatever you experience, you'll tell me, and I'll help you in whatever way I can."

Leo looked down at his feet, considering her proposal. "You believe me then?" His voice was so quiet, Sid almost didn't hear him.

She took a moment before answering him. She'd never believed in ghosts at any point in her life. She'd grown up in St. Augustine, had been on numerous ghost tours, had heard stories from the locals, but she'd never had any experiences of her own. Leo stood before her, head hanging down and eyes averted. What she *had* seen was his panic, his fear. That much was real. "Yes, Leo. I believe you. I don't understand it, but I believe that you are telling me the truth." She shrugged. "Maybe you can teach me about it as we go along."

Leo looked at her through his long, dark lashes. "Okay."

"Good." Sid moved to the staircase and grabbed her towel off the banister. "I'm going to take a quick shower, and then you and I are going to get to work."

Leo smiled. "The ACC?"

Sid clomped up the stairs. "Yep, the ACC."

———

Twenty minutes later, Sid and Leo strolled down Saragossa Street and turned right on Cordova. It had been eight years since Leo last toured St. Augustine, and it all looked vaguely familiar to him. He let Sid lead the way and kept his head-phones around his neck, although he desperately wanted to put them on and crank up the music.

The building on the corner of Cordova and Hypolita streets was a weathered, wooden structure with a wrap-around porch. A faded sign that swung from the porch eaves read, "Bonney's Bar." The smell of beer and fried food wafted over to them, blown their way by the ceiling fans spinning frantically on the porch and the faint breeze coming off the nearby Matanzas Bay. Several tables had been pushed together on one side of the porch, and a dozen or so customers laughed loudly as a waitress approached them with a tray full of beers. Two men began stacking empty pint glasses to make room for the incoming round of drinks.

"This is a drinking town with a history problem." Sid winked at Leo. "At least, that's what it says on the T-shirts in the tourist shops."

"More like a drinking town with a ghost problem." Leo turned his head away from Bonney's Bar. "I bet those folks don't know they have two spirits with them. One male and one female."

"Really?" Sid looked over her shoulder at the revelers on the porch. "Is one of them Anne Bonney?"

"Who?" Leo didn't turn his head.

Sid pointed to the bar. "She was a famous pirate. There's a plaque on the wall inside that says the ghost of Anne Bonney haunts that building."

Leo took a quick peek over his shoulder. "I don't think so, unless Anne Bonney is a teenage girl wearing a fancy pink dress." Sid's smile faded. "The boy is wearing a tux. My guess would be that they died at a wedding or something like that." He shrugged.

"There were several teenagers killed in a collision on prom night a while back," Sid said. "Maybe ten years ago, give or take. Two couples. One of the boys was a star on the high school baseball team. It was him and his girlfriend and his twin sister and her boyfriend. The boyfriend was also a baseball player. The brother and sister came from a big family, all local. I remember Wes talking about it. It had the whole department really shaken up. Some of the deputies knew the families, and a few were distantly related. St. Augustine may be full of tourists most of the year, but it's a small town at heart."

Leo nodded. "Maybe those spirits are the sister and brother. That would make sense if those people hanging out at the bar are their family members." He shrugged again.

Sid placed a hand on Leo's arm. "Do you want to say something to them? Let them know about the spirits?"

Leo gripped his headphones so tightly that Sid could see his knuckles turning white. He'd made that mistake in the past, letting people know that there was a spirit near them. None of the three times he'd done it had gone well. One person had had called him cruel; another had called him crazy. And the third went on a loud, expletive-filled rampage that had attracted the attention of onlookers and caused Leo to run away. He'd vowed never to do it again. And he hadn't, until this afternoon in Sid's office.

Sid held up her hands. "Okay, okay. I was just asking." She glanced back again, her heart aching for the group of people lifting their beer glasses in a toast. She nudged Leo with her elbow. "Come on, we've got work to do."

They continued to walk south on Cordova, past a line of small shops that included a used bookstore, Old City Books. The door of the bookstore was propped open, and a white cat sat in the entrance, grooming itself and frowning at passersby. The cat watched Leo and Sid as they strolled along the opposite side of the street. It suddenly hissed and darted into the shop, and Leo felt an icy chill slice through him. A spirit had passed through him and crossed Cordova, heading in the direction of the bar. The apparition was faint and difficult for him to see in the bright sunlight, but it was clear enough to discern that it was a large man with shoulder-length dark hair tied back at the nape of his neck. The spirit was wearing a torn white shirt, dark breeches, and boots. The back of the white shirt was stained a dark color. He'd been shot or stabbed by the looks of it. The spirit stopped in the middle of the street and began to slowly turn back in Leo's direction, as if he could sense Leo looking at him.

Leo quickly spun back around and was grateful for the sunglasses that Sid had insisted he wear. He gripped his headphones again and was sorely tempted to put them on. He would do exactly that if the pirate came anywhere near him.

"Slow down, Leo." Sid tugged his arm. "Take it easy. You want to fit in, not draw attention to yourself."

Oh, if you only knew, thought Leo. "I just want to get away from here." Sid swiveled her head to look back at the bar. "Don't look!" he hissed. "There's a pirate standing in the middle of the road, and I really don't want him to know that I can see him. Can we please just get out of here?"

"A pirate ghost?" Sid took another quick look and saw nothing but a portly man exit the bar, lumber down the porch steps, and retrieve a pack of cigarettes from the front pocket of his Hawaiian shirt. "I'm not surprised. There's bound to be quite a few ghosts around here—I mean, spirits. In fact, this town must be swamped with them. Can you see any others?"

Leo lifted his gaze to take in the street, the shops, and the tourists, but he promptly lowered his eyes again. "Yep."

Sid noted his grip on the headphones. "Do you want to put those on?"

"Only if one decides to talk to me." He lowered his hands, shoving them into his pockets. "Please don't be mad if I put them on. I'm not trying to ignore you. I'm just trying to ignore them."

Sid nodded. "Do what you have to do, Leo."

The west side of Cordova Street bordered the east edge of the campus of Flagler College, a small liberal arts college with a couple thousand students. In the middle of summer, the campus was quiet. The school's main building was an old, repurposed luxury hotel built by industrialist and oil magnate Henry Flagler. The east side of campus was all cream-colored stucco and red tile roofs, conspicuously devoid of student activity. In another month, though, when the students returned, the St. Augustine locals and tourists would share their streets, bars, and restaurants with swarms of young adults eager to soak up the sun and their freedom in equal measure.

Before they reached the intersection of Cordova and King streets, Sid took Leo by the arm and led him across the road and through a shady park that sat between Cordova and the Governor's House Museum. Leo gazed longingly at the fountain in the center of the park. Its water looked cool and inviting as it bubbled and sparkled in the bright afternoon sun.

Across King Street from the park stood the Casa Monica Hotel, another old luxury hotel built in the time of Henry Flagler. This hotel, unlike the one that housed college students across the road, found its renaissance through enough enthusiastic investment to restore it to something akin to its former glory. Similar to the other buildings in the area, it had bright, off-white stucco with red tile roofs, but it also had a distinctive Moorish Revival twist added to its Spanish-style architecture. The combination made for a grand, showy façade that looked decidedly more upscale and modern than many of the other old buildings in town. The Casa Monica was enjoying its reign as a busy resort in the heart of St. Augustine. A valet stand was located next to the porte cochere, and a young man in a crisp, white shirt and shorts spoke to the driver of a sleek, black sports car.

"Fancy," said Leo, noting both the sports car and the grand hotel.

"Sure." Sid pursed her lips. She took up position under a massive oak tree, whose branches stretched across King Street as if they were reaching for the hotel. Under the oak was an old cannon, painted black and mounted on a short pedestal. Sid leaned against the cannon and pulled out her phone. "See that salon across the street?"

Leo shuffled into the shade of the oak and looked across the road at the façade of the Casa Monica. Next to the porte cochere was a shop that fronted King Street. Its windows were filled with colorful bottles and rolled towels, all of it placed artfully on stands or spilling out of baskets. Gold letters stenciled onto the shop's door read, "Cielo Spa." The "o" was shaped like a sun with many rays of light beaming from it. The name also appeared on the sign hanging above the entrance, a yellow square in an electric-blue frame similar to those of the other shops sharing King Street frontage with the Casa Monica. There was an art gallery, a wine shop, and a Starbucks. Their yellow and blue signs stood out against the white stucco of the block-long hotel building. Everything a wealthy tourist could want to spend their money on, thought Leo.

He looked over at Sid. "I don't want a haircut."

Sid smiled, thinking that's exactly what he needed. "That's not why we're here." She handed him her phone. The photo on the screen had been pulled from Instagram. A leggy blonde in a bright red bikini was draped over the lap of a shirtless, soft-bellied man sporting light blue swim trunks and a receding hairline. Leo looked up at Sid with raised eyebrows and gave back the phone.

Sid pointed to the man in the photo. "That's the ACC."

"Really?" Leo looked at the photo again, zooming in on the man's round, sunburnt face. "And the woman?"

Sid folded her arms. "His wife."

"Seriously?!" He zoomed out and studied the blonde again. She was prettier and fancier than any woman he'd ever seen in person. "She looks like a model or a movie star or something. How did she end up with that guy?"

Sid grunted and glanced again at the photo. The ACC's wife was pretty in a pampered, monied sort of way. Dyed-blonde hair, manicured nails, and a figure likely sculpted by high-priced Pilates classes with a private trainer named Sven. "How'd she end up with him? Well, *she* is Mrs. Josette Clement of Savannah, Georgia. Apparently, Josette's mother's family is old money. Her father's family is new money. And Mr. Jasper Theodore Clement, who prefers to be called J. T., has been enjoying the benefits of both ever since he and Josette, who goes by Josie, met in Charleston. Josie was a junior at the College of Charleston at the time, and J. T. was twenty-nine. They dated for a year and a half and then got married at her family's house in Savannah's historic district just two weeks after she graduated college. Now, after eight wonderful years of boats, cars, houses, vacations, and, of course, marital bliss, J. T. suspects that his beloved Josie is cheating on him."

"Is she?" Leo handed the phone back to Sid.

Sid shrugged. She reached into her bag, pulled out a folded tourist map, and proceeded to fan herself against the heat. "That's what I've been hired to find out. Given that this is an election year, J. T. wants to determine whether his suspicions are true so he can decide how best to contain the situation."

Leo removed his sunglasses and wiped his face with the hem of his T-shirt. "You mean he wants to know whether he should divorce her?"

"Oh no," Sid said. "Nothing so pedestrian. He wants to know whether he needs to pay off the boyfriend and send his wife on an extended vacation so the whole thing can be hushed up. There will be no divorce as long as her money is still green and plentiful."

Leo shook his head and slipped his sunglasses back on. "J. T. sounds like a douchebag."

Sid smiled. "Well, he is the aptly named ACC, after all. Nevertheless, since *his own* green and plentiful money is what I need right about now, I've agreed to take the case. We're going to tail Josie, find out where she goes and what she's up to, and take some pictures."

"Okay." Leo looked back across the street. "And she's in there? The Cielo Spa?"

Sid nodded. "She is. She has appointments every Monday, Wednesday, and Friday."

"Jesus." Leo whistled softly. "How much does that cost?"

"A small fortune apparently," replied Sid. "Manicures and facials every Monday. Massages every Wednesday. And hair on Friday. Blowouts or highlights or whatever women like her have done." She fought the urge to smooth her own flyaway strands that had escaped her ponytail. Instead, she studied her watch. "Today's appointment was for two o'clock. I called and asked how long it would take for a manicure and pedicure and was told sixty to ninety minutes."

"What?!" Leo screwed up his face in disbelief. "It's just nail polish. I can paint a whole room in that amount of time."

"I don't know what to tell you, kid. Apparently, it's all about the pampering." Sid continued to fan herself. "We'll wait here until she comes out, and then we'll see where she goes."

Leo rolled his eyes and settled in to wait.

Twenty minutes later, they were still standing under the oak tree. Leo, sweating and bored, was listening to his music and studying the tourist map while Sid scrolled through Josie Clement's social media accounts. Their clothes were soaked through with sweat, thanks to the summer heat and humidity.

A high-pitched "Yoo-hoo!" reached them over the din of traffic, and Sid looked up to see a blonde woman in a white sundress being embraced by a petite redhead in front of the Cielo Spa. With his headphones on and his attention focused on the map, Leo hadn't noticed anything.

Josie Clement stood on the sidewalk, arms out and fingers splayed so as not to ruin her new manicure. The redhead released her from the hug and immediately began talking. The two women linked arms and headed toward the crosswalk. They waited for the light, the redhead talking the entire time and Josie nodding and smiling, and then they crossed King and disappeared around the corner on St. George Street.

"Come on." Sid nudged Leo and began walking toward her mark.

Leo pulled his headphones off, silenced his music, and stuffed the map in his pocket. "What's happening?"

"Josie is on the move."

They rounded the corner, and Sid caught a glimpse of Josie's golden-blonde head as she entered the pedestrian-only section of St. George Street. The redhead was still jabbering away, hands gesturing wildly. "The blonde up ahead. White dress. Walking with a short woman with red hair wearing a green top."

St. George Street ran the length of the historic downtown district of the Old City, as St. Augustine was known. In the pedestrian-only section, which was several blocks long, people roamed in and out of clothing stores, ice cream shops, and restaurants. A heady mix of scents assailed them. St. George Street smelled of pizza and waffle cones and stale beer. It also smelled of sunscreen, perfume, and sweat. Faint music wafted from some of the storefronts, a dizzying blend of pop songs and Latin music and the occasional Disney-esque pirate tune.

Leo stuck closely to Sid as they weaved through clumps of families and tourists, dodging baby strollers and dog leashes. There were spirits all over the place. Some were tagging along with tour groups; others were hovering close to couples or families. There were spirits of all ages, and many of them appeared dressed in clothing that was not modern.

Leo's eyes went wide at the sight of a spirit hovering in the doorway of a small dive bar. Like the spirit he'd seen on Cordova Street, this one also wore a white shirt, dark breeches, and boots. He had unruly, dark hair and a thick beard. The front of his shirt was stained a dark color, and the reason was obvious. The man's throat had been sliced from ear to ear. Leo looked away and reached for his headphones, ready to pull them on if the spirit decided to leave the bar and approach him. Mercifully, they made it past the bar and down the street without the pirate moving from the doorway.

Josie and her friend disappeared into a trendy restaurant about halfway down the strip. Sid slowed her pace and stopped in front of the shop next door. It was some sort of candle and soap shop, and the sweet, suffocating scents wafting from the open door made Leo want to gag. They also made him think of his mom. If she were here, she would make a beeline for this shop, spending hours smelling each and every item on offer, while Leo was forced to trail in her wake with his shirt pulled up over his nose.

Sid stood gazing at the display in the shop's front window for a few moments and then inched her way down until she could peek inside the restaurant. Leo took up a place next to her, and Sid pretended to fix her ponytail in the window's slightly reflective surface as she watched Josie and her friend take seats at the bar. They place their orders with a muscled bartender sporting a tattoo sleeve and shoulder-length blond hair tucked behind his ears. He smiled as he poured white wine into two glasses for the women, and then he drifted away to refill another barfly's beer.

An hour later, Sid and Leo were sitting on a concrete bench about twenty feet north of the restaurant's entrance on the opposite side of the pedestrian thoroughfare, having each finished a slice of pizza. Head bent low and eyes shaded by her dark sunglasses, Sid looked as if she were studying her phone, but she was dutifully watching the entrance to the restaurant. Foot traffic had picked up a bit as happy hour specials began at four o'clock. Leo was slumped forward, one elbow resting on his knee with his chin in his hand. Sid had encouraged him to blend in, so he adopted the posture of a cranky teenage boy who was bored out of his mind—which he was. But behind his mirrored shades, he, too, watched the restaurant. At half past four, Josie Clement left the restaurant alone and retraced her steps back down St. George Street.

Leo followed Sid as she crossed in front of the restaurant, slowing to look inside. The redhead was chatting to the bartender who was leaning toward her, arms resting on the bar. "Looks like this place was the friend's choice," said Sid. Leo nodded in agreement as he watched the redhead place her hand on the bartender's arm and smile up at him.

Sid and Leo hustled back down St. George Street, weaving in and out of throngs of tourists who had grown cranky in the late afternoon son. They tailed Josie Clement back to the valet stand in front of the Casa Monica Hotel, where she handed her ticket to the young man in white shorts. He disappeared into the porte cochere and returned a few minutes later, driving a shiny, red SUV that was equal parts supercar and military tank. He held the driver's door open as Josie swung her long, tanned legs up into the vehicle. She handed him a tip and slipped smoothly out into traffic. Sid pulled out her phone and snapped a few photos of Josie driving away, making sure to get a clean shot of the license plate.

"Well, that's a start." She put her phone away and turned to Leo. "The ACC is supposed to email me tonight with a more detailed itinerary of his wife's usual movements. Apparently, she keeps quite a strict schedule. Besides the fancy grooming and spa treatments, she also plays tennis, goes to the gym, participates in at least two book clubs, volunteers at the library, and lunches regularly with friends and a local women's group. It's going to mean a lot of hours following her around, and I could use your help with some of it. For today, though, I think we're done."

"Wait," said Leo as Sid turned to head for home. "What do I do now?"

Sid shrugged. "Whatever you want. We'll pick it up again tomorrow morning. First, check with Burt to see if he needs you around the house. If he doesn't, meet me in the office at nine o'clock, and we'll go from there."

She took a few steps and glanced back at him. "You headin' home?"

Leo shook his head.

"Okay then, be safe. See you in the morning." Sid waved and strolled back through the park next to the Governor's House Museum, heading for her garage apartment.

Leo turned in the opposite direction, not because he necessarily wanted to go that way, but because he didn't want to go home just yet. He headed east on King Street and crossed over into the oldest public park in the United States, immediately lowering his gaze and donning his headphones.

Chapter Ten

P laza de la Constitución was situated in the heart of the Old City. The park was long and narrow, running from St. George Street along its western edge to the Intracoastal Waterway and Matanzas Bay at its eastern end, and it was littered with small fountains, gazebos, war memorials, and monuments to the town's history. Several old cannons were positioned throughout the park, and most of them had children climbing on them or tourists using them for photo ops. Spirits lurked around some of the memorials; others lingered under the old oaks or crossed the surrounding streets, paying no attention to traffic signals or rights of way.

Leo followed the sidewalk as it cut a diagonal across the park and headed toward its eastern end. His plan was to wander toward the old fort, Castillo de San Marcos, for lack of anything better to do, although there were probably more spirits there than in the park. They seemed to be everywhere in this town. None had approached him yet, but it was only a matter of time. He wondered if spirits gossiped, if word would get out that he could see and hear them, and then they'd start flocking to him in droves. So Leo kept his head down, eyes shielded by his mirrored sunglasses, and tried his best not to look directly at the spirits in his vicinity. He reached for his phone, planning to crank up the music. Better safe than sorry.

"There are better ways, boy."

Leo's toe caught on a crack in the sidewalk, causing him to stumble off into the grass, but he managed to stay on his feet. He knew those words were meant for him, but they didn't sound like words from a spirit. They sounded like they had come from someone very much alive. He stood in the grass, still holding his phone, and very slowly looked around.

"Over here, boy. Over here." The elderly woman sat cross-legged on a folded blanket underneath a massive oak tree no more than twenty feet away.

Leo hadn't even noticed her as he passed by. She must be homeless, he thought to himself. Her skin was dark and weathered, and her gray hair was worn in thick dreadlocks that poked out at odd angles under her wide-brimmed straw hat. Her oversize dark sunglasses hid her eyes, but Leo knew she was looking at him, looking *into* him. She smiled to reveal a mouth full of more gums than teeth. "You have to learn to keep them away. It's much easier than trying to hide all the time." She pointed at him with a crooked finger. "Besides, you'll go deaf if you keep that up. But it still won't keep out their voices."

Leo stood stock-still as his heart threw itself around in his rib cage and his breath came in quick, shallow bursts. How did she know? He opened his mouth to speak, but no words came.

The old woman chuckled. "Has no one ever taught you about your gift, boy?" Leo found himself shaking his head before he realized what was happening. The old woman clucked her tongue. "Damn shame. How long you been seein' 'em?"

Leo tried to swallow, but his mouth had gone dry. He shrugged as his words failed him again.

"For as long as you can remember, I'm guessin'. Ain't that right?" she asked. Leo nodded. "Lordy." She frowned. "Well then, I'll give you one for free."

She beckoned to him with a crooked finger, and Leo took several slow steps toward her. At ten feet away, Leo expected to pick up the stench of body odor, based on the state of the woman's clothes and dirty feet, but he was assailed instead by the coconutty scent of sunscreen. He blinked in surprise.

"Don't be relyin' on those foul things. They'll do more harm than good." She pointed to his headphones, and he slid them down around his neck and shoved his hands into his pockets. "Get yourself a hat." Leo frowned, and the old woman chuckled. "You got a hat at home? One of them baseball caps, maybe?"

Leo nodded. There were several baseball caps sitting on the top shelf of the closet in his father's old bedroom. Leo had pushed the caps to one side to make room for some of his stuff, but he hadn't bothered to look at them. Sid had told him to wear a hat, too. He hated wearing them, but maybe getting the same advice twice meant they were onto something.

The woman nodded again. "Good. You get that hat, and you put it on. And when you do, you say, 'No spirits can speak to me now. None can come near me.'" She leaned toward him. "And you got to say it like you mean it. Be real intentional about it. Say, 'Stay away. You are not allowed near me now.' You say those words out loud to start with. After a while you can just say 'em in your head, but right now, you say 'em loud and forceful." The old woman leaned back against the tree and tilted her head to study him. "You got that?"

Leo frowned and looked around. There were no spirits in

the immediate area. Was that just a coincidence, or was she doing something to keep them at bay?

"I told 'em to keep away from me," she said simply, as if she knew what he was thinking. "When I put on this hat, I tell 'em they can't talk to me. When I sit on this blanket, I tell 'em they can't come near me."

"And that works?" Leo's voice was so soft, he barely heard the question himself.

The old woman nodded. "It does. But only because I mean it." She shook her finger at him. "You got to be intentional, boy. *Real* intentional. And don't let it slip. You got to keep it up, you got to keep meaning it, or they won't believe you and will just keep on botherin' you."

Leo shook his head. "It can't be as easy as that."

"Why not?" The old woman placed her hands on her knees and smiled. "You're makin' too big a deal of it. Life ain't that complicated. Death ain't that complicated either. So don't make 'em so difficult."

Leo frowned and rocked back on his heels.

The woman leaned toward him again. "Good and evil, those things are complicated. And rightly so, I guess." With her crooked finger, she drew an imaginary line in the grass in front of her. "There's a long, long line with good at one end and evil at the other. Now, everyone and everything falls somewhere on that line, and we're always moving up and down it. Nothin' and no one is ever only good or only evil. It's always a mix of both. And Lord knows, there's plenty of both 'round here. Bound to be, seein' as how this town is so old." She spread her arms wide and smiled her toothless grin. "This Old City was built on both, y'know. Sometimes there's more good than evil, and sometimes it's the other way 'round."

She lowered her arms and rested her hands on her knees,

still smiling. "Life and death, though, both of them are pretty simple. You're either living or you're not. One or the other. Treat 'em that way. You hear me?" Leo nodded. "Good. You go home and get your hat, and you give it a try. Let me know how you get on." She leaned her head back against the trunk of the tree, and Leo suspected she had closed her eyes.

"Thank you," he mumbled as he turned to leave, but then he stopped. He chewed his bottom lip, trying to decide whether to ask his question.

"Spit it out, boy," said the old woman.

Leo turned to face her again. "How did you know?"

"You're wearin' your fear." She lifted her head from where it rested against the tree. "I can practically see it on you, like a big fur coat. You've been wearin' it for years, I'm guessin'. Probably most of your life. Time to take it off. It's got to be heavy by now." She shook her head slightly. "Can't be livin' life if you're weighed down by fear all the time."

"Is it that obvious?" asked Leo, looking down at himself.

"It is to me." The old woman smiled at him. "Don't have to be like that, though."

He nodded. "My name is Leo, by the way."

"Pleasure to meet you, Leo. I'm Hattie. Everyone 'round here calls me Mad Hattie. You can, too, if you want. Don't bother me none." She tipped her head back again against the tree trunk. "That first one is free. Next lesson will cost you. You want to learn more? You bring me a little somethin' next time."

Leo sighed and shook his head. And there it was, the con. Just a scam to get him to give her money. He should have known it would be something like that. He rubbed the back of his neck, wiping away the sheen of sweat. "How much?" he asked, not even trying to hide the annoyance and disappointment in his voice.

"Large cup of coffee. Cream and lots of sugar. And don't go

gettin' it from no Starbucks. You go get it from Pirate Joe's on Aviles Street. Coffee's cheaper there, and it's better, too. And then you go next door to Fire in the Hole, and you get me a datil-pepper-glazed donut." Hattie licked her lips. "That's my price. You want another lesson? You bring me coffee and a donut."

———

Leo stared down at his father's collection of baseball caps. He had spread them out on the bed to get a good look at them. There were seven in total. He picked up the one that looked the most worn. The once-dark blue cap was faded and frayed; its yellow brim curved just right. Leo ran his fingers over the embroidered logo, a white baseball with red stitching surrounded by yellow sunrays. How many times had his dad worn it? Had he used it the way Leo planned to use it now? Probably not, thought Leo.

He took a deep breath and, before he could change his mind, spoke Hattie's words aloud: "No spirits may talk to me or come near me while I'm wearing this hat. You must stay away from me." He pulled on the baseball cap, surprised at how well it fit his head, and smiled to himself. Time to see whether it worked.

Leo clomped down the stairs and shot out the front door as his grandfather hollered at him to be back by seven o'clock for dinner. Leo jogged down the street and didn't stop until he reached Bonney's Bar. The teenaged spirits were gone, but the old pirate with the stab wound was still lingering on the porch. Leo slowed to a walk and turned to look right at the pirate. It took only a moment for the spirit to realize that Leo could see him.

The spirit suddenly materialized in front of Leo, sending a

shiver over Leo's arms despite the summer heat. An image appeared in Leo's mind of a long blade being wielded by another man with dirty blond hair and a full beard. Leo felt a sharp pain in his chest as his heart squeezed and his breathing became labored, but Leo grabbed the brim of the cap and tugged it a little lower on his head. Gasping for air, he hissed, "No, you will not speak to me or approach me. Stay away." The pirate pulled back, and the pain in Leo's chest eased just enough for him to widen his stance, lower his chin, and take a deep breath. "When I am wearing this hat, you will stay away from me. Now go!" he growled.

The pirate vanished, only to reappear on the porch, staring at Leo. It said nothing and made no further moves toward him. An elderly couple passed Leo on the sidewalk, throwing curious glances his way as he glowered at the seemingly empty porch of Bonney's Bar.

It worked! The advice from Mad Hattie had really worked. Leo smiled to himself and headed for St. George Street, breathing easier and feeling more alive than he had ever felt before. He'd been seeing spirits for most of his life, and this was the first time he'd ever had an encounter on his own terms. Pulling his phone from his pocket, he called his mom. Wait until she heard what he'd just done. If he could control the spirits, keep them from bombarding him, it would be a game changer. Maybe his mom would come and get him; maybe he could travel with her and Brooklyn and that ridiculous little white dog.

He found a small patch of shade under the sun-bleached green awning of an ice cream shop and took a deep breath as the ringing finally stopped. His mom's voice came through the phone, "Hi!"

"Mom, guess what! It was amazing! It really worked. I can't

believe it." Breathless with excitement, Leo blurted into the phone, pressing it so firmly against his ear that it hurt.

"This is Paizley Roberts. I'm sorry I can't chat now, but I'm probably scoping out cool places to visit, shop, and eat. Leave a message or, better yet, find me on social media and reach out to me there. Thanks a lot! Wishing you many delicious adventures!"

Leo stumbled backward, bumping into the glass window of the ice cream shop. He stabbed at his phone, disconnected the call, and frantically pulled up the PB&J Instagram page. There were half a dozen photos posted already. The first one was of the jeep and little camper; both vehicles were white, but the camper's bottom half was painted turquoise with white polka dots. The second photo was of Jezebel with a pink bow on her head, sitting on top of Paizley's pink suitcase. There was a pair of pseudo-artistic closeups of fingernails painted with bright pink polish and strands of bright bleach-blonde hair. The last two photos had been taken at the beach. One showed Jezebel curled up asleep on a turquoise beach towel while still wearing the same stupid bow, and the other was a photo of pale, thin legs stretched out on the white sand with pink toenails pointing toward the blue ocean in the background. Those were his mother's legs. She'd taken a photo of herself. She'd been at the beach.

Leo scrolled through the other social media pages he'd set up for them and finally to their website, where he found a brief blog post outlining their preparations so far: manicures, pedicures, hair color, and highlights; shopping, shopping, and more shopping; and some much-needed relaxation at the beach. Colorful banners and notices had been added to the PB&J landing page, announcing that their travels would officially begin next weekend. *First stop: Key West! Stay tuned for more updates. Paizley, Brooklyn, and Jezebel wish everyone many delicious adventures!*

Leo's arm went limp, falling to his side, and he almost dropped the phone. Glancing down, he closed the screen and slid the phone into his pocket.

His mom hadn't called him once since she dropped him off on his grandfather's doorstep three days ago, but she'd managed to find time to change her voicemail message, get a manicure, and go to the beach. He slid to the ground and sat with his head between his knees and his hands pressed to the top of his baseball cap. He squeezed his eyes shut, willing the tears not to fall.

"Hey, are you okay?" The female voice came from the door of the ice cream shop.

"I'm fine," he replied without looking up.

"Are you sure? 'Cause you don't look like it." The voice paused. When Leo didn't respond, the voice continued, "Are you feeling faint? Do you need some water?"

Still hunched over, Leo shook his head.

"Okaaaaay," said the voice. "Then you must be bummed out about something. Let me guess . . . Your girlfriend dumped you?" Leo shook his head again. "Boyfriend dumped you?" Another shake of the head. "Your pet iguana dumped you?"

Leo sighed heavily and slowly turned his head. He saw a pair of beat-up Chuck Taylors and tan legs. Tilting his head up even higher, he saw that the voice, as well as the sneakers and the long legs, partially hidden beneath a professional-looking apron, belonged to a girl. A very pretty girl. Leo felt himself blush, and he hoped with all his might that he was already so flushed from the summer heat and his anger at his mom that this girl wouldn't notice his cheeks redden.

"Nice Jacksonville Suns hat. Is it vintage?" The girl tilted her head to one side, and her long, straight ponytail fell across the shoulder of her N'Ice Day Ice Cream Shop tee. Redhead or blonde? Leo couldn't decide. His mom would probably have called it something like strawberry blonde. A smattering of freckles swept across her cheeks and the bridge of her nose, and her eyes were dark green with a gold ring around the pupil.

Leo shrugged. "I don't know."

"Well, it looks vintage. I'm Ellie, by the way," she said, holding out her hand to him. "Ellie Owen."

Leo rose and wiped his sweaty hand on his shirt before shaking hers. "Leo Roberts."

She smiled, and Leo noticed that one of her incisors slightly overlapped its neighbor in what would have otherwise been an absolutely perfect smile. Leo found himself smiling back at her. Ellie tilted her head to the other side, her ponytail swishing as she did so. "Is your mom a Leonardo DiCaprio fan?" Leo shook his head. "Leonardo da Vinci?"

Leo shook his head again. "Lions."

Ellie nodded. "Oh. Born in August, I guess?"

"Nope. June." Leo shrugged. "She just likes lions."

Ellie giggled. "I see. Well, happy belated birthday, Leo-as-in-lion and not Leo-as-in-DiCaprio." She tilted her head to one side and then beckoned him closer. "Hey, come with me." She stepped back into the shop, and Leo followed.

Fifteen minutes later, Leo left the ice cream shop after being crowded out by a large family of tourists that included six children, two of whom were still in diapers. Ellie was the only one working in the shop, and they'd had to cut their conversation short so she could take orders and scoop ice cream. He waved to her as he left, watching her pour colored sprinkles on a triple scoop of vanilla, and smiled to himself.

The free kid-size birthday cone filled with salted caramel ice cream dripped onto his hand, melting quickly in the heat, but he ignored it. He focused instead on the photo of the smiling girl with green eyes and strawberry blonde hair. Ellie had snapped a selfie when she'd put her number in his phone.

The day had been a filled with highs and lows. And while Leo was now exhausted by the emotional rollercoaster of it all, he also felt hopeful. That was a unique sensation for him. He hadn't felt hopeful about anything in a very long time. Perhaps living here in St. Augustine wasn't the worst thing in the world. Leo smiled at Ellie's photo, licked the ice cream now dripping down his wrist, and walked home.

Chapter Eleven

S id pulled into Burt's driveway around noon the next day. She had spent the morning tailing Josie Clement around town. First up was coffee at Pirate Joe's at eight o'clock with a female friend, a middle-aged brunette with a diamond ring so large and sparkly that it could probably bring down an airplane in bright sunlight. After forty-five minutes of chatting over coffee, Josie and the brunette had driven to their tennis club, where they disappeared inside for two and a half hours. When the pair emerged from the club with two other women, Josie looked as fresh as a daisy while the others looked like flowers that had wilted in the Florida heat. Josie went straight home after tennis and, according to the schedule her husband had shared, didn't have another social engagement until that evening.

Normally, Sid would have packed a sandwich and hunkered down to do surveillance two doors down from their bayfront mansion, but her refrigerator was empty and her pantry bare. Embarrassingly, she had cobbled together breakfast from the small packets of cookies and cheese crackers she kept stocked in her office. Rather than allow herself to get cranky from hunger, she called off the tail and returned home. Not an auspicious start, but a start nonetheless.

"You left without me!" Leo shouted from the open kitchen door as Sid exited the car. "I came to the office at nine o'clock like you told me to, but you were already gone."

"I needed to get an earlier start." She walked across the yard toward Leo. "I came to get you a little after seven this morning, but Burt said you were still sleeping, so I had to leave without you." She squeezed past Leo, who was still standing in the doorway. "Have you had lunch yet?"

"No," he grumbled. "You could have woken me up, or you could have told me last night."

Sid sighed heavily as she yanked open Burt's refrigerator. "I didn't know last night, Leo. J. T. didn't email me until after midnight. Besides, you didn't miss anything. I sat in the car all morning while Josie had coffee with a girlfriend and played tennis for a couple of hours with some other women. She's home now. Has another engagement tonight. One of her book clubs. Where's Burt?" Sid pulled out deli meat, cheese slices, and the jar of mayonnaise.

"He's working. Doing some renovations for the Crane's Roost." Leo picked up a note that Burt had left for him that morning and waved it in the air.

Burt had retired a few years ago, selling his construction business to a large outfit based in Jacksonville, but he'd immediately set up another enterprise to do local remodeling jobs. The Crane's Roost was a bed-and-breakfast at the end of Saragossa Street. Together with its rival across the street, La Señora, they had kept Burt busy on and off for the past two years.

"Can you make us a couple of sandwiches while I jot down some notes?" asked Sid as she sat at the kitchen table. The kid sulked as he unwrapped the loaf of bread on the counter.

"Honestly, Leo. You didn't miss anything." He nodded and began making the sandwiches.

After they'd eaten, Sid washed the dishes and headed back out to her car. The kitchen door slammed behind her, and Leo thumped down the steps, jogging across the yard to catch up to her. "Are you going to watch the house?" he asked.

"Nope." Sid fished her keys out of her bag and opened the car door. "Grocery shopping."

Leo halted, his hand hovering over the car door handle. "You think Josie's meeting someone at the grocery store?"

Sid couldn't help the grin that slid across her face. "No. Nothing that scandalous. I just need groceries." Leo frowned, looking back at the house, and then dropped his gaze to his shoes. Sid sighed. "It's not going to be very exciting, but you're welcome to join me."

"Okay." Leo bolted for the kitchen door and locked it, then sprinted back to the car. "It beats sitting at home by myself."

"Maybe you should get a hobby," replied Sid, tossing her bag on the back seat.

Leo snapped his seat belt into place and smirked. "Helping you *is* my hobby, seeing as you don't pay me. Can't very well call it a job, now can I?"

Sid groaned and turned the key in the ignition. "I'm going to regret this arrangement, aren't I?"

"Most likely, yes." Leo turned his head away from her and bit his lip to keep from smiling.

———

Sid pushed the shopping cart right past the fresh produce section toward the bakery, where she selected a bag of dinner rolls, a box of apple turnovers, and a container of chocolate chip cookies. Leo had made a beeline for the candy aisle as soon as they'd entered the store, and Sid was grateful for the reprieve. She liked the kid, but she wasn't used to having a shadow. She was used to being by herself all day, every day. Having a teenage boy following her around was going to take some getting used to. For now, however, she turned down the next aisle and was content to enjoy the peace of shopping for boxed macaroni and cheese all by herself.

As she held up two boxes, debating between the original recipe and the white cheddar version, she heard a pair of men's dress shoes come to a stop behind her. "Sidney," a voice belonging to the shoes called.

Sid turned, still looking at the boxes. "Yeah?"

"How are you?"

Sid tossed both boxes into the cart and looked up. Her jaw went slack, and she felt herself list to the left. Seizing the cart's handlebar with all her might, she nodded once. "Deputy Davis." She felt her face flush and heard her heart pounding in her ears.

"Tony. Please call me Tony." He smiled at her. It was that same smile that most people gave her, the one of sympathy and pity mixed with a little relief that they weren't her. "I thought it was you. How are you?"

"Fine, Tony. I'm fine. You?" She saw his eyes flick down to where her hands white-knuckled the shopping cart. "How's Naomi?"

"Good. She's good. I'm good. We're all good." He shrugged with a little laugh.

Sid tried to loosen her grip but couldn't. Desperately grasping for both the shopping cart and a change of conversation, she noticed he was in dark gray slacks and a light gray golf shirt. "Day off?"

"Naw." Tony glanced down at his clothes. "I made detective a few months ago. I'm in major crimes now."

Sid nodded. "Congratulations."

Tony had been Wes's new partner. At least, he would have been if Wes hadn't died that night of the party. Tony had transferred up from the Alachua County sheriff's office, where he spent two years in marine operations and the prior four years as a patrol officer. But before becoming a cop, Tony had been Antonio Davis, starting tight end for the Florida Gators.

At six foot four inches tall and a solid two hundred thirty pounds, Antonio Davis had been the one to watch, the one who was expected to turn pro, the one who would likely be selected in the first round of the NFL draft and emerge with a hefty contract and a line of companies wooing him with endorsement deals. People had shown up to the games wearing jerseys with *his* name and number on them. Kids had asked him for his autograph. Girls had thrown themselves at him. Middle-aged men who donated huge sums of money to the University of Florida football program had slapped him on the back and asked him about his plans for the future while their fancy-dressed wives smiled and winked at him.

All of that changed one Saturday afternoon in early December of his senior year.

At the start of the second half of the Southeastern Conference championship game, the crowd in Atlanta was the loudest Tony had ever heard, and he was used to playing in the Swamp. The Swamp was the University of Florida's home stadium, known for being loud and raucous and unkind to the Gators' opponents, but the vibe that day from the SEC Championship crowd was insane. The Gators were the underdogs, trying to upset Alabama's four-year winning streak. And they might have done it, too, if it weren't for what happened next.

By a freak act of God, and a brutal hit by a 'Bama defensive end, Antonio Davis went down. He didn't get up.

He was put on a stretcher, driven off the field and straight to the hospital, and then taken into surgery, where the bone that was sticking out of his leg was put back in place with rods, pins, and screws. His team lost the game, he missed the NFL draft, and he never played football again.

Instead, Tony Davis had two more surgeries and a long, painful stint in rehab. The bright spot in all of that had been meeting Naomi, a nursing student at Shands Hospital in Gainesville, at one of his countless doctor's appointments. Because of Naomi, Tony stayed at UF and finished his degree in criminology. Because of her, he never missed a physical therapy appointment and was up and running again in record time. Because of her, he passed his exam and became a sheriff's deputy. Because of her, he transferred to St. Johns County to be a marine deputy with the SJSO Marine Unit. And because of her, he had accepted the position as Wes Stone's new partner.

Sid looked him over. "You look good, Tony. I guess detective work agrees with you." She had liked Tony when she met him the first time. He seemed smart and capable, like someone who would have had her husband's back. Until he didn't.

Tony smiled. "It does. I miss the Marine Unit, but . . ." He looked down at the two foot-long deli sandwiches—lovingly called Pub Subs by most Floridians—in his hands. "Well, I better get going. Still on the job. I'll see you around, Sid."

Sid nodded and stepped to the side. "Stay safe, Tony." He had a wife and kid, after all. For their sake, she hoped he would stay safe, even if he hadn't kept *her* husband and kid safe. She watched Tony walk up the aisle toward the cash registers.

"Who was that?"

Sid turned to find Leo standing next to the cart, his arms filled with barbecue potato chips, peanut M&Ms, and Twizzlers. Sid frowned. "No peppermint patties?"

Leo scrunched up his face. "No one eats peppermint patties."

"I do." Sid pushed the cart, dropping in two more boxes of macaroni and cheese.

"Was that the guy from your wall? The cop?" Leo shifted the items in his arms so he could hike up the shorts that had slid down his narrow waist.

"It was." Sid turned the corner and saw Tony stride out of the store with his grocery bag in hand. "Deputy—I mean, *Detective* Tony Davis. He was going to be Wes's new partner when Manny retired and Wes got promoted. Tony transferred up from Gainesville to take the position. Wes was so excited. The great Antonio Davis. Wes had been a fan from when Tony played football at UF." She turned down the cereal aisle and selected three boxes at random, tossing them into the cart. "Tony had only been on the job one week when Wes died. After that, I heard he transferred to the patrol division. Not sure if it was his choice or if he was moved." She shrugged. "Doesn't really matter. He made detective a few months ago, apparently. Major crimes."

Leo walked alongside Sid, watching as she turned down another aisle and tossed bags of potato chips and pretzels into her cart. "You don't like him very much."

"Do I? I don't know." Sid selected two twelve-packs of soda from an endcap and turned down the next aisle. "I didn't get to know him well enough to like him or dislike him. He . . . he was sort of involved in Wes's death."

Leo's eyes went wide. "Did *he* shoot Wes?"

Sid took the chips and candy from Leo and tossed them into the shopping cart. Pointing down the next aisle, she gave him instructions. "Pick out two loaves of bread, a big jar of peanut butter, and some jelly, whatever flavor you want. Oh, and get some plastic sandwich bags. We're going to have to start packing lunches for our stakeouts. Make sure you pick stuff you will actually eat. I'll meet you up front at the registers."

Leo stood next to her, not moving. "Did he?"

Sid shook her head. "Apparently, he was at home when Wes was killed. So, no, I don't think he did."

Leo lowered his chin and looked her in the eye. "But you're not sure."

"No, I'm not sure." Sid sighed and pushed the cart toward the dairy aisle. She deserved some mint chocolate chip after this afternoon's unexpected encounter.

Chapter Twelve

Sid and Leo followed Josie Clement for the next few days. Just as the ACC had said, his wife adhered to a very strict schedule. She went to the gym precisely at the times stated in the digital calendar she shared with her husband. She lunched with her girlfriends exactly as planned. She attended her book club meetings as scheduled: one on Tuesday evening at the home of the redhead she'd met for drinks on Monday and one on Thursday at noon in the restaurant of the Casa Monica Hotel. She also attended a meeting of the Women's Advancement Guild, a philanthropic organization for the well-to-do and well-connected known around the Old City as the WAGs. The WAGs meeting was on Wednesday evening precisely as calendared, following Josie's afternoon massage at Cielo Spa and an early dinner with another girlfriend. Sid wondered how much time Josie and J. T. actually spent together, because Josie's busy schedule didn't seem to allow for much marital interaction. Perhaps that was by design.

Sid had been only mildly surprised to learn that Josie's dinner date was with Emmaline Colquitt, wife of Sheriff

Colquitt. They met at a fancy tapas restaurant one block off St. George Street, where they sipped wine at one of the outdoor tables. The two women then walked to the WAGs meeting, which started promptly at seven o'clock in the pretty, two-story white building with dark green shutters where the WAGs held all their fundraising events.

Josie Clement never deviated from the joint calendar. She was where she said she was, precisely on time, each and every time. By Friday morning, Sid was beginning to think that there was nothing at all mysterious about the lovely Mrs. Josette Clement.

The morning began with an early tennis lesson at seven o'clock, followed by coffee at Pirate Joe's at nine with a woman Sid recognized from the WAGs meeting on Wednesday night. After half an hour of watching the door, Sid decided to go inside to buy a coffee and do some eavesdropping. Waiting for her latte, Sid heard the two women talking about the upcoming WAGs luncheon and silent auction, the proceeds of which would buy school supplies, clothing, and shoes for local school-children in need.

Sid remembered the WAGs' yearly donations to the children. She had taught a number of kids who had shown up on the first day of school with brand-new backpacks, colorful sneakers, and bright, happy smiles—all thanks to the WAGs and their robust fundraising efforts. That had happened in her other life, back when Sid actually had a life. She'd been a teacher, a mother, a wife. She'd been all those things one day, and then the next day, she'd become none of those things.

Her daughter, Iris, had started kindergarten a few weeks before she was killed. Iris had been so excited to go to school, so excited to learn new things and to make new friends, and she'd been thrilled to be able to leave her classroom at the end of each day and walk down the hall to her mother's classroom.

Iris helped Sid straighten up each afternoon, and then she played while Sid marked papers. Iris would tell Sid all about her day, who she played with and what she learned, and then the two of them would leave school hand in hand and drive home.

After Iris died, Sid couldn't step foot inside her classroom. She couldn't bear to see the little faces of her students light up with innocent smiles, hear their laughter as they played, watch them work silently at their desks. She never went back to school after that fateful night. Someone collected her things from her classroom and brought them to her. They'd collected Iris's things, too. All of it went into boxes exactly as it had been delivered, and those boxes had been taped shut and stored away.

The thoughts of Iris, of her former students with their new backpacks, and of her own first-grade classroom with its colorful bulletin boards had her struggling for breath. Sid tugged her baseball cap down, grabbed her steaming coffee, and rushed for the door. She walked quickly down the block to where she'd left Leo sitting on the stoop of an antique shop not yet open for the day.

Leo looked up from his phone as she approached and frowned at her. "You okay? You look terrible."

"I'm fine," Sid wheezed, trying desperately to keep the anxiety at bay. "Keep an eye out. She's not scheduled to be anywhere for a while, so I don't expect her to leave anytime soon."

Sid kept walking until she reached her car, parked two blocks over in a public lot. She yanked open the door, slumped into the driver's seat, gripped the steering wheel as hard as she could, and screamed until she felt the tension finally ease. Hands still trembling with the aftereffects of adrenaline, she sipped her coffee, wishing she'd added some sugar to it before she fled the shop.

She had barely closed her eyes for a moment's rest when her phone dinged with a message from Leo:

On the move

———

A few minutes later, Sid watched as Josie Clement strutted across the half-empty parking lot toward her shiny red SUV. As Josie backed out of her parking spot, Leo arrived, having crept around the back of the lot to keep out of sight.

"Where's she going?" Sid wondered aloud as Leo climbed in next to her. "She's not due at the library until eleven o'clock."

Leo shrugged. It was the first move Josie Clement had made so far that didn't track precisely with her calendar.

Shortly after ten o'clock, Josie pulled into the parking lot of the main branch of the county library, located less than a mile from the heart of the historic downtown. Sid followed and chose a shady spot away from Josie's SUV but with a good view of the front door. Josie entered the library almost a full hour before she was scheduled to be there.

"New plan." Sid swiveled in her seat to face Leo. She reached up and took off his baseball cap and messed up his hair so that his lazy curls stood out at crazy angles.

When the cap left his head, Leo felt his heart skip a beat. He did a quick scan of the parking lot. Mercifully, there were no loitering spirits.

Reaching into her bag, Sid pulled out a pair of eyeglasses and handed them to Leo. "Take off the shades and put these on."

Leo shook his head. "I don't need glasses."

"They're not prescription." She waved the glasses in front of him. "They're for your disguise."

"My disguise as what? And how do you even see out of these things?" Leo used his T-shirt to wipe the smudges off the clear plastic lenses in the dark frames.

"You're going in there. Pose as a student taking a summer class. You're here to do some research. Pick a subject you already know something about so that you can bullshit a little if someone asks you a question." Leo frowned, and Sid rolled her eyes at him. "Just make something up. Go in, look around for Josie, and try not to be too obvious. Just see what's going on. If she's with someone, take some pictures. Just don't let her see you doing it."

"How long do I have to stay in there?" Leo fiddled with the glasses, trying to get them to sit comfortably on his face.

"Until you find out what's up. Josie has her meeting at eleven o'clock. Library volunteers or something like that. Just go see what you can find out. But keep your head down. And try not to talk to anyone. And don't be too obvious. And don't—"

"I got it!" Leo snarled. "Go in and spy, but don't get caught. Right?"

Sid held up her hands in surrender. "And sign up for a library card while you're at it."

"Why?" He opened the car door and grabbed his backpack. "Do I need it for spying?"

Sid smiled and shrugged a shoulder. "Everyone should have a library card."

Leo shook his head, slammed the car door, and sauntered into the building.

———

It didn't take long for Leo to locate Josie Clement. Her golden-blonde head and pale blue sundress were easy to spot at the bank of computers behind the checkout desk. The computer center was organized in an L-shape, with four machines in an alcove and the rest set up along a wall of picture windows that looked out onto a neighboring parking lot. Josie Clement had chosen the first computer behind the desk, the one most hidden from view. She was still easy to find, though. The library was neither that big nor that crowded.

Two elderly men were seated side by side at computers in the middle of the row along the windows. Leo sat at a computer three down from Josie's and placed his backpack between his feet. The glasses slipped down his nose when he lowered his head to look at the keyboard, and Leo pushed them back up, using the opportunity to glance at Josie's computer screen. It was a website with a white background, a green logo in the upper right corner, and a lot of text. No photos or graphics. Leo's fingers hovered over his keyboard. What was he supposed to look up? What kind of summer class project should he claim to be researching? He chewed his bottom lip, hoping inspiration would come to him.

And then the idea hit him. He typed in a search, scanned the results, and clicked on website after website as he researched pirates known to have died in and around St. Augustine. He looked through photos and sketches, museum pages and local enthusiasts' blog posts, but he didn't find any pirates that resembled the one he'd seen at Bonney's Bar—the dark-haired pirate who'd been run through the chest with a sword.

He'd almost forgotten where he was and why he was there when he heard a soft voice say, "Pirates, huh? Well, you're certainly in the right town for that."

Leo turned toward the voice and found Josie Clement smiling at him. She was even prettier up close. He noticed her eyes were the same bright turquoise as his mother's mini camper. "Yeah . . ." He cleared his throat. "Pirates."

"Just a fan, or are you researching something specific?" Josie tilted her head to get a better look at Leo's screen, which currently showed some sketches of pirates dying of various gruesome injuries. She scrunched her nose at the sight.

"It's for a research project," blurted Leo, a bit louder than he meant to be. He lowered his voice and explained, "I'm taking a summer class. I have a paper due. Pirates of St. Augustine."

"Oh." Josie smiled, nodded, and turned back to her own computer.

Leo scrambled for something to say. If he could get her talking, maybe he could sneak a better peek at her screen. "I don't know anything about them. I just moved here, so I'm starting from scratch. I could take one of those pirate tours they offer, but I don't think my teacher will allow me to use some old guy dressed up as a pirate as a legitimate source of information."

Josie's laugh actually sounded like tinkling bells. How was that possible? His mom tended to snort when she laughed, and his grandmother Camille had had a funny horselaugh. He hadn't heard Sid laugh yet. Not a proper, hearty laugh, anyway, and he wondered what it would sound like.

"No, I guess you couldn't really cite Pirate Bob as reference material, could you?" She smiled as she removed her purse from where it hung on the back of her chair. Then she cleared her computer screen, sending it back to the home page. "Where did you move here from?"

"Norfolk, Virginia." The words were out of Leo's mouth before he could stop them. Why had he said that? Was it too much information? He didn't know how much he was supposed to lie. Sid had told him to stay quiet, but Josie had started talking to him. He was just being polite.

"That's a long way away. Why did you move down?" She

turned in her chair to face him and hooked her purse over her arm.

"My mom and I moved down here." Leo's thoughts spun as he tried to carefully craft his answers. "We're staying with my grandfather. It's just temporary." This was true. "I came in here to use the computers. My grandfather doesn't have one." Not true. Burt had a brand-new laptop and said Leo could borrow it anytime he needed it. Besides, Leo had his own laptop. It was old and slow, but it still worked. "And I needed some peace and quiet to study." Also not true. His grandfather's house was extremely quiet during the day, when Burt was at his remodeling job at the Crane's Roost.

"I see." Josie fished around in her purse and pulled out a slim, gold case that contained a small stack of business cards. She fanned them out, looking for something specific. The cards were varied, in all manner of colors and designs. Finding the one she wanted, she plucked it from the stack and handed it to Leo. "Give this to your mom. Tell her that when she's ready to look for a place, a house or condo or whatever, to give me a call. I'd be happy to help her." She smiled and stood, pushing in her chair and straightening the keyboard so as to leave the workstation in perfect order. She hesitated before walking away, pressing one of her perfectly manicured nails to her bottom lip. "Don't give that card to anyone else, okay? Just your mom. I . . . I don't work with many clients, so I . . . I don't . . ." She paused and gathered herself. "Just don't share it with anyone else. Please."

Leo looked at the card and began to frown, but he caught himself and schooled his expression to one of delight. He nodded and tucked the card into the side pocket of his cargo shorts, zipping the pocket to hide the card from the rest of the world. "Thank you very much. And don't worry. I won't give it out." A lie. He'd give it to Sid as soon as he got back in the car.

Josie smiled in relief. "Good." She turned to go but stopped again. "What's your mom's name, by the way, in case she calls me?"

Leo smiled. "Paizley. With a Z." Not a lie, but only a recent truth.

"Pretty," cooed Josie. "I'll definitely remember that. Well, good luck with your pirates." She waved and left the alcove, heading toward a meeting room on the other side of the main area, where a few elderly women were gathering.

Leo waited until Josie and the other women had entered the room and shut the door before he slid into her vacated seat. He opened the search engine and pulled up the browser history, then, after looking left and right, snapped a photo of the list of websites. Tutting to himself but grateful that Josie hadn't cleared her history, Leo opened the last website she had visited and frowned. He snapped a photo of the page, leaped up from his seat, and charged toward the front door. It was only when he reached the parking lot that he remembered he hadn't signed up for a library card.

Chapter Thirteen

S id paced back and forth in her office, flicking the business card against her palm. "I don't understand. Josie Clement gave you this card and told you to call *her*?"

"Yes," Leo answered. He sat at Sid's desk in front of her computer and pulled up the website listed on the business card.

Sid continued pacing. "I don't understand."

"You keep saying that." Leo blew out a breath and scrolled through the list of agents on the website for Colquitt Dobbs Realty.

"Well, who is Liesel Winfield?" Sid came around the desk and stood behind Leo. "Did Josie give you the wrong card?"

"I don't think so. She carefully looked through all the cards and picked out that one. I don't think she made a mistake." Leo tapped the screen, pointing to an entry. "Here is Liesel Winfield. No photo, though."

Sid studied the screen. "So Liesel Winfield is a licensed agent at Colquitt Dobbs Realty. Looks like she's new. Just joined this year."

Leo pointed to the photo of Emmaline Colquitt, an attractive woman with high cheekbones, a pointed chin, and wavy, honey-blonde hair that grazed her shoulders. "Is she related to Sheriff Colquitt?"

"His wife." Sid began pacing again. "Search for Josie or Josette Clement."

Leo scanned the list and then did a general search of the entire website. "Nothing. She's not listed anywhere."

Sid pinched the bridge of her nose. "Okay, let's go through what we know. Josie took this card out of her purse, this specific card, and gave it to you. She then told you to give it to your mother and have your mother call her, call Josie *herself*, if she wanted to buy a house."

"Or a condo," added Leo.

"Right. Or a condo." Sid smirked. "Then, she told you not to tell anyone else. That she, Josie, only takes on a few clients, so she didn't want you sharing her information with anyone but your mom." Leo nodded. "And the last website Josie visited was for a company specializing in study programs for the real estate license exam in the state of Georgia."

"Correct," added Leo.

Sid rubbed her temples. "Is that it?"

Leo nodded again. "That's it."

Sid twirled her long ponytail around her fingers. "You told her your mom's name is Paizley?" Leo nodded. "Did you tell her your last name?"

"Nope. I didn't tell her my name either," replied Leo.

"Okay. I can work with that." Sid pulled open the top drawer of one of the filing cabinets and pulled out a cell phone. With the business card in hand, she dialed the number listed for Liesel Winfield. The call went straight to voicemail, so Sid left a message: "Hi, Ms. Winfield. My name is Paizley Rogers. You met my son today at the library and gave him your card. This is such great timing! I would really love to start looking at houses or condos in a decent school district. Somewhere close to downtown, if possible. My son and I don't need anything too big. Two or three bedrooms with two bathrooms preferably, but I can be flexible. I'd love to set up a time to meet you. Please give me a call or text me at this number. Thanks so much. Speak soon!"

Sid hung up and looked at Leo, who was covering his mouth with his hand to keep from laughing out loud. "What?"

"Hi, I'm Paizley Rogers." Leo imitated Sid's affected singsong voice. "Three bedrooms, please, but I'm flexible. Call me!"

She flicked the card at him. "Staple that to the inside of the case file. And for your information, that's how you do it. Burner phone, fake name, disguised voice. I can't very well use my own voice, now can I?"

"Not if you want her to call you back." Leo smirked and pounded the stapler with his fist.

"Very funny." Sid opened the mini fridge and pulled out two sodas, handing one to Leo. "I want you to search everything you can on social media for Liesel Winfield. Let's see if we can find a photo of her. And search Josie Clement's social media pages for her, too."

Leo nodded and went to work. Two snack bags of cheese crackers later, he swiveled the monitor toward Sid. "Found something." He tapped the screen. "This is a photo from last year. It's from some fancy fundraiser in Savannah. I found it on an account owned by Charlene Winfield. Next to her is a guy named Carter Winfield."

Sid studied the photo and its caption. A married couple, she assumed by the way they were standing, rather than brother and sister. They were both tall, thin, and tanned. The man had a thick head of salt-and-pepper hair and was dressed in a tuxedo; the woman wore a floor-length, emerald-green gown with her platinum-blonde hair swept up in a twist. Sid guessed they were in their late fifties, early sixties. "How did you find this?"

"Josie Clement liked the photo." Leo sat back and rocked, the desk chair screeching in protest.

Sid nodded. "Liesel's parents? Look 'em up. See what you can find."

Leo nodded and continued typing and scrolling.

The burner phone rang, and Sid greeted the caller with her singsong voice. "Oh, thanks so much for calling me back, Ms. Winfield!" Sid listened for a moment and then began answering questions about her preferred number of bedrooms, square footage, and neighborhoods. Then she made an appointment to meet with Liesel Winfield at a Starbucks over on Anastasia Island at one o'clock on Saturday afternoon. As she hung up the phone, Sid smiled to herself.

"You're not actually going to go meet her, are you?" asked Leo.

"Nope." Sid slid the case file toward her and checked her notes. Josie Clement's calendar had tennis matches scheduled on Saturday from eight o'clock until noon and then lunch scheduled until two o'clock. After that, she had a barbecue scheduled at her house beginning at six o'clock in the evening. "I just want to get a look at whoever shows up at Starbucks. I'll cancel once I know she's arrived."

"How will you know who she is?" Leo looked over at her. "You don't know what she looks like."

Sid smiled. "I have a pretty good idea." She picked up the empty snack bags and cans of soda and deposited them in the trash. "You should go get ready. I understand Burt wants you to play roadie for the band tonight."

Leo's face lit up. "Yeah, he's going to let me help set up." He headed for the door. "Are you coming to the show?"

"Of course." Sid smiled. "I'm one of the Geezers' biggest fans. I'll see you there. Save me a seat, okay?" Leo nodded and left the office.

Sid sat down in front of the computer and closed out of the social media sites that Leo had been scrolling through. Launching the website for the Historic Savannah Foundation, Sid began her own search for Carter and Charlene Winfield.

Three hours later, she turned off the computer, rubbed her eyes, and studied the business card stapled to the inside cover of the case file. She was tempted to keep the appointment tomorrow, to just go inside Starbucks and sit down for a chat with Liesel Winfield, but that was not how it was done. She bit her bottom lip. Something didn't feel right, but the investigation was still young. Hopefully things would become clearer soon. She glanced at her watch. She had a report to give, and the ACC was not going to like it.

———

By the time Sid arrived at Granny Oak's Music Park, the sun had dipped below the horizon, the opening act had finished his set, and Recent Geezer was taking the stage. Leo waved her over, sliding down to make room for her on the bench beneath the giant live oak that stood in the center of the open-air music venue.

The three-hundred-year-old tree, the second oldest live oak in the Old City, was so massive that its boughs extended to all corners of the venue. Colored lanterns were strung from the branches, casting the park in ethereal shades of gold, blue, and pink. A soft breeze off the bay made the lanterns sway ever so slightly, and the shadows cast by the giant oak and its decorative lights danced along the ground and over the faces of those in attendance. On nights like this one,

Granny Oak's Music Park looked like a rustic, magical fairyland.

The venue was located on the northern end of St. George Street behind a nondescript, six-foot-tall concrete wall painted the color of faded sunflowers. When it was open for business, a dark wooden door in the wall was propped open so patrons could come and go as they pleased. Admission was free, and live music was played every Thursday, Friday, and Saturday night without fail. Several rows of wooden benches stood in front of the tiny stage, which was just barely big enough to hold the Geezers and their equipment.

Behind the rows of benches were several more rows of picnic tables, and behind them and along the sides of the park were small benches and concrete planters filled with azalea bushes and colorful perennials. Every available seat and perch in the park was taken, and plenty of people were standing along the outer edges. Several small children made good use of the narrow space in front of the stage, happily dancing and clapping even though the music hadn't started up again. Two tiki bars, one on each side of the park, were doing a brisk business pouring beer, wine, cocktails, and sodas for lines that were constantly ten people deep. Granny Oak's was hopping, as it always was when Recent Geezer played.

Leo smiled and handed Sid a greasy cardboard box from the takeout counter of Old City Seafood Company, the restaurant next door. "Grandpa said you like fried shrimp. His treat. It might be cold by now, though."

Sid smiled and took the box. "Thanks, Leo. That was very thoughtful." She opened the box and found fried jumbo shrimp, two large hush puppies, and the Seafood Company's famous datil pepper coleslaw. Her mouth watered at the sight. "Any ghosts out tonight?"

Leo winced. "Spirits, not ghosts. And yes." His eyes darted

to the tiki bar on the left side of the stage, where the spirit of an old man was hovering near a group of young men, and then he glanced over his shoulder at the entrance, where four different spirits wandered among the patrons standing at the very back. "A few."

Sid gently elbowed him in the ribs. "Well, the music should be loud enough to drown them out . . . if they start talking to you."

"Let's hope they don't." Leo tugged on the brim of his baseball cap and looked back at the stage.

"Ever seen them play?" She nodded to the stage, where the Geezers were warming up.

"Nope." Leo shook his head. "I mean, I watched them rehearse on Wednesday night at Guppy's place, and I've seen some videos that people have posted online, but this is my first time seeing them live. They sound pretty good."

"Just pretty good?" Sid laughed. "Don't let the Geezers hear you say that. Guppy's ready to take them on the road, and Cesar's usually got a couple of groupies hanging around the place." She scanned the crowd and found two middle-aged women in full makeup and low-cut tank tops lounging by the tiki bar closest to Cesar's side of the stage. "Those two." She pointed in their direction. "And occasionally a couple of others."

A wide smile flashed across Leo's face. "Really?" Sid nodded as she bit into one of the hush puppies, which was still warm thankfully. "Cool," Leo mumbled, his eyes lighting up as he watched his grandfather and the three other men take their positions.

Eli Williams stepped up to the microphone, introduced the band, and was immediately drowned out by whistles and applause. Without further ado, the Recent Geezers launched into their version of Molly Hatchet's "Flirtin' With Disaster."

Leo watched the band with giddy delight. Before tonight, they had just been four old men, sitting around and playing tunes for fun. But now, as Leo took in the crowd, which was dancing, clapping, and singing along, these men became something else. They were still four old guys, with their gray hair and paunches, but they could rock.

Sid finished her fried shrimp and coleslaw and glanced at her watch. It was time for her report. Scanning the crowd, she found the ACC at one of the picnic benches behind her, surrounded by other former frat boy types in their casual Friday work attire. J. T. Clement caught her eye, picked up his half-full beer, and drained it. He made a show of standing up and offering to get the next round.

Sid picked up her takeout box and Leo's empty cup. "Want a refill?" Leo nodded but didn't take his eyes from the stage. "Okay, I'll be back in a few." She crossed the venue, tossed the empty containers in the trash, and headed for the line at the tiki bar on the right side of the stage.

J. T. Clement slid in line behind her. "Ms. Stone." He was standing so close that Sid could smell the beer on his breath. "I hope you have something to tell me."

Sid crossed her arms and angled her body so that she was facing away from the stage and would appear to be reading the bar's simple chalkboard menu. "She hasn't deviated from her calendar." Until she had a better sense of what was going on, Sid wasn't ready to reveal Josie's early arrival at the library. "I haven't seen her meet with any men. No one but her girlfriends, her tennis partners, her book clubs, and the WAGs. It's been less than a week, so I'd like to stay on the case a little longer just to see if she does deviate, as you suspect." She also wanted to dig a little deeper into her new and growing hunch. "You okay with that?"

She glanced over her shoulder and saw J. T. Clement

admiring her legs. He swayed a little on his feet, and, after realizing that she'd ceased speaking, he lifted his gaze and smiled at her. "You look lovely this evening, Sidney. Mind if I call you Sidney?" He swayed a little again and stared at her with half-closed eyelids.

Sid managed to refrain from rolling her eyes at him. It was a little early in the evening to be drunk. J. T. smelled of sweat and beer, and she wondered if he had spent his afternoon on the golf course. "Sidney is fine. Did you hear what I said? Your wife has stuck to her schedule so far, but I'd like to stay on the case for another week. Do you agree?"

J. T. waved his hand dismissively. "Fine, fine. Keep going. You can give me another report next weekend." He took a step closer, leaning in to look over her shoulder at the chalkboard menu. "Maybe we can meet somewhere a bit more private next time."

His suggestion made Sid's skin crawl. There was no way she was meeting this man anywhere but in a wide-open public space.

Sid stepped up to the counter and away from the ACC. She thought about ordering one of the specialty cocktails, all of which featured booze from the local distillery, Old City Spirits, and came with plastic swords speared with olives or fruit slices. But with the ACC currently staring at her ass, Sid didn't want to wait for the bartender to mix a drink, so she placed her order for one beer and one soda and handed over some cash.

"People might get suspicious if we keep meeting in person, J. T. I think it's probably best if I call you at work next Friday afternoon and give you my report. If I have any photos or evidence to share, I'll make an appointment with your office." She picked up her drinks and turned to go. "Enjoy your evening, Commissioner."

J. T. gave her a mock salute as his gaze slid over her body.

"Always a pleasure to meet with my constituents, Sidney. I look forward to working with you." He licked his lips. "For the good of our wonderful community, of course." Sid began walking backward, away from the ACC, before turning around and colliding with Detective Tony Davis.

"Whoa there," said Tony. He grabbed Sid by the arms to steady her, and her beer sloshed down the front of his shirt.

"Shit! Sorry!" Sid stared at the large, wet spot on the front of Tony's black T-shirt. "That's not good."

Tony chuckled. "You okay?"

Sid nodded and stepped back, and Tony released his grip.

"Lovely to see you again, Sidney." J. T. Clement winked at her as he sauntered past them, his eyelids still at half-mast. He quickly flashed his best politician's grin at the detective and then went back to concentrating on not spilling the four beers he was balancing in his hands.

"You have some business with Commissioner Clement?" Tony watched J. T. navigate his way back to his friends at the picnic table. "Is he drunk?"

"No. And yes," replied Sid. "Sorry about your shirt. I'll have it cleaned."

Tony snorted a laugh. "It's a cotton T-shirt. And that's just beer, right?" He pulled the front of his shirt up to sniff it. "Yep, just beer. Don't worry about it. I'm gonna toss it in the wash when I get home. Besides, Dante spilled a lot more than that on me already this evening." He pointed to a ketchup stain on the hem of his shorts. "See? Kids, man. What can you do?"

"Dante?" Sid blinked at Tony. "Is he . . ." She looked around, feeling her breath coming quickly. "How is he? Is he good?"

"Yeah, he's great. He's right over there with Naomi and my mom." Tony pointed to one of the concrete planters toward the back of the venue. Two women were sitting on the edge of the planter, holding on to a little boy who was standing between them. He was dancing to the music and trying to jump off the edge of the planter.

Sid felt a sob welling up inside her. "He's getting so big."

"He's almost four. Has a birthday coming up in September." Tony moved to stand next to Sid as she watched the little boy dance and clap. "He's a handful, that's for sure."

Sid nodded. Dante had been just shy of one year old when Tony transferred to the SJSO Marine Unit. Tony had brought his wife and the baby to Manny's farewell party, where Sid met them all for the first time. Iris immediately fell in love with Dante and tried to help him walk by holding his tiny hands. Dante would manage two or three steps before he'd topple over and begin giggling. Now, that baby had become a precocious four-year-old with dimples in his pudgy cheeks and a bright, happy smile.

"How's Naomi?" asked Sid. She watched Tony's wife smile adoringly at Dante. Naomi Davis was a beautiful woman with smooth, dark skin and wide-set eyes that turned up slightly at the outer corners. Tonight, she was still wearing her scrubs, having apparently just finished her shift as an emergency room nurse at Flagler Hospital on the south side of town.

"She's good. Come say hi!" Tony placed a hand on Sid's shoulder and took a step toward his family.

Sid shook her head, sliding away from him. "I can't. I . . . I'm sorry. I can't, Tony." She shook her head again and felt her throat start to constrict as she watched Dante dance next to his mom and grandma. "I have to go."

"Okay." Tony nodded. "Maybe next time then."

"Next time, yes." Sid turned and launched herself into the crowd.

When she reached Leo, she handed him the soda and gulped down half of what was left of her beer. Recent Geezer was in full swing, and the driving beat of the music clashed with Sid's racing pulse. "I have to go, Leo. I'll see you tomorrow."

Leo shot to his feet. "What's wrong? Why are you leaving? The Geezers just got started."

She placed a hand on his shoulder and squeezed gently. "I know. I'm sorry. Nothing's wrong. I just . . ." She glanced again toward the back of the venue. Tony was dancing with his son in his arms while Naomi and Dante's grandmother clapped along. "I just can't tonight. I'm sorry. I'll see you tomorrow."

Sid left Leo standing by himself, soda in hand, and wove her way through the crowd. She tossed the remainder of her beer in the trash and headed for home.

Chapter Fourteen

Leo put his cereal bowl in the sink and left the house at ten o'clock the next morning. Clomping down the back steps, he found a white SUV parked in the drive next to Sid's car. It hadn't been there when he and his grandfather arrived home the night before. As he approached, a man got out on the driver's side and lifted a little boy from the back seat, hoisting him over his shoulder. The little boy giggled.

Leo smiled. "Hello." He stood at the front of the vehicle. The man shut the car door and turned to face him, causing Leo to stagger back a few steps.

"Good morning. I'm here to see Sidney Stone." He patted his son's back and lowered him so that he held the little boy in his arms. "I'm Tony Davis. This is my son, Dante."

"Hi!" squealed the boy, waving a small, well-loved bunny in one hand.

Leo waved at the child. "Hi. I'm Leo, Burt's grandson." Tony nodded, and Leo cleared his throat. "Do you have an appointment?"

A slow grin crossed Tony's face. "No, we don't. I was hoping Sid would be able to squeeze us in. Won't take long."

Leo hesitated for a moment before nodding and moving to the office door. He knocked and then opened the door a crack. "Sid?" He heard her mumble something from her upstairs apartment. Leo looked back at Tony and Dante. "Give me a minute. She's upstairs. I'll let her know you're here." Tony nodded and set down Dante, who immediately picked up a stick and began scraping at the dirt next to the driveway.

Leo slipped inside the office as Sid descended the stairs, coffee mug in hand. "We're going to stake out Josie Clement today. I want to follow her to her lunch with her friends, and then we'll head to our meeting with Liesel Winfield."

"Um . . ." Leo shoved his hands in his pockets and rocked back and forth on his heels. "Someone's here to see you."

"Oh?" Sid crossed to her desk and set down her mug. "New client?"

Leo shook his head. "I don't think so. He says he just wants to talk to you for a minute."

"Okay, let him in." Sid pointed at the door and shuffled the files on her desk into a neat stack.

Leo chewed his bottom lip. "It's . . . uh . . ." Sid looked up at him and raised an eyebrow. "It's Tony Davis and his son."

Sid froze. When she finally began moving again, she knocked over her mug and sent coffee spilling across her desk and onto the floor. "Shit!" She grabbed the bottom of her shirt and tried to mop up the coffee before it reached her computer.

Leo leaped into action, swiping some napkins from a stack on the shelf next to the mini fridge and slamming them down on the desktop. He grabbed the rest of the napkins and began mopping up the coffee pooling on the carpet. "Do you want me to tell him to go away?"

Sid shook her head. "No. Let me go change my shirt, and

then you can let him in." She dumped the soggy napkins in the trashcan under her desk and held it out for Leo to do the same. "Just give me a few, okay?"

Sid hurried upstairs, selected a nicer, cleaner shirt and pair of shorts, and put them on. She brushed her hair and changed into a pair of pretty sandals she hadn't worn in three years. After a few deep, calming breaths, she went back downstairs and nodded for Leo to let in their guests.

Tony Davis entered holding Dante's hand. "Mornin', Sid."

"Hi," said Dante, smiling shyly.

"Good morning, Dante." She smiled at the little boy, feeling the familiar ache in her chest that always accompanied thoughts of her own losses, and then turned to Tony. "What can I do for you?"

"Can we talk for a minute?" Tony's eyes darted to Leo and then back to Sid.

Sid took a deep breath and nodded. She stepped forward and squatted to be eye level with Dante, her heart pounding in her ears. "What's your bunny's name?"

Dante smiled, showing a mouth full of baby teeth, and held out the stuffed rabbit for Sid to see. "Hopper. He's my favorite."

"I can see that." Sid smiled at the stuffed toy, noting the careful repair stitching in some of the worn spots. "Do you like cheese crackers, Dante?" The boy nodded and hugged the rabbit to his chest. Sid reached behind her and plucked two snack bags from the makeshift kitchen. "Leo loves cheese crackers, too." Dante's eyes went wide as he looked up at Leo. Sid held out one of the snack bags to Dante. "Why don't you and Leo go sit outside and have some crackers? Would you like to do that?" Dante took the bag and looked up at Leo.

Leo took the other bag from Sid and held out his hand. "Come on, Dante. I'm super hungry. Let's go eat some crackers."

"'Kay!" Dante held out the hand that was clutching his rabbit. "You hold Hopper."

"I can do that." Leo took the rabbit and held Dante's hand as he led the little boy outside to the wrought iron table and chairs under the branches of the neighbor's big oak tree.

Once they were gone, Sid waved to the guest chairs. "Have a seat." She pointed Tony toward the dining room chair. "Actually, take that one. I don't trust the other one not to break."

Tony smiled and looked around. "Nice digs."

"Thanks." Sid knew he didn't mean it. "Burt was kind enough to let me set up shop here." She sat in the desk chair and cringed as it squealed in protest. She was going to have to invest in some WD-40. "What can I do for you, Detective?"

"Look, Sid." Tony leaned forward, resting his elbows on his knees and clasping his hands together. "I don't want to interfere in your business or anything, but I got to ask. Are you involved with J. T. Clement? Are you workin' for him or something?"

Sid started. "I can't talk about my clients—confirm or deny, I mean." She drummed her fingers on the desk, trying to hide her annoyance at the flub. "Why do you ask?"

"Just a hunch." One side of Tony's mouth pulled up in a half smile. "The fact that he was talking to you at Granny Oak's last night. I saw you two in line at the bar. That's why I came over. I thought he was either trying to put the moves on you"— he shrugged one shoulder—"or he'd hired you for a job." Tony rubbed his hands together but kept his eyes fixed on Sid. "J. T. Clement is not a man you want to mess with."

"Are you suggesting he's dangerous?" Sid cocked an eyebrow and leaned back, a move she instantly regretted when her chair squeaked again.

Tony shook his head. "I don't think you're in any physical danger from him. J. T. isn't the kind of guy to get his hands dirty like that. But he's not a man you can trust."

Sid put a hand to her heart and feigned disbelief. "What?! But he's a man of the people! A beloved citizen of St. Augustine. A loyal servant of the community."

"He has a huge mansion on Vilano Beach that overlooks the St. Augustine Inlet. He's neither a man of the people nor a beloved anything." Tony sat back. "You should be careful."

"Why?" She held Tony's stare and waited.

Tony pursed his lips and gripped the arms of the chair, seeming to decide whether to continue or to get up and leave. "Okay. What I'm about to tell you needs to be kept secret. Agreed?"

Sid narrowed her eyes, studying him but saying nothing.

Tony sighed in annoyance. "Sid, please."

She sighed. "Fine. Spill it."

With a nod, Tony began his story: "My first weekend on the job here was Labor Day weekend. I had just arrived, and I was sent right out with Wes and Manny to learn the ropes. Labor Day weekend is always busy for the marine unit, so they were happy to have the extra hands. It was crazy busy, just as expected. There were so many drunk boaters out on the water." He shook his head. "We pulled up to one boat that was driving erratically and ignoring the lateral markers. J. T. Clement was driving. He was drunk, probably stoned, too." Sid nodded once, not surprised at all by this revelation.

Tony continued, "I didn't know who the guy was, but Manny and Wes did. Wes wanted to bring him in on a BUI, boating under the influence, but Manny convinced him not to. Manny let J. T. off with a warning, and I got the impression that Manny had done it before, let him off rather than arrest him. Just a feeling I had. Anyway, Wes made J. T.'s wife drive the boat back in. We followed to make sure they docked. J. T. has a big house near Porpoise Point, right on the inlet like I said. We told him we'd be back and forth in the inlet all day. If we found the boat wasn't at the dock, we'd track him down and arrest him. The boat stayed moored all day, thankfully. The next morning, I showed up to work and found Wes talking to J. T. Couldn't hear what they were saying, but the conversation looked a bit heated. As I got to the boat, J. T. was leaving. He didn't say anything to me. Neither did Wes . . . until the end of the day."

Sid twisted the hem of her shirt and forced herself to take slow, steady breaths. Listening to this man talk about working alongside Wes had her heart beating erratically. It took all of her effort to focus on Tony's story when what she really wanted to do was cover her ears, yell at him to leave her alone, and hide away from the rest of the world.

Tony wiped his palms on his shorts and dropped his gaze to the stack of files on Sid's desk. "At the end of our shift, the three of us agreed to go for a beer and grab a burger. Manny drove his own car, and I rode with Wes. When I asked Wes about what went down with J. T., he told me that J. T. was still drunk that morning, that he could smell the liquor on his breath, and that J. T. tried to bribe him."

"What?!" Sid shot forward in her chair. "Are you suggesting my husband took a bribe, Detective?"

Tony held up his hands. "No, Sid. I'm saying J. T. *tried* to bribe him, and Wes told him to go fuck himself."

Sid felt her shoulders slump in relief. "What kind of bribe?"

"I don't know exactly." Tony rubbed the back of his neck. "Wes said J. T. wanted to make sure that Wes kept his mouth shut and didn't spread it around about him almost getting arrested. He tried to offer Wes money." He shrugged. "That's what it looked like to me, anyway. J. T. pulled out his wallet, but Wes waved it away. It looked like J. T. was trying to give him cash, but Wes wouldn't say anything else to me about it. I don't know exactly what went down, but I always thought there was more to the story. I mean, I got the impression that that was not the first time J. T. had gotten himself into trouble. Not even the first time he'd been threatened with arrest for BUI. It seems like letting that guy off the hook is just standard operating procedure around here."

Tony leaned forward. "Sid, if J. T. was trying to bribe Wes, then I think it was for something more than just keepin' quiet about drunk boating. I'm pretty sure of it. I don't know why he wanted to buy Wes's silence, but it took balls to find Wes the next morning and offer him money like that, out in the open." Tony shook his head. "J. T. knows a lot of people. He's got money and power. What if he's got dirt on other people? If he tried to bribe a cop, then he's probably tried to bribe other people—and probably with more success. Guys like that are dangerous, Sid. You get what I'm sayin'?"

The blood was now pounding in Sid's ears, but she was determined not to let her anxiety show. "Thanks for the warning, but I can take care of myself." Sid studied him, unnerved by the concern showing in his eyes. "Really, Tony. I'm a big girl. And don't worry, J. T. hasn't offered me any bribes." She held her arms open. "And I have nothing of value that he can use against me, so . . ."

Tony shook his head. "But what if someone else thought you knew something? What if they thought J. T. was running his mouth off to you? You're a PI now. You're in the business of secrets. You may not be in danger from J. T., but what about someone who's scared of what J. T. might tell you?"

Sid chewed her bottom lip. "I'll be careful. I appreciate the concern, Tony."

Tony held up a hand. "There's something else I wanted to tell you." He sat back again, more at ease. "I wanted to let you know that I've been looking into Wes's death. I've never stopped looking into it, to be honest, but since I made detective, I've taken a closer look at the file. On the sly, of course."

Sid's eyes went wide. "Why?"

"Come on, Sid. Why do you think?" Tony frowned. "That was no accident that night. I know about the voicemail message Wes left you. I was not drunk at the gun range. I was home with my family, asleep in bed. If someone called Wes telling him to go pick me up, they were lying!"

Sid nodded. "I know." The investigation, such as it was, had cleared Tony. The police had arrived at his house to find him asleep with his wife. He was also stone-cold sober at the time.

Tony sighed. "I didn't know Wes very well, but I got to know him well enough that first week to know he would never shoot himself with your daughter in the car. He would never pull out a gun and fire a bullet into his head instead of trying everything he could to help Iris and whoever else might be injured, even if he was injured himself. He would have at least called it in." He rapped the arm of the chair with his knuckles. "All he talked about from the first day I met him, the only thing he really talked about, was you and Iris." Tony held Sid's wide-eyed stare. "He wouldn't leave you like that, Sid. I may have only known Wes for a week, but I knew enough about him to know that."

He stood to leave. "Just thought you should know." He walked to the door but paused before opening it. "J. T. tried to bribe Wes one week before he died. What if someone else besides me knew about that? I'll keep looking into Wes's death, and I'll let you know if I find anything. Just wanted you to know."

Tony stepped out of the office and shut the door, leaving Sid alone with her thoughts. He found Dante chasing Leo around the yard. The little boy was running with Hopper held tightly in his small fist. Both he and Leo were laughing and smiling. Tony watched for a few moments before calling out to his son, who came running over on his short legs. "Time to go, little man."

"Can Leo come?" asked Dante as Tony swung him up into his arms.

"Not this time." Tony smiled at Leo. "Thanks for watching him."

Leo brushed the hair back from his face. "No problem."

"You ever do any babysitting?" asked Tony as he walked toward his car.

Leo shook his head. "This was it. First time ever."

Tony chuckled. "Well, think about it. If you're up for it, we can always use a good back-up babysitter when Grandma isn't available."

"Maybe." Leo smiled at the boy and waved. "Bye, Dante."

"Bye, Leo." Dante waved Hopper in the air as his dad placed him in his car seat. "Bye, Leo. Bye, Leo. Bye, Leo!"

Leo couldn't help but chuckle. "Bye, Dante."

Tony shut Dante's door and climbed into the driver's seat. "Bye, Leo." He winked at the teenager and pulled out of the driveway. Leo could still hear Dante's farewell chant through the open windows as they drove away.

When Leo returned to the office, he found Sid staring at her Wall of Shame. "Everything okay?" he asked.

Sid nodded. "Tony said he, Wes, and Manny almost arrested J. T. Clement for drunk boating one week before Wes died."

"Drunk boating? Is that an actual thing?" Leo tossed the two empty cracker bags into the trash.

"Yep." Sid nodded, still studying the wall. "Wes had wanted to arrest J. T., but Manny decided to let him off with a warning. They made Josie drive the boat back to the dock. Apparently, she was the only sober one. J. T. offered Wes a bribe the following day. Money in exchange for Wes keeping his mouth shut."

Leo's eyes went wide. "To keep quiet about drunk boating?"

Sid shook her head. "Tony doesn't think so. He thinks J. T.'s drunk boating was public knowledge. He thinks J. T. was offering money for Wes's silence on something else."

Leo blew out his cheeks. "Did Wes take the bribe?"

"No," answered Sid, a hard edge in her voice. She heaved a sigh and turned to look at Leo. "Tony has been looking into Wes's death. Unofficially. He doesn't think it was suicide either. He thinks Wes was murdered."

Leo stared at Sid. "By J. T. Clement?"

Sid shrugged. "Maybe. Or someone else who knew about the bribe attempt."

Leo studied the Wall of Shame. "Now what do we do?"

Sid crossed to the desk, grabbed her oversize purse from the bottom drawer, and shoved the ACC's file into it. "We get to work. We have a lady of leisure to follow and a house we need to pretend to buy."

Chapter Fifteen

Sid and Leo pulled into the empty parking lot of the dermatologist's office that sat across the road from El Sabor, a Latin fusion beachside restaurant on Anastasia Island, just half a mile south of Josie Clement's tennis club. They watched as Josie, who had driven by herself to lunch, trailed the other ladies into the restaurant at precisely twelve o'clock on Saturday.

Sid lowered the windows to let in the sea breeze and shut off the engine while Leo opened the insulated cooler bag he had stowed behind his seat and handed her a peanut butter and jelly sandwich. They ate in silence, Sid watching the door and Leo scrolling on his phone.

He checked the PB&J website and social media accounts. There were more photos now. Lots of shots of luggage and shopping bags and Jezebel wearing various colored bows. There was a short video shot early that morning of Brooklyn driving and jabbering about it being so early that they were watching the sun rise as they drove south on I-95 heading toward Miami and, eventually, Key West. Paizley was asking questions off camera, and Brooklyn was detailing their plans for the day.

When the video was over, Leo went back to scrolling through the photos. His mom had dyed her hair blonde. It had always been a lighter brown than Leo's, but now it was so blonde it was almost white. Brooklyn's hair was even blonder. They were both wearing tons of makeup, something Leo's mom had never really done before. She liked to look at makeup and talked about buying it, but they never had money for her to spend on it. Now, however, his mother was wearing so much makeup it was hard for Leo to recognize her. Apparently, this was Paizley with a Z. This was who she was now.

"How's it going?" Sid nodded at Leo's phone. "Any good fashion tips I need to know about?"

He scowled. "No."

"Hmmm." Sid stuffed her trash in the cooler bag and sipped her drink. "Have you heard from your mom?"

"Yes," he mumbled. It was technically the truth. In the week since she'd left him at Burt's house, Paizley had sent Leo a grand total of three texts. Each one contained a photo of some aspect of their preparation: packing the camper, shopping for groceries, and filling up the jeep's gas tank. He angled the phone away from Sid. "I talked to her last night." Also technically true.

But Paizley Roberts hadn't called her son. Leo had been the one to call her. He knew that she and Brooklyn had planned to head out at sunrise to officially begin their tour of Florida. He'd learned this from a blog post his mom had written on Thursday.

At ten o'clock last night, he'd broken down and called her. She answered on the fourth ring. She sounded happy to hear from him and confessed that the day, the whole week in fact, had gotten away from her, and she was sorry that she hadn't been in touch. She promised to call more often once they were on the road. She talked for half an hour before she asked Leo any questions. Was he minding Burt? Were there any problems? Was he staying out of trouble?

Leo told his mom he had a job helping a private investigator and that they were working on a really big case involving powerful people. Paizley had "mm-hm'd" at the appropriate spots in Leo's story, but he knew she wasn't listening to him. Not really. She was probably packing or editing photos or doing something else that was more important than paying attention to her son. He pretended that Burt was calling him from downstairs, said goodbye to his mom, and hung up. Then he tossed the phone on the desk, hugged his pillow to his chest, and cried until he fell asleep.

"She's fine," said Leo. "They're on the road to Key West today. I'll probably talk to her tonight if they don't get in too late." He scrolled back and forth on her Instagram profile, scanning post after post, hoping to catch a glimpse of the mom he knew. Did she miss him? Was she thinking about him? He hoped to find some evidence that this was the case.

Sid stared out the window, grinding her nails into the palms of her hands in an effort to control her anger. "So everything is going good then? All according to plan?"

"Yep."

"Good."

"Yep."

"Great."

"Yep."

"Fantastic."

Leo blew out a breath. "Just say it. I know you want to."

Sid shrugged, the movement so unnatural as to feel like a flinch. "Say what?"

"Whatever it is you want to say about my mom." Leo

slapped the phone down on his leg and turned to face Sid. "This is her job now, and she needs to focus on it. As soon as she has the hang of it, she's going to come and get me, and we're going to travel around the country together."

"Right. I heard." Sid nodded, not looking at Leo.

"She *is* coming back here, you know. In a few weeks, she'll be in St. Augustine, and then I'm going to go with her."

Sid nodded again. "So you've said."

"It's *true!*" Leo's voice cracked, and she remembered this young man, her employee, was just a kid.

Sid shifted in her seat to face him. "I don't know your mom at all, and I've only known you for a week, but you're a good kid. If you were my son, there is no way in hell I would drop you off on your grandfather's doorstep, as lovely as he is, and take off for God-only-knows-where without you."

Sid gritted her teeth to keep from shouting. And, boy, did she want to shout. She wanted to pound something with her fist —preferably Paizley's face—and then run hard and fast and long until her legs and lungs burned with effort and anger.

"I don't understand how she could leave you here. I'll never understand it. And I don't care what her reasons are or what she's going through. I get that she's grieving, but you're grieving, too. Hell, we're all grieving something, but that doesn't mean you abandon your kid and go on vacation."

Leo started to kick against the floorboard but thought better of it. "She didn't abandon me!"

"Yes, she did."

"No, she didn't! And she's not on vacation!"

"She did abandon you! And she is on vacation!"

Leo turned away from Sid, trying to hide the tears now streaming down his face. The tension drained from Sid's body as she watched him wipe his cheeks with the back of his hand. What swept over her now was regret and shame. Why was she yelling at this poor kid? He was the victim of his mother's self-ishness and folly.

"I'm sorry, Leo." She pinched the bridge of her nose. "I'm really sorry. That was out of line. You're right. Your mom is not a bad person." A lie, she thought. Paizley-with-a-Z absolutely was a bad person. "She's grieving. I certainly know what that's like. I'm sorry for what I said." She watched Leo's back as his breathing became smoother and steadier. "For what it's worth, I'm glad you're not on that trip with her. I'm glad you're right here."

He turned his head slightly but didn't look at her. "Why?"

Sid sighed. "Like I said, you're a good kid. I like having you around. Burt likes having you around. So do the Geezers and Kitty. We're all happy you're here. I'm hoping that your mom doesn't come back too soon to take you away because I would miss you if you went. We'd all miss you." She smiled as Leo faced forward in his seat, pretending to scan the view beyond the windshield for their mark. "Besides, you're not bad at this PI stuff. With more training, you could be pretty good. Maybe there's a career in it for you."

He glanced sideways at her. "Really?"

Sid nodded. "Really. And if you can get the ghosts to help us and tell you the solutions to all our cases, then we'll be the biggest PI firm in town."

The corners of Leo's mouth twitched up. "I don't think it works like that."

"Too bad. If it did, we'd be rolling in money." She punched him lightly in the shoulder. "Try to work on that, will ya?"

Leo smiled and shook his head.

At 12:50, Josie dashed from the restaurant with a white Styrofoam to-go container in one hand and her car keys in the other.

Sid smiled. "Here we go." She started the car but waited

until Josie had pulled out of the parking lot and driven a block up the road before following.

"Don't we have to meet Liesel Winfield in a few minutes?" said Leo. "We're going to be late."

"We won't be late. Don't worry." They were heading south, farther onto Anastasia Island. Five minutes later, Josie Clement pulled into the Starbucks parking lot.

Leo glanced at Sid. "What's she doing?"

Sid smiled again. "She's taking a meeting."

They watched as Josie exited her vehicle, smoothed the pale yellow skirt over her hips, and strode inside the Starbucks. Sid pulled into the lot of the strip mall next door and parked, but she kept the car running. They had a clear view of Josie, who took a seat at a window table and began scrolling through her phone, glancing up whenever anyone entered or left.

Sid pulled the burner phone from her purse and dialed Liesel Winfield's number. "Watch." She nudged Leo's arm and pointed to Josie in the window.

They watched as Josie reached into her own purse and retrieved a second phone. She answered on the third ring. "Hello?"

"Ms. Winfield? This is Paizley Rogers." Sid affected her singsong voice.

"Oh, yes! Hi. Are you here? I'm sitting by the window. White blouse, yellow skirt." Josie Clement looked around the coffee shop with the phone held to her ear.

"Oh, Ms. Winfield," said Sid, "I'm so sorry to have to do this, but I need to cancel. I got into a fender bender on my way to meet you, and I'm afraid I'm not going to be able to make it. The police are on the way, and I need to call my insurance company to report the damage. That's my whole day shot, I'm afraid. Can I call you next week to reschedule?"

"Of course, of course. I understand." Sid and Leo watched

as Josie slumped back in her seat and leaned her golden head against the window. "I hope everyone is all right."

"Everyone is fine. Just shaken up, that's all. But now I have to deal with the insurance and get the car fixed. Again, I'm really sorry. I'll call soon. Thanks for understanding."

"No problem. Good luck with everything." Josie lowered the phone to her lap as Sid hung up.

"She looks sad," noted Leo. Sid nodded her agreement. They watched Josie as she stared at the phone in her lap for a long minute. "How did you know?"

Sid tossed the burner phone into her purse. "It's amazing what you can find online these days. Josie Clement was born Josette Elizabeth Winfield of Savannah, Georgia. Carter and Charlene Winfield, from that photo you found, are Josie's parents. Josie made up a new name for herself using Liesel, which is a nickname for Elizabeth, and her maiden name."

"But why use a fake name to sell real estate?" Leo tilted his head against the headrest and watched as Josie gathered her phones and purse and returned to her car.

Sid shrugged. "Why sell real estate at all?"

"Right. I mean, she's loaded. She doesn't need to work." Leo pulled off his baseball cap and ran his fingers through his mop of hair. "I don't get it."

"I think I do, or at least I have a hunch." Sid watched Josie leave the parking lot and head back toward the bridge between Anastasia Island and the historic downtown district. "The Winfields are members of the Historic Savannah Foundation. Big donors, from what I can tell. Josie's mom, Charlene Winfield, whose maiden name is Harper, has four sisters. The Harper sisters are all women who have married well, given birth to children who all look like cover models for *Town and Country* magazine, and devoted themselves to sitting on philanthropic boards and hosting charity events. One of the Harper sisters has a daughter named Clara Talcott. Clara appears to be the black sheep of the family. She doesn't seem to fit the mold of the others. Clara, to her credit, married well. She also divorced well. Three times. Now, it appears that she has become a successful businesswoman with her own real estate brokerage firm, specializing in high-end properties. Based on her listings, business appears to be very good."

Leo frowned at Sid. "So, what does that have to do with Josie pretending to be Liesel?"

Sid put the car in gear and headed for home. "I think Josie Clement is planning to follow in her cousin Clara's footsteps. I think she has passed the real estate exam in Florida, and Emmaline Colquitt has allowed Josie to join her agency using a fake name. I'm not sure why Emmaline would do that, but that's a question for another time. You found out that Josie was researching study programs for the Georgia exam. I think Josie's plan is to become a licensed agent in Georgia, join her cousin's real estate firm in Savannah, and become self-sufficient." Sid looked over at Leo. "So she can divorce J. T."

Leo whistled. "The ACC is not going to like that."

Sid smiled. "No, he's not."

"What do we do now?" asked Leo as he got out of the car and stood outside Sid's office. Burt's truck wasn't in the drive, which meant he was still on the remodel job. Leo knew he should walk down to the Crane's Roost and see if his grandfather needed any help, but he liked investigating more than construction work.

"I don't know." Sid jingled her keys and stared up at the clouds floating lazily overhead. "I want to know whether my hunch is correct before I decide what to do. And if I am correct,

I'd like to know why Josie is planning to divorce J. T. and run back to her family in Savannah. Is she in danger? Is J. T. violent or controlling? He's a bastard, for sure, but is there something more?"

Leo caught movement out of the corner of his eye. Kitty Lonigan's dead husband was standing at the fence in the front yard, staring at him. "Do you need me for anything else today?"

Sid shook her head. "No, kid. You're off the hook. I'm going to do some more research. The Clements have their big barbecue tonight. Starts at six o'clock, and I don't really see the need to stake it out. If Josie's having an affair, it's unlikely she'll be doing it at her own house with her husband and all their friends there."

An enormous, black pickup truck pulled up to the curb in front of the house, and a man got out. Sheriff Colquitt, clad in a blue-and-orange-striped golf shirt and his trademark sunglasses, came around the front of the truck and leaned against the passenger door. He crossed his feet at the ankles and shouted, "Sid, got a minute?" He waved a hand, beckoning her over.

"Now what?" mumbled Sid under her breath. She and Leo both walked toward the sheriff. When Sid nudged Leo in the ribs, he peeled off and headed for the front door of his grandfather's house. Even so, he took his time climbing the steps and fishing the key from his pocket.

Sid stood at the wrought iron fence and picked a wilted jasmine blossom from the vines that covered it. "What can I do for you, Sheriff?"

"Just wanted to see how things were going with your new case. How's our good friend, J. T.?" His smile was slick and leering, and Sid had to fight the urge to curl her lip in disgust.

"It's going well. Thanks again for the referral." She forced a smile. "Remind me again, Sheriff, how do you two know each other?"

The sheriff licked his bottom lip. "Are you investigating me now?"

Sid laughed. "I have no need to investigate you. That is, unless *you* are having an affair with the commissioner's wife."

"I am a happily married man, Sid." His nostrils flared in annoyance. "But since you asked so kindly, as I told you before, I knew him from college. We were at UF around the same time. He was a couple of years behind me. Different fraternities, but we knew a lot of the same people." He shrugged. "Anything else?"

Sid tilted her head to one side. "Why did you really refer me to J. T.?"

The sheriff stilled his face and stared at her through his mirrored sunglasses. "I told you. I thought you could use a break."

Sid picked another wilted flower. "Have there been any domestic dispute callouts to the Clement house?"

A slow grin crossed the sheriff's face. "To the best of my knowledge, there have been no arrests for domestic violence against either member of the Clement household." He raised his hand to wipe the sweat from the back of his neck, and Sid noticed the tattoo on his right forearm. It looked like a cross with some flowers around it, but she was too far away to make out the fine details.

Sid narrowed her gaze. "That's not what I asked."

"I know." The sheriff continued to grin at her.

"Any drunken disorderlies of any kind?" Sid plucked another flower and then another.

The sheriff pursed his lips. "I don't believe there have been any arrests involving alcohol or any illegal substances."

"Not what I asked."

"I know."

Sid twirled the bouquet of dead flowers between her fingers. "Any arrests at all? For anything?"

One shake of the head. "No criminal arrests to my knowledge." Before Sid could speak, the sheriff patted the hood of the truck and walked around to the driver's side. "Of course, I can only speak to criminal arrests or charges filed in St. Johns County. If there were, say, a civil suit of some kind filed in another county, well . . ." He stepped up on the running board. "I wouldn't know anything about that."

Sheriff Colquitt ducked into his truck, gunned the engine, and pulled away from the curb. Sid shook her head and turned back toward the house. Leo was already crossing the front lawn to meet her.

"Well, did you hear?" she asked him.

Leo nodded. "What was all that about? Was he talking in code or something?"

Sid sighed. "Not code. But he was trying to steer me toward something." She dropped the wilted blooms and dusted off her hands. "I'm not sure what's going on, but I've got some work to do." She patted the kid on the shoulder. "You can take the afternoon off. If I need you tomorrow, I'll text you." She walked to her office and disappeared inside.

Leo took one look at the empty house and decided not to spend the afternoon inside it. Construction work with his grandfather was better than being alone. He turned to reach for the front gate and came face to face with Kitty Lonigan's husband.

"Yoo-hoo!" Kitty Lonigan waved to him from her front porch swing. The gray tabby cat was curled up on her lap. "Leo? Yoo-hoo!"

Leo froze. The spirit standing before him lingered only a moment before slipping back across the street, coming to rest on the porch swing beside Kitty. The cat picked up its head, swished its tail once, and then curled back up on Kitty's lap.

Leo took his time crossing the street. He climbed up onto Kitty's front porch and leaned against the post at the top of the steps. "Hi, Ms. Lonigan. How are you? Do you need help with anything?" Burt had mentioned that Kitty often called him over for help with small things around the house, like opening jars or reaching something on a top shelf. Leo was told to offer to help her whenever he saw her.

Kitty giggled. "Aren't you kind?" She stroked the cat, who was now purring. "No, thank you. I just wanted to see how you were settling in. How do you like living in St. Augustine?"

Leo tried not to look at the spirit sitting on the porch swing. "It's nice. Really hot, but nice."

"And how are you getting on with Sidney?" The elderly woman tilted her head to one side, a look of concern clouding her face. "How does she seem to you?"

"She seems fine. Nice." Leo nodded, unsure of what else to say. "She has a big case, and I'm helping her with it."

Kitty's eyes went wide. "Nothin' dangerous, I hope."

"Oh no, ma'am. Nothing dangerous." At least, he hoped not. Leo noticed Kitty pull her cardigan a little tighter around her neck. Swallowing hard and hoping he would not regret his decision, Leo asked, "How long ago did your husband die?"

Kitty blinked in surprise. "Jerry? Why . . . oh, he's been gone five years now. Goin' on six. He died just before Christmas. The holidays are so hard now." She shook her head, and her gaze fell to the cat. She stroked the soft fur, and the cat purred in response. "Sometimes it feels like he's still here, though. Like I can feel him sittin' here with me or watchin' me cook dinner or sittin' with me when I'm havin' my mornin' coffee." She shook her head again. "I know that makes me sound crazy . . ."

"No, it doesn't, Ms. Lonigan." Leo looked over at Jerry Lonigan, and the spirit looked back at him. Leo slowly reached up and removed the baseball cap from his head. An image of an enormous bouquet of yellow roses popped into his mind. "Do you like yellow roses, Ms. Lonigan?"

Kitty looked up at him, blinking in surprise. "Why yes! Th-they're my absolute favorite. Jerry used to buy a dozen for me on my birthday every year."

Another image quickly filled his head. This time, a rosebush with bright red blooms, not a bouquet but a bush. Leo balled his fists and tried to calm his breathing. Was he really doing this? "What about red roses? A red rosebush?"

"Oh . . ." Kitty's hand fluttered at her throat. "Well, I do love roses. As you can see, I have dozens of them planted in the yard. Every year for our anniversary, Jerry would plant a new rosebush for me." She pointed to one in a pot at the other end of the porch. "That one there, it's a red one. Makes the most glorious red roses you've ever seen. Just breathtaking." Her voice cracked, and her fingers flew to her lips. "That was the last one he bought for me. We had so many planted in the yard already that I asked him to put it in a pot on the porch so I could see it when I was out here on the swing."

"Happy anniversary."

The words sounded inside Leo's head. A soft, kind voice.

"Did you have an anniversary recently?" Leo pressed himself into the post. He couldn't believe he was doing this.

Kitty nodded. "End of June. Just a few weeks ago."

"Well, your husband says, 'Happy anniversary.'" Leo slammed his eyes shut and braced himself for the reaction that would inevitably come.

"Did he tell you that?" Kitty's voice was barely more than a whisper. Leo opened his eyes and saw her staring at him hope-fully. "Your grandfather once told me that your father could speak to the dead. He also said that you have a similar gift. Can you speak to my Jerry?"

Leo's mouth was suddenly dry, and his heart was pounding louder than Guppy's drumming. "I can't speak to them so much as see them and hear them. Sometimes they tell me things or show me things. Like the yellow roses and the red rosebush." He pointed to the potted plant behind him. "And I heard, 'Happy anniversary,' in my head just now."

"Can you see him?" whispered Kitty, her eyes going wide.

Leo nodded. "He's sitting right beside you. I saw him sitting with you on that swing before, on the day I arrived. And he was with you when we had dinner with the Geezers at Grandpa's house."

Kitty nodded. "How does he look? Does he look okay?" Her eyes were filling with tears.

Leo smiled. Jerry Lonigan was looking lovingly at his wife. "Yes. He looks very nice. He's all dressed up, wearing a gray suit and a pink bow tie."

Tears spilled down Kitty's cheeks. "That was his favorite suit. He always looked so handsome in it. I had him buried in that suit." She nodded and patted the empty seat next to her. "I'm glad he's here with me." She looked up at Leo, wiping the tears from her cheeks. "Can he hear me when I talk to him?"

Jerry Lonigan continued to smile at his wife, and Leo heard in his head:

"I hear everything."

Chapter Sixteen

Leo found his grandfather wrapping up early at the Crane's Roost and told him about his conversation with Kitty Lonigan and Jerry. Burt folded him into a big bear hug, said he was proud of him, and told him not to be late for dinner. Twenty minutes later, Leo found himself standing in front of Mad Hattie with a large cup of coffee, heavy on the cream and sugar, a bottle of water, and two datil-pepper-glazed donuts.

Hattie was sitting cross-legged on her folded blanket, resting against the trunk of the same oak tree she'd been sitting under the last time Leo saw her. Her wide-brimmed straw hat was pulled down over her face.

Leo cleared his throat. "Um, excuse me?" He waited, but Hattie didn't move. "Miss Hattie?" Nothing. Leo kneeled in the grass and contemplated whether it would be appropriate to feel for a pulse. "Miss Hattie?"

"What is it, boy?"

Leo almost dropped the coffee. "I brought you something."

"Lots of cream and sugar?"

He nodded even though Hattie couldn't see him. "Yes,

ma'am." When she sat forward and pushed the hat back onto the top of her head, Leo held out the cup and one of the small, wax paper bags containing a donut.

Hattie licked her lips and took the proffered goodies. "I take it this means you want another lesson."

"Yes, ma'am." He sat cross-legged in front of her and opened the bottle of water.

"You got something in mind, or you want me to tell you what I think you need to know next?" Hattie pulled the lid off the steaming coffee and inhaled deeply.

Leo worried his bottom lip. After the success he'd just had with Kitty and Jerry, he had wanted to ask her about the best way to control a conversation with a spirit, but now he wasn't so sure. The old woman had been right about what he needed to know last time. He'd been practicing every day, donning his baseball cap and making his declaration, and his life had become markedly better as a result.

"I don't know what to choose," he confessed. "I was going to ask you about something—well, tell you about something that happened and then ask you what I should do—but . . ." His fingers touched his baseball cap. "I've been doing what you told me to do, and it's really helped. It actually works."

Hattie chuckled. "Of course it does, boy. Did you think I would tell you a lie?"

"Oh no, I didn't mean that. No, I just meant that I . . . I can't believe it worked. And I mean it *really* worked! That pirate at Bonney's Bar came right up to me, but I pushed him back just by wearing this hat and saying what you told me to say." Leo couldn't help but smile. "It's been great! They're actually leaving me alone."

Hattie flashed her toothless grin. "See? Mad Hattie knows what she's talkin' about." Leo nodded, and Hattie raised a crooked finger. "How about I tell you what I think you should learn next, and if you don't agree, you can ask me your question instead? That sound okay?"

Leo felt himself relax into the ground. "Yes, that sounds great."

Hattie set the coffee cup down in the grass and folded her hands in her lap. "Let me ask you some questions first, before we begin. You can see 'em, right?" Leo nodded. "What do they look like to you?"

"They look like themselves, I guess." He shrugged. "Sometimes they are really see-through. Sometimes just a little bit see-through. And sometimes it's hard to tell that they're spirits at all. They look real and solid. I've been fooled a couple of times by spirits that I thought were living people." Leo rolled the water bottle between his palms. "A lot of them look bad, like how they died, with blood and stuff, but some don't. They look fine. No blood or missing body parts. Just . . . normal. I don't know why."

Hattie nodded. "And you can hear 'em, too?"

"Yes," said Leo. "Not all the time, though. Sometimes it's words in my head. They'll sound male or female, but not always like a real voice. A lot of times, though, I just get images in my head. Like flowers or stuff like that. The pirate at Bonney's Bar showed me another pirate with a sword."

"And these thoughts and pictures, do they make sense to you?" Hattie studied Leo carefully as the boy shook his head.

"No." He sighed. "I know what yellow roses look like, so I know that's what the spirit is showing me, but I don't know what it means to the spirit."

Hattie nodded. "Do you feel their pain or their emotions?"

Leo crunched the bottle in his hands and lowered his gaze. "Sometimes, if it's really powerful. I'll feel a sharp pain in my chest, or my head will hurt real bad, and I assume that's how they died. A few times, I've learned afterward that it was how they died, that they had a heart attack or a stroke or something like that. Sometimes I'll feel their fear." He gripped the bottle even tighter. "I don't like feeling that stuff."

"Me neither." Hattie nodded when he looked up at her. "How about dreams? Do you ever dream about something, and then it happens? It can be when you're sleeping or awake, don't matter which."

Leo shrugged. "I can see things that have happened in the past. Like that pirate, I think he was trying to show me how he died, but I stopped him." Hattie smiled at him. "Sometimes it's stronger if I touch something that belonged to the spirit before they died or if I'm in their house or standing in the place where they died. But it's not always very clear, kind of like I'm looking through a dirty window or trying to work out a puzzle with a lot of missing pieces. It's pretty frustrating. Then, every once in a while, I'll see something that happens in the future. It doesn't happen to me very often, but when it does, it's usually a vision, like a daydream. I don't really dream at night, or at least I don't remember my dreams."

Hattie blew out a breath. "Well, you're lucky that way at least. I remember all my dreams, and it ain't no fun, let me tell you."

She opened her wax paper bag, took out her donut, and dunked it in her coffee. Leo opened his bag and took a bite of his own donut. The sugary glaze had a surprising amount of heat that kicked in after a few seconds. Hattie winked at him.

"Anyone ever tell you about datil peppers?" she asked.

Leo shook his head and took another bite.

Hattie smiled. "Most of the datil peppers produced in the world are grown right here in this county. Used to be exclusive to this area for a long time, but you can find 'em in other parts these days. There's different theories about how they came to be here, but the prevailin' one seems to be that the Minorcans brought 'em over from Europe in the eighteenth century."

"Really?" Leo's eyes grew wide, as much from the donut's heat as from the history lesson.

"That's right. We use datil peppers in everythin' 'round here. You like hot sauce?" Leo shrugged. "Well, I suggest you try some. There's plenty of good ones made locally usin' these peppers." She held up her donut. "But I think *this* is my favorite way to eat 'em." She took another bite, closed her eyes, and savored the spicy-sweet pastry.

Leo licked the last of the glaze from his fingers and wiped his mouth with a napkin. That was merely the first of what would be many more datil-pepper-glazed donuts to come, he was sure of it.

"How do you feel when you're denyin' your gift?" Hattie dunked her donut again and watched as Leo frowned and looked around him. "When spirits are comin' at you and tryin' to talk to you, and you're tryin' to ignore 'em. How does that feel?"

"I usually feel really anxious, and my heart starts racing or I start sweating. I start to panic, especially when there's a lot of them and it's really loud in my head. Lots of images and noise." Leo picked at his napkin. "Is that normal?"

Hattie chuckled. "It's normal. But you'll find it's better if you embrace your gift. It's easier on you if you try to help spirits than if you try to shut 'em out all the time. Lots of spirits just want to get a message to a loved one. It's good to help those spirits if you can." Hattie wagged a crooked finger. "But there's dark beings, too. They may be wicked spirits or ghosts . . . or things even darker still. They'll try to show you bad stuff and talk about evil things. Those are the ones you got to shut down. Tell 'em to go away, and don't let them in your head."

"Like the pirate at Bonney's Bar," offered Leo.

Hattie shrugged. "That one's mostly harmless. Lost his life defending the honor of the woman he loved, so he ain't so bad. A bit dark maybe, seein' as how he was a pirate and all, but no. I'm talking about the really dark things. You know the ones?"

Leo shuddered reflexively. He'd come across a dark and dangerous entity only once, and he hoped to never do so again. He nodded to Hattie.

"Thought so." She dunked her donut in her coffee again. "The sooner you make peace with your gift, the sooner you'll find peace for yourself."

Leo looked up at Hattie through his long, dark lashes. "Okay." They'd do this her way.

"Right." Hattie wiped her hands on her long skirt and fixed her gaze on Leo. "When a spirit comes up wantin' to talk to you, you take a deep breath in and let it out real slow. Calm yourself. Calm your mind. Try to clear everything out."

She held up a finger. "You got to take control of the situation. That's very important. You ask 'em what is it that they want to tell you, and then you say whatever it is that they say. Talk it out loud to start, like you're repeatin' it back to 'em. If they're going too fast, you tell 'em to slow down. If you don't understand, you ask 'em to show you something else to help you understand. Sometimes it helps to write things down. Write down the words as they come to you or draw what shows up in your mind, but get it *out*. And when you've had enough, you tell 'em to stop. Put your hat back on and say, 'That's it. I'm done. We ain't talkin' no more today.'"

Hattie leaned forward. "You understand what I'm sayin', boy? You got to open yourself up. Let it flow through you, and then shut it down. And be real selective about who you let in." She pointed at Leo, whose eyes had gone wide with fright. "You do that, and you'll feel better. What you have is a gift. You embrace it, and it will get easier. It won't be so scary anymore. Can you do that?"

Leo nodded. "Okay. I'll try."

"Good. Remember what I told you when we first met? Life and death ain't complicated. Don't go makin' 'em complicated." Hattie smiled. "You do what I told you and let me know how you get on." Leo gathered his trash and stood to leave. "And boy, if you need more lessons, or even if you just need someone to tell your troubles to, you can find me here." She winked at him. "You don't need to bring me coffee and donuts no more."

Leo smiled. "I don't mind." Walking away, he called over his shoulder, "Thank you, Miss Hattie!"

Hattie chuckled and took a sip of her coffee. "Good luck to you, Leo."

———

Leo wandered along St. George Street, hoping to run into Ellie on his way home. She'd replied to a text he sent while waiting in line at Pirate Joe's for Hattie's coffee. He'd asked if she wanted to hang out, and she answered that she couldn't because she was working at the ice cream shop until five o'clock and had to babysit after that, but he should stop by the shop to say hi.

At a quarter to five, Leo arrived at the N'Ice Day Ice Cream Shop. It was crowded inside, which wasn't a surprise given the strong, sugary scent of waffle cones that wafted out from the open doorway. Ellie and another girl were frantically scooping ice cream while a bald man with wire-rimmed glasses and heavy jowls manned the till.

Leo waited outside as a family of four with a baby stroller exited. As the customers inside reshuffled themselves at the counter, Leo caught sight of a golden-blonde head. He stared through the window at the back of the now-familiar figure of Josie Clement.

The woman stood at the counter, studying the tubs of ice cream on offer and chatting with Ellie. Josie had changed clothes. She was now wearing a very short skirt and high heels. Not her usual outfit, thought Leo. He glanced at his watch. Ten minutes to five. Wasn't she supposed to be getting ready for her barbecue? It was starting at six. Leo frowned as he watched Josie gather her hair up on top of her head with one hand and fan her neck with the other. He couldn't be sure from this distance, but it looked like Josie had a small tattoo behind her left ear.

Leo slipped inside the shop for a better look. A mother with two preteen boys stood at the counter next to Josie, and an elderly couple stood behind them, waiting their turn. Leo stood behind the couple and glanced over at Josie, keeping his cap pulled low over his eyes and hoping she wouldn't recognize him. It was a butterfly. The tattoo behind Josie's left ear was a monarch butterfly.

Josie leaned to her right and spoke to a young girl standing next to her. "Bubblegum" was the child's response to whatever question Josie had asked. Ellie reached behind her to grab a kid's cone and begin scooping.

"Hey, Leo!" Ellie waved at him with the empty cone.

So much for remaining inconspicuous, thought Leo. For a split second, he debated bolting for the door, but Josie turned to look at him before he could move. He stared, mouth hanging open, and removed his sunglasses for a better look.

"This is my sister, Ava." Ellie pointed to the woman whom Leo had mistaken for Josie Clement. "And this is Ruby." The girl standing beside Ava waved at him.

Ava looked him over. "Hey," was all she said before turning back to Ellie, who had started scooping blue-and-pink-swirled ice cream into the kid's cone. "Thanks for taking over babysitting duty, Ellie." She reached into her purse and took out some folded bills. She gave the bald man at the register a few dollars for the cone, deposited the change in the tip bucket, and held out the rest of the money for Ellie. "I won't be long. Maybe an hour or so. I'll meet you guys at home."

"Got it," said Ellie, taking the money. "Ruby and I are going to get pizza after this." She winked at the little girl, who couldn't have been much older than nine or ten, and handed her the ice cream cone. The little girl took it with wide eyes and moved to sit in an empty chair by the window. Ellie turned back to her sister and lowered her voice. "But you really shouldn't go. It's not cool that he calls only when it's convenient for him."

"Stop it," ordered Ava. "You don't know what you're talking about, and I don't need a lecture. I get enough of that from everyone else."

"Well, maybe you should listen once in a while," mumbled Ellie.

Ava huffed and flipped her long golden hair over her shoulder. Leo stared at her. With a bit of distance, the resemblance to Josie was uncanny. Same hair color, length, and style. Same height and build. Up close, however, the differences were noticeable. Ava was still a teenager. Probably a college student, thought Leo. Josie was at least ten years older. Ava's skin was fairer than Josie's but not by much, and Ava had the same smattering of freckles that her sister Ellie had. Josie's complexion was freckle free, as Leo recalled, and Josie didn't wear skirts that were this short or heels this high.

"Whatever. Gotta go." Ava turned her back on Ellie. "I'll see ya in a little while, Ruby Red." She waved at Ruby, who had ice cream on her chin, and Ruby waved back. Ava sashayed out of the ice cream shop and onto St. George Street.

Ellie rolled her eyes. "Ava's got a date. I keep telling her it's a bad idea to get involved with an old married guy, but she won't listen to me." She shoved Ava's money into the back pocket of her shorts and began to untie her apron. "She's supposed to be babysitting Ruby tonight, but I told her I'd help her out and watch Ruby for a while. Want to join us for pizza?"

Leo wanted very much to say yes, especially given that Ellie was smiling at him, but he shook his head. "I'm having dinner with my grandfather tonight, but I'll walk with you guys."

"Great!" She leaned over the counter and pointed to Ruby. "You stay put, Ruby Red. I'll be right back." She disappeared into the back of the shop to clock out.

Ruby sat quietly by herself. The cone was almost gone, and she was sucking the last bit of the melted blue ice cream out of the soggy tip.

Leo took the empty chair next to her. "I'm Leo."

"I know," replied Ruby as she wiped her face with a napkin, managing to miss the ice cream smear on her upper lip. "That's what Ellie said. I'm Ruby. My daddy's the sheriff. Do you know him?" She shoved the last bit of cone into her mouth and chewed.

"I've met him." Leo nodded. "So your last name is Colquitt?" Ruby nodded. "And your middle name is Red?" Leo studied the girl as she swung her legs back and forth, looking for any resemblance to Sheriff Travis Colquitt but finding none.

Ruby snorted. "No. That's just what people call me. My sister Scarlett started calling me that because she used to have this lipstick called "Ruby Red," and one day she came home from school, and I had smeared it all over my face and all over my doll's face, and there was lipstick everywhere." She shrugged. "I knew the lipstick was called Ruby Red 'cause Scarlett had told me, and I liked it 'cause it was a pretty color and it had a shiny gold case and 'cause it was my name. So Scarlett started calling me Ruby Red, and now everyone calls me that. Do you know my sister?" She looked up at Leo, who shook his head in response. "Scarlett's in college. She goes to Florida. That's in Gainesville. That's where I'm going to go to college, too, when I get big." She swung her legs back and forth. "Are you Ellie's boyfriend?"

Leo coughed and sputtered. "No! I, uh . . . no."

"But you like her?" Ruby smiled and waggled her eyebrows.

"I . . . uh . . ." Leo shot to his feet, his face blazing, eager to remove himself from this conversation.

"You ready?" Ellie asked, emerging from the back of the shop and coming around the counter.

Ruby stood and reached for Ellie's hand with her own sticky one. "Yep. I want pepperoni."

"Me too," said Ellie. "Let's go." She led Ruby out of the ice cream shop and turned back to Leo. "Coming?"

Leo stuttered again as Ruby smiled at him and waggled her eyebrows. He shook his head. A kid that young should not be that precocious. "I can't. I really have to get home. Thanks, though." He took a couple of steps backward. "You two have fun."

Ellie's face fell. "Okay. Well, text me tomorrow then."

Leo nodded and turned away. As he did, he walked straight through the spirit of an old woman who was drifting down St. George Street. He shivered with the sensation, tugged at the brim of his hat, and repeated Hattie's words in his head. Then he darted around the corner before Ruby Red Colquitt could embarrass him further.

He jogged up Hypolita Street, heading for home, but slowed as he approached Bonney's Bar. The pirate hovered in the corner of the porch, close to a rowdy table of drinkers, but he made no move to approach Leo. As soon as Leo turned the corner onto Cordova, he saw Ava sitting on the steps of Grace Methodist Church across the street. The large church in the Spanish Renaissance style was another Henry Flagler commission, a gift from the tycoon to the city of St. Augustine.

Ava sat on the steps, her long, bare legs stretched out in front of her, and she stared at her phone. She was wearing sunglasses now, and Leo was struck again by her resemblance to Josie Clement.

A shiny, black Mercedes rolled to a stop at the corner of Cordova and Carrera, next to the church. As it did, Ava stood up and walked toward it. Leo quickly stepped off the sidewalk and ducked into the shaded outdoor patio of a breakfast café that was closed for the night. Leo pulled out his phone, lowered his head, and waited. As Ava got in the car, Leo snapped photos. He thought he recognized the driver of the car but wasn't certain. He got several good shots of the man with Ava sitting next to him in the passenger seat, plus another two clear photos of the license plate as they drove away.

Chapter Seventeen

F ive minutes later, Leo knocked on Sid's door, winded from sprinting all the way home. After hearing her muffled voice, Leo stepped inside.

"Got a minute?" he asked as he plopped down in the guest chair in front of Sid's desk.

She rubbed her eyes, which were dry and sore from sitting in front of her computer screen for the past few hours. "Sure. I could use a break anyway." She pushed her chair back and nodded to him. "What's up?"

Leo wasn't sure why he felt the urge to show Sid the photos. Maybe he was excited that he'd played PI all by himself, or maybe there was something more to it. Regardless, he held out his phone. "Do you recognize this guy?"

Sid reached across the desk and took the phone from Leo. "Yeah, it's J. T. Clement. Why?" She scrolled through the dozen photos and held the phone back out to Leo, who was staring at her, wide-eyed.

"Are you sure?" he asked.

Sid scrolled through the photos again. "Yes. J. T. and Josie Clement."

"No, not Josie." Leo pointed to the woman in the passenger seat. "That's what I thought, too, but that's not her. It's a girl named Ava. She's Ellie's sister."

Sid gripped the phone in both hands now. "Who's Ellie?"

Leo blushed. "A girl I met at the ice cream shop. You know, the one on St. George Street with the faded green awning. 'Have a N'Ice Day' or something like that."

"I know the one," replied Sid slowly. "Tell me what happened."

Leo recounted the tale, beginning with his arrival at the shop, when he saw the woman he thought was Josie, through to snapping photos of Ava and J. T. Clement as they drove away in his car. Leo left out the part about Ruby teasing him.

Sid went quiet, letting him finish his story before asking, "When?"

"Just now. Like, five minutes ago. Maybe ten." Leo took the phone from her. "I'll send these pics to you."

Sid stood and began pacing. "He's supposed to be hosting a barbecue at his house tonight. Did they cancel it? Why is he driving around town with someone who looks just like his wife? What is he up to?" She rubbed her face with her hands. "I've been looking into J. T.'s past, trying to find any prosecutions or civil lawsuits like the sheriff suggested, but I haven't found much."

"But the sheriff made it sound like there was something out there. Maybe something big," offered Leo, not looking up from his phone.

"I know, right?" Sid continued pacing. "I found a lawsuit filed against him in Alachua County, back when he was at UF, but it was nothing major. His landlord sued him for damages caused to the house he was renting. The lease was in his name, and he got sued for something like thirty thousand dollars. The suit never went to trial, so I assume they settled out of court. I looked up the address of the house, and it was only a couple of blocks from his fraternity house. I'm pretty sure he didn't cause the damage all by himself. Based on the photos I've found online from some of his old fraternity buddies, I think J. T. must have enjoyed quite the reputation as a partier. That's all I've been able to find on him."

She plucked a sheet of paper off the desk and handed it to Leo, a printout of an article from the *Sun Sentinel*. "I did find this, which is kind of interesting. J. T. has an uncle down in South Florida who is a real estate developer. The uncle was charged with bribing a Palm Beach County commissioner about ten years ago. The charges were dropped in exchange for the uncle's cooperation with the police and the State Attorney's Office. They went after the commissioner, who apparently had been taking bribes for years. That guy was convicted and sent to jail for five years. Doesn't seem like long enough to me, but whatever. The uncle is still a developer and doing quite well, apparently."

"Well, we know J. T. is bribing people. He tried it with Wes, right?" asked Leo as he stood up and tossed the article on the desk. "Do you think he's taking bribes, too?" He crossed the room, heading for the door.

Sid shrugged. "I don't know. I wouldn't put anything past him, but I can't find anything scandalous. No arrests, no other lawsuits, nothing."

She reached across the desk and grabbed the case file, placing the article inside and adding some notes about Leo's sighting of J. T. and the woman who was a dead ringer for his wife. She pulled her sweater tighter around her shoulders with one hand as she wrote. "Leo, where did you say you saw J. T. pick up this girl? In front of Grace Methodist, right?" There was no response. "Leo," she huffed, "I asked—" But when she looked up, she stopped.

Leo stood pressed against the wall, frozen in place and drained of color.

"What is it?" she asked. She recognized that terrorized look on his face and registered the drop in the room's temperature. She heard her voice lower its volume on its own. "Who's here?"

Leo shook his head, eyes wide.

"Leo, we made a deal. Now, tell me what you see." Sid came around the desk and stood next to him. "I can't help you if you don't tell me."

Leo snapped his eyes shut, opening his mouth and then shutting it again without saying anything.

Sid placed a hand on his shoulder. "There's a spirit here, yes?" The kid nodded. "Just one, or more than one?"

"One," he whispered.

Sid swallowed hard. "Is it Iris?" When he kept his eyes shut and shook his head, Sid blanched.

She was not excited about ghosts haunting her office and upstairs apartment, but the spirit of her daughter was something she thought she might learn to accept. Abiding some other random spirit, however, would be much more of a challenge.

"Do you recognize the person?" Sid asked slowly.

Leo nodded.

"Okay, so . . . tell me," she murmured. "Who's here, Leo?"

Leo opened his eyes and held Sid's gaze. "It's your husband."

Chapter Eighteen

"Wes?!" Sid froze where she stood. Only her gaze moved around the room. "Is he . . . is he okay?" she asked Leo.

Leo swallowed hard. The spirit of Sid's dead husband was translucent, barely visible, and that was a blessing. Leo couldn't tell Sid what he was seeing. He couldn't explain to her that Wes was standing only a few feet away from her with part of his skull missing. He couldn't tell this grieving woman that her husband's shirt was covered in blood, that his temple bore powder burns around the gunshot wound. And he definitely couldn't tell her that Wes was angry. He looked so very angry at this moment.

"He looks fine," whispered Leo. "He's very faint. I can barely see him, but I can tell it's Wes."

Sid nodded. "Is he saying anything?"

No, thought Leo. He's just scowling. "Not yet." With a shaky hand, Leo removed the baseball cap from his head and ran his fingers through his sweaty curls. Seconds later, Leo saw two images in his mind. He didn't understand them, and Wes was offering nothing further. No words, no feelings, just the two images.

Sid looked at Leo, her eyes wide and hopeful. He shrugged. "He's not saying anything, Sid. But I think he's showing me something. I don't know what it means."

He held up his hands to show her. "I see this. Two hands forming a T, like calling a timeout." When Sid inhaled sharply, he asked, "Does that mean something to you?"

"It was our symbol for getting the other one to stop something." Sid wrapped her arms around herself, suddenly chilled by more than the drop in the room's temperature. The flood of memories was threatening to drag her under. "Whenever we'd fight, one of us would do that with our hands. We'd call timeout on the fight. Or if one of us was annoying the other in some way, ranting about work or whatever, we'd call timeout. It's how we kept things in check, kept them from going too far."

Leo nodded. "Okay, so he's calling timeout. On what, though? The investigation?"

Sid shook her head. "I don't know. Maybe." She hugged herself even tighter. "But why? I don't understand what he wants me to stop doing." Her eyes darted to the Wall of Shame hidden behind the heavy curtains.

"There's another symbol, but I don't know what it means." Leo rubbed the back of his neck and stared at the floor, trying to make sense of what he was being shown. He moved to the desk and drew the symbol on a scrap of paper. "Do you know what this is?"

Sid took the scrap of paper and studied the two vertical lines, connected at the top and bottom by two curved lines running horizontally. "It's the symbol for Gemini." When Leo stared back at her blankly, she continued. "It's the astrological symbol for Gemini. It was Wes's sign. His birthday was the second of June. He was a Gemini."

Leo shrugged. "So maybe he's confirming for you that it's really him."

Sid shook her head. "Wes didn't believe in that stuff." She waved the piece of paper. "He thought it was crap. Every now and then, I'd read out our horoscopes from the newspaper or a magazine, and he'd make fun of it all." She looked at the symbol. "Why would he show you this?"

"Maybe that's exactly why he's using it—because he knew it would be something you'd recognize." Leo remembered his lesson from Hattie earlier in the day. He'd have to ask Wes to show him something else so that he could understand. But before Leo could form the questions in his mind with clarity and intent, he felt the air shift and knew that Wes was gone.

"Can you ask him—"

Leo cut her off. "He's gone. Sorry."

Sid nodded. "Right, well, I guess we'll just add it to our growing list of mysteries." She paced back and forth across the office, trying to release all the emotions and nervous energy that had built up in her after learning that Wes was haunting her office. But the pacing wasn't working, and she felt like she needed to get out of there. Sid really wanted to go for a long run, but she had work to do.

She shoved the scrap of paper she was still holding into her pocket and grabbed her keys and purse from the desk drawer. She also pulled a camera bag from one of the drawers in the filing cabinet. "I'm going to go stake out the Clements' house. I'd like to know what's going on over there."

"Maybe we'll catch J. T. when he comes home," offered Leo as he held the door open for her.

"Not *we*, kid. Just me." Sid locked the door and headed for the car. "We'll catch up tomorrow. Come see me in the morning, but not too early. In fact, why don't you stake out the church tomorrow?" She set her bags down on the passenger seat and walked around to the driver's side. "The Clements usually attend Sunday service at the Presbyterian church two blocks down the street." She pointed to Sevilla Street, heading south. "I think Josie has it in her calendar for ten or eleven o'clock. Look up the times online. When you get there tomorrow, find a location outside that's inconspicuous, and see if you can spot them arriving. Pay attention to who they talk to. Take photos if you can, but don't get caught. And then change positions for the end of the service when everyone leaves. Find a different place to stand or sit, and change your shirt and hat. You don't want to look like the same person who was hanging around at the beginning of the service. Got it?"

Leo kicked at the edge of the driveway with the toe of his shoe. "Yeah, I got it."

"Good. Come see me after church. We'll swap stories." Sid slid into the driver's seat and pulled out of the driveway.

Leo cursed under his breath as he watched Sid turn the corner and drive away, wishing she'd let him tag along.

"Leo!" called Burt, sticking his head out the kitchen door. "Come help me with dinner. I thought we'd head down to Granny Oak's tonight, if you're up for it. There's a new band playing, and I'd like to check them out. You in?"

Leo nodded and shuffled toward the house.

———

Sid spent the evening parked down the street from the Clements' bayside mansion. When she arrived a few minutes after six o'clock, the street was already lined with cars, most of them shiny and expensive and all of them belonging to party guests. She managed to find a spot about three doors down that had been recently vacated by someone not attending the

Clements' soiree. She cut the engine, pulled out Trip's old camera with the telephoto lens, and settled back in the seat.

At 6:15 p.m., J. T. Clement rumbled past in his Mercedes and pulled into the drive. The garage door rolled up, but he left his car in the driveway. Sid snapped away with the camera as J. T. exited the car alone, popped the trunk, and removed two twelve-packs of beer. He made a total of three trips into the garage, carrying in more packs of beer and bags of ice, before the garage door came down and he disappeared inside.

Sid scrolled through the photos she'd taken. J. T. Clement was dressed in a pressed shirt with the sleeves rolled up, crisp khaki shorts, and boat shoes. There wasn't a wrinkle on him, nor a hair out of place. Sid sighed. What was the bastard up to?

She watched the house for another hour, hunched down uncomfortably in her seat. The Colquitts arrived at six thirty, and Sid recognized a handful of couples among the other late arrivals. By half past seven, it seemed all the guests had arrived, and none of them were look-alikes for Josie Clement.

———

The next morning, Leo sat cross-legged under the now-familiar oak tree in Plaza de la Constitución. He handed Hattie a cup of coffee. "Lots of cream and sugar," he said. "And a donut." He removed one of the datil-pepper-glazed donuts from the wax paper bag and then held out the bag with the second donut for Hattie.

"I told you that you don't need to bring me coffee and donuts no more." Even so, Hattie took the bag from Leo and placed it in her lap. "It was just a test. My way of makin' sure you were serious and not just playin' around."

"I know." Leo shrugged. "But I don't mind, and the donuts are really good." He took a bite and smiled at her.

"Thank you." She smiled back, removed the lid from the cup, and inhaled deeply. "So, did you come to Ol' Hattie with a question, or are you just here for a social call?"

Leo swallowed. "I have a question." With his index finger, he drew in a small patch of dirt near Hattie's seat under the tree. "Have you ever seen this before?"

Hattie studied the drawing as she sipped her coffee. "Looks like Gemini." Leo nodded. "Where'd you see it?"

"In my head." Leo sat back and wiped off his finger on his shorts. "A spirit showed it to me. He showed me two symbols, actually, but I think I already know what the other one meant."

"He?" asked Hattie, raising her eyebrows. Leo nodded. "Do you know this spirit?"

"No. I mean, I know who he is. I've seen his picture. He's the husband of my . . . my friend." His choice of word caught him by surprise. He hadn't said "employer." No, he'd called Sid his friend. But was she? Honestly, he wasn't sure. All he knew for certain was that he didn't miss his mom quite so much when Sid was around.

"And you're sure the spirit was tryin' to get a message to your friend?" Leo nodded, and Hattie took another sip of coffee before she continued. "Did the spirit say anythin' to you? You hear any words in your head? Feel anythin' from the spirit?"

Leo shook his head. "No words, but he felt very angry."

"And how'd he look?"

A shiver went up Leo's spine as he remembered Wes standing in front of him. "Like he'd been shot in the head. All bloody and stuff. And really angry."

Hattie pointed to the symbol. "It can mean a lot of things. The trick is what it means to the spirit. Gemini can mean a birthday, either of the spirit himself or the person he's trying to communicate with. Or it could mean two, as in two of something. One, two. Or it could mean twins. Two people. Actual twins, or two people who were close like twins, or maybe siblings that looked a lot alike or were close in age. Something like that. Any of that make sense?"

Leo furrowed his brow. "Not yet."

"What was the other symbol?" asked Hattie as she opened the bag. When Leo held up his hands, Hattie almost dropped her donut. "You tellin' me the spirit did *that*! It called timeout?!"

Leo nodded. "Yeah, why?"

Hattie shoved the donut back in the bag, breaking it in two in the process. Wagging her finger at Leo, she hissed, "Then you take it as a warnin', boy. If that spirit was as angry as you say, and he appeared to you the way he looked when he died, then he ain't settled. He ain't at peace. He may even be a ghost who hasn't moved on, either because he can't or because he won't. Looks like that spirit was callin' for a timeout, and you'd best listen to him. Whatever it is you're doin', or whatever it is your friend is doin', you should stop it right now." Hattie clucked her tongue. "Don't know what the Gemini means, but you tell your friend it's probably a warnin', too. And when spirits send warnin's, you'd be smart to heed 'em."

Leo nodded as his eyes grew wide. The phone in his pocket buzzed, and he pulled it out, noting the alarm. "I gotta go." He stood up and dusted off his shorts.

All of Hattie's vitriol seemed to have leaked out of her with her speech. She tapped her chin as she studied him calmly. "Just thought of another possibility." She leaned forward. "Gemini usually means two, but maybe it's not two separate people or things. Maybe it's only one person or thing with two sides to it. Two personalities, maybe."

When Leo frowned in confusion, Hattie continued. "Good and evil, boy. All of us have both those things inside us. It could be that somethin' that seems good at first is secretly evil." She shrugged. "If the spirit is tryin' to warn you off, I think you got to consider that there's some evil involved someplace. So you be careful, Leo. Don't go messin' around with evil."

———

Leo left Hattie sitting under her oak tree and jogged several blocks to Sevilla Street. Located on the southwest corner of Sevilla and Valencia, the Flagler College library nestled among some other college buildings, all of them distinguishable by their white facades, red-tile roofs, and red trim details.

The back of the library faced the Memorial Presbyterian Church across Valencia Street. The church was an ornate composition of grayish-white buildings decorated with gold detailing and topped with a green dome. Its website bragged that it was constructed in the Second Renaissance Revival style by Henry Flagler, who took his inspiration from Saint Mark's Basilica in Venice. Leo didn't care about any of that, but he was willing to admit that it was a pretty church, so far as churches went, and he liked the green dome at the very top.

In a shady section of the library's grounds, Leo found a small set of concrete steps leading to a rear exit. He took up his position there, leaning against the wall, with a view of the church and its parking lot. He watched as worshippers arrived for the eleven o'clock service, many of them lingering on the church steps despite the bright morning sun and climbing late July temperature.

Leo spotted Sheriff Colquitt and his family among the loitering congregants. His wife, Emmaline, was recognizable from her photo on the real estate agency website, and Ruby stood between her parents in a pale pink sundress with her nose in a book. The crowd shifted as people greeted one another and began to drift inside, lured by the promise of air-conditioning. Leo watched as Emmaline waved her hand in the air and was soon greeted by Josie Clement. J. T. held out his hand to Sheriff Colquitt. The two couples chatted animatedly while Ruby turned the pages of her book.

Eventually, the Colquitts and the Clements found their way inside along with the other worshippers, and the doors of the church were closed to all those who did not have the good sense to arrive early and be seen. Leo sat in the shade for a while, enjoying the peace and quiet and the soft breeze from the bay. Since beginning his stakeout, he'd only noted two spirits, neither of which went near the church. That was a common trait of the spirits he'd observed over the years. They didn't tend to congregate around churches, nor did they hang out in graveyards or cemeteries. He wasn't sure why that was, but he was grateful for the reduced spirit traffic on this particular block of the Old City.

At half past eleven, Leo left his shady spot on the back steps of the library and made his way through the church parking lot. He strolled past J. T.'s black Mercedes and found a small bench under a shade tree at the back of a small, two-story clapboard house that was now a converted administration building for the college. He pulled off his white T-shirt and vintage Jacksonville Suns baseball cap and swapped them for a black T-shirt and Jacksonville Jaguars cap.

While he waited on the bench for the worshippers to be sent forth into the world, renewed and refreshed from the morning's service, Leo scrolled through his mother's Instagram account. One week had passed since she'd left him at Burt's house and taken off for a life of adventure. There were a dozen new photos now—the campsite, several bars and restaurants, a few clothing shops, and two photos of either a sunrise or a sunset, Leo couldn't be sure which. Each photo featured one or both of Paizley and Brooklyn, both of whom were now sporting slight sunburns on their noses and shoulders. They were smiling and laughing, trying on colorful straw hats or holding up cocktails with tiny umbrellas. Jezebel, sporting an array of hairbows and rhinestone collars, appeared in ten of the twelve photos.

Leo closed the app and pulled his headphones out of his bag. Scrolling through a playlist that the Geezers had helped him create, he turned up the volume and let the music carry him away from thoughts of his mother and Brooklyn, of their polka-dotted camper, of sun hats and Key West cocktails, and of that stupid little dog who would probably see more of this country than he ever would.

When the service finally ended, the doors of Memorial Presbyterian Church were flung wide, and the congregation spilled out into the midday heat. The parishioners didn't linger as long now on the steps as they did before. Eager to get home, or at least find refuge from the sun and humidity, the crowd departed in a long line of cars filing out of the parking lot. The Clements were no exception. Sure, they waved to a few people and shook the hands of a few others, but all while making a beeline toward their car.

As they neared a dark gray minivan one row over from where their Mercedes baked in the sun, J. T. suddenly put his arm around Josie's waist and spun her toward the two closest parked cars. Josie stumbled slightly, but she recovered as J. T. took her hand and led her zigzagging between cars on their way toward their own. The act was so abrupt that it caught not only Leo's attention but that of the Owen family, loading themselves into the minivan—including Ellie and her sister, Ava.

Ava leaned against the side of the minivan, arms folded and legs crossed at the ankles, tracking J. T.'s movements across the parking lot. She was wearing a white sundress, similar to one

Josie had worn earlier in the week, and her hair was styled like Josie's in long, soft waves that cascaded down her back.

As J. T. opened the car door for his wife and waited for her to fold herself onto the scalding leather seat, Ava smiled at him. J. T. looked away and didn't return her smile. Once he was safely ensconced in his sports car, Ava slid into the back seat of the minivan next to Ellie.

The Mercedes was soon sitting in the line to leave the lot with the air-conditioning cranked so high that Leo could see Josie's hair fluttering in the breeze. The minivan was two cars behind them. A few minutes later, the Clements headed in one direction out of the parking lot, and the Owens family drove away in the opposite direction.

When all was once again quiet, Leo crossed the now-empty lot and headed for home. He thought about what Hattie had told him. Wes was sending them a warning. And Gemini meant two of something. Two people . . . twins, perhaps. Or maybe two people who looked like twins, at least from a distance. Josie and Ava certainly fit that description.

Chapter Nineteen

For the next several days, Sid stayed on the Clement case from sunup until well past sundown, but she wasn't following Josie around town.

She was tailing J. T.

After Leo gave his report on the Sunday church crowd and the goings-on in the parking lot, Sid began her surveillance of the ACC.

J. T. Clement spent less time at home than his wife did. If he wasn't on his boat, he was on the golf course. If he wasn't on the golf course, he was meeting his buddies for drinks or lunches or dinners. And on the rare occasion that he wasn't doing any of those things, he was at his office attending to the business of his constituency. J. T. Clement clearly fancied himself a man about town. Thankfully, St. Augustine was a relatively small, quiet town, so keeping up with his antics wasn't too difficult. It did mean, however, very early mornings and very late nights.

Before Sid left the house on Sunday afternoon to begin the tail on J. T., she gave Leo his marching orders. He was to find out everything he could about Ava Owen. Since then, Sid hadn't been home long enough to chat with the kid. She only came back to her apartment to shower, change clothes, and catch a couple hours of sleep. They'd exchanged text messages a few times, with Sid asking for a report and Leo replying that he hadn't learned anything yet.

By Wednesday evening, she was getting cranky. She sat on a bench on St. George Street, watching the entrance to an upscale tavern that had recently opened. J. T. was inside at the bar with some of his drinking buddies, and Sid was outside finishing off a slice of pizza from the shop behind her, which boasted the best slices in the Old City. She wiped the grease from her fingers, wadded up her napkin, and groaned. This job couldn't end soon enough. Her body was actually beginning to crave vegetables, and she desperately wanted to go for a long run. Her watch read seven o'clock, and she was willing to bet that the ACC and his entourage wouldn't be quitting the pub until at least nine. She groaned again, rubbed her eyes, and debated walking home.

Then she felt someone sit down next to her on the short bench. "Hey," he said.

Without opening her eyes, Sid smiled and replied, "Hey, Leo."

When she finally turned her head to look at him, he frowned. "You look like shit."

"Thanks a lot, kid." Sid brushed a few pizza crumbs from her shorts and stole a glance at the entrance to the tavern. No sign of the ACC.

Leo shrugged. "Sorry, but you do."

"Yeah, I know. What's up?" She kept her eyes on the door.

"I talked to Ellie." When Sid gave him a quick sideways glance, Leo rolled his eyes. "Ellie is Ava's sister, remember?" Sid nodded, refocused on the pub's entrance, and waved her hand for him to continue. "Well, according to Ellie, Ava goes to Flagler. She'll be a sophomore when classes start up again, and she works part time at the Cielo Spa."

Sid spun her gaze back to Leo, raising an eyebrow.

"I know," Leo said. "She paints nails apparently. She works afternoons during the week and occasionally on the weekend. Ellie says she's really good, whatever that means. Anyway, I mentioned that I thought I saw her and her boyfriend last Saturday and asked if the boyfriend drove a Mercedes. At first, Ellie got real quiet, but then she told me that the guy is married and that he's some big deal in town. Their parents don't know, and Ava has tried to keep it a secret from everyone. Except that Ellie knows and some of Ava's friends know . . . and we know."

Sid shook her head. "I doubt J. T. will be able to keep it a secret for much longer."

"That's just it," replied Leo. "Apparently she's been dating him since she was a senior in high school."

Sid grabbed Leo's arm. "Are you serious? He's been sneaking around with this girl for, what, over a year?"

"Almost two. They met at a Florida football game in Gainesville. Ava went with a friend of hers and the girl's family. They tailgated with J. T. and Josie at the game, and Ava and J. T. started sneaking around right after that." He leaned forward, resting his elbows on his knees, and lowered his voice. "She was only seventeen then. Isn't that, like, illegal or something?"

Sid ran her hands down her face, terrified by the implications. "If they were having sex? Yes, it's very illegal. The age of consent in Florida is eighteen."

"Well, there's more. Guess who Ava's friend is, the one she went to the game with?" Leo kept his voice low, and Sid leaned forward, mimicking his posture. "Scarlett Colquitt . . . Sheriff Colquitt's daughter."

"Shhhhit!" hissed Sid. She hung her head, placed her hands on the back of her neck, and tried to massage out the tension that was quickly forming into a throbbing headache. Another quick glance at the restaurant's entrance revealed no sign of the ACC.

Sid sat up and looked at Leo. "Sheriff Colquitt recommended me to J. T. to help him confirm whether or not Josie is having an affair, but all we've discovered is that the sheriff's wife, Emmaline, is helping Josie set herself up as a real estate agent under an assumed name. And J. T. is the one having an affair."

Leo nodded. "Yep. That's about it."

Sid shook her head and looked around. "Does this seem right to you?" She stood up and paced back and forth in front of the bench. "Because it doesn't seem right to me. I'm missing something." The tension in her neck and shoulders was continuing to build. "Or maybe I'm getting played."

"How?" Leo worried his bottom lip. "Why?"

"I don't know." Sid sat back down, pulled her pink folio out of her bag, and began jotting down notes. "Something is definitely not right."

Leo watched her for a few minutes and then pulled out his phone and opened PB&J's Instagram account. The latest photo showed Brooklyn and Paizley lounging in front of the polka-dotted camper and holding up wine glasses. The caption read, "Just relaxing this evening. Last night in the Keys. Tomorrow . . . South Beach, baby!"

"Oh!" Leo sat upright and spun toward Sid. "Ellie said that Ava and Scarlett Colquitt are best friends. Have been since the third grade. But they had a falling-out in their junior year of high school. Apparently, Ava and Scarlett went to some party over Labor Day weekend. Scarlett got drunk, and Ava had to drive them home in Scarlett's car."

"And?" Sid tapped her pen against her notebook.

"And," continued Leo as he lowered his voice again. "Ava got into an accident. She rear-ended another car. There wasn't much damage to the other car, but the front of Scarlett's car got scratched up pretty bad. Broke the headlight, too. The other driver called the police, and the cops came out. When they saw Scarlett and that she was drunk, they called Sheriff Colquitt."

Sid shrugged. "Was Ava cited for the accident?"

"No." Leo smiled. "It was all covered up. Ellie said that no one was hurt, but Ava was kind of a mess afterward. She was worried that it was going to come back to haunt her somehow. She and Scarlett fought about it, and they stopped speaking to one another for several months."

"That's great, Leo, but how do you think this fits in with our case?" Sid's knee began to bounce as she itched to get back to her notes.

"I don't know. It just struck me as curious, that's all. Scarlett gets drunk, so Ava drives home. Ava wrecks Scarlett's car, and the sheriff covers it up. Just seemed interesting, I guess." Leo shrugged. "And it happened the same weekend as Wes and Iris's accident."

As soon as the words left his mouth, he wished he could've pulled them back. He saw Sid stiffen at the mention of their names. "Sorry," he whispered.

She smiled at him, though it wasn't convincing. "It's okay, Leo. Don't be sorry. Besides, it wasn't the same weekend. You said Ava's accident was Labor Day weekend. Wes and Iris died the weekend after that."

"Oh." Leo felt his body go limp. "I forgot. Sorry."

Sid patted his arm. "Don't be. It's okay. Really." She resumed her notetaking and added the story about Ava's accident in Scarlett's car since Leo thought it was worth mentioning—just in case his hunches were linked to his other gift. "If you don't mind me asking, how did you get all this info out of Ellie?"

"She likes to talk, that's all." He glanced up S George Street to the ice cream shop. Ellie was working until closing, and Leo had left her once the shop started getting busy.

Getting the information out of her had been easy. He'd mentioned seeing Ava get in the black Mercedes, and Ellie had offered up the rest. It had taken only one or two other questions from Leo, prompts really, to keep her talking, and the story had simply spilled from her lips. Leo wondered who else she'd told. Maybe no one. Maybe that was why she'd been so eager to share the gossip about her sister; she had no one else to talk to about it.

It had been clear to Leo that Ellie was concerned about her sister—concerned Ava was being taken advantage of, that she was in over her head, that the fallout would damage her sister's reputation and perhaps that of her whole family. Ellie was right to be concerned, thought Leo. If J. T.'s wife was really trying to get away from him, then Ava was playing a very dangerous game.

Leo hung his head and glanced sideways at Sid, watching as she made notes. He wrinkled his nose. The pink notebook seemed so out of place, so out of character for her. "Can I ask you something?"

"Shoot." She didn't look up.

"How did you get into this, being a private investigator?"

Sid stopped writing and sighed. "It's all Burt's fault."

Leo's eyebrows shot up. "Really? What did Grandpa do?"

"One day, Burt dragged me out of bed and drove me to his friend's house and told him that I needed a job and that he was going to hire me. His friend was a PI named Trip Murdock." She shrugged. "Neither Trip nor I had much say in the matter, to be honest. You know how your grandfather is, so I'm sure that doesn't come as a shock."

Leo snorted. "Sort of like me and you working together."

"Exactly like that." Sid nodded and stared out at the crowds and the night sky, at everything and nothing. "I've known Burt my whole life. He and my dad grew up together, played ball together in high school, started in construction together after they graduated. My dad was the best man at Burt and Camille's wedding. Dad died, oh, about fifteen years ago now. Mom died a few years after that, and Burt and Camille sort of stepped in. Took on the role of pseudo-parents. Even after Camille passed away, Burt was there for me whether I liked it or not.

"After Wes and Iris died, I lost my job because I couldn't go back to teaching, not after what happened. It wasn't long before I was out of money and had to sell the condo. I didn't make much on the sale, not off the mortgage. I had nowhere to go, so Burt took me in. He let me stay in his guest room while he fixed up the apartment over the garage. I moved in there when it was ready." A faint smile crossed her lips. "Burt got tired of me sleeping all day and wandering around the house at night like a ghost, so one day he dragged me over to Trip's place and announced that I was coming to work for Trip and learn how to be a private investigator. Just like that. He never asked me if it was what I wanted to do. We never had a conversation about it. He just made it happen."

Sid shook her head at the memory. "I didn't have the energy to argue with him, so I just went along with it. I worked for Trip for two years. When I qualified to take the exam, I took it and got my license. I didn't do it because I wanted to. I did it because it was what Burt and Trip expected me to do. I never cared about becoming a PI. I was beyond being able to care about anything, and I didn't have enough strength or interest to do anything else." She shrugged. "So here I am. For better or worse, Burt gave me a place to live and something to do, something to focus on, when all I wanted to do was wallow in self-pity. He's the reason I'm a PI. He's the reason I have somewhere to sleep at night." Slowly, she swung her gaze to Leo. "And he's the reason I'm still here. If he hadn't intervened, well, I don't know where I'd be . . . or *if* I'd be anymore. Without Burt, I'd have no one."

Leo nodded. He understood. Without Burt, he'd have no one either.

They were quiet for a few minutes, watching a ghost tour wander past. A man dressed in full pirate regalia was leading the tour, regaling his group with tales of some pirate believed to haunt the area. Leo suppressed a grin as four different spirits, none of them pirates, passed right beside the tour guide.

After tugging on the brim of his cap and reciting Hattie's words in his head, he turned to Sid. "Do you even want to be a private investigator?"

"I don't know. Maybe." Sid continued to watch the tour group. She tapped the notebook with her pen. "There are worse jobs, I guess. And who knows? One day, it may even pay the bills."

"So, what do we do now?" asked Leo, nodding toward the tavern, which the ACC still hadn't vacated.

"You can head home. I'm going to wait until J. T. leaves the bar and then follow him. Hopefully, he goes straight home so that I can call it quits and get some sleep." She smiled at him. "Tomorrow, I think I might get my nails done."

Leo smirked. "That ought to be interesting."

"Indeed. Hopefully, Ava will be as chatty as her sister." She turned to a clean page in her notebook, ready to gather her thoughts on how to proceed with the case.

Leo stood and folded his arms. "No, I mean it ought to be interesting seeing you with painted nails." He smiled as he looked her over—sweat-stained baseball cap; oversize, long-sleeved T-shirt; frayed jean shorts; flip-flops; no make-up; hair tied in a low knot and looking like a rat's nest. "You do realize you'll need to shower before you go." Sid reached to swat him with her notebook, but he jumped out of the way.

"Go home, kid." Sid shook her head at him, but she couldn't keep the smile from her face. "And nice work today."

"Thanks." Leo gave her a mock salute and turned toward home. "'Night, boss."

Sid watched him disappear into the crowds, still smiling to herself. The kid was growing on her, she had to admit.

Shortly before nine o'clock, J. T. Clement and his little band of merry men left the tavern and parted ways. J. T. headed toward a parking lot over on Cordova Street. Sid had parked her car in the same lot, but at the opposite end from J. T.'s car. She blended in with a cluster of women heading to their own cars and quickly slipped into the shadows.

When J. T. pulled out of the lot, Sid followed, feeling instant relief the moment he turned onto San Marco Avenue in the direction of the Vilano Causeway and the bridge leading to Vilano Beach. He was heading home. She sighed happily.

Her relief was short-lived, though. Half a mile later, J. T. Clement pulled into the dark parking lot of the Villa Rosa Motel, one of the last remaining old-time Florida motels left in the Old City. It was a small, family-run place with about seventy rooms, and it had managed to stay alive thanks to its location, within walking distance of the downtown tourist attractions. The Villa Rosa was not seedy or run-down. It did not rent rooms by the hour. It was tidy, freshly painted, covered in blooming bougainvillea, and almost always busy.

Sid slowed to a crawl and shut off her lights as she watched J. T. drive to the back of the lot, park in the last space at the end of the long, single-story building, and get out of his car. He walked toward the open door of the room farthest from the lobby. A woman waited in the doorway—a woman who looked very much like his wife, wearing an absurdly short dress and stiletto heels.

It was just after nine o'clock. Josie Clement should have finished with her WAGs committee meeting over on Anastasia Island by half past eight. If there wasn't too much traffic, the timing would be just about right. There was a possibility here, remote as it was, that Josie had diverted from her well-planned life and pulled into this little motel on her way home to meet her husband for a spontaneous romantic evening. But that would mean that everything Sid had learned so far about Josie Clement was completely wrong.

Sid huffed aloud. "J. T., what the hell are you doing?" she muttered as she snapped photos of her client stalking to the motel room door, wrapping the woman in his arms, and planting a kiss on Ava Owen.

Chapter Twenty

Sid stared at the display case, her eyes blurring at the rows and rows of small bottles of nail polish. She was tired and in no mood to have her nails done. But she had showered and styled her hair and even put on mascara and lipstick—all to try to sway a teenage girl into spilling her most intimate secrets. Her stomach flip-flopped at the thought, but she smiled through the discomfort. "Maybe something subtle. I don't usually wear polish. What would you suggest?"

Ava Owen tapped one long, baby-pink nail on her chin and thought hard. "This one." She selected a bottle and held it out for Sid's inspection. "It's called Bridal Blush. It's subtle, classic, always on trend, and it goes with everything. My clients just love it. I can barely keep it in stock. It's probably my most popular color." Ava nodded encouragingly, waiting for Sid's approval.

"I'm not exactly a bride, though." Sid pursed her lips as she stared at the pale pink polish, shimmering in its tiny bottle.

Ava laughed, a girlish giggle that made her seem even younger than her nineteen years. "Oh, that's only the name of the color. It's not just for brides. It's for anyone, any time, any occasion." She patted Sid's hand and got to work filing her nails.

"Well, that's a relief," Sid said. It was an effort not to roll her eyes. "I'm not going to be walking down the aisle any time soon."

When she'd dressed that morning, something in the back of her mind had told her not to wear her wedding ring. She'd debated with herself for half an hour, not wanting to remove it. She hadn't taken it off since Wes placed it on her finger on their wedding day. In the end, when she'd removed it, she had been surprised to find a pale indentation where the ring had been.

The mark didn't go unnoticed by Ava. "Divorced?" she asked quietly, her face assuming a sympathetic expression. Sid simply shrugged. "Has it been long?"

"Seems like ages ago. My husband left . . . uh, almost three years ago now."

"Really?" Ava glanced at the pale mark on Sid's finger. "Are you dating anyone?"

Sid shook her head. "No, I just can't seem to find a nice guy. It's so hard these days. And all the good ones seem to be married already."

Ava sighed. "Isn't that the truth."

"You must have a ton of guys to choose from." Sid picked up the bottle of nail polish, pretending to study it, as Ava filed the nails of her other hand. "What are you, twenty-one? Twenty-two, maybe? If you don't mind me asking."

Ava smiled, pleased to be mistaken for being older and more mature than she really was. "Something like that, but it's still hard to find a nice guy. I'm lucky, though. My boyfriend is older. I think that makes all the difference. Guys my age are just useless."

"You are lucky, then." Sid placed the bottle of polish down in front of her. "What's he like?"

Ava giggled again. "He's wonderful. He's rich and successful, and he's got a really important job." She held out her wrist to display a diamond tennis bracelet. "He's always buying me jewelry and presents."

"Sounds like quite a catch," said Sid, eyeing the bracelet. She wondered how Ava's parents hadn't noticed it. Did Ava hide it in her jewelry box at home or play it off as costume jewelry? Did they really have no idea that their daughter was committing adultery with the county commissioner from District Five? "He must be handsome."

Ava's face scrunched up for the briefest of moments before she smiled coyly. "He's good-looking, yeah, but it's his personality that I fell in love with. He's so smart and funny and sweet, and he's really good to me."

Sid held in her smile. "Do you think you'll marry him?" She tapped the bottle of nail polish. "You already have the perfect shade of pink."

Ava lowered her head, pretending to focus intently on the nail she was filing. "I don't know. Maybe someday. He says he wants to marry me, but I don't know. It's not like he's bought me a ring or anything. We haven't made any plans. We're . . . taking it slow." When Ava fell silent, Sid waited patiently. It wasn't long before the young woman began talking again. "I want to finish college first, you know? I want to get my degree and get a good job. Not that I don't love working here, of course." She smiled. "But I have other dreams."

"Oh? Such as?" Hopefully, one of those dreams included dumping J. T. Clement on his sorry ass.

"Something in fashion, I think." Ava's gaze drifted toward the spa's front window, but her thoughts were miles away. "Not designing. Nothing like that. I don't have the patience for it. I'd like to write about it. You know, like, write for a fashion maga-zine. Go to all the fashion shows and write about what's in and what looks good and what I like and don't like." Ava shrugged. "Journalism, I guess. Something like that."

"That sounds really exciting." Sid winced as Ava went to work on her cuticles. "I'm sure your boyfriend would be very supportive."

"Probably," Ava replied without looking up. Another minute or so passed in silence before she spoke again. "I'm not stupid, you know."

Sid's breath caught in her throat. "Of course not. Why would you say that?"

Ava's eyes glistened, threatening tears. "Because that's what everyone thinks. Just because he's older than me and he's ma—" She caught herself and shifted in her seat. "They think I'm going to get hurt, that he's just using me. But it's not like that." She sat up straighter and sniffed. "He loves me. I know he does. And I'm not stupid enough to think that we can get married right now." She bit her bottom lip. "We might never get married. I love him. I do. But . . ." She looked out the window again. "I think I want more. I think I want to travel and see things and do things and . . . and maybe I can do all that without him."

Sid smiled at the girl. "I'm sure you can. In fact, I have no doubt in my mind that you can do all that and more. You're young with your whole life ahead of you. You've got lots of boyfriends in your future. Lots of travel. Lots of exciting stuff. There's no need to settle for a guy simply because he seems nice and buys you pretty jewelry and is, well, conveniently located."

Ava snorted with laughter. "That's exactly what he is! Conveniently located. Right here in little ol' St. Augustine." She smiled at Sid and picked up a bottle of clear coat. "You're right. I need to keep it all in perspective. He might not be Mr. Right, but he's a pretty good Mr. Right Now."

Sid said a small, silent prayer that Ava's "right now" would end very soon. Scrolling through her mental list of questions, she asked, "Are you in school at Flagler?"

"Yep," answered Ava, happy for the change of subject. "I'm going to be a sophomore this fall. I really wanted to go away to college, but my mom works at Flagler in the library, so I get a huge break on tuition. And since I can live at home for free, I don't have to pay for room and board. It just made sense financially to stay here and go to school."

Sid nodded, sensing Ava would fill in the silence now that they were talking about something other than her boyfriend dilemma. She wasn't wrong.

"My best friend goes to Florida," continued Ava. "I really wanted to go there, too, but now I'm glad I didn't. Her freshman year, she had to live off campus in this dingy little apartment with three other girls, all of whom turned out to be alcoholics. Partying all the time. Scarlett—that's my friend—she got put on academic probation after her first semester. Too much partying. She pulled up her grades in the spring, but that's only because her father put the fear of God into her." Ava leaned forward and whispered, "He's a scary dude, believe me."

Oh, I believe you, thought Sid.

Ava sat up, brightened her smile, and continued. "Scarlett stayed in Gainesville to take summer classes in order to bring up her grades. She wants to rush a sorority, but she can't do it until her grades get better. Anyway, I miss her. I was so bummed when she told me that she wasn't coming home this summer, but it's for the best. It's what she needed to do. She had me really worried last fall." Ava shook her head. "But she's doing much better now."

"That's tough," offered Sid. "It's hard to resist all that

freedom when you first start college. Hard to know how to best spend your time. And partying is an easy way to fill the time."

Ava nodded. "I know, but she really needs to watch it. She tends to get really drunk really quickly, and I was so worried when she told me she thought her roommates were alcoholics because I've worried the same thing about her in the past."

"That is scary." Remembering Leo's story about Ava's accident in Scarlett's car, Sid lowered her voice and said, "You can easily put yourself in danger when you've been drinking. And you can put your friends in danger, too, even if you don't mean to. It can happen so quickly."

"It can!" hissed Ava. She put the cap on the clear polish and grabbed the bottle of Bridal Blush, rolling it sideways on the table to mix the color. "That's exactly what happened with me and her our junior year of high school. She got drunk at a party, and I had to drive us both home." Sid watched as Ava rolled the bottle, her eyes glazing over as her thoughts flashed back to two years ago.

Ava whispered, "Scarlett had this old red BMW. It had been her mom's car, but her mom got a new one and gave the old one to Ava when she got her license. That was right at the start of school, and there was this huge party on Labor Day weekend. One of the seniors on the football team, Axel—his parents own this massive house over on Anastasia—well, he threw a party 'cause his parents were out of town . . ." Ava looked up at Sid. "Sorry, you probably don't want to hear all this kid drama."

"Oh no, I do," urged Sid. "It's been a long time since I was in high school, and it's bringing back a lot of memories. Parties and boys and, oh, all of it. Please, continue. Really, I'm all ears."

Ava tested Sid's nails to make sure they were dry and then began painting. "Okay. Well, this party was huge. Everyone was there. The kid, Axel, managed to buy two kegs and find the keys to his parents' liquor cabinet. Needless to say, there were a lot of drunk kids at the party. Scarlett got wasted. I swear, she had two beers and could barely stand up."

Ava leaned in conspiratorially. "I always wondered if someone put something in her drinks, but they poured the beer straight from the keg, so I don't know how that would be possible." She shook her head and sat back but kept her voice low. "Anyway, she got drunk, and I had to drive us home. Well, I'd never driven a BMW before. It's a lot fancier and faster than my parents' minivan. All those lights and buttons and stuff . . . whatever. The point is I had to drive, and I ended up hitting another car. This old guy just pulled out right in front of me, and I hit the brakes, but not in time. It was this big pickup with a massive bumper and a trailer hitch. His truck was mostly fine. Just a little dent. But Scarlett's car got banged up in the front. Not terrible, but bad enough that the bumper was bent and one of the headlights was broken."

"Was anyone hurt?"

Ava shook her head. "No, we were all fine. Scarlett's dad showed up to smooth things over with the other driver. Her dad was so pissed. Scarlett told me she'd never seen him so angry. She wouldn't tell me what he did when they got home. I don't think he hit her, but he might have come close. And he took her car away for, like, a month or something. Granted, most of that time it was in the shop getting fixed, but still. A whole month."

Sid nodded sympathetically, and Ava continued. "Anyway, I was really nervous that I was going to get in trouble because I was the one driving, but after talking to Scarlett's dad, the cops didn't give me a ticket. I think he also paid off the old guy or something like that. Scarlett thought I was being a big baby about the whole thing, but it was scary. It really was." Ava paused to test the dryness of Sid's nails and then continued painting. "Scarlett was being such a bitch about it. I know she lost her car, but still. She put me in a really bad position. She shouldn't have gotten drunk and made me drive home. She was being totally unreasonable about it all and disregarding my feelings, and we didn't speak for, like, three or four months after that." She shrugged. "But we made up and went back to being best friends."

———

By the time her nails were finished and she'd paid for her manicure, including a sizeable tip for Ava, Sid had a pounding headache and more information on Ava Owen and her family than she ever wanted to know. She was now fully up to speed on Ava's favorite music, her mother's talent for baking, her father's inability to grill anything without turning it into charcoal briquettes, and her sister's penchant for horror movies. That last detail was one she'd share with Leo, given that his eyes lit up whenever he mentioned Ellie by name.

When Sid reached her office and slipped the key in the lock, her headache had blossomed into a full migraine, and she was still uncertain whether to take the next step in her plan. Entering her office, she didn't bother to switch on the lights. Deciding how to proceed could wait until after she'd taken some ibuprofen and lain in a dark room for a few hours. She plucked the pill bottle from the shelf by the coffee pot and swore under her breath as she tried to open it without damaging her new, expensive nails.

A chill ran up her spine and down her arms as the cap popped off and tumbled to the ground. Sid held her breath for a moment, waiting to see if the cold persisted. When it did, she shook two pills into her hand and grabbed a bottle of water from the mini fridge.

"I don't know who's here," she said aloud, "but whoever

you are, you are just going to have to wait. I have a splitting headache, and I am not in the mood to be haunted right now. I am going to go upstairs and take a nap. Do not follow me! You are welcome to hang out down here, if you want, but don't even think about coming upstairs."

She popped the pills into her mouth, took two sips of water and stumbled up the stairs to the rhythm of the pain pounding against the inside of her skull.

Chapter Twenty-One

At lunchtime on Friday, Sid followed J. T. Clement as he left the county administration building and drove across the Bridge of Lions to Anastasia Island. J. T. pulled his shiny black car into the small parking lot located next to Ghost City Brewery, a local microbrewery known for beers with unique flavors and strong alcohol content.

Sid parked down the street and walked back to the brewery, which had a tasting room with large, plate-glass windows that fronted the road. A taco truck was positioned in front of the vacant laundromat next door, and brewery patrons were welcome to bring their tacos inside the tasting room.

J. T. and three other men, all sporting casual Friday khakis and pastel-colored golf shirts, ordered pints and tacos and spent their lunch hour in the tasting room, laughing heartily at each other's jokes. Sid spent her lunch hour sitting in one of the plastic chairs set up in front of the food truck. She chose one in the shade of an umbrella that also afforded her a clear view of J. T.'s window seat inside the tasting room. It was not a bad way to spend an hour. Her mac-n-cheese tacos were so good that she went back for seconds. When it looked like J. T.'s luncheon was winding down, Sid entered the tasting room, approached the bar, and ordered two IPAs. She smoothed the material of her white sundress over her hips and gathered her long, dark hair across one shoulder.

Carrying the two pints, Sid approached the table as the gentlemen stood to leave. Three of them smiled at her. J. T. Clement did not.

"Good afternoon, gentlemen," said Sid, returning their smiles. "I was wondering if I could have a few minutes with the commissioner . . . alone." She winked at them and turned her smile to J. T. "The bartender said this was your favorite." She set the beer down in front of him and cooed, "Have a drink with me? Just one."

The other men mumbled their goodbyes and thumped J. T. on the back as they left. Sid slid into the vacated seat across from her client and crossed her legs. "Have a seat, J. T.," she said, all good humor gone from her voice. "This won't take long." She took a long sip of her beer, happily noting the slight citrus flavor, and watched as the commissioner slumped back down into his chair.

Reaching for his beer, he scanned the room. There were two old-timers sitting at the bar loudly debating the merits of a new porter as well as a young couple seated at a table in the far back corner, sipping their beers and scrolling on their phones. The bartender was the only other person in the room, and he quickly disappeared into the back when he realized no one was in need of a refill.

"We shouldn't be meeting like this," whispered J. T.

Sid watched him gulp his beer, finishing half the glass. How interesting, thought Sid, that he wasn't as excited to see her now as he had been at Granny Oak's after a day of drinking with his golfing buddies. "Relax." Sid wound her hair around her finger and smiled. "I'm just a concerned citizen looking to bend my commissioner's ear for a few minutes about a very important issue in his jurisdiction." She leaned forward, resting her elbows on the table. "And I am due to deliver my report."

J. T. nodded and scooted closer to the table. "Well?" He looked again at the other patrons, none of whom were paying them any attention.

Sid lowered her voice. "Your wife does not appear to be having an affair."

J. T.'s gaze spun back to her, and his eyes went wide. "Are you sure?"

"As sure as I can be. I have seen no activity that would lead me to conclude that there is another man in her life. She sticks to the schedule in your shared calendar. She does not deviate from it in any significant way. As far as I can tell, she is where she says she is, when she says she's supposed to be there, so I don't think you have to worry about her cheating on you with another man." Sid smiled at her client. There was no way she was going to share what she'd learned about Josie's secret side gig as a real estate agent or her suspicions about Josie leaving him and returning to Savannah.

J. T. furrowed his brow and swirled the beer in his glass, but he didn't say anything.

"You seem disappointed, Commissioner," Sid noted.

J. T. shook his head but still said nothing.

Sid studied him. "Confused, then?"

The commissioner sighed heavily and finally looked up. "Well, that's that, I guess. Thanks for your hard work. Do you have a bill for me?" He held out his hand, offering to shake hers.

Sid narrowed her eyes. "J. T., did you honestly think your wife was having an affair?"

The man ran his hands over his face. "I don't know." He

sighed again and slumped back in his chair. "Something is up, but I can't put my finger on it. To look at it from the outside, Josie's acting perfectly normal. But I know her." He looked Sid in the eye and added, "I'm worried she might be getting ready to leave me."

"Okay," replied Sid, keeping her voice low. "Is that such a bad thing?" J. T.'s eyebrows shot up, and Sid took a sip of her beer, allowing the question to hang in the air. "I know about your affair with Ava Owen." Sid swore he stopped breathing momentarily.

She leaned toward him. "So I'll ask again. Is it such a bad thing if you and Josie split up?"

J. T. leaned forward until their faces were a foot apart. "How did you find out?"

"It's my job, J. T. It's what I do." She frowned at Commissioner Clement, whose face had begun to flush. A sheen of sweat was breaking out across his wide forehead. "I don't care about your affair . . . except for one very important thing." Sid held his gaze. "You began the affair when she was a minor. She was only seventeen, J. T."

"But we didn't . . . we didn't . . . not until she was eighteen, I swear." Sweat trickled down the side of his face.

"Maybe," said Sid. "But that would be a hell of a thing to prove." J. T. hung his head, and a drop of sweat hit the tabletop. "I have photos."

"Shit!" he hissed. With a quick motion, he gulped down the second half of his beer.

"Want another?" asked Sid.

The commissioner shook his head. "What are you going to do?"

"Nothing. Unless you give me a reason to," said Sid as she placed her hand over his, where it clutched the empty glass. She cringed at the clammy feel of his skin. "Two things." Sid waited for him to look up at her before she continued. "Number one: if Josie does decide to divorce you, you should let her go without putting up a fight." He cringed at the suggestion, but she pressed on. "It seems that you are unhappy in your marriage, enough to have a long-standing affair, so I think it would be fair of you to consider that Josie may be unhappy as well. If you try to drag her through the mud, I'll share the photos with her."

"You can't do that!" J. T.'s face turned an even deeper shade of pink, and he tried to pull his hand away, but Sid held tightly to it. "I'm the one who hired you!"

Sid clucked her tongue. "You hired me to investigate her. You did not hire me to investigate you."

"That's blackmail!" he hissed.

Sid shrugged. "Maybe it is, but at least it's not statutory rape." J. T.'s jaw slackened, and she felt her lip curl in disgust and disbelief. "I don't get it, J. T. Why did you hire a private investigator to investigate your wife for infidelity when you yourself were having an affair?"

"I had a hunch," he mumbled. "I just wanted to be sure."

Sid shook her head. "Regardless, there's my second thing. Number two: I would like some information."

"What?" J. T. stared at his empty glass. Sid released his hand and slid her own beer toward him. He took it without hesitation.

Sid wiped her hand on her dress, trying to remove the sticky feel of J. T.'s sweat. "Did you try to bribe my husband?"

The commissioner almost choked on the beer. "What? No. What are you talking about?"

"Labor Day weekend. Three years ago." Sid clenched her fists so tightly that her newly polished nails dug into her palms. "My husband, Wes, and his partners in the marine unit almost cited you for BUI. They gave you a break and let you go, but someone saw you the next day trying to give my husband money. So I'll ask again. Did you try to bribe him?"

J. T. shook his head. "That wasn't about the BUI, I swear."

Sid frowned. "No? Then what was it about?"

"I can't say. Please don't ask me."

"Do you make it a habit of bribing people, Commissioner?"

"No!" J. T.'s gaze darted around the room again, checking to make sure no one was listening in the wake of that outburst. "That was the only time *ever*. I swear!" He pressed his lips together, and Sid was afraid he might start crying. "I said something to him I shouldn't have. Or . . . or at least I thought I had." Sid raised an eyebrow and waited as J. T. took another gulp of beer. "I wasn't trying to bribe your husband over the drunk boating. I was asking him not to repeat something. I was trying to buy his silence."

He squeezed his eyes shut and shook his head. "Your husband wouldn't take any money. He told me he didn't know what I was talking about, but I didn't believe him. I could tell by the way he looked at me that I had opened my stupid fucking mouth and said something I shouldn't have."

Sid fought the urge to grab him by the collar and shake him until his teeth rattled. "For God's sake, J. T., what could you possibly have said that would make you want to try to bribe a law enforcement officer?"

"I can't tell you." He opened his eyes and looked at her. "It'll put you in danger."

Sid pinched the bridge of her nose and took a deep breath. "J. T. Clement, you had better start making sense right this minute, or I am going to drive to your house and have a nice chat with your wife."

"Okay, okay." J. T. held up his hands, the same way he might have approached a wounded animal. "Don't do that.

Please." He drained the rest of Sid's beer and leaned toward her. "But you've got to promise me that you'll be careful."

"Fine. I'll be careful." Sid rolled her eyes. "Now, spill!"

The commissioner nodded once. "Travis Colquitt didn't want me to hire you." When Sid frowned at him, he continued. "Travis was the one who told me Josie might be having an affair. He told me I should hire a private investigator. He gave me a few names, but I made up conflicts with all of them." He tapped the table with his index finger. "See, I had already been thinking that I might hire a PI. Josie'd been acting weird for a while, and the thought that maybe she was cheating on me had crossed my mind. I looked up PIs in the area and realized you were working for that Murdock guy.

"So I mentioned to Travis that I had heard your name tossed about by a friend of mine and asked if he knew you. I knew full well that he did, but he told me that you weren't really a PI and not to even consider it. But I said I wanted someone Josie would never recognize, and maybe it would be better if a woman did the investigating. So on and so forth. Eventually, he relented and agreed to make the referral."

Sid sat back and stared at her client. "Sheriff Colquitt told me that he had recommended me to you. He said he thought I could use a break, given that you're such a big fish in this small pond."

J. T. shook his head. "No. I was the one who pressed him to make the referral."

She licked her dry lips and wished she hadn't forfeited her beer to J. T. "Why me?"

"Well, I needed a PI. I really did want to find out if Josie was cheating on me." He ran his hands through his hair and blew out a long breath. "And I felt guilty."

Sid furrowed her brow. "Guilty about what?"

"Look, Sidney," said J. T. as he held up his hands again. "I've known the sheriff a long time. Since we were kids."

"Yeah, I know," she sighed. "You both went to UF. Different fraternities, but you knew each other. Blah blah blah."

"No. Before that." J. T. looked around again. "We knew each other as kids down in South Florida. We lived on the same street in Juno Beach. We played together. Me, him, and his brother." He nodded once. "You know what happened to his family, right?"

Sid nodded. "Vaguely." Most people knew about the tragic death of Travis Colquitt's immediate family. He had campaigned on it in the race for sheriff: orphaned at a young age, raised by a maternal aunt right here in St. Augustine, graduated from the University of Florida with a degree in criminology, and returned home to commit himself to serving the public good.

"I was better friends with his brother, though," whispered J. T. "That's what I accidentally told your husband."

"So what?" Sid threw up her hands. "Why the hell would you need to bribe someone about that?"

J. T. shook his head. "You have no idea. Honestly, Sidney. I shouldn't be telling you this." He wiped his mouth with the back of his hand, and Sid noticed that it trembled slightly. "Travis and Troy might have been identical twins, but otherwise, they were nothing alike."

At the mention of twins, Sid's heart began to hammer. "Gemini," she whispered, her breath catching in her throat.

"Sorry? What?" mumbled J. T.

"Nothing. You're saying Travis was a twin?" She licked her lips again and looked for the bartender, who was nowhere around.

"You couldn't tell 'em apart. Not until they opened their

mouths, at least." J. T. stared out the window. "Travis was the nice one, the funny one. Everyone liked him. Troy, on the other hand, was always getting into trouble. He got into fights. Damaged property. Shoplifted. It was bad enough that he got expelled from school in sixth grade and was picked up by the cops twice. His father held big sway down there at the time. Family were big landowners, had a lot of money. His father was able to smooth things over for him, but it would only have been a matter of time before Troy got himself into serious trouble."

"Why are you telling me this?" asked Sid.

"Because Travis and Troy looked identical, except for one thing." J. T. held her gaze. "Troy had a scar on his right forearm. It was about an inch and a half long. I was with him when he got it. The three of us were on Travis's bike. I was standing on the rear foot pegs, Troy was sitting on the handlebars, and Travis was pedaling. We were going pretty fast and coming up on this one house when the car on the driveway started to back up. Troy yelled something about the car. Travis swerved, and we all went down. I cut my ankle pretty bad when I slid off the peg. Travis sprained his wrist. And Troy went flying, took a tumble, and ended up with a two-inch nail embedded in his forearm. There was blood everywhere. The homeowner yelled at us, but then he loaded us up in his car and took us to the emergency room where they called our parents."

"Fascinating." Sid bounced her leg under the table, eager for J. T. to make his point.

The commissioner shifted his gaze out the window. "That happened right at the start of summer vacation. My parents forbade me from playing with the Colquitts for a month." He squinted into the bright sunlight. "By the end of the summer, our injuries had healed. I ended up with a bad scar. Still have it. Troy had a scar, too, from where the nail had ripped the skin when it went in. He had made this big deal of comparing our scars, saying his was worse, but it wasn't. Mine was."

J. T. wiped his mouth again, and Sid noticed that the trembling in his hand had eased, likely from all the alcohol. "Two weeks before school started, the Colquitts were in that boating accident in Jupiter Inlet. Only Travis survived the accident. He suffered a lot of injuries. Broke his hand, lots of cuts and gashes. With his family all gone, he moved up here to live with his aunt, and I didn't see him again until college. Ran into him at a rush party at his fraternity my freshman year. Pretty sure he's the reason his frat cut me. I pledged another fraternity, and we saw each other from time to time on campus. I lost track of him once he graduated and didn't realize he'd become a deputy in St. Johns County until I moved here after graduation."

"J. T., you're killing me here." Sid rubbed her temples. "Please, just get to the punch line."

"Okay, okay." He returned her stare. "I've always remembered Troy's scar because he made such a big deal about it. When I was at that rush party at Travis's frat house, Beta Lambda Chi, I realized Troy's scar looked like the Greek letter lambda. You know the sheriff's tattoo, the one on his forearm?"

"Sure." She knew the sheriff had a tattoo, but she'd never bothered to look at it.

"He didn't have it at that rush party. Got it soon after, though. Had it by the time I saw him again maybe a month or so later. It's a cross with some lilies, a banner wrapped around it, and three small doves. The names in the banner are 'Mom, Dad, and Troy.'"

"Awesome." Sid pursed her lips.

J. T.'s nostrils flared. "You're not getting it! The tattoo is on Travis's right forearm, which is no coincidence. It hides some scars from the boating accident. At the frat party, I saw that he had a few small scars that still showed markings from the stitches. The tattoo does a nice job of covering them up." He paused and leaned a bit closer. "But you can still see the lambda scar."

Sid frowned. "But I thought Troy had the lambda scar, not Travis."

J. T. nodded once. "I always liked Travis better than Troy. Troy scared me. He still does. *That's* what I think I said to your husband, Sidney." When he spoke again, his voice was so soft that she barely heard him. "Your husband was dead a week later. And I think . . . I *think* it was my fault."

Chapter Twenty-Two

Sid barged into her office, tossed her purse in the green velvet guest chair, and lunged for her computer. She had left Ghost City Brewery with both her head and heart pounding relentlessly and with J. T. Clement remaining behind, trying to drown his guilt in yet another pint of citrusy IPA. He had given her more information before she left: dates and locations, names of old friends, and more slurred apologies than she could stomach. In turn, she had promised to send him an itemized bill for her services at the earliest possible opportunity. J. T. waved her off, saying he just wanted the grand total. He'd pay whatever she asked.

She banged on her keyboard and scoured the search results. The printer whirred to life, spitting out key pieces of information in colorful ink on bright white paper. After several hours of researching, Sid stuck a small wad of adhesive putty to the back of a printed photo and affixed it to the Wall of Shame along with the rest of the afternoon's internet trawling haul. There was precious little empty space remaining on the wall, which should have made her feel better. Unfortunately, the holes in her understanding were larger than the remaining blank spaces. There were connections she wasn't making, things she wasn't seeing, and she wasn't sure what to do next.

Goose bumps began to rise on her arms, and she folded them tightly around herself without thinking. It wasn't until the chill seeped in enough to cause her to reach for her sweater that she realized what was happening. Someone was in the office with her. Wrapping the sweater around her shoulders, she stood in front of the Wall of Shame and let the cold settle around her.

"Wes?" she whispered. "Is that you?"

Nothing stirred. There was no sound, no fluttering of papers, no dimming of the lights, and yet the chill in the air persisted. She felt stupid, standing there talking to an empty room. Maybe it was nothing more than the air conditioner kicking on. If there was an actual spirit in the room, it might not even be her dead husband. Or her dead daughter. It could be some dead stranger. She shivered at the thought.

But what did she have to lose? No one was watching. No one was listening. No one was judging. "I know you told me to stop, Wes, but I can't. There is a connection here. A connection to you and to Iris, and I have to keep digging. I understand that this is dangerous, but I have to find out what happened." She took a step forward and pressed her fingers to the photo of herself and her daughter in the center of the wall. "But what do I do next? I'm out of my depth here, Wes. Give me a hand, will ya? Just point me in the right direction."

A knock on the door caused her to jump. Pressing her hand to her mouth and willing her heart to drop from her throat back down into her chest, she drew the curtains over the Wall of Shame and then opened the door.

"Hey!" Leo stood in the afternoon sunshine grinning from ear to ear and holding a wriggling ball of honey-colored fur.

"We have a new client." He walked into the office and set the cocker spaniel puppy on the floor. Sid closed the door and watched as the dog began sniffing every square inch of the space.

"Don't let him pee on anything," she warned.

"I don't think he will. He just peed on every bush in the yard, so we're probably okay." Leo folded his arms across his puffed-up chest, and they watched as the puppy lifted his fuzzy, little leg on the green velvet guest chair. "See, nothing left."

Sid lunged for her bag when the puppy sank its sharp, tiny teeth into one of the straps and began trying to pull it off the chair. "Feel free to start explaining, kid."

"Well . . ." Leo took a deep breath. "I was helping Grandpa this morning down at the Crane's Roost, and the owner came by and asked if I could stop painting and help some guests look for their dog. There's this old couple staying there, and the woman was hysterical, crying and blaming her husband for letting the dog get out of the room. Turns out that he took the dog for a walk and brought him back inside, and then he went back out to their car to get something but didn't close the door all the way. The dog escaped, and they couldn't find him."

"And you offered to help," added Sid, trying to speed up the story.

"Yep." Leo beamed with pride. "I told them I happened to work for a private investigator and that we specialized in finding lost pets, so the man asked the going rate. I didn't really know, so I said it was fifty bucks to spend the day looking for him, plus another fifty if I found the dog safe and sound and brought him back."

Sid raised an eyebrow. "And he agreed to that?"

Reaching into his pocket, Leo pulled out a fifty-dollar bill and held it up. "He did. To be honest, though, I think he would have paid more if he thought it would make his wife stop crying."

The puppy began trying to climb up the stairs, but his little paws kept slipping on the metal steps. Losing interest in the staircase, the dog continued his exploration of the room. "So, where did you find him?"

"Believe it or not, I found him in our yard. He must have slipped through the fence. He was just wandering around, lifting his leg on every tree and shrub." Leo rocked back on his heels and made the split-second decision not to mention that he had seen Iris's spirit wandering around the yard with the puppy trotting along behind her. He was pretty sure Iris was the one who had found the dog and lured it into the yard. The little girl's spirit had filled Leo's head with laughter and feelings of delight mixed with longing. As soon as he had picked up the dog, Iris vanished.

From another pocket, Leo now pulled out a well-chewed, blue ball, which made a loud jingle and squeak when he bounced it on the carpet. The puppy spun toward the sound and charged for it, his pink tongue lolling out the side of his mouth. Leo tossed the ball and laughed when the puppy missed. "This is his favorite toy, according to his owner. The little guy came right to me when he heard it. His name's Hercules, by the way. Do you want to open a case file?"

Sid smiled. "I'll let you do it, kid. And you can keep the fee."

Leo's eyes went wide. "All of it?"

"All of it." Sid pulled an empty folder, a blank intake form, and two blank receipt forms from the top drawer of the nearest filing cabinet. She placed the papers in the folder and handed it to the teen. "When you return the dog, ask them for some details. Just the name, address, and phone number should suffice. Fill out the two receipt forms and have them sign both copies. One is for them; the other is for the file. You can fill in your notes on the intake form later. No need to do that in front of them. Got it?"

"Got it!" Leo tucked the folder under one arm and scooped up the puppy, who wriggled and tried to lick his face. "I'll go return Hercules to his owners. Hopefully, the woman has stopped crying by now." He turned to leave, but Sid placed a hand on his shoulder.

"Leo, can I ask . . ." She paused and glanced around the room, which she realized was warmer now. "Is there anyone else here?"

Leo shook his head. "No. Just us. Why?" He cocked his head to the side.

Sid shrugged. "No reason. I felt chilled earlier and was just wondering. It's fine now, so no worries." She opened the door for him. "Congratulations on bringing in your first case. We should celebrate."

"Oh, that reminds me. Grandpa said the Geezers are playing tonight at Granny Oak's. Someone cancelled, and they're going to fill in. He wanted me to tell you. Wanna go? I'm going early to help them set up, but I can save you a seat." Leo practically beamed. "Like last time."

Sid leaned against the doorframe. "Don't you want to ask the girl from the ice cream shop?"

Color flooded the boy's face and neck, and he kicked at the grass with the toe of his sneaker. "She's working 'til nine."

Suppressing a smile, Sid nodded. "Well, in that case, I would love to go." She watched as Leo trotted across the yard and through the gate to the sidewalk, Hercules bouncing glee-fully in his arms.

Stepping back into the office, Sid stood once more in front of the Wall of Shame and pulled the curtains aside. The blue ball rolled across the floor, and Sid swore under her breath. She grabbed the ball and charged out of the office, hoping to catch Leo before he made it all the way to the end of the street where the Crane's Roost was located.

She skidded to a halt on the sidewalk as a black pickup pulled up in front of Kitty Lonigan's house. The sheriff was out of the truck and striding across the road before Sid realized what was happening. "Sheriff," she said, trying to feign calm indifference. "What can I do for you?"

"I hear you wrapped up your investigation for J. T." Colquitt stood at the curb, only a few feet from Sid, his legs in a wide stance and his arms folded across his chest.

Sid squinted, pretending the sun was bothering her, and raised her hand to shield her eyes. She flicked her gaze to the tattoo on his right forearm. It was just as J. T. had described, a cross wrapped with a banner and lilies. The sheriff wasn't quite close enough for Sid to read the names written in fancy script, but it looked like there were three of them. Sid had a hunch they might be *Mom, Dad,* and *Troy.*

She took a breath to steady herself. "Just a minute, Sheriff." She looked down the street and found that Leo was close to two hundred feet away, walking slowly and rubbing Hercules's soft head against his cheek. The pup's tail wagged with frantic delight. "Leo!"

The boy turned around and froze when he saw Sid standing next to the sheriff. She held up her hand and waved the ball in the air. She cocked her arm back, and Sheriff Colquitt snorted with laughter. "What?" she demanded.

"You really think you can throw it that far?" He smirked, and Sid could see her own annoyed expression reflected in his mirrored sunglasses.

"Yes." She lowered her arm. "Maybe." He raised an eyebrow. "Okay, probably not. Can you?"

"I have a better shot at it than you do." He held out his

hand, and Sid placed the blue ball, scored with tiny slashes from Hercules's razor-sharp puppy teeth, into it. The sheriff's lip curled at the slightly moist feel of the ball, and he took a few steps out into the middle of the street.

Sheriff Colquitt waved his arm, pointed at Leo, and whistled. As he waited for Leo to set his file folder down on the sidewalk, shift the dog to his other arm, and move into position in the middle of the road, the sheriff tossed the ball from one hand to the other, clearly relishing the idea of showing off his athletic prowess. Sid rolled her eyes as she watched him rotate each shoulder in turn. When boy and dog were standing in the middle of the quiet road, the sheriff studied the distance, cocked his arm back, and threw the blue dog toy in a long, graceful arc down Saragossa Street. It bounced once about ten feet in front of Leo, who caught the ball on its upward movement. Hercules began squirming as soon as he heard the jingle and squeak of his toy.

"Nice throw," said Sid.

Sheriff Colquitt grinned widely. "Nice to know I've still got it." He rotated his right shoulder, pretending to massage his flexed biceps.

Sid forced her face into a bright, happy smile. "Certainly looks like it, Sheriff." She did not comment on the fact that he had used his left arm to throw the ball. "Thanks very much for that. Now, you were asking about J. T.?"

"Right, right. I heard you wrapped up his case." He walked back toward Sid and placed one foot up on the curb, removing his sunglasses.

Sid squinted and raised her hand again to shield her eyes. The gesture had less to do with the brightness of the day and more to do with the need to try to hide her expressions. "News travels fast in this town."

Sheriff Colquitt chuckled. "I saw him earlier. He said you

did an excellent job, but he seemed a bit shaken. Hope you didn't have to deliver bad news."

"I don't think he was shaken much by the news, Sheriff." Sid kept squinting. "And if I had to guess, I would say that his condition was not so much shaken as intoxicated. I think his lunch at Ghost City Brewery had a lot to do with it." She smiled, keeping her hand over her eyes.

"Yes, that is probably true." The sheriff pursed his lips. "He did say that he was satisfied with your work and that you were very professional and discreet."

"I aim to please." Sid turned and walked through the gate, closing it once she was back in Burt's front yard. It felt a bit safer to have a barrier between them, though the simple jasmine-covered iron fence wouldn't stop this man if he wanted to get to her. "And thank you for the referral. It was kind of you to recommend me, especially given that I'm so new to the business. I appreciate the vote of confidence."

Sheriff Colquitt nodded, stepped up onto the curb, and onto the sidewalk. When he placed his hands on the fence, Sid took two slow steps backward. "I'm glad it worked out. I'll keep my eyes and ears open for more opportunities for you. From time to time, things come up that aren't worth wasting department resources on, like J. T. thinking Josie was cheating on him. Poor bastard." He shook his head and chuckled. "You may be just the person to take on that kind of work." He winked at her, grinning like a Cheshire cat. "You never know."

"That would be ideal, Sheriff." She smiled back at him and felt the sting of bile against the back of her throat. "Please keep me in mind."

"Oh, I will." He winked again and then turned back to his truck.

As he placed his hand on the door handle, Sid called out, "You must have played baseball as a kid." She mimed a throwing motion. "Is that where you learned to throw like that?"

"I played Little League when I was young. Was pretty good, too." He opened the door and stepped up onto the running board. "Still play league softball. We were undefeated last season."

"I heard you played ball with J. T.," she blurted. "You and your brother." The sheriff stilled, perched up on the running board with one foot in the cab. "Heard you were the best athlete, though. Of course, I can't imagine J. T. was much of an athlete to look at him now."

The sheriff ran his tongue over his bottom lip and stared at Sid. "He tell you that?"

"He did." Sid swallowed hard, still tasting bile, but she pressed on. Any guilt she had about throwing J. T. under the bus was starting to ebb as the feeling of dread began to rise. "He said he knew you as kids. Grew up in the same neighborhood, I think, but that you moved up here and you two lost touch until you met again in college."

There was silence for a long moment. Then the sheriff shifted his gaze down the street. Sid glanced in the same direction and whispered a small prayer of thanks that Leo was no longer in view. When the sheriff spoke, all joviality was gone. "I don't remember much from my childhood. Not before the accident." He shrugged. "If J. T. said we were friends back then, I'll have to take his word for it. I only remember him from our time at UF. And, like I said before, we didn't hang out much. Different fraternities and all that."

When he fixed his gaze back on Sid, she felt her heart drop to her stomach. "That must be hard sometimes," she offered. "Losing your family, your past. Sort of like having two lives. One before and one after. I certainly know what that's like." She stared back at him. "Do you ever miss it? Your life before?"

"Naw," drawled the sheriff. He slipped his sunglasses back on. "No sense in looking back at something that doesn't exist anymore, is there? Nothing good can come from that." The Cheshire grin spread slowly across his tanned face. "Besides, I like my life now. Wouldn't want anything to change that." He slipped into the driver's seat, closed the door, and pulled away slowly.

Sid's ragged breathing didn't ease until Sheriff Colquitt's black pickup reached the end of Saragossa Street and turned left onto Cordova. Then, she folded forward, hands on her knees, and gulped in heaping quantities of hot, humid air.

Chapter Twenty-Three

S haken by her encounter with the sheriff, it took Sid twice as long as it should have to finalize the bill for J. T. Clement. The invoice ran for three pages, itemized and notated, before Sid slipped it into the file. The first text she sent to J. T. included only the final amount. No dollar signs. No explanation. Her second text read:

ASAP, please. Method?

J. T.'s response was immediate:

Cash. Tonight. Granny Oaks.

Sid almost choked on her soda and wondered if J. T. had that much cash lying around or if he needed to make a trip to the bank. Hopefully he'd pay in large bills. She didn't want to have to carry a big stack of small bills around all night. She pulled out two blank receipt forms and quickly filled in the necessary information. She doubted that she'd be able to get him to sign them, but she'd ask nonetheless.

By the time Sid arrived at Granny Oak's Music Park, the opening act was thanking her audience, and Recent Geezer was waiting to take the stage. The crowd wasn't as large as it had been the week before, given that Recent Geezer's substitution had only happened that afternoon. Still, people were beginning to pour in the door and fill up the empty benches and picnic tables.

Sid found Leo stuffing his face with fried shrimp. He nodded to the takeout container on the bench next to him, holding her seat. He'd also gotten two cold drinks, both of which had sweated onto the wooden seat, leaving damp rings. Sid wiped the water off the bench before sitting. "Thanks for dinner, kid."

With his mouth full, Leo simply nodded. Sid picked up her container of fried shrimp and coleslaw and glanced around the venue. J. T. Clement was nowhere in sight. The Geezers took the stage, and Sid finished her dinner and sweet tea. When they took a short intermission halfway through their set, Sid stood to stretch her legs and offered to buy Leo a drink. Granny Oak's was now full to bursting, and the lines for both bars stretched nearly to the back of the park. It shouldn't have mattered since she was stuck there until J. T. arrived, but Sid didn't relish standing in line for half an hour just for one soda and a beer.

Her phone buzzed in her back pocket, and she pulled it out. Whoever called didn't wait for her to answer and hung up after only one ring. Sid stared at the unfamiliar number and debated whether to return the call. Glancing up and noticing the line had not moved an inch, she swore under her breath and hit redial.

The phone rang six times before a man answered. "Hello?"

"Hi," said Sid, surprised that someone had actually picked up. "I think you just called me. I was calling you back." Pause. Silence. "Just wanted to check to see if you meant to call me or if that was a misdial or something." Silence again. "Hello? Anyone there?"

"Who is this?"

Sid gave a laugh, deeply regretting having returned the call. "I asked you first."

"Sid?"

The voice came from all around her. She spun around and saw Tony Davis standing about ten feet away from her. Beside him, Naomi was balancing Dante on her hip. Both Tony and Naomi were frowning at her, and Tony had a flip phone held to his ear.

"Hey," said Sid as she gave them a little wave.

Tony held up his hand and pointed to the phone. "Why are you calling me?"

His voice sounded in her ear, and she almost dropped her own phone. "Why are you calling *me*?"

Tony shook his head and closed the phone. He pointed to the exit and then whispered something to Naomi. Sid followed Tony outside, leaving Naomi and Dante standing at the end of the line for the bar. Tony marched up St. George Street and turned right onto Fort Alley, a narrow, pedestrian-only lane that was largely deserted. He didn't stop until he was halfway down the long block.

"What is this?" He shook the phone at Sid, who came to a stop in front of him.

Sid shrugged. "How should I know? You called me."

"This isn't my phone." He shook it again. "We found it in Naomi's bag when it started ringing. It doesn't belong to us."

"Well, it doesn't belong to me either," said Sid, standing with her hands on her hips. "I didn't recognize the number. It rang, like, one time. That's it. I don't know why I even bothered to call it back, but I did. I thought maybe it was someone wanting to hire me. I don't know. But then you answered and got all grouchy on me."

Still gripping the phone in one hand, he pressed his fists to his eyes. "Sid, this phone could be from anywhere. It's a burner. Who knows who owned this thing before now? Someone dropped it in Naomi's bag, either by accident or on purpose. My money's on the latter."

Sid folded her arms and frowned. "Can you take it to the station and dust it for prints?"

Tony rolled his eyes. "If it was planted, then I'm pretty sure the only prints we'll find on it are mine and Naomi's."

"Well, what's on it? Any other calls or texts? Any history?" she asked.

He sighed and flipped open the phone. Navigating through the limited features, he found a single outgoing call from a few minutes ago, sent to a saved contact labeled SS. There was only one other saved contact, listed as WS. Tony held out the phone to Sid. "Recognize these?"

Sid stared at the contacts list. "That's me, SS. That's my number." Swallowing hard, she pointed to the second number. "The other one is Wes's old cell phone. The one he carried for work."

"You're sure?" Tony pulled his own phone from his pocket and scrolled through his contacts. "Fuck."

"What does that mean?" Sid glanced up and down the lane, but no one was close enough to hear their conversation.

"Let me think." Tony paced back and forth across the width of the alley, gripping the flip phone so tightly that Sid was afraid he'd crush it in his large hands. After nearly a minute of pacing, he stopped. "How long did you wait before calling back?"

"Maybe a minute. Why?"

"Whoever dropped this phone in Naomi's bag had to have done it in Granny Oak's. We'd only been inside a couple of minutes when we heard it ringing. Probably happened as we were entering or standing around looking for a place to sit." Tony ran his hands back and forth over his short hair. "Could have been anyone. People kept bumping into us. Lots of people leaving at the intermission, more people coming in."

"Anyone familiar?" she asked.

Tony's eyes went wide. "J. T. Clement. He and his wife were walking in right behind us." Sid worried her bottom lip, and Tony blew out a long breath. "Maybe it's no big deal. Maybe the phone is his and he accidentally dropped it in Naomi's bag. Or maybe it's his wife's. Could be nothing."

"I can't imagine the phone belongs to Josie. She doesn't know me, and she never knew Wes. As for J. T., I could understand it if it only had my number. But why would he have Wes's number?" Sid pinched the bridge of her nose. "That doesn't make any sense. Were they with anyone?"

Tony nodded. "Looked like three other couples. One I didn't recognize. One was Buddy Rizzo, the St. Johns County property appraiser, and his wife. Don't know her name. And then Sheriff Colquitt and his wife, Emmaline."

Sid felt her breathing change to short, rapid bursts, and she pressed her hand to her chest as if willing her lungs to fill with more air. "I don't think it was J. T." She turned and walked quickly back up Fort Alley toward St. George Street.

"Sid!" Tony was right on her heels. "What's going on?" She slowed as she approached the crowded entrance to Granny Oak's, and Tony grabbed her arm, spinning her around.

"I think it might have been the sheriff," she said, as loud as she dared. Recent Geezer had begun playing again, and their cover version of Creedence Clearwater Revival's "Have You

Ever Seen the Rain" filled the night. Tony's brow creased as he began to shake his head, and Sid pulled her arm out of his grip. She stood on her tiptoes and spoke into his ear so she could be heard over the din. "Can you get ahold of Wes's case file?" He nodded. "Good. Come by my office tomorrow. Bring the file."

Before Tony could say anything else, Sid ducked in front of two large families jostling with each other to enter the music park. She found Leo sitting by himself, filming the Geezers with his phone. He was still saving the seat next to him. She smiled to herself and scanned the rest of the audience, easily locating Josie Clement, the Colquitts, and the Rizzos. The fourth woman sitting with the group was someone Sid recognized from Josie's tennis club, but Sid didn't know her name. Emmaline and Josie were watching the stage, but Sheriff Colquitt was holding court with the others, trying to talk to them over the music.

She found J. T. Clement and the missing fourth man standing at the end of the line to the left of the stage. That drinks line was largely in the shadows, given that there were only a few lanterns strung from the overhead branches of the giant oak in that section of the park. She slipped through the crowd and came up behind J. T. The other man noticed her and nodded, and then he turned back to J. T. and continued talking. J. T. didn't turn around. He was swaying slightly, possibly still drunk from his long lunch at Ghost City Brewery.

The line inched forward for the next few minutes, and the mystery man kept talking. By now, he had revealed himself to be an attorney with a local firm specializing in land use law, bragging about a deal he was about to close. He reached for his phone and began scrolling to find a photo of the condominium project.

"Excuse me." Sid felt a tap on her shoulder. Emmaline Colquitt, with her honey-blonde hair and high cheekbones, smiled at her. "You're about to lose something." Sid felt Emmaline's fingers brush the back of her shorts, and then Emmaline held up a pale gray business card with the familiar yellow logo of the Cielo Spa on it. "It looked like it was getting ready to fall out of your pocket."

Sid shook her head and patted her back pocket. "Nope, don't think so. That's not mine."

"No? It was in your pocket. Just barely, but still." Emmaline glanced at the card and then held it up for Sid to read. "Is that your name?"

Sid frowned as she read the handwritten details. "That's my name, but..."

"Well then, surely it's yours." She smiled and held out the card for Sid to take. "I hate to ask this, but would you mind?" Emmaline pointed to the two men standing in front of Sid. "I'm with them."

Sid stepped aside and slipped the card into her pocket.

Emmaline moved forward and tapped J. T. on the shoulder. "J. T., your wife and I want to change our order. We don't want beer. Be a darling and get us two white wines instead, please."

J. T. rolled his eyes. "You already said you wanted white wine. You never said beer."

"No, I'm sure we said beer before."

He shook his head. "Nope. You said wine." He began to sway a little and quickly widened his stance to try to hide it.

"Don't get sassy with me, J. T. Clement." Emmaline swatted his arm playfully. "Two white wines, please."

"Got it." He gave her a mocking bow. "Anything else, milady?"

With an exaggerated flick of her hand, she smiled and turned to go. "That will be all. Thank you kindly." She sashayed off in the direction of the rest of the group.

J. T. shook his head again and gave Sid a wink. The other

man ignored the encounter and continued scrolling on his phone. Once the elusive photos of the condominium were located, J. T. moved so that he was standing slightly behind the man and looking over his shoulder at his phone. The attorney prattled on about the condo project, and Sid watched as J. T. slipped his hand into his pocket and pulled out a folded wad of cash.

She stepped forward and palmed the money, then slipped out of line without bothering to ask if he wanted a receipt. She shoved her hands into the pockets of her shorts as she crossed the park and slid onto the bench next to Leo.

"Did you get the drinks?" he asked, noticing Sid was empty-handed.

"Line's too long," she answered. "Maybe later."

Leo nodded and went back to filming the Geezers. Sid slumped down on the bench.

She stole occasional glances at the Clements and Colquitts out of the corner of her eye. The sheriff put his arm around J. T., who laughed heartily at whatever story Travis Colquitt was telling. Gone was the earlier look of fright and paranoia J. T. had worn; gone was the sheriff's annoyance and menace. From the outside, they looked like best friends. Sid wanted to spy more closely, but she didn't dare risk it. Maybe J. T. wasn't to be believed. Maybe the sheriff wasn't actually pretending to be his dead brother. What was the real story? Sid's head hurt, and the music wasn't helping.

She desperately wanted to go back to her office and have some peace and quiet to think, but she would wait. She'd wait until the band's set was over. She'd wait and help the Geezers pack up their equipment, and then, she'd head home with Burt and Leo. It was safest that way.

Sid couldn't shake the feeling that things were getting out of hand. Asking Tony for his help was probably the smart thing to do. She just wasn't looking forward it, because involving him meant sharing more information with him than she was comfortable with. The best she could hope for was that Tony would think she was nuts but would help her anyway. The worst case would be him saying she was in grave danger and insisting that she stop investigating.

But Sid knew one thing for certain—there was no way she was backing off now.

Chapter Twenty-Four

Tony Davis showed up at Sid's office the next morning with two large cups of coffee from Pirate Joe's, a box of donuts from Fire in the Hole, and the pilfered copy of Wes Stone's case file. Sid cleared her desk and motioned for Tony to spread out the file, but he kept it close to his chest.

"I'm not going to show you everything, Sid, so don't even ask." He pulled out a piece of notepaper upon which he appeared to have scribbled his thoughts. "You know the basics, of course, so we don't need to go over everything, but I do have some questions. There were a few things I found, small details, that weren't followed up. They may be nothing, but . . ." He shrugged.

"Just spit it out, Tony." She rocked back in her squeaky chair and bit into a donut. The datil pepper glaze tickled the back of her throat, and she chased the sensation with a sip of coffee. "I can take it. Go."

Tony removed the lid from his coffee cup and took a sip. "Okay, here goes. There were a couple of things about the car that were interesting."

"The car that hit them?" asked Sid with her mouth full.

"No, Wes's car. The whole scene in the car." Tony watched as Sid set down the rest of her donut and wiped her fingers on a napkin. He took a breath, trying to tread carefully. "The key was in the ignition."

"Okay."

Tony held up his finger. "Wes kept his service revolver locked in the glove compartment, right?" When Sid nodded, he continued. "Right. I saw his routine when he got in and out of the car. It was always the same. Getting in, he'd unlock the glove box, put the revolver in, lock the glove box, then turn on the ignition. Getting out of the car, he'd turn off the ignition, unlock the glove box, check the revolver, put the gun in his holster, lock the glove box, and then get out of the car." Tony jabbed the folder with his finger. "I rode with him for a whole week, every day. That was the routine. He never deviated from it."

"Sounds about right," said Sid as she sipped her coffee.

Tony set the file down on the end table next to his chair. "Let's set it up. On that night, Wes pulls to a stop on Big Oak Road a little ways past the Church of the New Dawn assembly hall. He's still a third of a mile away from the shooting range, but he just stops. Puts the car in park, turns off the engine, cuts the lights." Tony mimed each step as Sid watched. "We think his car was still in the roadway or maybe only a little on the grass. There isn't much of a shoulder on that stretch of road, and there was a small patch of roadside construction right there and the beginning of a temporary concrete barrier. At some point, the other car hits him from behind.

"Now, the skid marks were short and curved to the right, so we think the other car was going extremely fast and didn't see Wes's car until the very last second. It's dark on that stretch. No streetlamps. And Wes's lights were off. We're not sure why the other driver swerved to the right and toward the construction work. It seems more logical that he'd swerve to the left to avoid Wes's car, but that's not what happened. Perhaps there was oncoming traffic in the left lane at that moment, but if so, no one stopped and stayed at the scene."

Tony leaned forward and moved the box of donuts and both coffee cups into position on Sid's desk to simulate the accident. "On impact, Wes's car is slammed forward and to the right into the end of the concrete barricade. The other car ends up down in the ditch. Coroner said the other driver was killed on impact."

Sid nodded, and Tony passed her a photo from the case file. The photo showed the front of Wes's dark blue SUV pushed up against the concrete barricade. The passenger side of the front bumper was wrapped around the barricade, and the whole front of the car was a crumpled, tangled mess. "See anything odd?"

Sid stared at the photo. The windshield was mostly out of frame, and what little was showing was a spiderweb of shattered glass. She was thankful she was not able to see inside the car. "No."

"The front bumper is crumpled on both sides, the driver's-side headlight is broken, and there is damage to the driver's-side front panel." Sid looked up at him, and the vertical crease between her brows deepened. Tony nodded. "Exactly. Why is the driver's side so badly damaged when it was the passenger side that hit the barricade? What did Wes hit on the driver's side?"

"Was this ever investigated?" Sid stared at the photo.

"I don't think so." Tony flipped to his notes in the file. "And there was a bit of red paint on the driver's side of the front bumper. Someone made a note in the margin that the damage was consistent with the impact against the concrete barrier and that the red paint was preexisting. No initials on that note, and I don't recognize the handwriting as belonging to any of the detectives or other personnel identified in the file." He looked up at Sid. "Did Wes have an accident before this one? Any damage to the car, even if it was slight?"

Sid sat forward and shook her head. "No, no way. Wes loved that car. It was old, and we couldn't afford a new one, so he babied that thing. Washed it almost every weekend. It was spotless inside and out, even with hauling around a five-year-old. He had even washed it that day, before Manny's party. If there had been any red paint or even a small scratch on it, I would have heard about it. Wes would have moaned and groaned about it until he finally had it buffed out or whatever else he had to do to fix it."

"Okay, so that's definitely one point worth looking at." Tony took the photo back and placed it carefully in the file. "Now, upon impact, Wes's seat failed and fell backward." Sid's breath hitched, and Tony winced. "Sorry."

She waved the apology away. "Don't be. It's okay."

It wasn't okay, not by a long shot. When the other car hit them from behind, Wes had been thrown forward, but crashing into the concrete barricade a split second later had thrown Wes back against his seat. The force of that impact caused the seat to break and collapse backward, crushing Iris, who was asleep in her booster seat. The coroner believed she was killed instantly, that she never felt a thing, and Sid clung to that belief with all her might.

Tony continued. "Wes had a number of injuries, to say the least, including several deep lacerations on his right forearm. On the top and the underside."

"I remember," said Sid. "I received the report of all his injuries."

"I had Naomi look at the report, too. She said he would

have been losing a lot of blood from those cuts. The lacerations also nicked the tendons in his arm and might have had an impact on his ability to open and close his hand."

Sid's eyes went wide. "Meaning he might not have been able to fire his gun?"

"Fire it. Hold it." Tony held up his finger again and reached for his notes. "When deputies arrived at the scene, he wasn't wearing his seat belt, but his injuries suggest that he was wearing it on impact. Bruising and such."

Sid picked some of the glaze off the remnants of her donut. "I saw the report. The conclusion is that he took off his seat belt to get his gun."

"And he unlocked the glove box to get to it."

"Right."

"But his keys were found in the ignition." Tony sat forward. "That wasn't Wes's routine. His keys would have been in the glove box's lock or maybe in his lap or on the seat next to him, not back in the ignition. And to reach the glove box, he would have had to pull himself forward out of the collapsed seat and reach over, all while bleeding profusely from his arm and likely not being able to flex or extend his fingers." Tony shook his head. "Something's not right."

Sid ran her hands over her face and took a few slow, deep breaths. "So, what's your theory? I assume you have one."

Tony sat back, and Sid watched as one of his legs began to bounce. "I think someone else was there that night. I think that's why Wes stopped where he did, right in the road. I think they forced him to turn off the car and the headlights. I think he hit another vehicle when he was pushed forward into the barricade, and that's why there is damage to the driver's-side front. I think whoever was there removed the keys from the ignition, unlocked the glove box, and took out Wes's gun. They returned the keys to the ignition, not knowing Wes's routine." Tony looked Sid in the eyes. "I think someone else shot Wes. They put the gun in Wes's hand, closed his fingers around the trigger, and fired."

Sid pressed a hand to her mouth and slowly nodded. She wasn't going to cry. She hadn't cried in almost three years, and this wasn't enough to make her do so now. Tony's theory was not so different from her own. Hearing him talk about the case felt like a series of sharp stabs to her heart, but she wasn't going to cry.

"I think you're probably right." She reached for her coffee, which had cooled somewhat during their conversation. "I've been thinking something similar." She thought for a moment, staring at the drawn curtains over her Wall of Shame, trying to picture where each photo and news clipping hung. "What about the burner phone? Do you think it ties in with this?"

"Yes." Tony reached into his pocket, removed the burner phone, and placed it on the edge of her desk. "This is the phone that was used to call Wes that night."

Sid leaned forward. "You're sure?"

Tony nodded. "The fact that it had Wes's number saved in it was suspicious enough, but at the time of the investigation, we got the IMEI number for the phone." He picked up the phone and pressed buttons until he found what he was looking for, then turned it so Sid could see the screen. "It's like a serial number, a fifteen-digit number that's unique to this phone. Every cell phone has one. We got it when we traced the call made to Wes. Unfortunately, the number IDs the phone, not the caller, but they're a match."

Sid let out a long, slow breath and willed her heart to stop racing. "So, why has it made an appearance now, after all these years?"

"I don't know." Tony shook his head and placed the phone

back on the edge of the desk. "Wes received a call that night. He then left you a voicemail that said—"

"I know what he said," she interrupted. "He said that he'd received a call telling him that his new partner—that *you* were drunk at the shooting range and that he needed to go take care of it. He said he was taking Iris with him, and as soon as he'd dealt with you, he would head home."

Tony's leg kept bouncing. "Except I wasn't at the shooting range, and I wasn't drunk."

Sid nodded. "I know. You were at home, asleep in your bed with your wife. Stone-cold sober."

"Right." He ran his finger down a page in the file. "Wes's phone showed one incoming call and one outgoing call that night. Both of them were brief. The outgoing call was to your number. The incoming call came from a prepaid phone identified as having been activated for the first time in Gainesville that morning. Someone must have turned it on, programmed in Wes's number, and then quickly turned it off again. The next activity was the call made to Wes's phone. We got a ping from a tower north of downtown near the airport, not too far from Big Oak Road. The call would seemingly have come from someone at or near the gun range."

"And it's the same phone number as the one that called me last night?" Sid reached for her phone and scrolled through the call activity log.

"No," replied Tony. "Hear me out. There was no more activity from the burner phone the night of Wes's death. However, there was another call made to Wes's phone the following Wednesday night. Wes's phone was in custody. No one got to it in time to pick it up, and the caller didn't leave a voicemail. The call pinged off a tower near downtown, but there's no way to tell exactly where it came from. After that, there was no further activity. It was assumed that the phone was tossed or destroyed. Any prepaid minutes that came with the phone when it was bought in Gainesville would have expired a long time ago. They would have only lasted a couple of months at the most."

"But someone reactivated it. Someone called me last night, so there must be more minutes on it now. Can we find out who did that?" Sid stared at the phone but didn't touch it.

Tony waggled his head back and forth in thought. "Maybe, but I doubt it. Anyone can add minutes to a phone like this without signing a contract or giving out personal information. If they wanted to fly under the radar, they could pay cash for a gift card and then call the provider and use the gift card to add more minutes to the phone. There are ways to do it." He shrugged. "However it was done, the phone was assigned a new number. The old one would have been burned by now, maybe even reassigned to another phone. Who knows? Regardless, the phone number that called Wes and the one that called you don't match."

Sid sat back. "All right, but it's the same IMEI number, the same phone. Likely still the same owner, right?"

"Likely." One side of Tony's mouth twitched upward. "At the time of the investigation, the phone number and IMEI number were used to track the burner to Gainesville, where it was purchased and activated that morning at . . ."

Tony paused to check his notes, flipping a page back and forth. "At a CVS near the corner of Southwest Thirteenth Street and Southwest Third Avenue. You may not remember, but that was the first home game for the Gators that season. They played Tennessee. Always a big crowd. Tailgating all day. It's a madhouse."

Sid nodded. She had been to exactly two Gator football games in her life and had told Wes that she wasn't going back for more. The Swamp, as the UF stadium was affectionately known, was a loud, enormous crucible of trapped heat and fanaticism. To say that the games were organized chaos was being generous. As she looked across the desk at Tony, Sid suddenly realized that she might have seen the great Antonio Davis play in person. The first game she attended would have been during his senior year, although thankfully it was not the one where he shattered his leg and his career.

"I remember," she said. "Wes watched the game before we went to Manny's party. He was yelling at the TV, so Iris and I watched Disney movies in the bedroom." Her heart squeezed as she remembered Iris singing along, blissfully out of tune.

"Kickoff was at noon. Tailgating would have started early," explained Tony. "Investigators checked the store's CCTV footage, which luckily was kept on file because of the increased foot traffic. They identified a college kid as the purchaser of the phone. Happened around ten o'clock that morning. He was wearing a T-shirt with Greek letters across his chest. Tau Beta Psi. The frat house is across the street from the CVS. Kid was a sophomore. He didn't live in the frat house but was there for the party. When he was interviewed, he said some old guy gave him a hundred bucks to buy a phone for him. Told him exactly what to buy. Said he could keep the change, and there was another hundred in it for him when it was done. So the kid did it."

Sid sat forward. "Did the frat boy give a description of the old guy?"

"Yeah, real specific," Tony said with a snort of laughter. He read aloud from the file, "Middle-aged white guy wearing a pale blue button-down. Probably long-sleeved. May have had the sleeves rolled up. Some kind of logo. Probably the UF logo. Khaki shorts. Maybe khaki pants. Not jeans. Blue UF baseball cap. Sunglasses with dark shades. No description of hair color or eye color. About the kid's height. Kid was six feet tall.

Heavier than the kid. Kind of bulky. No noticeable scars, tattoos, marks, or other traits."

Sid rolled her eyes. "Not very helpful."

"No, but this is." Tony tapped the file. "The man identified himself as a Tau Beta Psi fraternity brother at UF. The investigators had the kid look at the fraternity's old membership photos going back twenty years, but he couldn't pick him out with any certainty. Thought it might be any of about two dozen guys. To their credit, the detectives ran those guys down. All of them had alibis for the night of the accident. None of them were in St. Augustine."

Sid shook her head. "So, how is that helpful?"

"J. T. Clement was in Tau Beta Psi at UF. Graduated fourteen years prior to Wes's death." Tony tapped the file again. "He wasn't one of those identified by the kid from the old photos, but still, it's an awfully big coincidence."

Sid swirled the last bit of coffee in her cup. It was possible J. T. was the guy. He had met Ava Owen at a tailgate party in Gainesville, albeit a year later, and Wes had refused to take his bribe. "Could J. T. be so stupid as to tell this kid he was a fraternity brother, though? After being so careful to conceal his identity?"

Tony shrugged. "Maybe, if he needed to convince the kid to do him the favor. More inclined to do it for a frat brother than a total stranger, right?"

Sid nodded. "I guess. So J. T. then calls Wes to lure him to Big Oak Road?"

"He failed to bribe Wes," offered Tony. "Murder is another way to make sure someone keeps their mouth shut."

Sid chewed her bottom lip and stared at the Wall of Shame. "Let's assume you're right. But what if it wasn't J. T.?"

Chapter Twenty-Five

Detective Tony Davis let out a low whistle. "Damn, Sid."

"I know." Sid sighed. "You think I'm crazy, don't you?"

He shook his head. "I think you've been busy. Maybe borderline obsessed, but not crazy." Tony studied the Wall of Shame, starting with the photo of Sid and Iris in the center and branching out in all directions. "What's all this?" He pointed to the newest additions to the Wall, the ones closest to the spiral staircase.

"That is what I learned yesterday, thanks to J. T. Clement." Sid related her conversation with the commissioner, revealing only the details about his relationship with the Colquitt family and leaving out her discovery of J. T.'s own affair.

"You know the gist, right?" She pointed to a newspaper article about the boating accident. "The Colquitt family— parents, Don and Lani, and twelve-year-old twin boys Travis and Troy—were on their boat heading into Jupiter Inlet when the boat capsized. From my research, it looks like Jupiter Inlet is one of the most dangerous inlets in Florida. It has to do with how the Loxahatchee River empties into the Atlantic Ocean there. Apparently, it creates something called shoaling, where sand builds up and causes the waves above to be unpredictable, with really high swells. A lot of boaters get caught off guard by it as they pass over the sandbar. If you time it wrong, your boat ends up on top of the swell and then comes hurtling down."

Sid scanned the article, running her finger over the lines of text. "It's called pitchpoling. You come down the wave, and the boat sheers to the left or right, rolling over on its side. Or you come straight down, and the wave crashes over the boat, sinking it. That's what happened to the Colquitts. Don, Lani, and one of the boys died. Lani's body was found right away. She got trapped in the boat and drowned. Don's body was found a day later. The boy's body was never found."

Sid tapped the two photos she had printed. They were mirror images; each showed a boy in a yellow-and-white Little League uniform, holding a bat and standing over home plate. "Travis and Troy were identical twins. According to J. T., you couldn't tell them apart just by looking at them."

Tony looked closely at the photos. "And J. T. knew them when they were kids?"

Sid nodded. "He lived down the street from the Colquitts. J. T. was two years younger, but they all played together. J. T. liked Travis better." Sid tapped one of the photos. "He said Travis was a nice kid, did well in school." She tapped on the other photo. "Troy, however, was not as well liked. Always in trouble. Fighting, stealing. Got picked up by the cops a few times, but his daddy always smoothed things over for him. J. T. said that, at the rate Troy was going, he was bound to get himself into big trouble pretty quickly."

"Okay," said Tony. "This really isn't big news, though, is it? I mean, most people know the sheriff was orphaned. He's made no secret of it."

Sid squared her shoulders and faced Tony. "But what if I told you that the boy who survived the boating accident that day wasn't Travis Colquitt? What if I told you it was Troy?"

Tony frowned. Sid continued. "J. T. believes it was actually Travis Colquitt who died that day. Troy survived, but he led everyone to believe that he was his brother. After all, everyone liked Travis. He was the golden boy. Troy was the problem child. This would have been a fresh start for him, a chance to be the golden boy for a change, rather than the juvenile delinquent." She held up her finger. "There's just one small catch . . . literally." She pointed back and forth between the two photos. "Can you see what it is?"

Tony stepped forward and studied the photos again. He shook his head in confusion, but as he took a step back from the wall, it hit him. "Troy is batting left-handed."

Sid nodded. "Yes! Yes, he is."

"But the sheriff isn't left-handed, Sid." Tony shook his head. "I play softball with him. He bats and fields right-handed."

"He could have learned to use his right hand. According to J. T., Troy broke his right arm and several of the fingers on his right hand in the boating accident, so he would have had time to learn how to use it as his dominant hand when the cast came off. He could blame any weakness in his grip or bad handwriting on the accident." Sid crossed her arms. "What position does he play on your softball team?"

"Second base."

"So the farthest he would have to throw is to home plate?"

"Yeah. So?"

Sid smiled. "I watched him throw a ball yesterday. Far, like halfway down Saragossa. And he did it with his left hand. Could you do that with your nondominant hand?"

"Doubtful." Tony stared at the photo of Troy Colquitt. "That's pretty thin, Sid."

"J. T. said that Troy cut himself about two months before the boating accident. He was there when it happened. He, Travis, and Troy were all on a bicycle, and they took a bad spill." She held up her right forearm and pressed a finger to the skin about six inches above the wrist. "Troy got a nail stuck in his arm, and it left a bad scar. The sheriff has a tattoo on his forearm that covers up a lot of other smaller scars that he got from the boating accident, but you can still see the outline of the big scar. The skin is raised and bumpy, and it looks like the Greek letter lambda."

"Okay, then people would have figured it out. Troy cut his arm, and now Travis has the same scar." Tony shook his head. "How would he explain that?"

Sid nodded to the photo of Troy. "It all happened during summer vacation. That summer, J. T. was the only other kid from school the twins hung out with. And the hospital that Troy was taken to after the boating accident was different from the one he went to after the bicycle accident. If Troy told them he was Travis, there was nothing in the medical records to dispute it. The cut had already healed. He then had surgery to repair his broken arm, and on went the cast. Days later, he was shipped up here to St. Augustine to live with his aunt, and no one from South Florida saw him again . . . except J. T."

Tony dragged his hands down his face. "So Troy Colquitt has been lying all these years, impersonating his dead twin brother, Travis. Is that what you're saying?"

"Yes." Sid nodded. "And I think he's the one who killed Wes."

Tony almost laughed. "You're serious? The sheriff of St. Johns County murdered one of his own deputies. Really? That's what you think?"

"Yes, and so does J. T." Sid persisted, even as Tony shook his head and stepped away from the wall. "J. T. did try to bribe Wes. He told me so. That day you stopped him for drunk boating, he thinks he let something slip to Wes as he was trying to talk himself out of trouble. He thinks he told Wes that he was childhood friends with the sheriff and that Wes could call him and it would all be taken care of. But, because he was really drunk, he said something about being *better* friends with Travis, and too bad he was the one who died."

Tony blew out a breath. "I never heard J. T. say any of that."

"How close were you in proximity to them that day?" asked Sid.

Tony rubbed the back of his neck. "I stayed on the patrol boat. So did Manny, at first. Wes was the one who boarded J. T.'s boat. Manny joined him after a bit to settle things down when it looked like Wes might actually make an arrest."

"So J. T. and Wes were speaking together, but you couldn't hear what they were saying."

"No, not really." Tony sighed. "Wes had J. T. alone in the cockpit. The others were told to stay up on the bow. But come on, Sid."

"I know it's crazy, but it's possible," she replied. "J. T. was always a little bit scared of Troy. Still is, apparently. What if Wes did some digging and confirmed the sheriff is really Troy, not Travis? I'll be the first to admit that Wes could be smug and self-righteous when he wanted to be. What if he confronted the sheriff about it?"

Tony shook his head. "I don't know." He took a sip of cold coffee and put the cup back down. "Okay," he sighed. "Let's assume that Wes said something to the sheriff about it. The sheriff is afraid that Wes will say something to other people, too. He could then be in big trouble. Depending on the evidence, he could be charged with false personation for pretending to be a dead person. Possibly fraud."

"Murder," added Sid.

Tony shook his head. "We've got no proof of that."

"Well, let's get some." She began pacing. "What about the red paint on Wes's car? He must have driven a red vehicle to Big Oak Road to confront my husband. It would have been damaged when Wes's car hit it. We can track that down."

"You're talking about trying to track down repairs on a red vehicle from three years ago. We'll be lucky if even half the body shops in the area have records going back that far, and I doubt many would be willing to share information with us anyway. They'll probably want to see a warrant." Tony picked up a donut and took a bite. "That's a big job, Sid. I don't really have a lot of free time."

"Fine," she huffed. "Then *I'll* track it down."

"It might take you a while."

Sid threw up her hands. "What else have I got going on, Tony? I have no current clients, and all of my prior cases except for one have involved finding lost pets."

Tony wiped his hands on a napkin. "Sid, have you been listening to yourself? You just told me that you think the St. Johns County sheriff murdered your husband because the county commissioner for District Five let it slip in a moment of drunken pleading that the sheriff has been masquerading for years as his dead twin brother. If any of that is actually true, then this is stuff you don't want to be messing with. Let me continue to work on the case. I'll do it discreetly so that no one is put in danger, and I'll keep you updated."

Sid glared at Tony for a few moments and then said, "Fine. Let me know what you find out."

"Yeah?" Tony frowned.

"Yes!" Sid walked around the desk and plopped down into her squeaky chair. "You're the detective. You handle it."

"Okay." Tony nodded once, tossed his napkin in the trash, and picked up his case file and the burner phone. "I'll handle it. I promise you, Sid, I'll find out what happened to Wes. Just keep your head down for now and stay safe. I'll be in touch."

Sid gave him a thumbs-up as he headed for the door. "Thanks for the coffee and donuts, Detective."

He gave her a half smile in return. "Any time."

Sid plucked a donut from the box and ate it while counting down on her watch. When five minutes had passed, enough time to ensure Detective Davis was no longer in her driveway, she snatched up her purse and keys and locked the door on her way out.

Chapter Twenty-Six

Sid pulled into the only vacant spot in the small parking lot in front of Hernandez Auto Body. She found Cesar Hernandez, of Recent Geezer fame, elbow-deep in the engine of a late-model Mustang.

"Hey, Sid. Give me a minute, will ya?" He stepped back and motioned for the young mechanic sitting behind the wheel to start the engine. It roared to life, and a grin spread across Cesar's face. The young man cut the engine and nodded with approval. "Love that sound," said Cesar. "Almost as beautiful as the guitar." He gave the young man instructions for finishing up and then led Sid into his office. "What can I do for you?"

Cesar's office was neat and tidy. The furniture was old and worn, but there was no mess. No piles of loose paper, no stacks of files, no jumbled boxes of parts or old coffee cups still half full. She smiled as she sat in the chair opposite his desk. "I was wondering if you keep records going back at least three years."

"I have records going back to the beginning." Cesar grinned. He rocked back and forth, and the lack of squeaks and squeals coming from his desk chair was not lost on Sid. "You need a receipt or something? I worked on your little car only about a year ago, I think."

"No, no." Sid waved her hand. "Not me. I, uh . . . I need a favor."

Cesar cocked an eyebrow. "Legal or illegal?"

She shrugged. "Not sure."

"Try me." He smiled at her.

"Okay," Sid began as she took a deep breath. "This would've been three years ago. I'm wondering if someone brought in a red vehicle involved in an accident. Would have needed some bodywork. Traded paint with a dark blue vehicle."

Cesar blew out a breath. "That's pretty vague. Any chance you got a specific date in mind? Or are you looking for anything that year?" He rolled up to the computer and started typing.

"The weekend after Labor Day. The vehicle would have come in sometime shortly thereafter." Sid chewed her bottom lip. "And the vehicle may have belonged to someone in law enforcement."

Cesar froze and slowly turned his gaze to Sid. "Law enforcement?"

Sid nodded. "I know you give a discount to law enforcement."

"I do." Cesar folded his hands in front of him on the desk. "Care to tell me why you want to know about repairs to a red vehicle that may belong to someone in law enforcement who was involved in an accident three years ago, right around the time of your husband's death?" He pursed his lips. "And don't think I don't remember that your husband drove a dark blue SUV."

Sid smiled. "New information has come to light."

"I don't think I like the sound of that."

"You'd like it even less if you knew the details."

"Do I want to know the details?"

"Definitely not. So, what do you say, Cesar? Can you help me?"

Cesar frowned at her for only a moment before resignedly turning back to his computer. "Let's see what I've got."

Sid's gaze wandered around the office for a minute while Cesar typed away, but she snapped back to attention when she heard, "Shit!"

"What is it?" She lunged across the desk and swung the monitor toward her.

"I don't think this is a good idea, Sid." Cesar was shaking his head.

"Just tell me what I'm looking at here," she demanded.

"Okay, okay. Sit down. You're wrecking my office." He straightened the mail tray that Sid had pushed aside and waved at the guest chair.

Sid pulled the chair up as close as she could to the desk and sat down. "Better?"

"Yes, thank you," replied Cesar. He moved the screen so they could both see it. "This is a record for a repair that was completed at the end of September that year. The vehicle had a broken headlamp and damage to the front bumper."

Cesar clicked on a folder and opened a series of photos. He pointed out the damage to the red BMW sedan, one photo at a time. He then clicked back to the record page. "The vehicle was brought in on Friday following Labor Day. My notes say that the damage was incurred the prior holiday weekend and that the owner was not filing a claim with the insurance company."

Sid's leg began bouncing. "I'm not looking for vehicles involved in accidents *on* Labor Day weekend, though. I need the weekend after that."

Cesar nodded. "Yeah, I got that. Here's what I'm trying to

tell you." He tapped the screen. "We didn't get to this vehicle right away. We were swamped, and there was a line of cars ahead of this one. The owner dropped it off, and we left it parked in our lot over the weekend, right out front. We started working on it the following week."

Sid shook her head. "How do you remember all this?"

"Because the car ended up receiving additional damage after the owner dropped it off." Cesar opened another folder of photos and clicked through them slowly so Sid could see them all. "I teach all my guys to compare the vehicle in front of them to the photos and notes in the file before they start working. If anything doesn't match, they're supposed to tell me. When my guys got started on this vehicle, they found all this. None of this damage was on the vehicle when it was dropped off. I know because I took all of those photos myself."

Sid blinked at the photographs—a broken right taillight, dented bumper, crumpled right rear panel. "Damage to the rear."

"Yep."

"Is that dark blue paint?"

"Yep." Cesar clicked back to the record page. "I made a note that this damage was new. I assumed someone had taken the car from our lot and gone on a joy ride with it. When they got into an accident, they decided to bring the car back and then took off." He frowned. "I had security cameras installed soon after that."

"Did you call the owner?" asked Sid.

Cesar nodded. "Of course. I said we wouldn't charge to fix the damage to the rear since it happened on our watch."

Sid's brow creased. "And they were okay with that?"

Cesar nodded again. "Yep. They said no hard feelings."

Sid blinked in amazement, and her leg began bouncing again. "Did you call the police and file a report?"

"No." Cesar shook his head. "Owner told me not to bother."

"What? Why?"

"Said it didn't matter."

"Didn't matter? Why not?" Sid stopped bouncing and leaned forward. "Who's the owner?"

He sat back in his chair and shook his head.

"Just tell me," Sid growled.

Cesar blew out a breath. "Emmaline Colquitt."

———

Sid pulled up in front of the Crane's Roost. She removed her handbag from the passenger seat and placed it behind her own seat, careful not to spill the file that Cesar had given her. He'd graciously printed out the records and all of his notes. Plus, he'd emailed her all of the photos of the damaged, red BMW.

Leo slid into the passenger seat, his T-shirt and shorts spotted with lemon-yellow paint, and Sid plastered a bright smile on her face. "Nice shirt, kid."

"Thanks." Leo looked down at his dad's old Tom Petty and the Heartbreakers concert tee, one of a collection of four he had found in his dad's old bedroom. Leo had selected this one to wear today because it already had a dozen small holes in it and a nickel-sized bleach stain on the left sleeve. At this point, a little yellow paint wouldn't make any difference. "Where are we going?"

"I need a favor." She kept her eyes straight ahead, taking side roads out of the neighborhood to avoid traffic. When she finally turned onto U.S. Highway 1, she asked, "You hungry?"

Leo grinned. "I'm always hungry."

Sid nodded and jerked the wheel, turning sharply into the parking lot of the Old City's only permanent hot dog stand,

The Sea Dog. She was out of the car before Leo had finished unbuckling his seat belt. They ordered food—a bacon chili cheese dog for Leo, a brat with sauerkraut and mustard for Sid —and ate at a picnic bench under the shade of a giant magnolia tree. Sid said very little, asking only a few questions about how Burt's renovations were going. Leo answered her but was happy to eat in relative silence. When they finished, Sid stacked up their trash.

"I need you to do something for me, Leo." She wadded up a napkin and placed it on top of the trash pile. "I know it's a big ask, and I'm not sure you'll be able to do it. Not even sure if it's something that's possible, but . . . I'd like you to try."

Leo eyed her cautiously. "What exactly do you want me to do?"

Sid held his gaze. "I want to take you to the crash site, and I want you to tell me what you can see."

———

Ten minutes later, Sid and Leo turned onto Big Oak Road. A little more than half a mile down the road, they came upon the Church of the New Dawn assembly hall. It was a nondescript, one-story, concrete-block structure with a tin roof, and it was home to one of those enigmatic Southern churches that tend to be found in the middle of nowhere. The building was painted a pale salmon color and was no bigger than the space of two double-wide trailers. The crash had happened not far from this church, and thinking of that—and of what Leo might see— made Sid's heartbeat begin to race.

As they passed the assembly hall, Sid slowed to a crawl and eventually stopped, turning on her hazard lights. They were about a third of a mile from the shooting range.

Sid had never been down this road. Not before the crash

and certainly not after it. For the past three years, she had stayed away because she wasn't sure if she could bear to see where it had all happened, where her prior life had ended so horrifically and her current life had begun without her consent. Sitting in the car now, she still wasn't sure if she could bear it, but she had no choice.

"I don't think this is going to work." Leo gripped his seat belt, not yet ready to unfasten it. "I don't know how to do this —*if* I can even do this. I don't know . . ."

"I'm just asking you to try," whispered Sid. "Please."

Leo noticed her white knuckles gripping the steering wheel and the hard line of her mouth as she pressed her lips together. "Okay." He unclipped his seat belt and opened the door. "I'll try."

He stepped out of the car and looked around. The road was narrow, only two lanes with no shoulders. The ground on either side of the road sloped away into drainage swales, which were dry but clogged with reeds and tall grass. Leo stood at the front of the car and waited, but Sid remained in the car. Her forehead was resting on the steering wheel, and Leo thought it might be a while before she joined him.

He took a few steps forward and removed his baseball cap, running his paint-speckled hand through his sweaty curls. Breathing deeply, he tried to remember Hattie's instructions about life and death—that the two weren't very complicated and that he shouldn't make them more difficult than they were. Easier said than done, he thought, standing all by himself on the deserted country road in the summer heat.

Leo didn't have to wait long, though, for the others to join him.

Chapter Twenty-Seven

Wes Stone and his daughter, Iris, stood at the side of the road, about thirty feet away from the car. Leo felt his stomach do a somersault, but he forced himself to breathe steadily in and out as he began walking toward them. Iris looked like she had when Leo had seen her before, smiling and wearing the same yellow dress with the red embroidered strawberries. Wes also looked like he had before—angry, covered in blood, and missing part of his skull.

Leo swallowed hard, fighting the urge to run in the other direction. He whispered, "She wants to know what happened here. Can you tell me?"

Immediately, his mind was flooded with blurry images and his body was racked with pain. Leo's knees began to buckle, and he gripped the sides of his head, digging his fingers into his hair and pressing hard. "Stop!" he yelled. "Stop it, Wes! Stop!" The pain subsided, the images faded, and Leo heard the car door slam shut behind him.

"Leo?!"

"It's okay, Sid." He looked back over his shoulder. "Just stay there. I need a minute. I have to try to figure out how to do this." He didn't want her coming any closer. At least, not yet.

Keeping his hands where they were on his head, he tried again. "Hello, Iris. Nice to see you. You look very pretty today." He heard her giggle, that girlish, lilting laugh that he'd heard before. He also felt Wes's anger subside a little. "Iris, I need to talk to your dad. Can you go stand over by your mom?" In a blink, the little girl was gone. Looking over his shoulder, he saw Iris sitting on the hood of the car, right next to Sid.

Leo turned back to Wes, and an idea struck him. "I'm not here to cause a problem." He slowly removed his hands from his head and held them up as if he were under arrest. "Please, don't hurt me." He felt Wes's anger subside a bit more. It was working. "Sid has asked for my help, and I want to help her." The anger flared again. "She hasn't left this alone for three years. Three long years. You've seen her. I know you have. She's a mess. She eats nothing but junk food. She's got stains on all her clothes. She doesn't shower. She's not living. Not really." The anger subsided, and a new feeling crept in. Leo felt it as sadness, maybe even regret.

Leo nodded. "But this past week or so, she's been better. She's been working. She's trying to figure things out, trying to get her life back on track, and I think she can do it." He swallowed hard and blew out a breath. "But she needs your help, Wes. She needs you to tell me what really happened that night." The sad feeling intensified, and the anger faded a bit more. "I know you don't want to. I know you don't want her to get hurt. But look at her, Wes."

Leo looked over his shoulder again at Sid and Iris. Sid had her arms wrapped around herself, as if she was cold. Given Iris's proximity, Leo was sure Sid was feeling the chill.

"Wes, Sid's been in pain for the past three years, and this might be the only way for her to stop. You need to help her. I'm asking you to trust me and—"

Leo turned his attention back to Wes and gasped.

Wes's spirit was no longer battered and bloody. He was standing on the side of the road, wearing a white camp shirt, khaki shorts, and flip-flops. He stood tall and broad, his body unmarked by injury. His blond hair was cut short and neatly combed, and his skin appeared tan and healthy. Leo assumed that this was what he'd been wearing at Manny's party. This was how he'd looked the night he was killed.

They must have been a striking couple, thought Leo, the kind of couple that you noticed when they walked past, all health and good looks. His heart ached for the woman who had lost this man and that little girl in the yellow dress. This life. Leo lowered his arms, widened his stance, and stood tall, taking a deep breath. "Okay, Wes. I'm going to call Sid over, and I want you to walk me through what happened. But I need you to go slow so that I can describe what you show me." He held up a cautionary hand. "Don't worry, I won't tell her the really bad parts. Okay?"

"Yes."

Leo gasped again. It was the first time he had heard Wes's voice, such as it was, in his head. The sound was low and deep, not at all like the soft, girlish sound of Iris's voice. Leo nodded and waved Sid over. Once she was standing beside him, he began, "Wes is here."

Sid nodded. "Iris?"

Leo looked around, but the little girl was gone. "No. She

was here earlier. She was sitting on the car next to you, but she's not here now." He turned back to Wes. "I don't think Wes wants her here for this part."

"Good." Sid nodded. "How . . . how is he?"

This time, Leo didn't have to lie. "He looks good." He smiled. "He's a big guy, isn't he? Tall and built." Leo mimed a bodybuilding pose, and Sid laughed. Leo felt a wave of joy coming from Wes. "He's wearing a white shirt and khaki shorts."

Sid nodded again. "That's what he was wearing the last time I saw him." Her voice hitched, and she pressed her fingers to her lips.

"Good. Excellent. That's great." Leo took a breath and shook out his hands, trying to release some of the nervous energy that was beginning to build. He wasn't sure if it was his alone or if some of the anxiety was coming from Wes. Either way, he had to press on. "I'm going to just talk out loud because I don't know how else to do it. I'm going to describe what he shows me. I'll point to you if I want to ask you a question, okay? Otherwise, assume I'm talking to Wes."

"Got it." Sid wrapped her arms around herself and fell silent.

"Okay, Wes. Let's do this." Leo rolled his shoulders, and as he did, the images began to appear in his mind. They flashed before him like memories, as if he already knew them. As if they'd been there all along.

The day became night, pitch-black night illuminated only by headlights. There was music playing, and someone was singing softly. Leo began to laugh.

"What?" asked Sid.

Leo smiled. "Did Wes like to sing songs from Disney movies?"

Sid's mouth fell open. "Only when he was alone in the car with Iris. She said he knew the words to all the songs, but he claimed that he didn't. We'd play Disney songs when we drove because she usually fell asleep to them."

Leo nodded. "He was singing to her in the car that night." An image of Iris flashed in his mind, a view of her in the rearview mirror. She was in her booster seat with her head lolled to one side. "She is asleep in the back seat." Sid nodded.

Leo looked around. "It's really dark on this road at night. There are no streetlamps. I can only see what's right in front of me in the headlights." A beam of light flashed ahead, sweeping back and forth across the road. Leo could see a car. "There's a car in the road with its lights off. It's stopped next to one of those concrete barriers they use for road construction. I can see a person standing behind the car with a flashlight." Leo winced, suddenly blinded.

"Shit!" He pressed his fingers to his eyes. "The guy just shined his flashlight in my eyes—in Wes's eyes—as he was driving. God, that's bright!" He saw Wes slow the car, coming to a stop. "Okay, so Wes stops behind the other car. About here." Leo walked to a spot about fifteen feet away, and Sid joined him. "The guy's still pointing the flashlight in Wes's eyes."

"How do you know it's a man?" asked Sid.

"I guess I don't," Leo admitted. "I can't see much of anything because of that damn flashlight." Leo squinted against the image of the light in Wes's eyes. "The guy—or whoever—he walks around to Wes's side of the car. But the guy's still shining the flashlight, keeping Wes from seeing him."

Leo blinked, another image flashing in his head.

"Red BMW," he whispered.

Sid's eyes went wide. "What did you say?!"

"The other car, the one parked in the road. It's a red

BMW." Leo could feel Wes turn his head away from the light. The car ahead was close enough for him to see that it was a red BMW. Leo squinted. "D, V, something something." He turned his head, as if that might afford him a better view. "There's a four. First two letters are D and V, I think. Last number is a 4." He shook his head. "I can't make out the rest."

Sid nodded. "That's good, Leo. That's really good. Keep going."

The flashlight beam was lowered, and Leo saw that it was a man. "It's a man. He's wearing dark clothes, but I can tell based on his size and shape."

The man rapped his knuckles on Wes's window, and Leo felt a wave of instant relief. "I think Wes knows him. He knows the man." Leo watched the window being lowered. The man waved his hand and pointed his finger, and Leo heard a muffled voice. "I think the man is telling Wes to turn the car off, to turn the lights off." He watched as the flashlight beam swung into the back seat, and Leo felt a rush of anger and fear.

"Something's not right." He closed his eyes, trying to make the images and feelings clearer. "Iris isn't supposed to be there. That's the feeling I'm getting. The man is shining the flashlight into the back seat. He can see Iris. I feel anger and fear, but I don't know who it's coming from, Wes or the other man. Maybe both? But I definitely get the feeling that Iris shouldn't be there."

"Is she awake?" asked Sid with a trembling voice.

Leo shook his head. "No, she's still asleep. I can see her in the rearview mirror. She doesn't know what's happening." Leo could feel Sid relax a little as she stood next to him, and he continued to concentrate on what Wes was showing him.

Leo flinched as he watched the man place a hand on the door and bend forward so that he was at eye level with Wes.

The man was wearing a black, zip-up hoodie, and the sleeves were pushed up to his elbows.

"What?!" asked Sid. "What do you see?"

Leo recognized the tattoo on his forearm, a cross with three doves. "The man . . . the man with the flashlight," he stuttered. "It's Sheriff Colquitt."

Chapter Twenty-Eight

"I can't hear what they're saying. It just sounds like mumbling," said Leo.

He was standing next to Sid at the side of Big Oak Road. The sun was unforgiving, and Leo could feel his skin beginning to burn. There was no one else around, not a car in sight. The only sound was the noise of cicadas, singing their song in the summer heat, and yet, in his mind, he was sitting in Wes's car in the dark of night with Iris asleep in the back, her soft snoring filling his ears. So strange, thought Leo, that he could hear Iris's snoring, but he couldn't hear the men's words being spoken.

"They're talking to each other?" Sid was pacing back and forth across the right-hand lane.

"Yes, but I can't make out what they're saying." Leo had his eyes closed, straining to hear, but he knew it was useless. It felt as if Wes was intentionally blocking that part of the scene, but Leo could still feel what was happening. "It's not an argument. I don't feel that at all. I feel worry, maybe fear, at first." He tilted his head to the side. "But then, it feels like relief." He nodded, feeling an ease in the tension between the two men.

"Secret."

The word came to him in Wes's deep baritone.

"There's a secret," said Leo. He watched as the sheriff held out his hand to Wes, and Wes took it. "They've agreed to something. They just shook hands."

Sid stopped pacing. "What do you mean, they shook hands? What did they agree to, Leo?"

"I don't know. It's like Wes doesn't want me to know what it is. He's not letting me hear what's being said." He shrugged. "But they've come to an agreement. They both seem relieved. I feel like Wes is smiling . . . or maybe even laughing."

"Laughing?!" barked Sid, and Leo's eyes flew open.

"Easy, Sid. I'm just telling you what I'm seeing and feeling. I don't know exactly what's going on. It seems like Wes doesn't want you to know the secret, whatever it is."

Sid began pacing. "I know what it is," she snapped. "You tell Wes that I know what it is." Her steps turned into stomps. "You tell him that I know exactly what it is, and how dare he keep it from me!" She was shouting now.

Leo kept his hands raised. "He can hear you, Sid. I don't need to translate."

"Oh yeah?" Sid stopped pacing. "Fine." She spread her arms out wide. "Gemini!" She screamed it. "Gemini! Isn't that right, Wes? Gemini! Twins! That's the big secret, isn't it?" Her face was bright red, and she was gasping for air.

"Twins."

Leo heard Wes's voice in his head.

"He's saying *twins*, Sid."

She continued pacing, nodding and looking over at Leo.

"Yeah, well, why the hell is Wes shaking hands and laughing about it?"

"*Secret.*"

Leo saw the image of the handshake again.

"I think they agreed to keep it a secret. Twins, Gemini . . . whatever. They agreed to keep it a secret. They're happy about it, like they agree it's the right thing to do, and everything is okay now."

"They agreed to keep it a secret?" Sid's mind whirled with disbelief.

Leo nodded. "Seems like it." He could feel the relief coming from both men.

In the next moment, the image in his mind changed, and Leo felt a wave of panic. "Something's wrong." He turned to look over his shoulder. "Someone's coming." Leo could hear the rumble of an engine getting closer. "Another car. The sound is loud, deep. Like a muscle car or something. Sounds like it's coming really fast."

Sid shuddered. "Camaro?" The car that hit Wes and Iris had been an early-model Camaro.

Leo shrugged. "I can't see it. I can only hear it." He watched as the sheriff took a few steps away from Wes's car, moving into the far lane, and swung his flashlight up.

In the next instance, Leo dropped to his knees, keening with pain.

"Leo!" Sid rushed over, kneeling in front of him, and took his face in her hands. "Open your eyes, Leo! Open your eyes! Look at me, kid."

Leo opened his eyes, and tears poured out. He shook his head at her, and she wiped away his tears with her thumbs.

"It's okay, Leo. It's okay," she soothed. "You don't have to do anything else. It's all right. I'm sorry. So, so sorry."

Leo gasped for breath, reeling from the images Wes had shown him. "Don't you want to know what happened?" he croaked. His throat felt raw, as though he'd been screaming. In that instant, he realized that Sheriff Colquitt had been screaming. "I've already seen it. It can't hurt me much now." He took in a ragged breath and felt a stab of pain in his ribs.

"Are you sure?" She noted how the boy winced when she helped him to stand. He nodded only once and then pressed his hands to his head. "Let's go sit in the car. Can you walk?"

"I think so."

Leo took a step and stumbled. Sid had to wrap an arm around his waist and help him to the car. Once inside, she cranked the air-conditioning, and they took a moment to bask in the cold air.

"The sheriff was standing across the road, holding up his flashlight." Leo pointed to the oncoming lane. "I think the sheriff blinded the other driver. I don't think he meant to do it or for the other car to crash into Wes's, but the car was going too fast. I heard brakes squeal and then a loud crash."

Leo pulled the front of his shirt away from his sticky skin and wiped the sweat from his face with the hem. When he lowered his shirt, he found Wes's spirit standing alongside the car, next to his window. The images resumed, moving slower this time. He stared ahead at the road, bright and hazy in the afternoon sun. In his mind, it was once again the middle of the night.

"It lasted only seconds. Less than seconds." Leo shook his head. "The first impact is in the back. Loud and hard. I feel Wes snap forward. And then there is another crash, almost immediately after the first one. But in the front of the car this time. I can feel Wes get jerked backward. It's like the seat gives way, and I'm just lying there. I don't feel any pain right away. Not at first. But it's like I can't clear my head. Everything is fuzzy. I can hear screaming. I think the sheriff is screaming."

"Screaming?" Sid's brow furrowed.

"Yelling." Leo nodded, his head pounding along with the images. "One moment the sheriff is at the window." He pointed to the driver's side. "Then he's gone. I'm not sure for how long. I can't get up. I can't sit up. I keep thinking about Iris, trying to call to her. I don't hear her."

Sid pressed her lips together and clenched her fists so hard that her pink-painted nails cut into her palms.

Leo turned to her. "Iris died instantly, just like they said." Sid nodded, and he whispered, "I promise, Sid. She didn't feel any pain." It was the truth. He was thankful that he didn't have to lie to her.

For the first time in almost three years, a tear rolled down Sid's cheek. "That's good."

"It's very good," said Leo. He turned his gaze back to the road ahead and made a decision. He would not talk about the pain. Wes's pain—his ribs, his arms, his legs, his head—none of it started right away. But it came eventually, and when it did break through, it was everywhere all at once. Not for too long, though. That was a mercy. No, Leo would not tell Sid about the pain.

"Everything is quiet for a while," he said. An image came into his head of Wes reaching for the steering wheel. "He's trying to pull himself up by grabbing the steering wheel."

"Which hand?" asked Sid.

"Left." Leo looked down at his own hands. "The right one's not working. There's a lot of blood, and I can't get my right arm to work." He felt a sense of urgency come over him. "I feel like I need to move, to do something, to get out of the car, but my mind isn't clear. I can't get my body to move." He hesitated then and sighed. "Before I tell you the rest, Sid, are you sure you want to hear it?"

"Yes." She shifted in her seat. "Tell me."

Leo turned his head to the left. "The sheriff is back and looking in the car." The voice was muffled again. "I can't hear what he's saying. I don't know if that's Wes blocking it again or if Wes really can't understand him. I can feel myself trying to speak, but I can't. I can't say anything." Leo looked down at his lap. In his head, he saw the sheriff reach across him and unlatch the seat belt. "He's taking off the seat belt."

"Wes is?"

"No, the sheriff. He's unhooked Wes's seat belt, but Wes still can't move."

Leo felt Wes's confusion, his desperation to move and to make sense of what was happening. Leo closed his eyes. He didn't want to look at Sid while he told her the rest. "I see the sheriff reach into the car and take the keys out of the ignition. Wes is confused. I can feel his confusion. My head feels fuzzy, so it all seems a bit warped. Sort of like looking in one of those carnival mirrors when it makes you look short and fat, but then you move a little and you're tall and skinny, you know? It feels like that."

Leo watched as the sheriff disappeared once more. "The sheriff is gone again. Not sure for how long. Then, I see him on the passenger side, and he's doing something with the glove compartment." He sucked in a breath. "I see a gun."

Leo felt as if his heart was lodged in his throat and he couldn't swallow. He kept his eyes closed. "He has my hand— Wes's hand. The right one. My hand's not working. I try to pull it away, but I've got no strength. I feel really tired." He paused for just a moment, deciding what to do. "I think the sheriff is saying something, but I don't know what it is."

That was a lie. Leo did know what the sheriff said. Wes had let him hear it, but Leo wouldn't tell Sid that part either.

Leo shook his head and gripped the hems of his shorts. "He has my hand. I see the gun in it now. And then, I lose sight of it. I just see the sheriff's face. He's leaning into the car. And then . . . there's nothing." He opened his eyes. Tears were streaming down Sid's cheeks. "I'm sorry, Sid. I'm so sorry."

Sid began sobbing then. Leo stepped out of the car and walked up the road, far enough away that he could no longer hear her crying. He'd give her some privacy and take these moments to clear his own head. He closed his eyes and tilted his head back, letting the sun beat down on his face. He didn't open his eyes until he felt Wes standing in front of him again.

"Thank you," whispered Leo. "I know you didn't want her to know all of that, but I felt she needed to." He felt a wave of love crash over him. "She'll be okay, you know. It may take a while, but she'll be okay." The waves of love kept coming. "The sheriff's plan wasn't to kill you, was it? Not initially, anyway. Right?"

The image of the handshake appeared in his mind. Leo nodded. "I hope you're okay with me not telling her the last part." Another wave of love swept over Leo, and he nodded again. "After the crash, Sheriff Colquitt knew he'd have to explain why he was out here with you. He knew you'd have to tell the truth about everything and that you wouldn't be able to keep the secret like you'd agreed." Leo blew out a breath. "He was worried his secret would come out, so he decided to kill you. He said he knew you wouldn't be able to lie for him and that he couldn't risk you telling everyone. You let me hear that part."

Leo laughed aloud. He couldn't help it. "Sheriff Colquitt is such a stupid prick, isn't he?" He shook his head and looked at

Wes. "He didn't have to kill you. You were already dying. You would have been dead in a few minutes, anyway."

Chapter Twenty-Nine

Sid drove Leo home, changed her clothes, laced up her sneakers, and went for a run. She ran until her legs wouldn't carry her any farther, and then she sat down and waited for her strength to return. When it did, she started running again. She stopped to buy water twice and food once, not because she wanted it, but because it was the only way to keep her body going. When she returned home around midnight, Burt was waiting for her in the backyard.

"How far did you run this time?" Burt took a sip of his beer. With his foot, he pushed an empty wrought iron chair out from the table. It made a loud screech as the legs scraped against the concrete pavers.

"No idea." Sid shrugged and took the seat. She opened the cooler at Burt's feet. Most of the ice had melted, and two empty bottles floated in the water. Sid grabbed one of the unopened beers and twisted off the cap. Burt had been waiting a while, but he'd paced himself. Only two and a half beers in probably twice as many hours, so he was practically sober. Sid lifted the bottle in a mock toast. "Until I didn't need to go any further."

They sat in silence for a few minutes, and Sid relished the taste of the beer. It didn't matter that it wasn't ice cold. She'd drink the rest of the six-pack if Burt would let her. "Did he tell you?" she asked.

"He did." Burt took another sip.

"I'm sorry," said Sid. "I'm sorry I asked him to do that. I didn't realize what it would be like for him."

"Oh, I think you had a pretty good idea, Sid." Burt picked at the label on the bottle.

Sid sighed heavily. "Yes and no. I thought he'd see things, but I didn't realize he'd feel any pain. For what it's worth, I am truly sorry for putting him through that."

Burt nodded. "I'm sure you are." He set his beer down on the table and leaned forward, resting his elbows on his knees and clasping his hands in front of him. "For what it's worth, he doesn't seem too damaged by it. If anything, he seems . . ." Burt thought for a moment. "Pleased. That might be the best word for it." He held up a hand before Sid could speak. "Not pleased to have experienced what he did, but pleased to have helped you. Pleased to have used his gift for something good. To not be scared shitless by it, like he usually is." He clasped his hands together again. "So for that reason . . . for *him* . . . I'm not gonna kick you out on your ass."

Sid swallowed audibly and held her breath, but Burt wouldn't look at her.

"I hope whatever you learned will help you find some peace, Sid. I really do." He shook his head. "But that boy is still just a kid, and you have him messin' with dangerous stuff."

"Wes wouldn't hurt him, Burt," she offered. "His spirit has been around several times, and Leo's never been in any danger."

Burt swung his gaze to her and held up his index finger. "One, you don't know that. You can't see what he sees, hear what he hears, feel what he feels. I saw the condition that boy was in when he got home, and it looked like he'd had the shit kicked out of him. So don't tell me he's not in any danger. You can't presume to make a statement like that because you don't know how it works."

Burt held up a second finger. "Two, according to what Leo told me, your husband was shot in the head by his own boss. He was murdered by the sheriff of St. Johns County, the very same man who is still sheriff today. So do not tell me that he is not in any danger when a murderer is driving around with a badge and a gun and a whole department of deputies under him and that same murderer is showing up on *our* doorstep, giving you cases."

Sid began to protest, but Burt held up a third finger. "And three, that boy desperately wants to feel like he belongs somewhere and that he has people around him who love him. He's lost his dad. His mom is off traipsing around the state dealing with her own life crisis, and all he has right now is a bunch of old fuckers—me and the Geezers and Kitty—and *you*. That's it. So it is up to us to protect him. To raise him. Now, if helping me raise that boy is something you don't want to be a part of, then pack up and get the hell out. But if you are going to stay, you need to get your head on straight. You were a mother at one time, or have you forgotten that? I'm not asking you to be Leo's mother. I'm just asking you to start acting like you remember what it was like to be one."

He rose and walked to the back steps. "By the way, there was something Leo didn't tell you, but I think he should have."

Sid looked up at him as he stood in the golden glow of the light above the kitchen door. "What's that?"

Burt sighed. "Leo said Wes was in a bad way after the crash. Even if he hadn't been shot, he wouldn't have survived his injuries. And even if the sheriff had called for help instead of . . . instead of doing what he did, it would have been too late." He nodded once. "I just thought you should know. Leo thought it would be better for you if you believed Wes might have lived. He wanted to give you hope. But I don't want you beating yourself up thinking that Wes might have survived or that things might have turned out different. That's not the case."

"I know." Sid nodded. "I read the reports. I know how badly Wes was hurt. I know he lost a lot of blood, and it wasn't very likely that he would have survived his injuries." Sid held up her beer in salute. "But I appreciate Leo trying to spare my feelings. That was very sweet of him."

Burt went inside, and she heard him lock the kitchen door. A moment later, the outside light went out, and Sid was plunged into darkness. She sat by herself in the dark and finished her beer. Then, she pulled another one from the cooler. At some point, between beers two and three, Sid felt the temperature drop a few degrees even though the summer night air was thick and humid.

"Hello, Wes," she whispered. "I think we should talk."

Chapter Thirty

The next morning, Sid awoke with a headache. She knew she was dehydrated from hours of running—and from drinking three beers. Her eyes were dry, her legs were sore, and her whole body ached with exhaustion, but for the first time in almost three years, her heart felt a bit lighter. It was a strange feeling, like something was missing. Like she had set down part of a heavy load . . . which was what she had done, in a way.

Sid chugged two glasses of water, took a shower, and then polished off the few donuts left from the dozen Tony had brought with him the day before. After that, she ate a bowl of cereal and drank half a pot of coffee.

She was making notes in her file when she heard Burt's truck roar to life. She dragged the end table over to the wall and climbed up on it to peer out the transom window. She watched as Burt and Leo pulled out of the driveway. No surprise, thought Sid. Burt was likely to keep Leo away from her for a while. She wouldn't be surprised if he called an end to Leo's internship either. Maybe that was for the best. There was no reason to put the kid in danger. No reason he should be learning how to spy on people, sitting around in a hot car eating peanut butter sandwiches, or spending his time hunting for old ladies' lost pets. Sid pushed the end table back into place.

But then again, why not? Why not learn how to be a private investigator? What else was the kid going to do around here? Wait for his mother to show up and finally lay claim to him? Follow Burt around on his one-man construction jobs or play roadie for Recent Geezer? And why shouldn't he learn how to hone his gift for talking to dead people? Yesterday's adventure on Big Oak Road was the first time Sid had seen Leo engage with a spirit without looking like he was ready to throw up or pee his pants.

And she had helped with that. The kid was definitely more self-confident now than he had been when Paizley-with-a-Z dropped him off on Burt's doorstep two weeks ago. Leo seemed happier now, more talkative, less argumentative and defensive. He had color in his cheeks. He was wearing clothes that fit him. He had even met a girl who made him blush whenever he said her name. And Sid had helped with all of that.

She stared at the Wall of Shame. Leo had helped her, too. He'd spoken to Wes. Well, maybe that wasn't the right word for it. He'd been a conduit, perhaps, a way for Wes to communicate. She'd finally learned what had happened to him; to Iris. Not knowing, not being certain, thinking that Iris may have been in pain, that Wes may have actually shot himself—that was what had been slowly killing her these last three years. But now she knew the truth, and Leo had given her that.

She wasn't going to give up on Leo. She wasn't going to let him go without a fight. Sid reached for her phone and scrolled through the latest photos from PB&J's social media blitz. The two women and their ridiculous dog had arrived in Orlando that morning, set up at a Disney campground, and posed for photos in front of a lagoon wearing sequined mouse ears and holding a couple of cocktails. Sid rolled her eyes and put her phone down.

Leo's mother had let go of him. Sid would never understand that about Paizley-with-a-Z, but the pain of grief could make people do crazy things. Sid had lost her husband and basically ceased living these past three years. Paizley-with-a-Z had lost hers as well, and yet she'd had the opposite reaction. The woman had dyed her hair, bought a new bikini, and dumped her only son with his grandfather in her pursuit of a wild and carefree youth that had never been spent the first time around. They had experienced a similar tragedy, but they'd reacted in completely different ways.

Going forward, Sid decided she would try not to judge Paizley. Well, that wasn't entirely true. Sid was certain she'd continue to judge the woman, but she would try not to be too harsh.

What Sid could do, though, was help take care of a boy who had lost his father and been abandoned by his mother. Sid would not let Leo think that she was abandoning him as well.

No, Sidney Stone was not going to give up on her new apprentice. Leo Roberts had a job with her for as long as he wanted one. Sid opened the bottom drawer of the file cabinet, pulled out the cashbox, and unlocked it. She removed two hundred-dollar bills from the stack of cash that J. T. Clement had paid her and stuffed them into an envelope, then scribbled Leo's name across the front.

And, in addition to helping Leo, Sidney Stone, private investigator, was going to rejoin the land of the living. She pulled an elastic tie from the top desk drawer and twisted her damp hair into a topknot. Then, with a clean notepad and a blue ink pen, she made a list. She jotted down everything that came to mind, just as it came, in no particular order. She filtered nothing. The list went on for four pages by the time she was done, and it included major items like creating a business plan, setting up a website, and designing an ad to run in the local paper. Other important items on the list included eating better, getting a haircut, and buying new underwear.

Sid dropped her pen on the pad and turned to look at the pale gray business card she had gotten at Granny Oak's two nights before. She snatched it from under the magnet she had used to affix it to the metal file cabinet and stared at it for a while. Then, she flicked it back and forth against her chin until she finally made a decision. Why not? What did she have to lose? She dialed the number on the card and waited.

"Cielo Spa. How may I help you?"

Sid cleared her throat. "Hi, yes, this is Sidney Stone. I believe I have an appointment tomorrow morning." She looked at the card again. "I think it's for eleven o'clock with Gia. I just want to confirm that I have that correct."

"Just a moment, ma'am, and I'll check for you." Sid could hear the sound of long nails clicking against a keyboard. "Yes, Ms. Stone. We have you scheduled for a massage with Gia at eleven o'clock. Did you want to book any other treatments with us while you're here? A facial or a mani-pedi?"

"No, thanks. The massage is good. That's all I need." Sid ended the call and smiled to herself. She had almost asked how much it was going to cost her, but she didn't want to ruin her good mood. She'd use some of the money that J. T. Clement had paid her. It would be her first indulgence in, well, ever.

The rest of the afternoon was spent organizing her office and finishing her notes on Wes's case. When that was done, she began the slow, meticulous cataloging of all the information she had collected. There wasn't much in the way of hard evidence, but there might be something usable amid everything she had compiled. There was the burner phone and Cesar Hernandez's photos and repair records. She typed up summaries of her conversations with Detective Tony Davis and Commissioner J. T. Clement as well as everything she had learned about the Colquitt family. Sid left out the information that Leo had gleaned from his conversations with the spirit world. There was no way she was going to drag him any further into this mess.

Slowly and carefully, she disassembled the Wall of Shame. She made copies of any information worth sharing and organized everything into two sets of ringed binders, using colored tabs and plastic sheet protectors.

One set of binders was for her to keep. Sid cleared out one whole drawer of a file cabinet and placed this set of binders inside. She didn't need to torture herself anymore by looking at them every day. Three years of that torment had been enough. She found the key for that drawer and locked it. Whenever the dust eventually settled, be it weeks, months, or years from now, she would put those binders into boxes, seal them shut, and store them someplace completely out of sight.

The second, smaller set of binders was placed in the large drawer of her desk. This set was to be given to someone, although she wasn't exactly sure whom. She'd figure that out soon. Maybe Detective Davis would have some ideas.

By the time Sid was done, the top of her desk was clear, the Wall of Shame was bare but for the holes from the pushpins, and her watch read a quarter to two in the morning. Sid bagged up the trash, placed it by the door and made her way up the stairs to her apartment. She shrugged off the sweater she'd worn all day and tossed it aside as she climbed into bed. The air around her was still noticeably cool.

"Good night, Wes. Good night, Iris." Sid closed her eyes and smiled.

Chapter Thirty-One

Sid stepped into the air-conditioned waiting room of the Cielo Spa and was greeted by none other than Ava Owens.

"Oh, hi!" Ava stood up from the desk and smiled at her. She held out her hand, palm up, and wiggled her fingers. "Let me see. How are your nails holding up?"

Sid cringed as she stuck her hands out. "I'm afraid I put them through the wringer yesterday."

Ava frowned. "No kidding." She tsked but then winked at Sid. "We'll just have to book you for another manicure this week, won't we?"

"Let me check my calendar and get back to you," Sid answered as she leaned on the frosted glass reception desk. "I'm here for a massage. Eleven o'clock with Gia."

"Lucky you!" Ava typed away and then nodded. "I'll let her know you're here. Have a seat in the lounge, and she'll come get you in just a few." She waved her arm toward an arched doorway leading to another seating area. "Help yourself to anything. Today's water is lemon and pomegranate." She smiled and disappeared into the back.

Sid poured herself a glass of water from the large beverage dispenser and selected a snack bag of trail mix before sinking down into one of the buttery-soft leather chairs. The lounge smelled like lavender and eucalyptus and was decorated in shades of silver and gold. Sid relaxed into the chair and sipped the tart water, letting the dulcet tones of the harp and pan flute music being piped through the speakers wash over her.

"Ms. Stone?" A petite woman with light brown skin; short, black hair; and wide, dark eyes walked toward her. "My name is Gia. I'm ready for you. Please come with me."

Sid followed the woman into the depths of the spa, making so many turns that she was no longer sure how to find her way out. Gia ushered her into a small room decorated in the same silver and gold and emitting the same lavender-eucalyptus scent and pan flute music. After she gave Sid instructions on how to undress and lie on the table, Gia left her alone in the dimly lit room. Sid stepped behind the privacy screen in the corner, slipped off her sundress, and then moved to the padded massage table in the middle of the room. She slipped in between the cool sheets and lay down on her stomach. The headrest squished her cheeks so much that it was difficult to see, and she wondered if she was using it wrong. Sid closed her eyes and tried to relax.

A few minutes passed, and Sid was on the verge of falling asleep before the door opened again and Gia returned. "Ms. Stone?"

"Yep," answered Sid.

"Perhaps it would be best if you sat up."

"Huh?" Sid hugged the sheet to herself and turned to look at Gia. She shot up off the table, wrapping the sheet tightly around her.

Emmaline Colquitt held up her hands as the masseuse apologetically left the two women alone. "Relax, Ms. Stone. I'm just here to talk."

Sid stared at the woman standing in front of the door in a fitted, peach dress and kitten heels. Sid sidestepped to the privacy screen and ducked behind it, dressing as quickly as she could. "What would you like to talk about, Mrs. Colquitt?" she asked, feeling very much like a cornered animal.

"Call me Emmaline, please." She heard Emmaline take a seat on a rolling stool that had been tucked in the opposite corner near a cabinet housing an assortment of oils, lotions, and rolled-up towels. She waited for Sid to reemerge.

Once Sid finally stepped out from behind the screen, Emmaline smiled at her. "Please, take a seat. Would you like me to turn the lights up a bit?" She waved her manicured hands in the air. "This is definitely a mood, but probably not the one appropriate for the occasion. Do you agree, Sidney? May I call you Sidney?"

"Sure," replied Sid flatly. She sat in the chair against the wall where she'd taken off her shoes. "But if you wanted to meet with me, Emmaline, you could have just called me. I'm not sure all this cloak-and-dagger stuff is really necessary."

Emmaline smiled. "Oh, I assure you, it is. And I think you are going to want to hear what I have to say." She reached up and slid the dimmer switch so that the room brightened. "Much better. Now, let's see." She crossed her legs and smoothed the material of her skirt. "I had this all rehearsed in my head, but now that we're here, I seem to be a bit flummoxed."

"Let's start with the reason you wanted to speak to me in secret," suggested Sid. She crossed her legs, mimicking the other woman's body language.

"You're right. I should just say it." Emmaline exhaled and

nodded once. "I know you were hired by J. T. Clement to spy on his wife."

Sid raised an eyebrow. "I beg your pardon?"

Emmaline waved her hand. "There's no need to deny it. I know all about it."

Sid smirked. "If that were true, and I'm not saying that it is, how exactly would you know about it?"

"Because I was the one who made it happen."

Sid leaned back in her chair and let her head fall back against the wall with an audible thud. "I feel like that is probably the end of the story, Emmaline, so perhaps you should start at the very beginning."

"Oh, my dear, it's not the end. Not by a long shot." Emmaline tilted her head, causing her honey-blonde tresses to sway. "It might be the middle, at best."

"Fine." Sid's head was beginning to throb from the lavender, the pan flute, and the espionage. "Just start at the beginning."

Emmaline folded her hands in her lap and straightened her spine. "All right then, from the beginning. Three years ago, a terrible thing happened here that changed a lot of people's lives, including yours, mine, and Josette Clement's." Sid stared at the woman, who sat ramrod-straight on the other side of the room. Emmaline held her gaze. "You may or may not know this, but on Labor Day weekend three years ago, your husband pulled his patrol boat up alongside J. T. Clement's boat and almost arrested him for drunk boating." Emmaline paused for a moment, looking for a response from Sid.

"Okay." Sid shrugged slightly, unwilling to share any of her own knowledge with this woman.

"Well," continued Emmaline, "I was on that boat. Josie had begged me to come out with her, so I agreed. I got a sitter for Ruby, that's my youngest, and I joined her. Travis was working that day. Labor Day weekend is one of their busiest times of the year. You know all about that, I'm sure. Well, J. T. got very drunk, which is no great surprise. Josie was keeping an eye on him. We were not in any danger because we were going pretty slow, but still." She shrugged. "Apparently, he swerved close enough to some other boats that it caught the attention of the marine patrol, and they stopped us. Your husband boarded the boat and took J. T. aside. Words were exchanged, I don't know exactly what was said, but your husband's partner—what was his name? I always liked him." She tapped a polished nail on her chin.

"Manuel Sandoval. Manny."

"Yes, that's it. Manny." Emmaline nodded at Sid. "Well, Manny came aboard and spoke to your husband, your husband went back to the patrol boat, and Manny asked Josie to drive the boat home. She got us back to the dock, we all got off, and everyone went home. We thought that was it. All's well that ends well, right?" She gave a half-hearted chuckle. "Boy, were we wrong."

Emmaline began fiddling with a three-strand pearl bracelet on her right wrist. "Josie called me the next day. After we had docked and everyone left, J. T. just kept drinking. She said he got completely wasted. He was stumbling around. At one point, he tripped on an ottoman in the den and fell and hit his head. He was bleeding but didn't need stitches, thank goodness. As Josie was cleaning him up, he told her that he fucked up." Her hand flew to her neck. "Excuse my language."

"I've heard worse," said Sid.

"I'm sure." Emmaline smiled at her, a fellow cop's wife. "J. T. said he had fucked up and said something to your husband that he shouldn't have. It didn't make any sense to Josie at the time—or to me, for that matter. J. T. said something about liking Travis better than his twin brother, Troy. Troy died when they were kids. I don't know if you know that. Anyway, J. T. said that he liked Travis better than Troy, and it was too bad that Travis was the one who died." Emmaline shook her head. "We had no idea what that meant at the time, but J. T. was sufficiently freaked out about it to drink himself stupid. I told Josie not to worry, to put it out of her mind. J. T. was just drunk and got mixed up, and that's all there was to it."

She fiddled with her bracelet again. "I also told Josie not to say anything to anyone about it. And she hasn't. Only me, that one time." Emmaline lowered her eyes. "On the following Sunday, I hosted a garden party for the Women's Advancement Guild at my home. We have a small pool house, a little cabana really, and I always make sure I clear it out before we have guests over." She looked up at Sid. "My husband likes to hide things in the pool house." She lowered her eyes again. "I've found money, mostly. A few hundred here, a few thousand there. Sometimes marijuana. Nothing worse than that. I found a set of keys once. Some notes on scrap paper." She paused and cleared her throat. "A few phone numbers."

Sid shifted in her seat. "Are you sure it was all his? I mean, you have two daughters. Maybe some of it belonged to them?"

"I know my girls, Sidney," snapped Emmaline. "Besides, I've watched Travis disappear into the pool house after coming home from work enough times to get suspicious and eventually check it out. Sure enough, he was stashing stuff out there. He always did a good job, too. Up high, in a spot the girls couldn't reach. I had to step on a chair just to reach it myself." She smoothed her skirt again. "I always cleaned out his stash before we had company over. I'd move it inside and lock it away in our safe, and then I'd put it back the next day. There was never a problem. He never caught me, and I never said anything. Until the day of the garden party."

When she went quiet, Sid prodded. "What happened, Emmaline?"

Emmaline's voice was softer when she next spoke. "I went to the pool house early that morning, before the caterers arrived. I didn't want them to find whatever Travis had stashed there." She shook her head once. "But there wasn't any money or pot. There was just . . . a phone."

"A phone?" Sid sat up straight. "Tell me about it."

"An old flip phone. It might have been what's called a burner phone. It was turned off, and I was afraid to turn it on. I've been married to a cop for almost twenty years and watched enough crime shows and movies to know that you can trace phones, even burners. So I took it and put it in the safe, like I always do." She bit her lip. "I didn't get a chance to put it back before Travis got home that night, though. The party ran long, and the caterers were still packing up the last of their things when Travis pulled up. He went straight out to the pool house, and the next thing I know he's swearing up a storm and tossing lawn chairs into the pool and acting like a crazy person. He stormed into the house and demanded to know who had been in the pool house. He grabbed me and shook me. I swear, I felt the fillings in my teeth loosen."

She placed a hand on her cheek. "I told him that I didn't know. There'd been close to a hundred people at the party, plus the catering staff. I told him anyone could have been in the pool house. Well, he didn't like that answer very much. He threw some things. Broke some things. And then he stormed out. Just drove off and didn't come back that night."

"So when he realized the phone was missing, he went berserk. Was that typical for him?" asked Sid, her brow furrowing. "Does he normally lose his temper?"

Emmaline looked around the room, as if the answer to the question was hidden among the towels or bottles of oil. "Sometimes. Travis is usually very much in control of his emotions. I've known him long enough to know that he works very hard to maintain his composure. But occasionally, he slips up, and when he does, it's like his whole personality changes. It's like he becomes a different person."

Emmaline held Sid's gaze for a long moment without blinking. "Travis doesn't talk about his childhood very much. He sticks to a few basic stories and doesn't tend to expound on them. But he has told me a few things about his twin brother, Troy. Not many, but a few. Troy seemed like a troubled young man, always getting into trouble. Fights. Shoplifting. That sort of thing. Travis worried that he was heading for bigger trouble, bigger crimes. He had a few run-ins with the law and was suspended from school. He would have probably ended up in jail. Travis thought it was just a matter of time."

Emmaline rolled her stool forward a couple of feet. "Whenever Travis lost his temper, I wondered if maybe that was what Troy had been like. I wondered if Travis had a bit of Troy's personality in him. And then Josie told me what J. T. said, and I thought maybe I hadn't been too far off." She hesitated a moment, as though she was nervous to share aloud what she'd been thinking for a long while. "Maybe Travis . . . maybe he actually was Troy."

Sid nodded once, and Emmaline took it as a sign to continue. "After Travis stormed out, I took the phone out of our safe and hid it. I put it in my box of tampons." A corner of her mouth twitched up. "I knew he'd never look in there. Anyway, I thought he might be having an affair. That's all I thought at the time, I swear."

Emmaline Colquitt straightened her spine again and uncrossed her legs. "I took the phone with me to the WAGs meeting the next Wednesday night. I thought if Travis was going to cheat, he'd do it with someone who was wealthy and well positioned. He wouldn't run the risk of getting caught with some pretty young thing who could ruin him. No, Travis would pick someone who could make a scandal go away."

"And that would have been one of the WAGs?" Sid smirked.

Emmaline shrugged. "I had no idea who it might be, but it was the best place to start looking." She began twirling her pearl bracelet again. "As everyone was coming in and getting settled in their seats, right before the meeting started, I moved to the back of the room and turned on the phone. There was only one number listed in the contacts, and only one call had been made to that number. So I called it." She cleared her throat again. "The phone rang, and I watched the room, waiting for someone to reach into their purse to pick up their phone and answer it."

Sid shook her head. "But no one did."

Emmaline shook her head, too. "No, no one did. It went to voicemail, and I hung up and turned off the phone as soon as I heard the message." She licked her lips. "Sidney, it was your husband's voicemail. My husband had hidden a burner phone in our pool house with your husband's number in it."

Sid knew this part of the story already, but she raised her eyebrows in mock surprise. "What did you do then, Emmaline?"

Emmaline's eyes were wide. "I left the meeting and drove straight to my office. I put the phone in a small cardboard box, taped it shut, and wrote on it, 'PRIVATE. DO NOT OPEN,' in big capital letters. Then, I put the box in one of my office safes."

Sid raised an eyebrow. "Why didn't you take it to the police?"

Emmaline barked a laugh. "The police? My husband *is* the police. He's the sheriff of this county. The *sheriff*. He *is* the law around here, and he's the one who hid the phone in my damn pool house!"

"Okay, you're right." Sid held up her hands. "I get that you didn't know what to do."

Emmaline reeled her emotions back in and tucked a wavy strand of hair behind her ear. "I knew enough about your husband's—his *case* . . . to assume that the phone was probably involved. I knew about your husband getting a call that night to go get his new partner out of trouble. I heard about that, and I thought it was nuts. Why would Antonio Davis be drunk at the shooting range? I had just seen him and his lovely wife and their beautiful little boy at Manny's retirement party."

Sid sat up. "You were there, weren't you?" She had forgotten that Emmaline and Travis Colquitt had been at the party. There were so many people coming and going that night, and the details had blurred in the aftermath of the crash.

"Yes, we stopped by on our way back into town. We'd gone to Gainesville that day for the Gators' season opener. We were such a mess, all sweaty from the game, but Travis insisted that we go, so we made an appearance. We stayed maybe half an hour, but that was it. I made Travis take Ruby and me home. He dropped us off and then went into work. Said he needed to check on things since he'd been gone all day." She shrugged. "I was too tired to ask any questions. Ruby and I got cleaned up, watched some TV, and went to bed. Travis came home late. I was already asleep. He was in the shower when the phones started ringing. People were calling him to tell him there was an officer down, so he got dressed and left again. I didn't see him until late the next morning when the caterers were setting up. He was only home long enough to shower and have a sandwich, and then he was gone again."

Emmaline pressed her fingers to her lips and shook her head. "I don't know why Travis had that phone with your husband's number in it. Honestly, I don't know any more about it than that. It's just . . ." She clasped her hands in her lap. "He hasn't been the same since he discovered it missing the night of the garden party. It's like he can barely contain his anger most days. He tries so hard. I can see him straining to do it, but he loses his temper a lot more often now."

Sid frowned. "Has he hit you?"

Emmaline shook her head. "No. He hasn't been violent toward me or the girls, but he's thrown things. Kicked things. Broken things. It's getting worse and worse." She sat up straight again and held Sid's gaze. "So I came up with a plan, and it involves you."

Chapter Thirty-Two

If Emmaline didn't have Sid's attention before, she certainly did now.

Sid shifted in her seat. "Well, don't keep me in suspense."

The sheriff's wife cleared her throat. "A few months ago, Josie and I went to lunch and got to talking as we usually do, and she mentioned out of the blue that she was thinking of leaving J. T." Emmaline held up her hand. "Now, Sidney, you have to understand what a very big deal that was for Josie. She never shares any personal issues about her marriage. Never. But there she was, telling me that she wanted out. When I asked why, she told me that J. T. was having an affair.

"She wasn't sure how long the affair had been going on, but she suspected it was for several months. And then she told me who it was. Well . . ." Emmaline shut her eyes and shook her head, trying to clear out the unsavory thought. "Let's just say, the woman is very young. Practically a girl. She *is* over eighteen, but still."

Sid bit her tongue. There was a lot that neither Emmaline

nor Josie knew, and Sid wasn't about to share. "That must have been devastating."

"Yes, it was." Emmaline nodded as if she had been the one devastated. "Josie said she wanted to divorce J. T. and move back to Savannah. She was afraid, though, of how her family would react to her coming back home, divorced and childless." Emmaline rolled her eyes. "She comes from old money, and scandal would not be welcomed in the family."

"And divorce is scandalous?" Sid raised an eyebrow.

"In some circles? Very." Emmaline smirked. "Especially when the ex-son-in-law has been spending that old money like it was going out of style." She sighed and waved a hand. "But Josie told me about a cousin of hers, Clara, who is sort of the rebel in the family. She's been divorced several times, so Josie was hoping that she could stay with her. Well, Clara owns a real estate firm that the family thinks is doing very well, but Clara let it slip to Josie that she's in financial trouble. Too much debt and too few sales."

Emmaline tossed her hair and set her shoulders. "So I devised a plan. I set Josie up to get her Georgia real estate license and added her to my agency here under a fake name so that she could get a little experience. My partner didn't care. We do very well under my leadership, so he defers to me on most things. Anyway, she is scheduled to take her license exam this week. Once she passes, she can move to Savannah and start working for Clara's firm."

Sid gave Emmaline a half smile. "That's very nice of you, to help your friend like that."

Emmaline waved the notion away. "Oh, it's not just for her. It's my ticket out as well. I'm divorcing my husband and taking the Georgia exam, too. I've convinced my partner to buy me out here. Then I'll use the proceeds of the sale to buy into Clara's firm at a fifty-percent stake. That will be enough to clear her debt and give the business a nice capital infusion."

Sid nodded slowly. "Sounds like a plan." Emmaline smiled, obviously pleased with herself. Sid held up a finger. "But where exactly do I come in?"

"Ah, yes." Emmaline's smile brightened. "I thought you could help us."

"I'm afraid I don't know anything about selling real estate." Sid shrugged. "Or any sort of wheeling and dealing for that matter."

"No, no, no. I need you to help us with our divorces. You see, I've been keeping tabs on you ever since . . . well, since your husband died." Emmaline's smile faded. "I knew you had taken over for that private investigator who retired. Murphy or something like that."

"Murdock. Trip Murdock," Sid offered.

"Right. Well, I thought since you were a PI, you must be trying to solve your husband's case." She leaned forward. "I don't think anyone around here believes it was a suicide. Why no one has pursued it further is a mystery to me." She shook her head. "Well, maybe it's not much of a mystery after all, if my husband . . ." She shook her head again. "Anyway, I needed to get you in the mix, but Josie didn't want you investigating J. T.'s affair."

Too late, thought Sid.

"No, she doesn't want that made public. She wants to be able to use it as leverage against him when she files for divorce," explained Emmaline.

Sid fought the urge to smile, thinking of all the photos she could share with Josie if the need arose.

"I suggested to Josie that we have you investigate *her*." Emmaline smiled again. "I knew you wouldn't find anything. Josie's as squeaky clean as they come, so I planted a seed with

Travis. I mentioned that I thought Josie had been acting strangely, that maybe she could be cheating on J. T., seeing someone else on the side." She shrugged. "I knew it wouldn't take much. He and J. T. are such gossips whenever they get together. I suggested to him that J. T. should hire someone to investigate, but that he'd better hire a woman. Otherwise, Josie would figure it out."

"And you recommended me?"

Emmaline batted the idea away with a wave of her hand. "I didn't need to. You're the only female private investigator in town, Sidney. I knew Travis would *have* to recommend you to J. T."

Sid nodded, wondering if Emmaline knew that J. T. had independently arrived at the same conclusion. He had thought it was his idea to hire Sid while Emmaline thought it was part of her own brilliant plan. Sid was pretty sure the only person who hadn't wanted Sid hired was Sheriff Colquitt.

Emmaline clasped her hands in her lap. "Well, sure enough, Travis tells me that J. T. has hired a PI, and Josie confirmed it was you."

Sid coughed and sputtered. "How was she able to confirm it?"

Emmaline smiled. "My dear, we set the whole thing up. We choreographed all her movements. Her calendar, all her meetings and appointments. She caught a glimpse of you following her one day."

"Shit!" Sid hissed under her breath.

"Oh, don't beat yourself up, Sidney." Emmaline chuckled. "Josie knew to look for you. If she hadn't known you were out there in the shadows, she never would have spotted you. She only saw you once, but we assumed you had been following her for days." She tilted her head to the side. "By any chance, did you call Liesel Winfield posing as Paizley Rogers?"

Sid's brow furrowed. "Maybe."

"I knew it!" Emmaline clapped with glee. "I won't tell Josie. She thinks she actually came close to landing a client, but I suspected it was you when the appointment was cancelled at the last minute." She clapped again, so pleased with herself. "Anyway, I thought it would be useful to have Josie investigated and cleared of having an affair. It will make her look better in the divorce, especially given J. T.'s own philandering."

Sid nodded. "And what about you? How am I supposed to help you in your divorce?"

Emmaline grew serious. "I needed to make sure you were looking into your husband's case. That's why I planted Travis's burner phone on Detective Davis's wife. My plan was to slip it into your purse, but then I saw Detective Davis and his wife and their little boy when we arrived at Granny Oak's on Friday, and I thought that Heaven must be sending me a sign. I knew he had been your husband's partner, and I knew he had recently made detective. I thought you might be able to use him, sort of like having a man on the inside."

Sid kept her breathing steady, trying to make sure she caught every word. "So *you* called me from the burner phone?"

"I did." Emmaline nodded. "I reactivated the phone. Turns out that prepaid minutes expire. Who knew? I certainly didn't. But I did some research, and I added minutes to the phone. I also added your phone number to the contacts so it would be ready to go."

"How did you do that?" asked Sid. "If you don't mind me asking."

"Not at all." Emmaline smiled. "When I decided to put all of this in motion, I fired up the phone again and discovered that it didn't work. No more minutes. Well, as it so happens, I have a stack of Visa gift cards in a drawer at home. I send Scarlett one a month in a little care package. Her father doesn't know I do this. He's got her on a strict budget, but sometimes a girl just needs a little spending money, you know?" She shrugged. "I called the phone carrier, can't remember which one now, and added minutes to the phone. It was pretty easy . . . and I did it from Travis's office at work."

A small, nervous laugh escaped her, but she recovered herself and continued. "Travis and I had plans to meet for lunch one day. This was about a month ago. I was supposed to meet him at his office at noon, but I arrived early. I knew he would still be stuck in a meeting, so I waited for him in his office. And I used his office line to reactivate the burner phone. It was risky, I know, but I thought, if my call was traced or they somehow tracked the burner phone, it would lead back to Travis. Once I added new minutes, I shut the phone off again, and I just waited. I carried that thing around with me in a little bag in my purse with my tampons and such." She winked. "As I said, no one would look in there.

"When I saw Detective Davis at Granny Oak's, I decided to give the phone to him instead of you. I made up an excuse to step away from our group. I said I wanted to call Ruby to make sure she was okay, but instead, I turned on the burner phone and dialed your number. I made sure it rang once, and then I hung up. Then I walked behind Detective Davis's wife and slipped the phone into her bag."

Sid swept her arm wide. "And you already had this appointment lined up and ready to go?"

"It's my usual appointment," Emmaline explained. "Every Monday at eleven o'clock with Gia. I had Gia change the name in the system to yours. I even had her fill out the little appointment card with your name on it. I've been doing that for several weeks now. I knew this would be where I'd be able to talk to you in secret. Gia can be trusted. I've been coming to her for years. Besides, I promised to give her a very healthy tip when I finally got you in here.

"I knew J. T. had terminated your investigation on Friday. Travis told me that afternoon when he got home, right before we left to go to Granny Oak's. He told me that the case was over, and that Josie was not cheating on J. T. I knew I needed to be ready just in case I saw you there." She waved her hand. "I saw the social media post from the venue saying that Recent Geezer was going to be playing that night. I love the Geezers, by the way. They are *so* good."

Sid sighed. "Mm-hm. So good."

"I know you live at Burt Roberts's place and that he's in the band, so I thought you might be there." She held up her hands in victory. "And you were!"

Sid sighed again. "Maybe *you* should be the private investigator, Emmaline."

"Ooh, wouldn't that be fun? I think I'd be pretty good, don't you?" Sid smiled and nodded, and Emmaline's chest puffed with pride. "Anyway, the other reason you are here today is because I'd like to hire you to investigate my husband. Specifically, I'd like to know if my husband is involved in your husband's death." She nodded once, all business. "I want a divorce, and I want it to be quick and uncontested, so I want you to find out what happened to your husband and whether my husband had anything to do with it. In addition, I want you to find out whether he really is Travis Colquitt or whether he is actually Troy, the twin brother who supposedly died in that boating accident all those years ago, as I suspect he might be. Either way, I want to use whatever you can find out about my husband as leverage against him in our divorce."

Sid bit her tongue again and wondered how many more times she could do it before drawing blood. "Emmaline, what if I find out that your husband killed my husband? We might be talking about murder here. That's much more serious than a simple divorce proceeding. You realize that this could result in criminal charges, right? It would be a huge scandal . . . for you, your family." Emmaline nodded, though her lower lip trembled. "And you're okay with that?"

"No, I'm not *okay* with that, Sidney." Emmaline's voice cracked. "But I'm married to a man who may be lying about who he is, pretending to be his twin brother who died almost thirty years ago. I'm married to a man who may have been involved in the death of a fellow law enforcement officer. And I am living with a man whose temper is getting more and more violent every day." Emmaline blinked rapidly, fighting against threatening tears. "I love Travis. I really do, but I'm scared for my girls. I'm scared for myself. Most of all, I'm scared about what all of this is doing to him. I see the toll it's taking on him. He's losing his grip, and I don't want to be in the line of fire when he's no longer able to hold on."

Sid nodded. "I understand. If I were you, I wouldn't want to be there either."

"I'll pay you whatever you want, but I need you to do one more thing for me, Sidney." Emmaline held her pointed chin high. "Please."

"What's that, Emmaline?" asked Sid.

The sheriff's wife smoothed the material of her skirt once again. "I want you to wait at least until the end of this week before you go public with anything." She held up a hand to stop Sid from speaking. "You can investigate all you want. I only ask that you be discreet about it. Josie and I are taking the Georgia real estate license exam on Wednesday. If you agree to help me, I will call my lawyer and have her file the divorce papers on Friday morning. The timing will work out perfectly. The papers are all ready to go. My lawyer drew them up months ago, both for me and Josie, and she's been holding them for us. She'll have our husbands served right away."

Her voice caught again, and she cleared her throat. "I already have plans for Josie to join me, Ruby, and Scarlett in St. Pete Beach for a little girls-only vacation. We're going to pick up Scarlett at UF on Friday morning because it's the end of her summer semester, and then we're all heading over to see my parents in Tampa for a night and then to the beach for a couple more nights after that." Emmaline smiled. "But now, we can head straight to Savannah instead, right after we pick of Scarlett. Clara's been on standby for a number of weeks, so she'll be ready for us. We can start getting set up there. It'll be the beginning of our fresh start."

She gave Sid a half smile. "You know, I got pregnant my sophomore year of college. Travis and I got married and moved into an apartment together. I dropped out of school to take care of the baby, but Travis kept going. Scarlett was nearly two when he graduated, and then we moved here to St. Augustine. He became a deputy, and I got my real estate license. I built my business, made a lot of money, and did it almost all by myself. My parents were so disappointed in me when I got pregnant. They helped us out financially until Travis got his first job, but when they found out he was going to be a cop . . ." She laughed. "They thought that kind of job was beneath them, that it was too low for them and their high society friends. It was one thing for their daughter to get knocked up and drop out of school, but it was quite another to have their son-in-law working in such a blue-collar job as law enforcement.

"I never told Travis about my parents' . . . distaste." She shrugged. "He had enough to worry about, like not getting killed on the job. You know what I mean, don't you? They softened up a bit more when Ruby came along, more still when Travis was elected sheriff." She shook her head. "But I often think . . . if I were that age today, the same age as Scarlett is now, I would make sure that I didn't get pregnant. I'd finish college, go to law school. Who knows? My life could have been very different."

"You seem to have done pretty well for yourself, Emmaline." Sid smiled. "Even if you had to fight for all of it yourself."

Emmaline nodded. "I did turn out pretty well, didn't I? And my girls are turning out well, too. Or at least, I'm hopeful that they will." She twirled her bracelet again. "But I worry that won't be the case if I don't leave him. I worry what will happen to them—and to me—if I stay. I can't take that risk, Sidney."

Sid held the woman's gaze for several moments and then blew out a breath. "Well then, as my new client, I think you and I should have a further chat about the case. After that, you can tell me exactly what you want me to do on Friday, Emmaline."

Chapter Thirty-Three

On the following Friday morning, Sidney Stone sat in an uncomfortable wooden chair in a noisy reception room in the St. Johns County judicial center, about a quarter of a mile down the road from J. T. Clement's office. Emmaline Colquitt had made a phone call to set up this meeting before she and Sid left the privacy of the massage room at the Cielo Spa on Monday. Now, Sid's foot bounced nervously, tapping the cardboard box that held her second set of binders.

The reception room's door opened, and Tony Davis poked his head in and looked around. He was wearing a suit, as was Sid. She'd had to buy one at the outlet mall near the highway the day before. Tony sat down next to her. "You ready?"

Sid nodded. "Yep. Did you bring it?"

He patted his jacket pocket where the burner phone was tucked neatly out of sight. "Yep." He blew out a breath. "Shit's gonna hit the fan after this."

"I know." Sid's foot continued to tap against the box. "It already is. Emmaline and Josie are filing for divorce right now. The sheriff and the commissioner should find out by the end of

"

the day. Apparently, Emmaline's lawyer is very good and has a process server ready to go."

Tony tilted his head back and rested it against the wall. "Those women may get what they want, but there's no guarantee you'll get what you want out of all of this." He shook his head. "There's not much evidence, Sid. A good defense attorney could probably poke enough holes in the case to allow Travis Colquitt to drive his big-ass truck through it."

"I know that, too." Sid smiled at the detective. "But he won't be sheriff anymore. There's no way he survives this politically. I'm going to make sure of that." She sighed. "As for criminal charges, I'm going to have to put that in someone else's hands. I've done my part to solve my husband's murder. Now it's time for others to get off their asses and do their damn jobs."

A wide grin crossed Tony's face. "Certainly is."

"By the way, thanks for coming to my office Wednesday night," she said, tilting her head back against the wall to mimic Tony's position.

He turned to look at Sid. "I can't believe you got Emmaline Colquitt to make a video statement implicating her husband in Wes's murder."

Sid smiled. "Me neither. I was sure she'd laugh in my face when I suggested it, but she didn't. In fact, she got all excited and told me she would sneak out of her WAGs meeting to do it. Besides, she'll be out of town for a while, so her statement should help speed things along." Sid nudged the box with her foot. "Brought it with me. Two copies, just to be safe."

Tony chuckled. "That was nice of her. It was also nice that she ID'd the burner phone and explained how it ended up in Naomi's bag."

"Wasn't it, though?" Sid grinned to herself. "Bless her heart."

Tony checked his watch. "Does Barnes know what this meeting is about today?"

Sid nodded. "She has a general idea."

Tessa Barnes was the state attorney for St. Johns County. Recently re-elected to a second term, Tessa was enjoying a high approval rating and favorable publicity from a few big wins, including a major drugs case and a human trafficking case. She also happened to be the law school classmate of Emmaline Colquitt's divorce attorney, Carleigh Sutton.

Emmaline and Carleigh graduated from high school together in Tampa, roomed together their first year at the University of Florida, and stayed friends despite one of them getting pregnant and dropping out of college. Carleigh Sutton graduated with honors and went straight to law school at UF, where she became fast friends with the talented and fiercely competitive, Tessa Barnes.

The two lawyers got jobs in St. Augustine right out of school, Carleigh with a boutique family law firm and Tessa as an assistant state attorney. On Monday, after Carleigh received the call from Emmaline telling her about Sidney Stone's investigation, she immediately called Tessa and suggested she take a meeting on Friday with the local PI. Tessa agreed without hesitation, and Sid received a phone call within an hour of leaving the Cielo Spa, confirming the ten o'clock appointment with State Attorney Barnes.

Sid folded her hands across her stomach and closed her eyes. Tessa Barnes was running late, but Sid wasn't worried. The meeting would happen today. There was no way the ambitious state attorney would miss out on the opportunity to blow this sordid affair wide open, so Sid would wait as long as necessary. Her box was full of binders, all of them painstakingly organized and color coded. She had Emmaline's statement on video, detailing everything that she'd told Sid in the massage room on Monday. She had Detective Tony Davis sitting next to her with the burner phone in his pocket, ready to give his own statement to the prosecutor.

And Sid had her two presentations—a quick, five-minute one hitting the highlights that she would use if Tessa Barnes was distracted or in a hurry and a second, twenty-minute presentation in which she would walk the attorney through all of the events, starting with the Colquitts' thirty-year-old boating accident down in Jupiter Inlet and ending with Emmaline's video from two days ago.

She inhaled deeply and exhaled a long, slow breath, trying to calm her nerves. Sid wasn't worried that she wouldn't be taken seriously. Her box of files, Emmaline's statement, and the presence of Detective Tony Davis would guarantee that Tessa Barnes, at the very least, would hear what she had to say. Sid wasn't even worried about the possibility that the case might go nowhere, that Travis Colquitt wouldn't be arrested or prosecuted or convicted. There was a very real possibility that Tessa Barnes would take one look at the information Sid presented and decide to do nothing with it. It was an unlikely possibility, but a real one nonetheless.

Sid could only make her pitch to Tessa Barnes here today and leave the rest in the prosecutor's hands. Travis Colquitt might indeed be arrested. He might be prosecuted for murder or fraud or false personation or any other crime that Tessa would come up with. He might go to jail, or he might walk free. Sid had no control over what would happen, but she was definitely going to make sure that all of it appeared in the newspapers. She would make sure the local news stations were tipped off, and she would make sure that Sheriff Colquitt spent his days dodging reporters for as long as possible. Sidney Stone would make sure that Travis Colquitt was never re-elected sheriff of St. Johns County, or any place else, ever again.

No, Sid wasn't nervous about any of that. There was only one thing that worried her, and that was Burt's reaction to what she was going to say to him when she cornered him this afternoon down at the Crane's Roost. She was going to tell him that she was staying put, that she was keeping Leo on as an intern because she firmly believed that it was the best thing for the boy, and that she was all in for helping make sure Leo thrived in his new home here in St. Augustine. She had no plans to step in as a surrogate parent to the boy, not like Burt had done for her, but she would agree to help. She would be one of the villagers it would take to raise the child and ensure he developed into a healthy, well-adjusted young man. Sid winced at the idea. How exactly that was to be achieved was eluding her at the moment, but she was convinced it included Leo's continued involvement in her private investigation business and her continued support of his ability to see and talk to spirits.

The glass door leading to the inner chaos of the office opened behind the reception desk and a tall, gangly young man in a navy suit emerged. His collar was unbuttoned, his pale blue tie was askew, and a sprinkling of acne decorated his jawline. Sid smiled. The young man reminded her of Leo.

She marveled at how her heart swelled at the thought. She'd gotten so used to it squeezing with a mixture of sympathy for him and sadness for herself whenever he was around that these new feelings kept catching her off guard. She hadn't felt such maternal things in a long time. Almost three years, to be exact.

Sid blew out a breath. Whatever was about to happen between Sheriff Colquitt and the justice system was out of her hands. A part of her understood that and knew she'd have to accept it. And yet she was still angry, so very angry. If not for the sheriff's selfish actions, both Wes and Iris would be alive right now. Sheriff Colquitt would have to pay for her loss one way or another. Sid hoped Tessa Barnes would see to it.

But rising to meet that anger was a feeling of relief. Sid was beginning to feel a strange sense of peace, and it was all thanks to Leo. The kid had given her something important, something she'd been missing for the last three years. He'd given her answers. He'd given her certainty. And he'd given her the opportunity to say goodbye to the two people she loved most in the world.

"Ms. Stone? Detective Davis?" The young man in the navy suit looked around the busy reception room. When Sid raised her hand, he motioned to her. "Mrs. Barnes will see you now."

Chapter Thirty-Four

Sid plucked a hush puppy out of her takeout container and handed it to Dante. The little boy happily took it from her and dunked it into a pile of ketchup. He wriggled a few inches closer to her and smiled up at her, his mouth now full to bursting with fried cornmeal. Dante was sitting between Sid and Naomi at the picnic table, and Sid wondered how soon it would be before the little boy's mountain of ketchup ended up all over him—and her.

Recent Geezer was getting ready to take the stage, filling in again for another band who had canceled at the last minute, and the crowd at Granny Oak's Music Park was beginning to swell. Tony and Leo returned to the picnic table carrying drinks from the bar and took up seats on the opposite side.

"What should we toast to?" asked Tony, handing a plastic cup of white wine to his wife and reserving a beer for himself. "To closing your first big case?"

Sid shook her head. "Let's toast to second chances." She looked around the table and smiled. That's how life felt to her at that moment: like a second chance. A second chance for friendship, for caring about people, for living life again.

"To second chances," echoed Naomi, lifting her cup.

"And to absent friends," muttered Leo. When the others looked at him, he shrugged. "It's what my dad always said." His eyes flicked to Sid, but he quickly lowered them. "Sort of seems appropriate."

"Agreed." Sid smiled at him when he glanced up at her again. "To absent friends." She clinked her plastic cup with his across the table, and everyone set about devouring their trays of fried fish and coleslaw.

Leo kept checking his phone every few minutes, so Sid nudged his leg under the table with her foot. "Hot date?" She chuckled when his ears turned bright pink.

"No," he mumbled and looked down at his phone. Sid nudged him again, and he smirked. "Maybe." Leo's phone buzzed, and he read the incoming text. "Um, Sid?" He glanced over his shoulder toward the entrance.

Sid followed his gaze and saw a teenage girl with a long ponytail, who looked suspiciously like Ava Owen, scanning the crowd. "Invite her over," she urged. Leo's eyes went wide, and his blush grew even pinker. "Go on! We're not going to bite." She held up her hands. "I promise we will not embarrass you."

Leo furrowed his brow, trying to decide whether to trust his boss. Tony nudged him with his elbow. "Don't keep the young lady waiting, son. Invite her over."

"Neither of them will do anything to embarrass you," Naomi reassured him. "If they do, they'll have me to deal with." She winked, and Leo broke into a bright smile.

"Okay. I'll be right back." He got up and snaked his way through the other picnic tables toward the music park's entrance.

"So the kid's going to keep working for you?" asked Tony, popping a fried shrimp into his mouth.

Sid nodded. "I can't pay him much right now, of course, but I'm hoping that will change soon."

"I imagine it will." Naomi lifted her cup. "Word on the street is that J. T. Clement was served divorce papers at a Rotary Club luncheon today, in full view of half the business-people in town."

"And the sheriff got served today in the office. It's all anyone can talk about. Didn't help himself by swearing and shouting and turning his desk over." Tony chuckled. "Poor bastard."

"Really? Is that what you think?" Naomi cocked an eyebrow.

Tony grinned. "If he's mad now, just wait until all hell breaks loose with the State Attorney's Office."

"And the local news hears about it." Sid smiled and took a sip of her beer.

"Poor bastard indeed." Naomi raised her cup again and took a sip.

Leo arrived back at the picnic table with Ellie Owen in tow. She sat next to him and was introduced around the table.

"I like your shirt!" announced Dante at full volume. Ellie was wearing a Rolling Stones T-shirt that someone—a vintage shop, Sid guessed—had made sleeveless. Dante stuck out his tongue to mimic the iconic logo and giggled as his mom quickly wiped the ketchup from his chin.

"Thanks. It's new," said Ellie, glancing down at the shirt and then over at Leo.

Leo blushed again. He'd bought the shirt for her online with the money he'd made finding Hercules for the hysterical couple at the Crane's Roost. Ellie had mentioned that his hair reminded her of Mick Jagger's, which he didn't quite understand. Did she mean young Mick Jagger or old Mick Jagger? Leo didn't think he had hair that looked like either version of Jagger, but he wasn't about to correct her. The Rolling Stones shirt popped up when he was searching for vintage tees, looking for others like his dad's old ones, and he bought it on impulse and paid for express shipping. He wrapped it in birthday paper and had given it to her earlier today at the start of her shift. He said it was a thank-you gift for the free ice cream cone she'd given him as a belated birthday present. In reality, it was a thank-you gift for helping him learn about J. T.'s extramarital affair, but he could never tell her that. Ellie had laughed, a sound Leo definitely wanted to hear more of, and she promised him free kid-size cones for life.

Ellie smiled at Dante. "It was a gift for my birthday."

"Happy birthday!" squealed Dante.

"Yes, happy birthday," said Sid. "Is it today?"

Ellie smiled and shook her head. "April." Sid frowned and glanced at Leo who glared back at her, shaking his head slightly in a plea for her to keep her promise not to embarrass him.

Recent Geezer took the stage to raucous applause and began playing. Dante danced a jig in his seat while continuing to dip his fries in ketchup. When Ellie reached for Leo's fries, he happily slid the container toward her.

Leo's phone buzzed in his pocket, and he removed it and looked at the screen. The incoming text was from his mom, and he read the first line.

Change of plans

Leo inwardly groaned. PB&J's latest posts were from St. Pete Beach. They'd arrived only yesterday, and yet they'd posted a dozen new photos of colorful shops, outdoor cafes, and bright beach umbrellas. Leo knew from her initial itinerary that they were supposed to head to Gainesville on Sunday and then over to St. Augustine. After that, they had planned to go to Amelia Island, then Savannah, and then on to Charleston, South Carolina. He opened the text and read on.

Skipping gainesville heading to panama city

Leo frowned as another text came in.

Then to nola

Leo leaned across the table. "Hey, Sid. Where's Panama City?"

Sid swallowed a mouthful of coleslaw. "In the panhandle. West of Tallahassee. Why?"

Leo ignored her question. "And 'nola'? Where's that?"

Sid sighed inwardly, the realization of what he was asking dawning on her. "New Orleans." She watched as his face fell and his shoulders slumped.

Sid wanted to scream. Paizley-with-a-Z was disappointing her son again, which likely meant she'd delayed her visit to St. Augustine. Sid wanted to find that woman in whatever beach chair or cocktail bar she was sitting in right now and drag her up here to spend time with her son, to learn how he was doing, to see for herself just how far he'd come in the weeks since she dumped him on Burt's doorstep.

Leo nodded. "Thanks." Another text arrived.

Not coming to st aug next week

Then another.

Might be a few weeks before we get there

And another.

Will keep you posted love you xoxo

Leo sighed, held the phone in his lap, and thought about how to reply. He was disappointed, he couldn't deny that. But the disappointment wasn't overwhelming, certainly not like it had been before. There was only a small part of him that was disappointed, and he realized that if his mom showed up right now and asked him to go with her, he'd probably say no.

Leo didn't want to be a third wheel to his mom and Brooklyn—or rather, a fourth wheel if you counted the fluffy, white dog. He didn't want to sleep in a tent beside the polka-dotted camper and share a sleeping bag with Jezebel and her stupid hairbows. "Huh," he mumbled under his breath as that revelation hit him.

Glancing around, he watched Dante dancing in his seat, wiping his ketchup-soaked fingers down the front of his shirt. He watched Tony and Naomi smiling at each other across the picnic table. He felt the brush of Ellie's leg against his own as she reached for another fry, and he watched Sid finish off the last of her beer and smile at him as she set her cup down.

Sid was looking better, he thought. In the past week, she'd showered every day, gone shopping, and gotten a haircut. He'd caught her smiling more these past few days, too. Her dimples now made regular appearances. Leo returned Sid's smile, knowing that he'd played a role in that change.

He had helped her find answers. Helped her say goodbye. Helped her move on.

And she had offered him a permanent job. She still wasn't really paying him, but she promised that would change if they began bringing in regular clients. Leo had a feeling that would happen soon, once news broke that she'd cracked the case of Wes's murder and Sheriff Colquitt's secret identity.

Leo glanced up at the stage, tapping his foot to the beat. His grandfather was rocking out with the other Geezers. The colored lanterns, strung from the limbs of the giant oak over-head, cast the scene in warm shades of gold, pink, and blue. People were clapping to the music; some were dancing in front of the stage. This was not a bad life, he thought. He let his gaze wander over the crowd, and it snagged on a familiar face.

Mad Hattie sat on a concrete planter off on the far right side of the park. She bobbed her head to the music. Gone was her big straw hat and flowing patterned skirts. She wore a billowy, black sundress and her signature sunglasses. Her dreadlocks were pulled back at the nape of her neck. When she caught Leo staring at her, she smiled her toothless grin. Leo waved, and she waved back.

Good and evil, he thought. That had been Hattie's lesson to him the first day he met her. She was right, of course. The Old City had been built by good and evil, and those two things were keeping it running.

Leo inhaled deeply, the scents of beer, fried food, and sweat hanging heavy in the humid night air. At this moment, the scales seemed to be tipping more to the side of good. If Sheriff Colquitt was arrested and sent to jail, there'd be a lot less evil around, at least for a little while. Thanks to Sid, thanks to Tony, thanks to Wes and Iris . . . and thanks to himself.

Recent Geezer finished their first song and launched into their rendition of George Thorogood & The Destroyers' "Who Do You Love?" Dante scooted off the bench and grabbed Sid by the hand, tugging her toward the stage.

"Oh, okay. We're dancing now, are we?" Sid scrambled out of her seat as Dante dragged her with him. She twirled the little boy around as he squealed with delight, and then Dante began clapping and busting out dance moves that made Sid blink in surprise. Tony burst out laughing, and Naomi groaned with embarrassment.

"The kid's got my moves," said Tony as he shimmied his shoulders.

Naomi rolled her eyes. "I wouldn't be braggin' about that."

Leo watched as Sid danced with the little boy. She looked happy. Honestly and truly happy. He picked up his phone and typed a message to his mother. One line.

Have fun

Leo smiled to himself. That was all he wanted to say to her right now. If she wanted more, she could call him. He knew she wouldn't, though, and he was okay with that. She could travel around in her tiny camper, taking pictures of cocktails and trying to find some peace of mind. He hoped she found it, too.

For Leo, he was beginning to find some peace of mind right here in the Old City, a town teeming with the spirits of the dead—as well as a handful of living people who cared about him.

Author's Note

St. Augustine is a unique town. It has several nicknames, but I chose to use "Old City" for this series. Founded in 1565 by Spanish explorers, it is hailed as the oldest continuously inhabited European-established city in the United States. It is also rumored to be filled with ghosts and haunted locales. There are plenty of ghost tours on offer within the Old City. I make no endorsement of any particular tour, nor do I make any claim as to their ability to accurately describe the spirits or ghosts...or darker things...that may or may not haunt St. Augustine.

If you've never visited, you should. Be prepared to bake in the sun, be assailed by the scents of pizza, beer and waffle cones, and watch as adults dressed as pirates stroll past you on St. George Street.

I took a lot of liberties with this story. It is a work of fiction, after all. The characters are not based on real people, and any seemingly similar mysteries or scandals that may have occurred in the Old City's history are strictly coincidences. The ghosts are not real, either. At least, I don't think they are.

My descriptions of Leo Robert's and Mad Hattie's abilities

to see, hear, feel, and experience spirits are not meant to be a definitive statement on how such things are done. While I researched paranormal experiences and spoke with people who have mediumistic gifts, I created my own set of rules and parameters for the things that would transpire within my story. This is not to say that it is the only way in which people experience spirits or ghosts. It is simply the way my characters experience them.

As for the setting of this story, I did try to accurately portray St. Augustine's streets, landmarks, monuments, and historical sites. . .and its general vibe. St. George Street is the heart of the downtown pedestrian district. The Casa Monica Hotel, Flagler College, Plaza de la Constitución, Bridge of Lions, Castillo de San Marcos, and the churches do exist and are located right where I describe them. You can listen to free music concerts under a giant live oak tree in a music park located off St. George Street. However, the music park is not called Granny Oak's.

In fact, none of the businesses I describe are meant to portray real-life ones, even if I've placed them in locations where these same types of businesses are located. For example, at the time of publishing, there may or may not be a bar located on the same corner as Bonney's Bar. The last time I checked, none of the ice cream shops (and there are a lot of them!) are called N'Ice Day Ice Cream. And, to my knowledge, there is no donut shop in the Old City offering datil-pepper-glazed donuts exactly as I envision them. But I wish there was!

Acknowledgments

There are many people to thank for their help in bringing this book to life. Therefore, I offer my sincere appreciation...

To my family for their love and support. There are times when they find the subject matter of my writing to be a bit frightening—they wonder if they even know me at all, I'm sure —but they continue to love me all the same.

To my brother, Scott, for his willingness to read my stories with a critical eye while at the same time sparing my feelings and boosting my spirits. His help was invaluable during the editing process. He has an amazing ability to see things others miss and to offer suggestions to make the story better without changing my vision for it.

To my editor Jessica Hatch for bringing all of her years of expertise to bear on my little ol' novel. I am grateful for her enthusiasm for the story, her hard work in making this book the best it can be, and her willingness to help me become a better writer.

To James at Bookfly for his wonderful cover art and willing-ness to listen to my suggestions, kindly ignore the ridiculous parts, and ultimately design exactly what I never knew I always wanted.

To Robin for her explanation of things that defy explanation.

To Lori Carr for her prosecutorial expertise and

suggestions, as well as her longtime friendship and encouragement.

To Daphne Berry for giving me her valuable time and feedback.

To the members of the Reading Between the Wines Book Club who have been wonderful in both their support of my writing and their offer of friendship—especially Cathy Klein, Tracy Tripp, Meg Balke, Charmaine Brooks, Leah Maltz, Donna Nuckols, Maritza Ochoa, and Christine Schmitt, all of whom were early beta readers and provided amazing feedback.

And last, but always first in my heart, to my husband, Matt. He is my first and most important reader, the reader I think about when I write my stories. He has been unwavering in his support of everything I do, and I am forever grateful for him.

About the Author

Stacey Horan writes about things that scare her, and her goal is to keep writing until nothing scares her anymore. Stacey is the author of the *Old City Mysteries*, an adult paranormal mystery series set in St. Augustine, Florida. She has written seven young adult novels, including two paranormal thrillers and an adventure/mystery series. Stacey also hosts *The Bookshop at the End of the Internet*, a podcast dedicated to helping book lovers discover new authors.

You can learn more about Stacey at her website (www.staceyhoran.com) or on social media (@staceyleehoran).